P9-DJA-567

Advance Praise for *Tropic of Kansas*

"Timely, dark, and ultimately hopeful: it might not 'make America great again,' but then again, it just might."
—Cory Doctorow, *New York Times* bestselling and award-winning author of *Homeland*

"Futurist as provocateur! The world is sheer batshit genius . . . A truly hallucinatorily envisioned environment."
—William Gibson, *New York Times* bestselling and award-winning author of *Neuromancer* and *The Peripheral*

"This stunning novel of a time all too easily imaginable as our own highlights a few of the keen-voiced, brave-souled women and men who balance like subversive acrobats on society's whirling edges. Read *Tropic of Kansas* for the sheer pleasure of sunning yourself in Brown's warm words; read it for its characters' heart-stopping-and-starting actions in the face of crushing oppression; read it for the way this book melts through years of glacial dread you didn't realize had accumulated. Read it to burn with the joy of realistic hope."
—Nisi Shawl, Tiptree Award–winning author of *Everfair* and *Writing the Other*

"*Tropic of Kansas* is the tale of a politically desperate USA haunted by a sullen, feral teen who is Huck Finn, Conan, and Tarzan. Because it's Chris Brown's own imaginary America, this extraordinary novel is probably more American than America itself will ever get."
—Bruce Sterling, award-winning author of *Islands in the Net* and *Pirate Utopia*

TROPIC OF KANSAS

Tropic of Kansas

Christopher Brown

HARPER Voyager

An Imprint of HarperCollinsPublishers

TROPIC OF KANSAS. Copyright © 2017 by Christopher Brown. All rights reserved. Printed in the United States of America. No part of this book may be used or reproduced in any manner whatsoever without written permission except in the case of brief quotations embodied in critical articles and reviews. For information, address HarperCollins Publishers, 195 Broadway, New York, NY 10007.

HarperCollins books may be purchased for educational, business, or sales promotional use. For information, please email the Special Markets Department at SPsales@harpercollins.com.

Harper Voyager and design are trademarks of HarperCollins Publishers LLC.

FIRST EDITION

Designed by Renata De Oliveira

Library of Congress Cataloging-in-Publication Data has been applied for.

ISBN 978-0-06-256381-1

17 18 19 20 21   LSC   10 9 8 7 6 5 4 3 2 1

For Agustina and Hugo

Contents

Prologue

HIDDEN IN THE TALL WEEDS OF AN EMPTY LOT OUTSIDE WINNIPEG, Sig watched the family eat dinner in the backyard of their new house on the other side of the fence. They were grilling pork chops, and it smelled good.

Sig had no house, and no food. He was hungry, dirty, and tired. He had been running for so long he forgot where he was going. Sometimes he forgot where he was from.

The kids were younger than Sig, maybe eight and ten, a redheaded boy and his dark-haired older sister. The mom was blond and the dad was bald. The lawn was an unnaturally bright green, and the picnic table was painted red. The family looked safe and happy.

The yard was filled with toys.

Sig had hopped a train in western Ontario, after a summer roaming the Quetico. The lakes were good to him until the people hunters found him, and he had to abandon the canoe he'd stolen and disappear into the woods. Now it had been a couple of days since he had a real meal, and surviving off the land was a different matter in the edges of a big city like Winnipeg. Easier and harder at the same time.

Sig watched the family for close to an hour, until they finished and went inside. The sun set, and the house glowed from the flickering white light of its electric hearth.

Sig jumped the fence and crouched behind the jungle gym, waiting to see if anyone noticed the sound of the chain link moving.

Quiet. He could hear the sounds of the family talking, and the strange voices from an interactive children's show.

He moved to the picnic table and found the food he had seen the children drop. Part of a pork chop, and some french fries. He brushed off the dirt and ate them.

He lifted the lid on the father's gas grill. There was some food left on there, too—three backup hot dogs. Sig ate those. They were still warm.

The sliding glass door opened. Sig ducked behind the grill. The father stepped out.

Sig watched the man scan his backyard, night blind from his house full of screens. If he could have seen Sig, he would have seen a skinny, unwashed thirteen-year-old staring back at him from under greasy, uncut bangs.

"Hello?" said the man.

A dog barked from another house nearby. Sig was glad this family did not have a dog.

The man went back inside. Sig stayed hidden. He watched and waited.

The parents carried the children upstairs. They left the television on.

Sig went to the glass door. He quietly slid it open. Listened, looked, smelled, and stepped in.

He crouched behind the sofa and scrambled to the kitchen.

There was a laundry closet there, with a hamper made of a cloth bag draped over a metal frame. Sig took the bag from the frame. It had some clothes in it. He raided the refrigerator and the pantry, filling the rest of the bag with food.

He ran out the back before the parents came back down. He forgot to close the door behind him.

Don't look back.

He threw the bag over the fence, climbed back over, and ran off toward the woods he had come from.

Later, he built a fire in a clearing at the bottom of a ravine. He cooked frozen ravioli, and hot dogs, and marshmallows. He ate graham crackers and Cheetos and a peanut butter cup. He drank Pepsi Cola and beer. He sorted through the family's clothes. He took a pair of the father's blue jeans, rolled up the legs, and cinched the waist with the string from the laundry bag. He put on three of the mother's T-shirts at the same time, and a big sweatshirt. He made a nest with the rest of the clothes, using it for bedding inside a lean-to he made under a fallen tree wedged into the muddy grade of the ravine.

Buzzed on beer, sugar, and animal fat, Sig curled up in a pile of the family's dirty clothes and forgot about his worries for a while. Their scents were so strong and clean, he felt almost like he was living with them in their house.

The police came in the morning. They found the lean-to, but Sig had already headed farther north.

Five years later

LOOKING AT THE BRIGHT BLUE SKY FROM THE BACKSEAT OF THE armored truck, which was more like a cell than a seat, Sig could almost believe it was a warm day. But the shackles around his ankles were still cold from the walk out to the vehicle, and when Sig put his head up against the bars to test for faults, he could feel the ice trying to get to him. And winter was just getting started.

"What day is it?" asked Sig.

"Deportation day," said the big constable who had muscled him out of lockup thirty minutes earlier. When he talked the red maple leaf tattoo on the side of his thick neck moved, like a lazy bat.

"Friday," said the Sergeant, who was driving. "December 1. The day you get to go back where you came from."

The thought conjured different images in Sig's head than his jailers might have imagined.

"Back to cuckoo country," laughed the constable. "Lucky you. Say hi to the TV tyrant for me."

The Mounties had nicknames for Sig, like Animal and Dog Boy, but they never called him any of those to his face. They didn't know his real name. When they trapped him stealing tools and food from a trailer at the Loonhaunt Lake work camp a month earlier, he had no ID, no name he would give them, and they couldn't find him in their computers. They still tagged him, accurately, as another American illegal immigrant or smuggler, and processed him as a John Doe criminal repatriation. They did not know that he had been up here the better part of seven years, living in the edgelands.

The memory of that day he ran tried to get out, like a critter in a trap, but he kept it down there in its cage. And wished he had stayed farther north.

He pulled his wrists against the cuffs again, but he couldn't get any leverage the way they had him strapped in.

Then the truck braked hard, and the restraints hit back.

The constable laughed.

They opened the door, pulled him out of the cage, and uncuffed him there on the road. Beyond the barriers was the international bridge stretching over the Rainy River to the place he had escaped.

"Walk on over there and you'll be in the USA, kid," said the sergeant. "Thank you for visiting Canada. Don't come back."

Sig stretched, feeling the blood move back into his hands and feet. He looked back at the Canadian border fortifications. A thirty-foot-high fence ran along the riverbank. Machine guns pointed down from the towers that loomed over the barren killing zone on the other side. He could see two figures watching him through gun scopes from the nearest tower, waiting for an opportunity to ensure he would never return.

Sig looked in the other direction. A military transport idled in the middle of the bridge on six fat tires, occupants hidden behind tinted windows and black armor. Behind them was an even higher fence shielding what passed for tall buildings in International Falls. The fence was decorated with big pictograms of death: by gunfire, explosives, and electricity. The wayfinding sign was closer to the bridge.

UNITED STATES BORDERZONE
Minnesota State Line 3.4 Miles

Sig looked down at the churning river. No ice yet.

He shifted, trying to remember how far it was before the river dumped into the lake.

"Step over the bridge, prisoner," said a machine voice. It looked like the transport was talking. Maybe it was. He'd heard stories. Red and white flashing lights went on across the top of the black windshield. You could see the gun barrels and camera eyes embedded in the grill.

"Go on home to robotland, kid," said the sergeant. "They watch from above too, you know."

Sig looked up at the sky. He heard a chopper but saw only low-flying geese, working their way south. He thought about the idea of home. It was one he had pretty much forgotten, or at least given up on. Now it just felt like the open door to a cage.

He steeled himself and walked toward the transport. Five armed guards emerged from the vehicle to greet him in black tactical gear. The one carrying the shackles had a smile painted on his face mask.

2

THE PILGRIM CENTER WAS AN OLD SHOPPING PLAZA BY THE FREE-
way that had been turned into a detention camp. It was full.

The whole town of International Falls had been evacuated and turned into a paramilitary control zone. Sig saw two
tanks, four helicopters, and lots of soldiers and militarized police through the gun slits of the transport. Even the flag looked
different—the blue part had turned almost black.

No one in the camp looked like a pilgrim. Instead they
wore yellow jumpsuits. There were plenty of local boys in the
mix, the sort of rowdies who'd have a good chance of getting
locked up even in normal times. The others were immigrants,
refugees, and guest workers. Hmong, Honduran, North Korean,
Bolivian, Liberian. They had been rounded up from all over
the region. Some got caught trying to sneak out, only to be
accused of sneaking in.

They interrogated Sig for several hours each day. Most
days the interrogator was a suit named Connors. He asked Sig
a hundred variations on the same questions.

Where did you come from?

North.

Where specifically?

All over.

What were you doing up there?

Traveling. Hunting. Working. Walking.

What did you do with your papers?

Never had any.

How old are you?
Old enough.
Are you a smuggler?
No.
Where were you during the Thanksgiving attacks?
What attacks.
Where were you during the Washington bombings last month?
I don't know. In the woods.
Tell me about your friends. Where were they?
What friends.
Tell us your name. Your true name.

They took his picture, a bunch of times, naked and with his clothes on. They had a weird machine that took close-up shots of his eyes. They took his fingerprints, asked him about his scars, and took samples of his skin, blood, and hair. He still wouldn't give them his name. They said they would find him in their databases anyway. He worried they would match him to records in their computers of the things he'd done before he fled.

They made fun of his hair.

3

THE IMPROVISED PRISON WAS SMALL. A ONE-STORY MALL THAT might once have housed twenty stores. The camp included a section of parking lot cordoned off with a ten-foot hurricane fence topped with razor wire. They parked military vehicles and fortification materials on the other side, coming and going all the time.

They rolled in buses with more detainees every day. A couple of times they brought a prisoner in on a helicopter that landed right outside the gate. Those prisoners were hooded and shackled, with big headphones on. They kept them in another section.

At night you could hear helicopters and faraway trains. Some nights there was gunfire. Most nights there were screams.

Every room in the camp had a picture of the same forty-something white guy. Mostly he was just sitting there in a suit, looking serious. Sometimes he was younger, smiling, wearing a flight suit, holding a gun, playing with kids and dogs. In the room where they ate there was a big poster on the wall that showed him talking to a bunch of people standing in what looked like a football stadium. There was a slogan across the bottom in big letters.

Accountability = Responsibility + Consequences

One of the other detainees told Sig the guy on the poster was the President.

They just tried to kill him, Samir explained. He whispered because he didn't want them to hear him talking about it. Said people got into the White House with a bomb. Sig asked what people. Samir just held up his hands and shrugged.

Samir was the guy who had the cot next to Sig. He was from Mali. Their cot was in a pen with an old sign over it. "Wonderbooks." There were holes in the walls and floors where once there had been store shelving. One of the guys that slept back there, a middle-aged white guy named Del, said they were closing all the bookstores on purpose. Samir said it was because no one read books anymore. Sig wasn't sure what the difference was.

The women detainees were in a different section, where there used to be a dollar store. Sometimes they could see the women when they were out in the yard.

One day a lady showed up at Sig's interrogation. Blonde in a suit. She said she was an investigator from the Twin Cities. Why do you look so nervous all the sudden, said Connors. They asked him about what happened back then. About other people who were with him. Sig didn't say anything.

Looks like you get to go to Detroit, said Connors.

Sig did not know what that meant, but it scared him anyway, from the way the guy said it, and from the not knowing. He tried not to show it.

That afternoon Sig found a tiny figure of a man in a business suit stuck in a crack in the floor. His suit was bright blue, and he had a hat and a briefcase. Del said there used to be a shop in the mall that made imaginary landscapes for model trains to travel through, and maybe this guy missed his train.

Del and Samir and the others talked whenever they could about what was going on. They talked about the attacks. They talked outside, they talked in whispers, they swapped theories at night after one of the guys figured out how to muffle the surveillance mic with a pillow they took turns holding up there. They talked about how there were stories of underground cells from here to the Gulf of Mexico trying to fight the government. How the government blamed the Canadians for harboring "foreign fighters," by which they meant Americans who'd fled or been deported. They told Sig how the elections were probably rigged, and the President didn't even have a real opponent the last time. Some of the guys said they thought the attacks were faked to create public support for a crackdown. For a new war to fight right here in the Motherland. To put more people back to work. Del said he had trouble believing the President would have his guys blow off his own arm to manipulate public opinion. Beto said no way, I bet he would have blown off more than that to make sure he killed that lady that used to be Vice President since she was his biggest enemy.

One of the guys admitted that he really was a part of the resistance. Fred said that lady's name was Maxine Price and he'd been in New Orleans when she led the people to take over the city. He said he joined the fight and shot three federal troopers and it felt good.

Sig asked the others what it meant when the interrogator told him he was going to Detroit. They got quiet. Then they told him about the work camps. They sounded different from what he had seen in Canada. Old factories where they made prisoners work without pay, building machines for war and extraction.

On his fourth day in the camp, Sig made a knife. It wasn't a knife at first. It was a piece of rebar he noticed in the same crack in the floor where he found the little man. He managed to dig out and break off a sliver a little longer than his finger, and get a better edge working it against a good rock he found in one of the old concrete planters in the yard. Just having it made him feel more confident when the guards pushed him around.

The seventh day in the camp, as the other detainees loitered in the common areas after dinner, Sig escaped.

He got the idea watching squirrels. The squirrels loved it behind the tall fences, which kept out their competition. Sig saw one jump from a tree outside the fence onto the roof, grab some acorns that had fallen from another nearby tree, and then jump back using the fence as a relay.

Del went with him. Samir said he didn't want to die yet.

They waited until the guards were busy after dinner. Samir took watch. They leaned Sig's cot up against the wall and pushed through the section of cheap ceiling Sig had cut out the night before. They carried their blankets around their shoulders. Del could barely fit when they got up in the crawl space. Sig didn't wait. They followed the ductwork on their hands and knees to the roof access and broke out into the open air. Sig half-expected to get shot right then, but the guards in the tower were watching a prisoner delivery.

He could see the black trucks driving by on the high road behind the mall.

They tossed their blankets so they would drape over the razor wire where the fence came close to the back of the building. Del's throw was good, but Sig's went too far, over the fence. Too bad, said Del. Sig backed up, got a running start, and jumped anyway.

The razored barbs felt like sharpened velcro, grabbing onto his prison jumpsuit in bunches, poking through into his forearm and hand.

Del didn't even make it to the fence.

Shit.

"You go!" said Del, curled up on the ground, groaning.

The sound of Sig's body hitting the chain link like a big monkey got the guards' attention, but by the time bullets came they hit torn fragments of his paper jumpsuit that stayed stuck when he leapt from his momentary perch.

The tree branch Sig landed on broke under his weight, and he hit the frozen ground hard. But he got up okay. Nothing broken. His blanket was right there, so he grabbed it.

He looked through the fence. Del was up on his knees, hands behind his head, hollering at the guards not to shoot as they came around the corner and from the roof.

Sig ran. He heard the gunfire behind him, but didn't hear Del.

They came after Sig fast, but he had already disappeared into the landscaping that ran along the side road. He heard them off in the distance as he crawled through a vacant subdivision of knee-high grass, broken doors, and gardens gone wild. He evaded capture that night moving through cover, the way a field mouse escapes a hawk.

He was glad it took them half an hour to get out the dogs.

He used torn chunks of his prison jumpsuit to bandage his wounds. They were little bleeders, but he would be okay. Then he cut a hole in the middle of the blanket to turn it into a poncho. He thought about where he could get new clothes, if he made it through the night.

Later, as he huddled in a portable toilet behind a convenience store just south of the borderzone, he wondered if what that Mountie said was true. That they had robots in the sky that could see you in the dark, tag you and track you, and kill without you ever knowing they were there. Sig thought maybe if he got cold enough, their heat cameras couldn't find him.

4

WHEN SIG WAS NINE YEARS OLD HIS MOTHER GOT ARRESTED FOR
her protesting. They said they suspected her of terrorist activities. They sent seven men in suits to take her away in a black Suburban. She said they just wanted to shut her up.

She was gone.

So was Sig's dad. He was a fugitive on the other side of the northern border, smuggling and poaching. So the judge sent Sig to the Boys School.

The Boys School was in an old summer camp on a small lake outside Duluth. It was a place where the court let the state send dangerous kids so the state didn't have to pay for their care.

The Boys School was run by an ex-Marine who had been the director of the summer camp until he got the idea he could do it year-round with troubled youth, funding from the Lutheran Brotherhood, and a government contract. His name was Barney Kukla. Before that he taught high school gym in North Dakota.

The Boys School was like the Marines for kids. They had inspections once a week where Barney would give out root beer floats to whichever cabin was best squared away. Sometimes Barney even tried to bounce a quarter off the bedsheets. Sig was not very good at inspection. He did better at archery, orienteering, and paddling. He was pretty good at making stuff out of leather and bone, too.

On weekends they had these big games that Barney and the other counselors would dream up. It started with a game of Capture the Flag spread across the whole hundred acres occupied by the camp, and then spun off into crazy variations. There was Border Guard, where one team tried to smuggle trunks full of rocks across a frontier marked with ball field chalk and guarded by kids with squirt guns and unlimited detention authority. In Mole Hunt, members of each team were actually covert agents of the other team. Barbary Coast was played on the lake in canoes and sailboats, with water balloons as cannons. On Barbary Coast day Barney wore a giant admiral's hat with a big yellow feather that the other boys dared Sig to steal. For MIA, Barney and the counselors built a little pine log and chicken wire jail on the other side of the little swamp. The older kids persuaded Sig to sneak through the swamp after sundown and break into the fake jail, which turned out to be a pretty stupid idea.

Even if he got caught sometimes, Sig was really good at all those games. But his favorite was Klondike Day, when the entire camp area was littered with gold nuggets they made by painting rocks yellow and hiding them like Easter eggs. At the end of the day you could trade in the rocks you'd found for special treats from the dispensary. Including a root beer float if your nuggets weighed enough. Sig got so many of the rocks that he couldn't even spend them all, so he hid them in a special spot behind the rifle range.

That was when he figured out a hole in the camp security perimeter—the area behind the backstop of the range. Later that week Sig got a letter from his mom saying she didn't know when they would let her out to come get him. That night he snuck out of his cabin through the loose floorboard he'd discovered during the last inspection, and disappeared.

Getting Mom out of jail was a lot harder.

5

SIG WOKE TO THE SOUND OF MEN TALKING OUTSIDE THE CONVE-
nience store, and when he opened his eyes he saw the slow
strobe of police lights bouncing off the ceiling of the plastic
john. When he heard the men go into the store, he ran, into
the woods behind. Morning came awhile later, which was
mostly good.

When he got far enough away from International Falls
and the detention center, Sig came back out of the woods and
stowed away in the back of a truck. He woke up in Bemidji,
then jumped a freight that took him back up north of Hibbing.
He walked from there, twenty-some miles in the dark, to the
last place they lived. The morning light broke just as he started
down the long gravel drive through the woods to the cabin by
Lost Lake.

The woods had burned. Maybe the year before, but you
could still smell it in the black pines. There had been fighting.

Mom's house was gone. Razed. Sig dug around in the dirt.
He didn't find much. There was one shoe, a broken mirror, a
soldier's shiny button, and a red ponytail holder. He dusted off
the ponytail holder. The smell of Mom was gone, washed out
by time. He put it in his pocket anyway. He might be able to
use it. He rarely cut his hair after he ran. Mom always liked it
long.

He kept the button, too, as a reminder. He made note of
the logo imprinted in the brass, a picture of an eagle swinging
a sword.

He walked down the road to Kong's place. The trailer was still there, but Kong wasn't. It looked like he hadn't been there in a long time. Kong was old even back when Sig was a little kid, so who knew.

The trailer was tucked in the woods, but with a clear view of the water. Sig remembered how they would fish right out there at dusk. Kong would look at the contrails in the burning-down sky and tell fortunes. They were mostly dark forebodings of war and struggle, except when he saw far in the future, when he said most of the people would be gone.

The trailer door was open. Animals had been through the place. It was a mess.

Sig rummaged around. He found some clothes that smelled like a nest. Kong used to be a lot bigger than Sig, but now it would be the other way around. Sig found a black hoodie that stretched out without tearing too bad, and a few mismatched socks. He shook the little rodent turds off the hoodie and put it on, then shoved the socks in the big stomach pocket for later.

The animals hadn't found the safe. It was right where Sig remembered, hidden in the floor under a box and a removable piece of plywood. It was a simple little safe, four-digit code that scrambled the year Kong's dead son was born. The code still worked. And Sig's tackle box was still inside.

The tackle box was small, too, just big enough for a day's worth of lures. But instead of tackle it had Sig's stuff. The stuff he collected when he was hanging out with Kong. Stuff they found on the lake and in the woods. Stuff guys left behind, mainly, the kind of stuff a boy would notice and pocket. Arrowheads, little bones, some weird rocks, a pocket watch that didn't run, spent pistol cartridges, and sixty-two dollars and thirty-five cents in vintage pocket change.

Kong always told him some of those coins were worth more as collectibles than as regular money, but today they were probably going to have to get back into regular circulation for someone else to discover, while Sig worried about getting to tomorrow without getting caught.

Sig was glad Kong kept his promise to keep Sig's secret stash but was bummed Kong wasn't there in person. Kong would know what to do. He had escaped from a lot worse situations than this.

The only other thing Kong left in the safe was his old knife. Sig remembered the story. It was a military survival knife from a war before Sig was born. Kong got it as a gift from a downed American pilot he helped. It was a good knife. Kong had given Sig another knife a long time ago, a Hmong blade, but they took that one away from him. This one he would borrow and not lose.

6

SIG WALKED INTO TOWER AND HUNG OUT AT THE PUBLIC DEPOT
until he found a ride. He bought some work pants, a ball cap
to hide his hair, cheap sunglasses to mask his face, and a clean
new T-shirt with the name of the business on it. Iron Country
Supply. He bought a fried walleye sandwich, too. The people
made fun of how long he took to count out his change on the
countertop. The lady told him we're not supposed to accept
cash but when she saw how old the money was she changed
her mind. When Sig was done he had a little over sixteen dollars left. He changed into the clothes in the bathroom, cut
what was left of his prison jumpsuit into pieces, and put them
at the bottom of the trash can.

He ate his sandwich under a leafless tree at the edge of
the parking lot. He hung out and watched from the margins
for about twenty minutes until he saw the big tanker pull up
and decided to give it a try. When he showed the driver the
buffalo nickel and said it was worth three hundred bucks,
the guy laughed and said sure, I'll give you a ride to Grand
Portage since I'm going there anyway. The way the guy smiled
Sig thought he was going to say keep your money kid but he
grabbed it and pocketed it while he was still smiling, then
showed Sig where to sit while the guy went inside to use the
head.

The trucker was based out of Thief River Falls, running
biofuels and other cargo between the NoDak fields and the

border forts. When Sig asked why he was making deliveries to an Indian casino the guy laughed and said you must have been gone awhile.

When they came up on a checkpoint at Temperance River, Sig tried to hide in the back of the cab. It didn't work. The guards shined a light on him. The trucker said that's my kid, taking a nap, we've been driving all night. Sig tried to play the part. Sat up, acted groggy. He could hear the gunmetal when the guards moved. The crackle of the radios, connected to base. The harsh white beam of the flashlight in his face. Maybe taking his picture.

When they were waved on and Sig got back in front, the trucker asked Sig what was that all about.

I don't like soldiers, said Sig.

Then you're in the wrong country, said the trucker.

Sig looked in the side mirror, back at a pair of border guards in their dark green fatigues. You couldn't tell through their shades, but it looked like they were talking and looking at Sig at the same time.

One of them got on the phone.

The truck hissed, then moved out, into gear.

The changed mood in the cab made Sig nervous. When he looked over the trucker was messing with the screen on his steering wheel, like he was looking something up.

They drove on for another twenty quiet minutes that felt like hours. The road cut through tall pines on either side. Every once in a while there was a sign.

FEDERAL BORDER SECTOR SUPERIOR
Access Restricted
All Vehicles and Persons Subject to Search

They passed through stretches where you could see the big lake off to the right. Cold blue water that dissolved into cloud along the horizon.

They passed through a little town that had been abandoned, or cleared. Same thing. The post office was bombed out, marred with big black scorches that licked out through the empty windows.

On the other side of the town they entered another thick patch of forest. That was when the soldiers walked right out of the woods with their machine guns ready, the leader waving at the trucker to stop.

The trucker looked at Sig.

"Guess you're worth a lot more than an old coin, kid," he said.

The brakes were so loud. The squeak of big hydraulics.

Sig went for the door, but the trucker locked it from his controls before Sig could grab the handle.

The guy smiled.

Sig leapt at the guy like a panicked animal. Stuck Kong's knife into the guy's leg. That drove his foot harder on the brake and knocked the truck out of gear. The lurch threw Sig up against the windshield. He kicked the trucker in the face. The door opened so fast Sig practically fell out onto the ground, hands first, dropping the knife.

The woods were right there. The guy had driven off the road.

Sig grabbed the knife from the dirt.

He ran, chased by bullets, into the labyrinth of trees, intuiting paths that would be hard to follow. The soldiers relied on machines to see their prey, but their electronic eyes had trouble seeing through the dense forest. Too much noise.

He heard a helicopter. It came in close. Maybe it saw him but couldn't get a clear shot.

He imagined what they saw on the screen.

He almost lost a sneaker crossing the swamp. The muck pulled on his feet, like the mouth of a hungry monster. He reached down and found the shoe when it came off, carried it in his hand until he could stop.

He heard more shooting. Not too close, but not far, either.

In a clearing at the other end of the swamp lay a dying moose. Juvenile male, maybe two-thirds of the way to full-grown, rack fuzzed out like a teenager's beard.

It had been shot. Three red wounds across the torso. From a big machine gun.

Sig kept moving.

When the moose cried, it sounded like the call of some ancient horn. A word in a language no one knows.

IT WAS LATE AFTERNOON WHEN SIG WALKED INTO SOVEREIGN territory. His clothes were soiled with dirt and pine sap, his pants wet to mid-thigh, but he had not been shot or captured.

Feeling suddenly safe just by stepping over an imaginary line that only existed on maps, he wondered why he hadn't come there a long time ago. Maybe because these weren't really his people. They weren't even really his dad's. Or maybe because he was a lot more scared back then.

The public part of the reservation was easy to find. He could see tall buildings over the treetops.

He cleaned himself off as best he could, then walked out of the woods and into a big parking lot.

They had built a ten-story office building next to the old casino. The casino sign said CLOSED FOR SEASON, but you could tell it had been that way for many seasons. The parking lot had more shipping containers in it than cars. Some of them were painted in camouflage patterns, others stacked three high.

Under new management. That was what the trucker said.

Sig walked past a row of tricked-out pickups and SUVs. Most of them looked new. Shiny and expensive, with high suspensions and all kinds of aftermarket add-ons. He was excited when he recognized one of them, a vintage black van converted for off-road running. He had slept in the back of that van more than a few times. Hard to forget the image airbrushed on the side, faded now from sun and winter, a wizard riding on the back of a giant owl. The tires looked brand-new.

He looked around, wondering where he might find its driver.

It was confusing seeing this place turned into an office park. He tried a few doors, all locked with security access pads. He tried looking in through the windows, but they were mirrors. He saw a few people coming and going, but they were too far off to even make out their faces. He found a building directory that listed companies he'd never heard of, some with tribal names:

Chippewa Development Group
Arrowhead Logistics Co.
Gichigami Salvage and Rescue Corp.
OJOCo Data Foundry
Superior Bank

He saw a couple of people walk into another building on the opposite side of the parking lot. The old hotel. He walked down there. The door said COMMUNITY CENTER. It was open. Inside it was more like a bar.

Sig sat at the counter. Behind it was an old white guy who'd lost his smile, leaned back watching the television over the bar. When he finally looked over at Sig, he looked right back at the TV, as if Sig weren't there. Sig took off his ball cap to see if that helped.

It didn't.

"Do you have food?" said Sig.

"Do you have money?"

"Some." He checked his pocket to make sure he still had the sixteen dollars.

The guy laughed at him. "You look a little lost, kid. And a little dirty. This isn't that kind of community center, as most

27

of the locals know. You just walk in off the portage or something?"

Sig nodded.

"Alone?"

Sig shrugged.

"Here," said the guy, putting a glass of water and a menu down in front of Sig. "You want a grilled cheese or something I'll hook you up. Then you need to get lost."

Sig took a long, thirsty drink, emptying the glass.

The television was tuned to live footage from a recon team crossing the Iranian Blast Zone. The only person at the counter was another old white guy, down at the other end nursing a tablet computer and a tumbler of brown liquor on ice. The guy looked up from his screen and sized up Sig with the eyes of someone who saw the world in numbers and bodies. He went back to his drink.

Three tables against the wall were occupied by a livelier crowd. Nine guys and two women, drinking and smoking, talking and laughing.

And there was Merle. Mom's old boyfriend, the guy that belonged to the wizard van, grown older and fatter, with gold jewelry over his shiny leather vest and a fancy black pearl snap shirt. Merle had his sunglasses on, even though it was pretty dark in the bar.

"Hey, Bob!" yelled Merle to the bartender. "Can you switch to the hunting channel or something? I can't stand all this war noise."

"No kidding, we got enough of that right here," said one of Merle's crew.

"Planet Kitten!" said another one.

They all laughed, except for Merle, who was staring at Sig.

Merle took off his sunglasses and squinted. He got up and

walked over, waving off two of his guys as they jumped out of their chairs to escort him. He came in real close. His eyes looked a little crazy. Bloodshot and wired.

"What the hell?" said Merle, grabbing Sig by the shoulders. "I can't believe it!"

Sig fought the slight smile that worked its way into the corner of his mouth. He noticed the big automatic pistol Merle had under his belt. It matched his jewelry.

"Where did you go, you little fucker?" said Merle.

"North," said Sig.

"Shit," said Merle. "I always knew it." He put his hand on Sig's shoulder. "You got bigger, boy. Still not as big as your dad."

"Where is he?" asked Sig.

Merle let out a mumbled groan and hid behind his sunglasses.

"Gone again," said Sig.

"Gone for good," said Merle. "Guess you came here looking for him. He's dead. But man, you should have seen him that night."

Sig stepped back. He felt another level of alone at the news, even if he wasn't surprised. He tried to imagine what Merle was referring to. He had never known much about what his dad was up to. Maybe because half the time Mom was dragging Sig off to some political gathering as far as possible from wherever Dad was going, when she wasn't dropping him off with strangers and calling them family.

"Get this guy a beer, Bob," said Merle. He looked at Sig. "Come on, kid, your dad wouldn't want you to get all mopey." He grabbed Sig's beer and dragged Sig over to their tables.

"Everybody, meet Siggy," said Merle. "The Mexican Muskie's boy, back from a long wander."

"You're Clyde's kid?" said one of the guys. "He always used to talk about you."

News to Sig.

"Warrior just like dad," said Merle. "Killed two cops before he turned thirteen."

"I remember your mom, honey," said one of the women. She was older, with a beat-up leather jacket and hair turned mostly silver. "That sucked what happened."

"Yeah, I guess he gets it from both sides," said Merle. "Even if he didn't get any of Erika's big blond hair."

Merle went to pat Sig on the head, but Sig pushed his hand away. Merle laughed it off.

"Never seen green eyes like that on either side, though," said the older lady, leaning in to look.

Sig looked away, at the wall covered with photos. Some were old pictures of the band and life on the lake. Others were more recent. One showed Sig's dad standing on top of a charred government SUV.

"That's the Full Metal Armadillo he took out with a home-made grenade," said Merle. "Crazy fucker crawled up on top of the goddam thing and dropped it through the hatch. They stopped sending their swamp drones in after that."

"They sent snipers instead," said one of the others, a burly white guy with a shaved head and a golden earring. "Counter-insurgency squads and yahoo militia from Wisconsin. Your dad killed about twenty of those nimrods on their way out."

"It was more than that, Holt," said Merle. "But how would you know. You were sleeping in that day."

"I was in Washington getting you more funding," said Holt. "Benjy and Cottonmouth were the ones on that run."

Benjy shrugged. He had crazy wiry hair, light brown skin, and a thick wild mustache. Cottonmouth sat next to him, a severe-looking Indian with face tattoos, rough lines drawn in a complex geometric pattern, the kind some guys got to beat the facial recognition.

"We got set up, man," said Benjy. "Motherland mofos all waiting for us there at our drop spot. I wouldn't be here if it wasn't for your dad, kid."

"We'd all be evicted," said Merle. "Or in the Supermax."

"More like the Island," said Cottonmouth.

Merle nodded, agreement in his crazy eyes, like the mental image made him even crazier.

"Freaking Clyde," said Benjy. "That was epic."

"That was definitely an epic quantity of shit you guys lost that night," said another guy sitting back from the group in a chair pulled away from the table. Thirty-something white guy with short hair and a black technical jacket.

"Thanks to your shitty intel, Dick," said Benjy.

"No shit," said a woman seated behind Benjy. She was Ojibwe, a couple of years older than Sig, long black hair woven into tight punk braids bunched up on her head. She had a pocket knife out, carving new patterns into the already ornate design on the wooden stock of the old assault rifle that lay across her lap. "We should be doing this for ourselves. We call ourselves sovereign but we work for the Dicks."

"Without our help you would have all been relocated, Betty," said Dick. "We're the ones who brokered your deal to be left alone. Let you enjoy your private little slice of free border-zone. So we just ask for a little help with our other projects."

"The Dick is our corporate sponsor," said Betty, looking at Sig. "Just flew in from Virginia."

"He's confused," said Benjy, laughing at Sig and smiling.

"You wonder why the casino is closed," said Merle.

"Because it's winter," said Benjy.

"Because we got a better business model," said Merle. "Revolution!"

"For profit, he neglects to mention," said Betty, raising her eyebrows.

"That's not our only business," said Benjy. "We have the native corporations, and the data center."

"And the bank," said Merle. "Tribal bank, under our own laws. So we can hold people's money—"

"Hide Dick's money," said Betty.

"Invest corporate money," said Merle. "And loan it back out to make more. Helps pay for our projects."

"You all talk too much," said Dick.

"We're recruiting," said Merle. "Sig, what we're doing is helping free Canada."

"Arming the people," said Benjy. "Helping them do self-help."

"First peoples," said Merle. "Helping them get real sovereignty, like we did."

"Like the Mohawks did first," said Betty. "Got their own real country."

"About the size of a small farm," said Benjy, smiling. "The next one will be a lot bigger. Then we'll move up there. Less polluted. Fishing's still good."

"We can just merge," said Betty. "Make an archipelago of nations."

"A what?" said Benjy.

"A network," said Betty. "Of free people. Helping share free information. Keep it growing. Restore our lands, take them back to wild."

Sig saw the bald guy, Holt, look over at Dick, the suit.

"You probably know all about it, from traveling up there," said Merle.

Sig had seen a camp northwest of Flin Flon and come across signs of fighting. He didn't know what it was all about, and had stayed clear.

"It started out just smuggling people who wanted to get out of the States," said Merle. "Then Dick and his guys told us how we could help deliver their loads to our cousins on the other side."

"And bring special goodies back," said Betty. "You gotta join us!"

"What's in it for them?" said Sig, pointing at Dick and Holt.

"Water," said Merle.

"For his frackers and factories," said Betty. "And rich fuckers who take long showers."

"Don't forget the golf courses," said Dick, not quite chuckling. "We pay market. And we buy mineral rights, too."

"Can he come with us?" Betty asked Dick. "I'll lay off you for a week."

"Make it a month and we can give him a tryout," said Dick. "But he needs to understand that, in this business, there are rules. Rules you need to follow if you don't want to end up dead. Discretion, honesty, and loyalty. Don't talk, don't steal, and don't cheat us. No freelancing we don't know about."

"He looks pretty reliable to me," said Benjy. "Definitely got the don't talk part down pretty good."

"I'll show him around," said Betty. "He'll open up."

8

THEY WENT FOR A WALK ALONG THE WATER.

When Sig said how quiet it was, Betty told him how the loons had been decimated by the cleaning agents they dumped in the lakes to try to kill the invasive aquatic plants that had gotten so out of control over all these freaky warm summers. Sig looked out over the dark water beyond the frozen-over part and wondered if any fish were left hiding in the stillness below.

Then a bunch of the guys came out and started tearing around on ice bikes, making enough noise for a race track, so Betty and Sig walked back into the woods.

They talked about kids Sig remembered from when he was a kid, and which ones were dead. Betty asked Sig about how his mom died, and whether he wanted to kill more cops because of it. Sig said it wasn't like that anymore.

She asked him if his dad was really Mexican, and Sig told the story how his grandpa, Clyde's dad, joined the Army and brought a wife back from Tijuana. They both died before Sig showed up. Betty said that made Sig a real mutt.

Sig asked more about these border runs they went on. Betty told Sig a secret. How she, Merle, and Benjy had a side deal. Bringing back illegal information to sell to underground networks. Sig asked how you smuggle information. Betty said depends what kind.

Sig asked Betty about the information carved on her gun. She called it her Kalashnikov, which she said was the name of the guy who invented it, and said how she liked the way it sounded. The carvings were images of all the animals she had hunted with it, and the imaginary animals that she associated with her dead friends. She said her grandpa had taught her how to carve, and when they went back to her cabin she showed him the special knife she used for that, and then they spent a sleepless night showing each other their scars, some of which were from other knives.

He still wasn't ready to tell her his own secrets.

9

SIG SLEPT MOST OF THE NEXT DAY. BETTY'S BED WAS SMALL BUT super-cozy, with clean sheets, a down comforter, thick wool blankets, and a huge pillow. She had a shortwave radio that played music from Tibet that sounded like sad old ghosts. She had teas that made your toes warm and your hair feel differ-ent. When she undid her hair, he could have sworn it had more wool than all of her blankets, but softer, and blacker, the color of a world without light. She made Sig wonder why he had spent most of the last six years sleeping alone in the woods.

Betty knew how to tune the radio so she never heard any news, except when she wanted to hear the worst news of the wars so she could get motivated to go try to make things better in her own destructive, acting-out way. She told Sig how she thought they should be arming other Americans to change things on this side of the border. Sig said guns never did any good, but they all already had them anyway. Betty insisted that wasn't true anymore, that they only issued guns to the people who joined the patriot militias, and the militia-men went around confiscating regular people's guns when they weren't busy hunting terrorists.

Sig told Betty how he wanted to make money so he wouldn't have to sleep outside and have a big house like the ones he had broken into in the Canadian cities. Betty laughed for a long minute and said maybe they could give him a job at the bank if he didn't mind wearing office clothes. She told him how most of the people at the bank and the data center were other Dicks who commuted from Virginia, and how she thought they were all about hiding money inside numbers and codes. Even if they had to hurt other people to do it.

Sig asked her how much they made for smuggling information. She told him. It was a lot. Could be a couple thousand for a good load. Sometimes it came in little plastic boxes, other times in notebooks, once in big reels of tape.

When they took another bath in her old tub Sig told her about the detention facility in International Falls and how he escaped when he heard they were going to send him to Detroit. She said if you think that sounds bad you should see the one they built in New Orleans.

No, she hadn't been.

She said Benjy told her that was where the smuggled information was supposed to end up. How you could get paid a lot more, full price, if you took it all the way there.

And that's when they decided they would hit the road together, and go there, to New Orleans. Follow the Mississippi all the way down. Take as big a shipment as they could put together. Maybe they could get a canoe. See if they could help the cause when they got there. Sig told her how he was worried about getting arrested again but she said it's easy to sneak around if you know how and he agreed. Then she hugged him again and said how excited she was and started working on her pack list.

It wasn't long after that when Benjy came around and told them Merle needed them to come help him make a run after dinner.

10

THEY RODE SNOWMOBILES UP THE OLD PORTAGE, SEVEN MILES from the big lake to the ruins of Fort Charlotte on the Pigeon River. They kept the guns and contraband up there in a camouflaged shed in the woods. The snowmobiles were special—superlight and quiet—paid for by Dick. Moving fast out on the open snow, they looked like they shifted from shiny black to the soft blue glow of the moon.

The section of the border that ran along the rez was one of the only stretches that hadn't been fortified. Betty acted like it was a point of pride—like it symbolized their hard-won freedom—but from Merle you got the sense it was more like the price of it.

They were eight—Sig and Betty, Benjy, Cottonmouth and Merle, and three younger guys Sig hadn't seen before. They loaded the guns into lockers, then tied the lockers down to the snowmobile trailer sleds, and put north. They carried extra fuel. Merle sent Sig and Betty ahead without trailers on the two smallest snowmobiles as scouts. The pair throttled full up the frozen river, looking at each other and at the way ahead, scanning the eerie tree line on either side, watching the sky when they could remember to.

They must have gone more than twenty miles through the luminous snow. A small aircraft flew over low at one point, but they were pretty sure it didn't see them. They rode up the river until the ice stopped and they had to continue on the right bank to a spot just short of where the concrete and metal bridge crossed over.

Merle and the guys caught up, then held back while Betty and Sig checked it out.

Betty had told Sig how they exchanged the lockers for duffel bags stuffed with English and Canadian cash money that they could exchange for American chits at black market rates. Or just use—most people were happy to take Queens. Benjy had told them they'd make three hundred bucks each. Betty and Sig figured that was enough to outfit their trip. Not counting the extra stuff Betty said she expected to get from her guy.

They stowed their rides and hiked up toward the road, staying under the tree cover and trying as best they could to walk on old snowpack where the icy crust was thick enough not to crunch underfoot. Betty had her Kalashnikov slung tight with the hand-tooled leather strap she'd made. Sig had Kong's knife in its sheath, and the old revolver Benjy loaned him under his belt at the crook of his hip. The metal was cold.

They crawled up the traverse to where they could see the scene on the road.

They heard the vehicle idling before they saw it. Betty tapped her penlight three times and the vehicle flashed its headlights back. It was an old blue van, the kind that didn't have any windows on the sides.

"Come on," said Betty, leading Sig out from the trees onto the road. As she stepped forward, she turned and whistled a jay call in the direction of downriver.

The two-lane bridge had low concrete walls on either side. There was no snow, just a few patches of ice and some dirty pack on the shoulders. You could hear the cold river running over the engine noise of the van. Sig looked down to the left, trying to see the guys through the trees. Then the driver turned on his headlights and blinded them. Sig blinked. The driver pulled forward and backed the van up so the rear end was facing them. Another guy opened the back doors from the inside to take on the cargo load.

"Hey, girl," said the guy as he stepped out of the van and onto the pavement. It was hard to make out his face in the dark. He had glasses on and a ball cap, and wore a black shell, work pants, and boots.

The inside of the van was lit up. Sig saw two big black duffels behind the guy, just like Betty said there would be.

"Hey, Pete," said Betty. "They should be up in a minute."

"They should hurry the fuck up," said Pete, tossing the duffels out onto the pavement. They hit with a soft thud. Sig imagined their contents.

"Got my other package?" said Betty.

"Oh, yeah, right," said Pete. "Hold on."

He grabbed something from inside the van and tossed it to Betty. A plastic bag. She pulled two small plastic cases from the bag and zipped them into her jacket pocket. Then she handed the bag to Sig. The contents were hard, the size of a book.

"Two little ones for me, one big one for you," she smiled.

Sig looked through the clear plastic. It was a videocassette. *Messages from Lemuria.* Sig shoved it behind his waistband.

The driver stepped out, standing in front of the open door. He held a black metal machine gun that flickered blue in the moonlight. It was a nicer gun than most cops had. The driver wore a black down jacket and his hair pulled back in a ponytail. He looked Asian, maybe indigenous from way up north.

"Crazy Betty," said the driver. "Who's your boyfriend?"

"Need to know, Nik," said Betty. She whistled again for Merle and the guys.

Sig looked back toward the woods behind them, at the other end of the bridge. He sensed something, like maybe an owl was watching them.

"Looks like your high school mascot," said the driver, smiling a mean smile.

"He's not, and we don't have one," said Betty. "What's your problem tonight?"

"Cranky from dealing with your boss," said crewman Pete.

"I don't have a boss," said Betty. "Maybe Merle does."

They heard the clanking of the lockers, then saw the guys bring them up over the edge of the hill and out from the trees. They carried them on their shoulders like boats, four guys on each locker.

"Hey, you brought your own coffins!" said the driver.

"Shut up, Nik," said Pete.

"We definitely brought a lot of death," said Merle, knocking the side of the locker with his free hand.

The driver sized up the crew while he watched the delivery. A couple of the guys Merle brought looked even younger than Sig. "Got a lot of interns with you tonight, Uncle Mo," said the driver.

"You didn't hear them coming, did you?" said Merle. They set the lockers down on the pavement. The metal boxes sounded even heavier than they looked.

The driver shrugged, and shifted his machine gun.

Merle and Cottonmouth went for the duffels.

Sig looked for the owl again.

Instead he saw lights come on in the woods. Headlights. Then another set, on the other side.

Sig pulled out the revolver they had loaned him.

"Fuckers!" yelled Merle.

Merle and his crew all went for their guns. Sig shot first, at the second car.

You could not hear the nightbirds flee as the bridge lit up with gunfire from five directions at once.

Cottonmouth and the other guys fired back hard, but it was hopeless, aiming at headlamps and shadows, taking it from two sides. Sig shot at the guys in the van, but they got him first.

The first shot felt like a hornet had dug its way up inside him and exploded.

The second shot felt worse.

The cacophony of gun chambers mostly stopped, replaced by moans and men barking instructions at each other.

Sig crawled toward Betty, who lay motionless ten feet away. He saw the corporate skinhead, Holt, walk up to her.

"You dumb shits broke the rules," he said. "Pissed off the people we work for. Make us do things I don't enjoy."

Holt aimed his pistol at Betty and put a bullet through her head.

"Videotape that," he said.

Then he saw Sig staring at him. Sig pulled out his knife. Holt kicked him in the face, then in one of the spots where he'd been shot, and everything went white.

SIG CAME TO WHEN HE HIT THE ICY WATER. GASPING FOR BREATH as the cold seized his chest, he saw them hanging Merle's body from the bridge, naked and carved with a warning that looked like a corporate logo.

He saw another body thrown over the bridge, and felt the impact as it hit the water near him.

He saw Holt look down at him. Sig went under and swam as best he could.

The cold made it hard to breathe but also made it easier to ignore the pain.

Then the cold took him, like a white tendril pulling him down into the darkness.

12

SIG WOKE UP WITH THE MORNING LIGHT, CURLED UP LIKE A BRO-ken baby on a cold wet bank.

He had lost his hoodie and one of his sneakers. He felt his belly. It felt like his T-shirt was glued to his insides with a layer of frozen mud between. The spot on his leg felt like there was a big rock in there, but when he touched it, it was all gooey. His mouth tasted like blood. Two of his teeth were loose. There was a lump at the base of his spine. He felt it and realized it was the videocassette, still shoved down his pants.

He vomited, blood and coffee, and felt like all of his internal organs were trying to climb out.

He curled up tighter, shivered, quivered.

An hour later he started crawling.

He pulled himself up the bank through the snow mixed with leaf litter and mud. He got up to where there was a gravel road. He didn't know what road it was, or even what country he was in.

He crawled out into the middle of the road, fighting sleep and looking up for turkey vultures, until, after what seemed like a really long time but could have been no time at all, a truck drove up. He could hear it coming from a ways away, enough to try to sit up, and he could remember the sound of a man's voice and the tires on the gravel from where he lay on the floor as the guy drove so far that Sig fell asleep.

He woke for a minute when the people were staring at him in their white smocks, then again later, when he was in a bed and the two old women and one old man were talking to him. They asked their questions very patiently, but he did not have any answers.

PART TWO

Spinoza and Mortimer Snerd

13

TANIA WAS THE ONE WHO HAD THE IDEA TO WALK DOWN AFTER lunch and take a look at the White House. What was left of it.

"Let me go with you," said Odile, leaning in and turning on that smile, the one that combined mischief and privilege in a way that usually worked to get her what she wanted, even when it shouldn't.

"You're dangerous," said Tania, smiling and shaking her head.

"You should try it," said Odile. "This town needs more dangerous people."

"You should try driving while black," said Tania. "Then tell me about living dangerously."

"Touché," said Odile. "I forget you got your fill of danger before we took the bar."

"You don't know the half of it," said Tania, looking down into what was left of her espresso and stirring the sugar back up with the little silver spoon.

"I promise to behave if you get me in there," said Odile.

Tania looked up and raised her eyebrows. "Maybe," she said. "I don't even know if they'll let me in. Just because I have government ID doesn't mean I have clearance for *that* zone."

Odile smiled at her. Behind Odile, Tania saw a room full of murmuring power lunchers, dark flannels and mostly pink faces against the posh white minimalism of the restaurant, watched over by well-groomed guards in their designer Kevlars. The outfits made them look like posable action butlers, maybe

49

because they seemed to spend more time looming over the patrons than checking who walked in the door. Odile swore there were no listening devices in the restaurant, that the customers were too powerful to put up with it, but every time Tania looked at that owl sculpture hanging on the wall she had to wonder.

Lunch with Odile, her best girlfriend from law school, was one of the only things that would get Tania downtown these days. Tania had settled into a more suburban reality, which suited her just fine. Her office was way out in Herndon off the toll road, her apartment up on Georgia Avenue just this side of Silver Spring, not far from the disabled veterans camp. That made her one of the drive-time Beltway bots who shuttled between different points in the outer limits, listening to banal hits of a mellower past when she couldn't stomach the news. She liked to go to the museums when she had a Sunday off, but with all the new checkpoints and barricades it was getting to be too much of a pain. Today was a special occasion: celebrating the payment of Odile's year-end bonus, which was more than Tania's whole salary.

Lunch was on Odile.

Odile worked at one of the big K Street firms, negotiating military merchant charters for $635 an hour and then bragging about how many nonbillable hours she spent on pro bono cases for the Detainee Project. They had met as section mates their first semester at the Liddy Institute for Law and Public Policy, bonded by a shared sardonic humor that bridged their divergent backgrounds. Odile was an affluent white girl who grew up behind so many layers of protection that she could afford to be an idealist, with a politician mother and businessman father whose access to power was the ultimate insurance.

This restaurant she picked was just Odile's kind of place, from the security that vetted you with your office before you could get a table to the way who saw you was more important than what you ordered. Even the name was pure Odile: Minerva, the preferred daughter of the most powerful man in the castle city that rules the world.

The stuffiness of the venue didn't hinder their laughing. They traded gossip about classmates, debated whether the miseries of private practice or public service were worse, and talked a ridiculous amount of time about the new show they were watching: *In My Eyes,* a stupid but charming romantic comedy about a drone pilot who gets a crush on one of the bad boys she's tracking. They enjoyed fancy-ass crab cakes on white tablecloths and told jokes about X-ray cameras and how people like to undress the last secrets they have left in their lives. They avoided politics and Odile's tendency to say the kinds of things most people know better than to say when the machines might be listening. Until it was time to pay the check.

"Who do you really think tried to kill that fascist?" she said, not even bothering to whisper. "And why couldn't they finish the damn job?"

"Okay," said Tania, trying to see who was around without really looking. "I knew it was a bad idea to let you order wine with lunch. Let's go. You can come with me if you promise to keep it cool."

Odile brushed off Tania's paranoia with a dismissive hand and a wry smile. As caring as she could be, Odile never really got it, never really understood the gulf between them. Odile could literally afford to say the kinds of things that would get other people arrested.

Tania couldn't. No matter how much she sometimes wanted to.

As they waited for their coats, Tania wondered if the guard who was talking into his hand was talking about them, but figured that was being overly paranoid, even for her. Outside, you could see, the sun was shining bright.

14

THE STREETS WERE CLOSED SOUTH OF EYE STREET. HAD BEEN since the event. So they walked to the checkpoint at Farragut Square, which had been converted into a staging area for the federal troops that protected the new perimeter around the White House. Marines, Motherland Guard, and uniformed Secret Service. The Secret Service were the most intense, with their black uniforms, patent leather, and chromed gunmetal.

"You know I dated one of those guys," said Odile, as they stood at the crosswalk and admired the scene. "A lieutenant. The algorithm said we had a ninety-two percent chance of compatibility."

"Seriously," said Tania. "Like that movie about the girl and her bodyguard. How'd that work out?"

"Fun at first. Lots of fitness fun. Then he got a little too strict."

Tania laughed.

"Don't even ask about the tattoos," added Odile.

The image that flashed in her head was darker than Tania expected.

They joined the queue of office workers headed back from lunch, lined up half a block along the barricades waiting their turn to get through. It was one of those winter days that were as sunny as they were cold. You could hear it in the harsh rotor chop of the helicopter patrol that flew over low while they waited.

"Seriously, though," said Odile. "What do you think really went down?"

There were a lot of theories. It had happened when Maxine Price, Vice President of the ousted administration that had come before—and more recently leader of the separatist political experiment that took root in New Orleans after the flood—led a delegation for cease-fire talks at the White House. That much everyone agreed on. Theories about who brought the bomb, or if there even was a bomb, varied widely. The less people really knew, the crazier the stories they invented to explain things. What Tania was sure of was that Maxine Price was killed that day, whether by her own hand as the ultimate American suicide bomber, by a heroic Secret Service agent, by a rogue corporate coup attempt, or all of the above, and what was left of the idea of a real change in this town, and this country, disappeared with her.

Tania made the sign for Odile to zip it. The bulletproof kiosk of the officer in charge was getting closer. She watched the people pass through and tried to reverse-engineer the protocol.

"I don't know about this," said Tania, sizing up the seriousness of the guards. "I need to get back to work anyway."

"We're here now," said Odile, gently tugging at Tania's arm. "It's no different than standing in line at a fancy nightclub. Just try to look like you belong there."

"Computers don't control who gets into nightclubs," said Tania.

"No, they don't," said Odile. "And they don't control it here, either. People do. That guy does. We just need to figure out what he wants to hear."

Tania nodded, got an idea for a safe strategy, and then it was their turn.

"IDs, please," said the unit officer, a thirtyish white dude who had taken his shiny helmet off but left his government-issue sunglasses on.

Tania looked at Odile, who registered no doubt.

Tania handed him her badge, and Odile her firm credentials, and they both flashed real enough smiles that they almost got one from the officer. He scanned their IDs, looked at his screen, looked at them, typed something, and made a cop face.

"Sorry, ladies," said the officer. "Heightened alert today, on-site personnel only, and you're not on the list."

"That's annoying," said Tania. "We have a meeting in the Annex, kind of last minute, and they were supposed to log it this morning."

She gave him her most innocent face and watched to see his reaction. What she said was not entirely untrue. Just mostly.

"Nope," said the officer, looking back at his screen. "Who's your meeting with?"

Two of the other guards moved in behind them.

"Andrea Fox in the Office of the Chief Procurer," said Tania, using the name of someone she really did work with on occasion.

"Okay, I will check on that." The officer closed the window to his kiosk so you couldn't see or hear what he was doing. Tania looked at her reflection in the black glass and didn't particularly like what she saw. As if the icy wind and the bright sun exposed the truth behind the lies you told yourself thinking others would believe them.

She looked away, at Odile's still-smiling face, which managed to show the cold in lush rosy cheeks, the kind of skin that was made to look good in cold climates. She looked at the Secret

Service soldiers, three of them now, clearly blocking them in. And she glanced at the growing line of workers behind her, starting to grumble at the delay.

When the officer opened his whole door instead of sliding back the window, he had shifted into a more alert mode. You could see it in his eyes.

"Deputy Assistant Secretary Fox is not in the office," he said. "Out all week."

"Right," said Tania, thinking on her feet. "But we're not actually having an in-person meeting. Just reviewing documents. Someone in her office was supposed to meet us."

"Uh huh," said the officer. "Why don't you two come with me and we can figure it out."

"Forget it," said Tania, getting scared now. "We'll just go back to our offices and reschedule. Sorry to hold you all up."

"Not that easy," said the officer.

Just then another officer walked up, plainclothes, kind of short for a Secret Service guy, blond hair working on gray.

"Inspector," said the officer. He handed them their IDs and pointed at the display on his screen, which Tania could not see.

"We just want to see it," said Odile, as the inspector assessed the situation. "To pay our respects. We didn't know it was so restricted."

The inspector looked up at Odile, then back at her ID, and the screen.

"Miss La Farge," he said.

"Yes, sir," said Odile, with the smile.

The inspector tapped on the officer's keyboard, then pointed him at something on the screen. The officer shrugged, and the inspector nodded.

"Okay, Miss La Farge," said the inspector. "You and your friend can go on in, up to the next perimeter, and take a quick look. Fifteen minutes. We'll keep your IDs here at the box and you can collect them when you leave."

"Oh, thank you so much, sir. You are so kind. Please tell me your name."

"Nichols. Inspector Nichols. You can express your appreciation to your mother, and give her our regards."

"Oh, I will," said Odile.

"Come on through," he said, guiding them to the radiation detectors.

When Tania stepped out of the machine, she saw Odile there smiling, as one of the shiny helmet dudes passed the wand over her body while another watched.

"All dressed up and nobody to shoot," she joked.

The guards gave each other a look but let them pass.

Tania shook her head and noticed the sweat under her armpits as she pulled her jacket back on. But the anxiety from lying to the law bled off quickly once you got through, aided by her friend's contagious smile. Odile probably knew this was how they would get in, but didn't want to spoil the fun of watching Tania freak. Tania should have been mad, but instead felt excited, like she was in on the prank.

They walked on, through public spaces turned into DMZ.

There were even more boots and armor in Lafayette Park, impeding their view through the layers of hurricane fence, bollards, and razor wire erected as temporary barricades. They elbowed and smiled their way to a spot where you could see the familiar profile of the main entrance and the East Wing. It was weird to see the big yellow earth movers and trenching machines parked on the ceremonial lawn, maybe waiting for it to get warm enough to start digging again in the big black scar where the West Wing used to be. Tania saw smoke there, which was surprising all these months later, until she realized it was just steam coming up from some heat exhaust vent.

"This is intense," said Odile. "Pictures don't do it justice."

"Kind of crazy they're spending all that money on rebuilding it," said Tania. "Everybody knows the real White House is underground."

"When it's not flying around in the air," said Odile.

And then, lucky day, almost as if it was because Odile asked for it, just as they were about to leave, it flew right in. Eagle One. The pitch of its turbines humming at a frequency that sounded like the future.

"No wonder the security is heightened," said Odile.

They waited to see if it would land on the front lawn. And if it was true. How he looked now.

"His scars are America's scars." That's what they said in the interstitials. And when she thought about it as it came into her head just then, Tania realized how true that was. Just not exactly the way they meant.

15

THE NIGHT BEFORE, TANIA FELL ASLEEP WATCHING THE PRESI-
dent on TV.

She hadn't meant to watch it, but when she sat down to find the numb after an intense few days fighting lopsided battles at work, she forgot that it was Third Thursday—time for *Hello America*, the President's monthly show where he talks to his people.

It was easy to forget, because it was so rare that it actually ran on Thursday anymore. Instead, it was whenever the President felt like, which seemed like it was more often than monthly, and usually Sunday.

When it was on, it was the only thing on, at least on the main channels.

It was already in progress when Tania turned on the Feed. *Hello America* had no time limits. It was scheduled for an hour, but it went on as long as the President wanted. For this episode he was sitting in the den of Rancho la Paz, the executive retreat he had carved out of the mountainous military range above Alamogordo. It was a nuke-proof bunker, but they made it look like some kind of fancy cabin, with antlers over the fireplace, wood furniture, and Navajo blankets, which Tania thought was kind of messed up. One time when Tania was watching, the President had gone off on a ramble about why all the U.S. military helicopters were named after conquered Indian tribes, "honoring their fierce spirit."

Tonight when Tania tuned in the President was sitting by the fire, badly lit—the way he often was since the bombing—talking to one of his bodyguards about some businessman in Texas who had earned his wrath. As the President ranted, the bodyguard flipped through a slide show of incriminating surveillance shots of the guy.

When the show first started at the beginning of his first term, people watched it mostly with hope, or at least an expectant curiosity. The leader was live without a script, talking with seeming authenticity about his plans for change, solutions for a country that felt increasingly broken, run out of frontier to tame. Tania thought it was like at work when a new boss would call an all-hands meeting and you went to hear what the new plan was, who got promoted, and who just got fired.

But at this company, you found out who just got arrested. And when he said so-and-so is no longer with us, he usually meant it literally. One time he announced a small invasion. He would also give out dispensations. Grants to worthy causes. Rewards and bonuses for special achievements. Or the ultimate prize of all, his attention. That was the highlight of every episode, the part where he would call one "lucky" American, and depending on how the conversation went, your future could be determined. Especially if, when he called, it was evident you hadn't been watching the show.

So Tania left it on, but started reading a book as well, and nodded off at some point when he was rambling on about the philosophy of property rights and how what we find in nature becomes ours, exclusively, as soon as we possess it.

It was only hours later, when she was awakened on the sofa to the jarring tones of a Citizen Emergency Alert blasting from her devices, that Tania learned what the big announcement was that evening. Counterterror raid in the heart of the Tropic. Some senior VP for the St. Louis Restoration Corporation had jogged a little too far south on the riverfront and got nabbed. Ended up on camera in a private upload with bad sound, but not so bad you couldn't hear he was reciting fragments of classified clauses and dronecodes. Cut to family members of alleged cell leaders the Chief had authorized SLoRC security to round up "for their safety" as they prepared to hunt down the kidnappers.

When they ran the hostage videos, Tania found herself looking for signs hidden in plain sight, signs of what was really going on behind the screen spectacle. The eyes of people she had grown up with peering out through the balaclavas. Evidence of false flag production stages, like the dissidents claimed. Tania came from both those worlds—the federal state and the restless zones it had given up on—but mostly felt like she belonged to neither. There was a time when she thought maybe she could help find a new third way into a better future, but these days she was just happy to find her way to Friday, working a good job doing things that could make a small difference, with a few trusted friends and a safe, comfortable apartment to come home to.

But when she woke up scared from dreaming about Him, it put other ideas back in her head, ideas that were getting harder to banish.

16

EAGLE ONE FLEW IN FAST FROM THE WEST, THEN YAWED BACK
over the East Lawn, engines whining overthrottle, blasting air
onto the ground.

Eagle One was the flagship of a new line of Anglo-American
tactical aircraft the President had promoted as superior to the
helicopter. It could fly faster and higher, with even better vertical takeoff and landing capabilities. All jet, no wings—just
stabilizers at the tail. Manufactured by a company he still had
stock in.

Tania tried to see through the cockpit window, to see if he
really was the pilot, but the glass was as opaque as the midnight blue fuselage.

It was a beautiful and scary thing, with its Luftwaffe '46
lines guided by twenty-first-century electrorobotics. Visitor
from a different tomorrow. She'd seen it on the big screens for
the last inaugural, when it flew in from Camp David, but seeing it in person was a whole different deal. Pure wonder. Like
some cross between a royal yacht, an experimental supercar,
and a unicorn.

Piloted by God.

"Dark Apollo has landed," joked Odile, barely audible
through the noise.

Tania had been close enough to see him once before—two
years earlier, on the day they swore him in for his third term,
wearing his medals. Tania had watched the parade, just down
the road, on an office balcony with Odile and a bunch of other

silk suits cheering on their sugar daddy in chief. Tania remembered the snowflakes melting on the military robots as they rumbled down the street. The big land drones with their black beret Engineer escorts walking alongside. The double-wide floats with their maudlin pageants of the martyrs of Tehran, Seoul, Panama City. She'd seen a guy in the crowd throw a snowball at the Vice President's limo, then watched the silver helmets swarm him.

"Which one's your boyfriend?" she teased Odile now, as they watched the soldiers mark out a landing pad with their regimented bodies, so close Tania could almost reach them through the fence.

They felt the thrust as the turbine turned down, like a hot hard wind. The craft dropped fast, then slowed just above the flickering turf, gently moving through the final phase into a soft landing.

There were no tourists on this side of the checkpoint, but everyone around turned to watch. The President, even just the idea of his imminent presence, compelled your gaze.

The Secret Service detail assembled around the rear of the aircraft, waiting for the door to drop. The sanctioned cameras were right behind them.

Tania's view was occluded, but she could see the colored light leak out from inside when they opened the hatch.

The personal guard emerged first. A detail of three. All tall, handpicked from the best corporate security firms. One of them, a blond woman with a white scarf instead of a necktie, looked right at Tania, through lenses that clearly read her face.

"Don't forget to smile," said Odile.

"You're the one she should be checking out," said Tania.

"Look," said Odile. "The dogs!"

Sure enough, the presidential pets trotted out on cue. The wolfhound, then the ridgeback. Everyone knew their names. Ulysses and Lee.

The man who followed looked like the President, but wasn't. Odile squealed.

"Newton!" she yelled.

Others joined in with shouts and whistles. Tania gasped.

The man turned, flashing a white porcelain smile. Newton Towns. The actor who played the President in the movies. The one that popularized Mack's narrative before he first ran for office, dramatizing his escape from the North Koreans after his fighter jet went down in the DMZ. Then the sequel, a miniseries about the Panamanian crisis of his first term. They were working on a third one now, about the retaking of New Orleans.

"He's fucking glowing," said Odile, and Tania laughed with her.

He wasn't, really, but he had that aura. Opposite of what Tania expected, he was even better-looking in person. Beautiful, in an unreal way, yet there he was, magazine cover model of a good-looking, friendly white man, the archetype they wanted you to believe in. He wore a suit, but no tie. One of those suits built to your scan, that draped elegantly and suggested superhero bulges all at the same time.

One of the cameras came in close for the star, then moved toward the crowd. Not that you could tell what it was filming. There was more than one eye behind the black glass of those rotored orbs.

As she thought of it scanning them, Tania got anxious for a second, then remembered how that inspector sucked up to Odile. If they were watching them, it was probably to protect her.

Two women walked out. The girlfriends. Newton's date, the country singer Ashley Lionel, and the presidential companion, triathlete Patricia Wood. They looked rich, unnaturally young, and happy.

Then *He* emerged.

The Commander in Chief, wearing an old-school bomber jacket with flight patches and the left sleeve pinned up over his stump. He didn't look back. All business, the busy boss headed back to the office. His hair was going white. It looked like some of his skin was, too, scar tissue you could see on the back of his neck. He was shorter than they made him look on TV. And something about seeing him in the flesh, feeling him that close, made all your deep down feelings about him come right up to the surface.

Tania wished she could see his eyes.

"Yo, Tommy!" she yelled, insanely, uncontrollably, as if momentarily possessed by the rabble-rousing spirit of her mom. "Look at your people, tyrant!"

Odile gasped.

And as soon as the words left her mouth, Tania could feel she had breached the terms of their unofficial permission to be here.

Shit.

Tania was right at the fence now, fingers through the chain link, eyes on, like some crazy starfucker. Or assassin. She suddenly realized how very close they were to the most protected man in the world.

She glanced at Odile's freaked-out face, and the uniformed dudes gaping behind her, all staring at Tania.

But she got what she wanted.

She got the President of the United States to look right

at her. They locked gazes. No more than a second, but long enough to register the judgment of those cold blue eyes.

It was not a safe feeling.

"Let's go," said Odile.

The President turned. Barked something at his guard. One of his dogs actually barked.

The blond lady bodyguard was really watching Tania then. So were half the people around her.

Tania felt the shudder of fear come up through her body.

She looked up and around, at the cameras you could see, and the ones you couldn't. One of the news cameras was on her now.

OMFG.

"Come on!" said Odile, grabbing Tania, pulling her hard.

"Yeah, okay," said Tania. They turned and headed back the way they came.

"What the fuck!" said Odile, glaring, as they walked as fast as they could without running.

"Sorry!" said Tania. "I think you just got me all riled up with all that crazy talk at lunch and hollering at Newton."

"That was all you," said Odile. "I say what I think sometimes, but in the right time and place. I thought you knew how this town works!"

"Same way the whole country works," said Tania. "I didn't do anything wrong."

She knew that was a lie, even if it was true.

When they got to Lafayette Square, they were waiting for them. Of course they were. The soldiers surrounded them, separated them, frisked them. Tania saw Odile crying as that same inspector, Nichols, escorted her back behind the checkpoint. Then four Secret Service agents took Tania away in a car with windows tinted so dark she couldn't see where they were.

She asked what cause they had to detain her, but they didn't say anything. As she knew, they didn't have to.

It was an emergency.

It had been an emergency for as long as Tania could remember.

THE SECRET SERVICE AGENTS TOOK TANIA'S PHONE, TOOK OFF her handcuffs, and locked her in a room without windows.

The room was cold. Sweater temperature, but they had taken hers away, along with her winter coat and suit jacket, and left her to shiver.

She waited there for a very long time. She couldn't be sure, because they took her watch, too, and her bag, and everything from her pockets.

The only things on the walls were the official portraits. An old one of the President, leading-man head shot from the first term, before the job started to really show on his face, way before they tried to blow him up. Next to him was an even bigger one of the General, chest garnished with the campaign ribbons of long wars over diminishing resources, stern eyes that had been staring at her since childhood.

They omitted the portrait of the President who came between. The one they deposed. They would have written him out of the books entirely, if he didn't provide such a convenient scapegoat.

He was still in office when the computers first tagged Tania for her "talents." She scored the way they liked on the tests, and they transferred her out of the combat zone and into the elite academy across town in St. Paul. That bought her a scholarship slot at university, where the professor for her senior seminar on Popular Defense and Ecological Struggles gave her name to a government recruiter. She took those tests, and a few weeks later people in suits were taking her to lunch. They said they needed people with her gifts, a compliment she devoured without really asking what it was they liked so much. They offered her a federal service package that would put her through law school, guarantee her a five-year employment contract, and get her out of the Blocks and into the capital. They said she would be able to help people, fight the nation's enemies, protect the people she loved. She took it, against her mom's advice. Tania wanted something better than the hard world of her childhood.

During summer vacation after her second year, while most of her law school classmates worked cushy clerkships at big firms, they sent Tania and a few others off for special training. They would crowd into conference rooms with trainees from other schools to learn computer forensics, predictive analytics, surveillance and countersurveillance. They spent hours writing their own algorithms to analyze data harvests, learn how to code their own little bots. People from Fleet trained them on the latest drone protocols. The year before the President had made some of the drones semiautonomous, and the teacher said getting one to really work your case was like having a cross between a supercomputer and a pack of bloodhounds.

At the end of the first month they put Tania and five other trainees in a room with two shrinks from Quantico to work on techniques of noncoercive interrogation. Being chosen like that felt good, and what you learned seemed so secret and so powerful, it converted you without you even knowing it. Or so it seemed.

They learned techniques for reading personality, signs of lying, signs of fear. They learned how to manipulate time, atmosphere, and language. They learned how to glean truth from bullshit.

The shrinks peddled some of the oldest knowledge. "Witchcraft and psychopomp," one of them joked. They taught Cold War interrogation breakdown strategies like Nobody Loves You, News from Home, Alice in Wonderland, and Spinoza and Mortimer Snerd. Tania didn't know who Mortimer Snerd was, until she looked it up, and then lost an evening watching early-twentieth-century ventriloquism videos and seeing if she could throw her voice.

They taught new strategies, too, tailored to the neuroses of the age. What's Your Movie, All Nine Eyes, Who Shot Yoko, We Have a Winner, Do You Know Who My Dad Is. The last one was Tania's favorite, tailor-made for penthouse provocateurs.

Tania scored high on all the tests. She proved a good shot on the firing range. She studied her butt off, as always, and had amazing grades. She was slotted for a choice job—maybe even an embassy posting. Until the semester before graduation, when they assigned her to the next class of Motherland special agents. When she imagined herself spying on her own people, on Americans, on people who still lived in places like the one she came from, she realized that was what they had wanted her for all along. And when she said no thanks, try again, they made her take more tests, and then posted her to an obscure office of the Defense Department providing investigative oversight of companies with military merchant contracts.

They thought it was punishment, but the tests failed to predict she be would so good at that job that they would want to fire her, and so good at it that they couldn't, at least until her contract ran out.

She was sitting there in the cold, wondering if maybe that's what this was really about, when she heard the steel door buzz open.

18

A MAN AND A WOMAN ENTERED THE HOLDING ROOM. THEY BOTH wore gray suits, the prosecutorial uniform of people who see the world in gradations of criminal guilt. The woman, who was taller, flashed her Secret Service credentials and said she was Agent Gerson and her colleague was Agent Breland. Breland looked like a cross between a soldier and an accountant. Gerson reminded Tania of a girl who picked a fight with her in middle school.

"Where's my friend?" said Tania.

"What were you doing at the White House today?" asked Gerson, making it clear who got to ask the questions.

"Looking at the White House," said Tania.

"You were inside a secure area," said Gerson.

"They let us through," said Tania.

"That doesn't make it okay," said Gerson. "Almost makes the violation worse."

"You tried to lie your way in," said Breland.

"Come on," said Tania. "We just wanted to see it. See how it looks now."

"It looks like a reason to clean up the country," said Breland.

"Was it your idea or your friend's?" asked Gerson.

"I don't know," said Tania. "Mine."

"But she's the real troublemaker, isn't she?" said Gerson. "A rebel in patriot's clothing. She wants to hurt him. Probably put you up to it. If you tell us what she's up to, this will go a lot easier for you."

"She—"

Tania could feel it, how everything her mom taught her about sticking up to authority crumbled in the face of indefinite detention. Along with all the lessons learned in law school about never talking to cops. Instead, everything she'd learned about pleasing teachers came out to say hello. Maybe they already knew how she would act. She assumed they had access to all her profiles.

"Ma'am, she's harmless. Talks big, but in the end she likes living in the tower. Hard to blame her. I'm the one who acted out."

"Why did you threaten the President?" said Breland.

"I did not threaten anybody, sir."

"That's not what he thought."

Tania looked Breland in the eyes, trying to convey disbelief. Instead she shuddered at the sense that it might be true.

"You want to see the video?" said Breland.

"I don't need to, sir, no thank you. I just want to get back to my caseload. I'm sorry if we caused any trouble. We didn't even know he was going to be there, and when I saw him, I just got excited, and—"

Every time she blinked, the President's eyes were there, burning a hole in her.

"What kind of cases do you do, anyway?" said Breland. "Office of Special Investigations."

"They think they're special," said Gerson. "They investigate our own troops."

"No, ma'am, that's not right," said Tania. "We investigate contractors. Corporate licensees, not uniformed service. For bad stuff. Fraud, charter violations, dark markets, vice."

"Working hotline snark from chickenshit whistleblowers," said Breland. "You should be investigating who put that hole in the ground, instead of gawking at it like some tourist."

Gerson laughed.

"I just do my job, sir," said Tania. "Ma'am. I don't make the laws."

The door opened, and another man walked in. He was black, and older, with white eyebrows and a charcoal suit. He wore a metal lapel pin, the flag-hued *F* of the President's party. The others looked up when he entered, but the man said nothing. Just glanced at Tania and then stood at the side of the room, watching.

Breland looked back at his tablet screen, scrolling.

"No wonder they washed you out of the elite services," he said. "Before you even started."

He held his screen up to Gerson. She smiled, a smile of adverse judgment.

"They knew better than to let her get close to the power," said Gerson. "Knew she's a threat."

"I am not a threat!" yelled Tania, suddenly steaming, repressed anger tripped, anger at a lot of things that were reflected in this moment. "I called out his name! I was excited. He was with Newton Towns! And the girlfriends!" She looked at the other man, who should have understood, but he registered nothing.

"I think you have serious loyalty issues," said Breland.

"Runs in the family," said Gerson.

Mom, thought Tania. That turned out to be only partly right.

"Like your brother," said Breland.

"My *what*?" said Tania.

"This guy," said Breland, turning his tablet to show her the screen.

The image was the mug shot of a man that looked nothing like Tania. For starters, he was white, or something close to it, with long straight hair and crazy green eyes. It took a kind of internal double take before her mind did the morphing, and she felt the blood drain. A face she had not seen in a very long time.

"I don't have a brother," she said, a legal truth that was also false.

Sig. The little fucker. He was alive.

"That's not what your mom told us," said Gerson.

Tania felt the air leak out of her.

"You talked to my mom?" she asked, weakly, after a long pause.

"We detained her for questioning," said Breland.

"Fuck!" said Tania, the crazy coming on.

"We think she has been helping him," said Gerson. "Harboring a fugitive."

"She runs a coffee shop!" said Tania. "And we have nothing to do with that kid."

"You lived in the same house," said Gerson. "Your mom was his guardian."

"Never for long," said Tania, caving all the way in, the words coming out like a sigh of surrender. "More like a stray dog than a brother."

"Modern family," said Breland, letting out a snicker.

"When did you talk to him last?" asked Gerson.

"Years. He disappeared."

"Escaped from custody, more precisely," said Gerson.

"He was just a little kid," said Tania. "A juvenile."

"A juvenile terrorist cop killer," said Gerson.

"You have no idea," said Tania. "His mom—"

"His mom was the leader of a cell," said Gerson. "What happened was as much her own fault as anyone else's. If she were alive today she'd be in prison."

"For her nonviolent protests?" said Tania.

"Like I said, loyalty issues," said Gerson.

"I am a loyal citizen," said Tania. "And so is my mother. You can be a good employee and not love the CEO."

"Not sure I agree, in this context," said Breland.

"Mom is definitely not on the team," said Gerson. "We've been learning a lot."

"You still have her?"

Gerson nodded. Held up the screen with Mom's intake photo, dated three days ago.

Tania imagined her sixty-eight-year-old mom in the interrogation chair, getting the treatment, being pressured to rat out people she knew.

"Would you like to prove your loyalty?" said Gerson.

"Will it get her free?"

"It should keep you both free, if we get the right results," said Gerson.

"We need you to find your brother," said the man with the white eyebrows, breaking his silence. "You have the training, and you have the access to that community."

Tania processed that for a long minute. She looked at the man, tried to intuit what his story was and what her real options were.

"Why do you need him so bad?" she asked. "What else did he do?"

"Maybe we just think he's going to go on to bigger and better things," said the man. "Predictive analytics are getting pretty good."

"And it will help us map the cells, all through the Tropic and the Sector N/C," said Gerson.

"Is that where he is?" asked Tania.

"Last seen in the sunny Minnesota borderzone," said Breland. "That's where they took this picture. Before whatever B-team knuckleheads they have running that igloo let him get away again."

"I see," said Tania. "You want me to capture my 'brother' and out my people."

"Help us find him, and you and your mother will walk, no charges," said Gerson. "Everything else you find along the way is extra credit."

Tania took a deep breath.

"You are helping us keep the peace," said the third man. "Keep these people safe, from misguided leaders who want to take us all down the path to chaos."

"Where do you think your brother would go?" asked Gerson.

Tania shrugged.

"Think harder," said Breland.

"I can find him," said Tania. "Just let my mom out."

"That comes after," said Gerson.

Fuck you, thought Tania.

"We already have three felonies on her," said Gerson. "Including a conspiracy charge. And we're just getting started. This is a nice deal we're offering."

"Put it in writing. Immunity for her, and for me. And for Odile La Farge."

"The deal is real," said the third man.

When she looked at him, Tania believed him.

"Agent Gerson has your paperwork," said Breland. "And you don't need to worry about Miss La Farge."

"Where is she?"

"We dropped your girlfriend off at her mom's," said Gerson.

"The office," smiled Breland. Tania imagined the scene.

"Your breach of presidential security wasn't the only reason we brought you in," said Gerson. "Though it made it a lot more fun, and conveniently gives us three felonies to pursue if you don't help us. But not on your cute rich friend. She's untouchable, for now."

"Unlike you," said Breland, standing up. "Agent Gerson is going to escort you out, and you are going to get to work."

"What do I tell my work?"

"You'll think of something," said the third man. "We'll be watching."

19

TANIA WAS SEVENTEEN THE FIRST TIME SIG STAYED WITH THEM. A bad age for babysitting, when Tania was more interested in taking the bus across town for "study halls" with the cool kids from the fancy high school she'd managed to get into.

Tania bitched at her mom about it from the get-go, asking why they had to adopt a weird little white kid as a pet when Tania wanted a cat. Mom said that wasn't nice, and it wouldn't be for long. They weren't adopting him, he wasn't really white, and it was their responsibility to help a sister in need. Even one with thick blond hair like the Viking-looking chick who first came by that night for coffee to drop off her brat. She seemed nice, but crazy, talking about how she had to go underground for a while. How the General had put her on a list. And that wasn't even the craziest thing she said.

Erika, the mom, had almost no control over her kid, as best Tania could tell. No wonder she wasn't taking him underground with her. When it was time for Erika to go, they found her little freak on the fire escape, holding a bird in his hands. A live bird.

Mom said he's kind of like a cat, right?

He let the bird go.

Tania knew Erika was part of the same movement as her mom and agreed to give it a try. Maybe she could get the kid to do stuff for her. Teach him. It was summer, after all, summer in Minneapolis. School was out and the days were stacked up in front of her like one big long afternoon that would never end.

It was the same summer that the local committee set up the mesh network in their neighborhood. They called it the Island. They put these little antenna units up on rooftops and telephone poles and gave everybody a box that turned their TV into a primitive computer. Keyboard and everything. It was secure, they said. No one else had access except for people in the neighborhood.

The neighborhood was not like the neighborhoods they saw on TV. It was a half-dozen apartment buildings spread over a couple of blocks, former public housing that got cooperatized after the feds cut the funding and the residents were on their own. Tania's mom was one of the leaders of the residents' committee that put it together. She took advantage of the opportunity to move to a bigger place where they each had their own bedroom, on the thirty-first floor of B Block.

The TV was in the main room, where little Sig slept on an air mattress on the floor. Most nights he would fall asleep right on the rug while Tania helped put the node to work. When she woke up in the morning he was usually gone, out hunting with the early birds or whatever it was he did before breakfast. Maybe Tania should have gone looking for him, but she just wanted to log back in.

They used the network for all kinds of stuff. Mainly, the people in the neighborhood got more organized than they had ever been. They shared information about food shortages and power outages, jobs and informal financial networks, traffic and weather, potholes and politics. They reported on police activity and arrests, and the incursions of the first militias as the bankrupt city, state, and federal governments started to look to citizen posses to do the jobs they could no longer pay for. The militia, unsurprisingly, were mostly white guys who already had their own guns. So the committee used the network to organize their own militia. Like a neighborhood watch with attitude, said Mom. They had their meetings in her coffee shop on the ground floor, which was also a bookstore, even if it functioned more like a library. They put a bunch of terminals in there for the people who didn't have the right kind of TVs. Tania made a program to track the books in circulation—mostly so she could find who had the copies of her Max Price books when she wanted to reread one. Tania spent a lot of her time "on air," as they called it, helping out as a community dispatcher.

This conveniently let her spend most of her time talking to her friends.

The kids figured out how to use the network to make their own computer games. Tania played the one they called Rat Race with her friend Esther, while Tania was at home and Esther was sitting in her apartment two blocks away. Tania showed it to Sig, and he kind of got it, but he didn't really seem to parse how the little dots and lines were supposed to be rodents and cats running through buildings.

The best thing about Rat Race wasn't the game itself. It was the pages it had where you could leave messages for each other. Like the August night when Esther told her about the meet-up at Arthur's. Tania said she was on babysitting duty, but Esther pressed, with the best Esther enticements, and Tania caved. She woke up Sig, made him put on his shoes, and said they were going out for candy.

That was a bad idea. Not just because there was rarely any candy at the corner stores, not just because it was after curfew, and not just because it was the hottest of a long summer of nights above 100 degrees. She knew all that before they left. What was really bad was that when they got two blocks from home, right around 11 P.M., the raid began.

When they came out of Topo's Grocery, each with a hand-wrapped chocolate drop in hand, Tania told Sig they were going to stop by her friend's place in the old office building. Sig pointed at the armored trucks rolling down the street, with their red and blue police lights spinning disco on the walls of the buildings. The men came out of the trucks, with guns and helmets, and ladders and wire cutters. They came to remove the network. They did not ask permission. They closed the streets and took over the neighborhood, four trucks per block, while they did it. The only explanation was that it was illegal. A violation of the Federal Communications Act. Tania and Sig were standing right there when Mr. Kingston, Mrs. Wilson, and rowdy Angie Brown came out and talked to one of the commanders. When Tania looked around, she realized there was a crowd of folks that had come out.

She never figured out exactly how it got out of hand. Part of it definitely was when they detained old Mr. Kingston for asking too many questions. But for sure some of the boys in the neighborhood were looking for a reason to fight and took up the opportunity to extract some justice. When the first of the police trucks went up in flames, the riot got going in earnest.

She tried to get Sig back to the apartment, using every secret route she knew, but she didn't. He freaked out, broke loose, and ran—between people's legs—like a crazy mini critter.

Rat Race.

Twenty minutes later, she was screaming, holding the little freak, trying to keep the bleeding under control with her hands and his balled-up T-shirt, the one with the picture of a moose on it. She held it hard against his stomach.

They said it was a stray bullet.

When they were at the hospital that night, Tania promised Sig she would never let anything bad happen to him again. No matter what stupid things he did, what trouble he got himself into, she would protect him. Even if she had to lock him in.

The government sent a check two months later for $21,000 for what happened to Sig. His mother, Erika, showed up just in time to cash it. She gave a thousand to Mom, saying maybe they could use it to help rebuild the network.

That night that Erika came back she was with two weird-looking dudes that Tania had never seen before. She said they had been in the country, planning. The guys didn't say anything. Just looked really uncomfortable. They didn't even spend the night, just grabbed Sig and the money and split.

Sig hugged Tania when he left but left the crying to her.

Mom said don't worry, you can bet he'll be back. He likes it here.

20

AS SOON AS SHE GOT HOME AFTER THE SECRET SERVICE RE-
leased her, Tania started looking for Mom.

She had asked Gerson for more info, but all her new covert handler had was a somewhat sketchy govspeak write-up
of their deal, a phone to use solely for staying in touch with
Gerson, and a promise to send more later.

Tania signed the deal, took the phone, and tried to collect
herself on the train home.

The new phone, she assumed, was also a tracking device,
a way for them to make sure she was keeping her part of the
bargain. She kept it out on the table while she worked. It was
like studying in public. It helped her focus, and keep the crazy
at bay.

If Mom's file was online, it was on a network Tania couldn't
access.

Mom was not the type of person you could track through
her public digital traces. She lived life in person, helping people she could see with her own eyes.

So Tania made some phone calls, on her own phone. Left
a pretty freaked-out message at the house. Talked to one of the
employees at the shop, who confirmed the detention but didn't
know where. Then she got through to Cousin Mell.

"You need to get home now!" yelled Mell. "They won't
even let her talk to a lawyer, and they won't let any of us see
her because we're not immediate family."

"I'm working on it," said Tania. "Do you know where they have her?"

"She's in the Box."

Tania's stomach turned.

The Box was the windowless federal annex out by the airport. The building that people joked was built without exits. Halfway house to the private prisons where they liked to send political criminals.

"I know how to get her out," said Tania. And after she hung up, that felt like a lie.

She sat there crying for a long time, the prisoner ID band still on her wrist. She thought about her options. About other ways she could get Mom out. People she could call who might have connections, or at least access. She took a long shower. She drank a glass of the strong stuff, the stuff she kept in a cupboard she could hardly reach.

She started looking for Sig.

She didn't have much luck. That probably meant neither had they. If Mom was a digital blip, Sig was invisible. But she looked anyway. You had to exhaust all options.

They had not downgraded her access level. They might even have upgraded it. She imagined them watching her as she searched. She thought about ways she could evade that. Maybe with her own encryption layer. Or a borrowed account, preferably with higher clearance. Todd at the office would know. And he owed her a favor.

Then a little box popped up on-screen. One of those annoying messages from BreakRoom, the workplace chat site. Looked like spam. *You gotta check this out!* A masked link. There was a note below the subject line, saying "*per our discussion today," and then she saw the handle of the sender—<gerson5991>. So Tania clicked it, and instead of turning her machine into a porno zombie, she got an under-the-table start kit of packed files.

It was Sig's detention file, excerpted. The file was thin on details. Standard deportation turned into order for indefinite holding via transfer to North Central Temporary Detention Center. Detroit. He escaped before the transfer.

There was footage of the escape loaded to the file. Grainy perimeter cam frames that looked black-and-white until the yellow jumpsuit popped into the middle of the frame like mustard splat on snow.

He looked even wilder than she remembered. The way he moved. Feral. The way he went over the barbed fence. Ouch.

She read the after-action report. He'd gone ghost. Back into the woods. They didn't know where to look.

She thought about those nature shows, where the dudes catch an animal, put a tag on it, and release it back into the wild, to find its true habitat, learn more about how it lives, and locate the entire social group of animals with which it interacts. She laughed to herself imagining doing such a thing to Sig, wishing she had done it to him when he was a kid. And then she realized that was exactly what they were doing to her.

Thinking about it that way made everything clearer, and made her a lot more pissed off. She should have been most angry at the people who were manipulating her, and the impersonal institutions that controlled them. But who she was really mad at was Sig, for putting Mom's and her lives on the line, even as she knew blaming him was like blaming that animal for escaping its captors.

She needed to find him.

Tania went to her closet and found the file box she had stuffed back in there the day she moved in and had not touched since. The orange plastic had faded. There were dead bugs curled up in the cracks. But the information inside was intact, if as incomplete as when she had given up all those years before.

This was the kind of information you didn't keep on your computer.

And as she started digging through it, trying to find her way to the present through the yellowed relics of the past, she began to wonder whether maybe they were right. Maybe Mom, and Sig, and all those people she left behind were in on something bigger than Tania or anyone else in Washington knew.

21

"JUST BECAUSE YOU GOT A CONVICTION IN THE REINBECK CASE doesn't make you immune," said Mike. "You really never want me to get a call like I got yesterday."

They were in Mike's office. Fifth floor, with a view of Dulles. A black and red AmLog cargo jet lumbered through the window frame behind Mike's head, carrying fresh heavy metal from the hub in Stansted. Bert and Tania were at Mike's breakout table, waiting to go over a file, but ten minutes in and Mike hadn't stopped laying into Tania about her candid camera moment.

"Who called?" asked Tania. She tried to keep it cool, wondering but figuring they hadn't outed her to her boss.

"You don't want to know," said Mike. "Somebody from the personal detail. You know, the people trained to *die* to protect their leader? Do you have any idea how strict they are about the perimeter they maintain around him now?"

"I waved at him!"

"You yelled at him, Tania! Called him a fascist!" He shook his head.

"Tyrant," muttered Tania.

"We both saw the footage," said Bert. "Not your best moment. You're lucky they censored it. That clip so wanted to be all over the Feed."

"People yell at him all the time," said Tania. "All those huge rallies he has. People go nuts. Call out his name. Slander his enemies. Chant the slogans."

"Careful," said Bert, pointing at the ceiling.

"You really don't get it," said Mike. "Those are his supporters, at events where everyone has been vetted. And coached. It's a potential felony just to be where you were, doubly so when you bullshit your way in. If you act out in there—"

"Room Twenty-Three," said Bert, laughing.

"Right," said Mike. "I guess. Put it this way. This little office of ours doesn't need this kind of attention. Got it?"

Tania nodded.

"We took you on here because of your skills, because we needed a third hand," said Mike. "And because the 'personality' matching—aka political demerits—that got you referred to us happen to be just the kind of thing we like to see—"

Bert pointed up again, more emphatically this time.

Mike turned on the white noise machine on his desk.

"Tania," said Mike, changing his tone, less agitated but even more serious. "We operate here on as tenuous a basis as some endangered bird. A table scrap thrown to the diminishing minority in Congress that doesn't go with the whole program of the party in power. There are just the three of us, sharing our resources with other offices that have very different agendas. Now we are working some angles that could help bring real change, and you're out screaming for adverse political attention. Do you fucking get it?"

If only he knew.

"Yes," said Tania. "I'm sorry. I don't know what got into me."

"Newton Towns is what got into you," said Bert, raising his eyebrows. "I wish he'd get into me."

"Jesus," said Mike.

"I knew you had a crush on him," said Tania. "Too bad. I saw him first."

"Can we talk about the cases now?" said Mike. "What do you hear from the Canadians, Bert?"

"They found them," said Bert.

"The guns?" said Mike.

Tania nodded, pointed at Bert. "P-B shipment. Got 'lost' in Chicago."

"I don't follow."

"Separatists," said Bert. "I found them in a raid two days ago. Manitoba. Anonymized but a definite match."

"Weird," said Mike.

"Maybe not," said Bert.

"Bert doesn't think they were lost," said Tania. "He thinks they ended up exactly where they were meant to be. I think he's right."

"Pendleton-Bolan guys are supplying Canadian guerrillas," said Mike. "The President's old company. That's what you're saying?"

"That's what RCMP thinks," said Bert. "It's a pretty good theory, actually."

"Maybe if you're a Canadian," said Mike. "There are many plausible explanations for those facts. But this is good. Anything else?"

"Funny you should ask," said Bert, adjusting his glasses. "I haven't even told Tania about this one."

"No secrets in the office," said Tania, wondering if she should tell hers. "First rule you told me, Bert."

"Had to wait for you to get out of jail, honey," said Bert.

Mike almost smiled.

"This also comes from the Mounties," said Bert. "Evidently the same gang that's running the guns for P-B is smuggling other contraband back in."

"What kind?" said Mike.

"Information," said Bert. "Content. Video, foreign media, porn, all kinds of stuff. Prohibited stuff."

"They'll love that downtown," said Mike. "Could earn us some points. But I'm not buying the idea that corporates are breaking the White House's own rules on command and control."

"I don't know," said Bert. "They have a source. Somebody they busted at this raid. Says they have one customer who's buying it all. Not sure where."

Tania remembered what the nameless Secret Service agent told her. *Figure something out.* Maybe he knew what they were working on. Maybe getting them off the trail was his real agenda. Maybe it was working.

"It must be there, in Minnesota," said Tania. She had never tried to steer the facts like this. It was illuminating.

"Could be," said Bert. "A relay station, or at least some good sources who know."

"We should find it," said Tania.

"You're killing me," said Mike. "I'm tempted, but you need to focus on the guns."

"Let me go out there," said Tania.

"You have other projects," said Mike.

"Not as hot as this one," said Tania. "Like you said, this could earn us some serious points. Might even get you a commendation."

"Handshake from the veep," said Bert.

Tania smiled. "Seriously," she said. "Besides, I know my way around out there."

Mike groaned.

"I like it," said Bert. "We can tag-team this one. Maybe put a bigger chunk of the puzzle together. I always feel like there's so much more going on."

Mike looked at Tania. Tania looked at the window.

"What aren't you telling me, Tania?"

She tried to banish the truth from her mind as best she could, but only started to blush. She tried a different tact.

"Trust me on this one, okay?" said Tania, giving him the most earnest face she could muster. "It feels right. I'll make it right."

She meant it, even if she wasn't sure she could deliver.

Mike stared at her. They listened to the white noise for a minute. Tania raised her eyebrows.

"Okay," said Mike. "You go to Minnesota. I'll order the travel pass today. And Bert, you go to Toronto or wherever."

"Winnipeg," said Bert.

"Whatever," said Mike.

"They're on complete opposite sides of the—"

"*Whatever.* See if you can find some better proof. Good enough to withstand crunching by the logic bots. This one has to be crazy solid to stick."

"Agreed," said Bert.

"Can I get some help from Todd?" asked Tania.

"If you want to go down there, knock yourself out," said Mike. "Just don't spend any more of our money."

"Thank you," said Tania.

"You're welcome, I guess," he said. "And Tania, I'm not fucking around here. If you get in trouble like that again?"

Tania looked down.

"Don't come back."

22

THE TELEVISION SET REMINDED TANIA OF THE ONE HER GRANDMA had. It was weird to see it here in Todd's computer forensics lab full of high-tech digital equipment. But Todd had a gift for the weird shit. Other agencies sent him theirs, the stuff for which there was no user manual.

"It was harder to find than I expected," said Todd. "These things have been obsolete since the MOFUC."

"The huh?"

"The Mandatory Open Format Universal Conversion," said Todd. "You remember, the 'Force Feed.' Where FCC and Motherland mandated that all media—broadcast, terrestrial, cable, online, you name it—operate on the new digital standard dictated by the government."

"The MOFUC, right," said Tania. "I had to buy a new personal phone and a hundred-dollar box for my TV."

"Exactly," said Todd. "Me, too. Except I was happy about it. It put everything on the same network. You can do so much more now. Especially the things we do."

He fiddled with one of the dials.

"Though I'm thinking this thing is actually kind of cool," he said.

It was tuned to technicolor snow.

"Not seeing it," said Tania. "It even smells kind of funny."

"Yeah, I don't think it was stored well. Electronics are a little gummy. Had to try four different thrift stores before I found one—they said people have been coming in and buying them. Past year or so."

"Weird. What use is a TV that only tunes dead air?"

"That's what I'm showing you."

He fiddled with an adapter attached to the back of the set, extended the antenna, and tuned two of the knobs.

"UHF," said Todd. "Totally illegal. And totally weird old over-the-air broadcast tech I barely understand. Here it is."

The picture was grainy. A black woman, sitting at a desk, in front of a map of the United States, reading a string of numbers out loud. The colors of an old Polaroid that had been sitting in a box.

"*Seven. Nine. Three. One. Three. Zero. Four. Seven.*"

"All it needs is a burning log," said Tania. "Code?"

"*Six. Nine. Zero. Nine. Three. Three. Three. One.*"

"Yeah, has to be," said Todd. "They use different channels at different times, with a few different readers. Sometimes they run test patterns that look like they might have some kind of steganographic stuff going on. I've also seen a lot of banned programming—foreign news, atrocity stuff, anti-Executive propaganda."

"Bert's lead."

"Exactly—that's how we found it—but other times they just have weird, random shows. Hunting videos, Mexican movies, police drone feed outtakes, warporn. The kind of prohibited stuff you'd buy in a truck stop. Once I actually saw a speech, just like a ten-minute rant about you know who."

Todd pointed his thumb at the framed portrait of the President hanging on the wall by the light switch. It was the new official portrait, the one where you could see the scars.

"I think the ranter was someone I've seen in the files. I'm working on a match."

"Really?" said Tania. "Tell me more."

"I'm kind of stuck," he said, shaking his head.

"Not very helpful. Can those guys you work with in Motherland help you?"

"Good idea. Maybe they'd let me access the DdB, look for matches."

"Why don't you let me help you," said Tania. "Get *me* access to the dissident database, give me some screenshots, I'll find them for you fast. While you focus on this." She put her hand on the TV.

"Maybe," said Todd.

"Think you could ask them about the other watch lists they keep?" said Tania. "The unofficial ones?"

"You sound like one of them," he said, pointing at the TV.

"Lighten up," said Tania. "They know you're a Boy Scout. Can you at least tell where the broadcasts are coming from?"

Todd made a face. "It's really hard to say. This stuff is so elusive. Ethereal, literally. Masked behind terrestrial relays, on platforms our gear doesn't track. I'm working on it as a math problem, but I bet the fastest way would be to penetrate the network. HUMINT."

Tania looked at the lady on the screen, and wondered.

"That makes sense," she said. "Where would you start?"

"Someplace in the Midwest, maybe," said Todd. "Lot of big old antennas out there in the zones. And that *is* where the insurrection is concentrated."

"The Tropic," said Tania. "Makes sense."

"We should look in St. Louis," said Todd.

"Mike's sending me to Minnesota," said Tania. "Can you look for possible sources there?"

Todd shrugged. "I guess," he said. "Could be a node there. Definitely a known dissident scene. Might get some tips from them."

"That's the plan," said Tania. She put her hand on the outlaw receiver. "Can I take this with me?"

"No," said Todd. "But I found something even better for you."

He reached over to the shelf and pulled down a portable set the size of a small jewelry box. She reached for it, but he pulled it back.

"What?"

"You just need to help me when they do the Calibration, okay? A couple of the guys we outed on Bert's last project are gunning for me."

The Calibration was the quarterly peer assessment that President Mack had implemented early in his first term. It applied to all federal employees and any corporation or state agency that received any funds from the feds. How it worked basically was everyone you worked with ranked you in whatever categories they picked that year. Competence, attitude, team spirit, loyalty, management skills, throughput. Not just the people in your own office. You could rank anyone you worked with from other offices. Vendors. Up and down the ladder. A good score meant money and status. A bad score and you could lose your job. Or a lot worse, as people were hearing. Because, you know, it meant you were a bad fit. Tania hated it, but had gotten by okay so far. Dishonesty on the Calibration was a violation.

"Of course," said Tania. "I'd do it anyway, for you. But I'm not sure I'm in the best standing myself."

"What do you mean?" He looked as if Tania had just said she had a contagious disease.

"Just kidding," said Tania, smiling. "I'll take care of you. Get me those login credentials and I'll fix your whole damn file."

Todd smiled back. He handed her the set.

When she turned it on, the picture came up like a beam of light from another reality.

23

ODILE CALLED HER THAT NIGHT.

"Are you okay?" she said.

"Sort of. I need to leave town."

"That bad?"

"I can't explain. It should be okay."

"Let's meet. You can tell me in person."

"I need to pack. I'll see you when I get back. Shouldn't be long."

"Promise?"

"Yes," said Tania, trying to convince herself. "What did they do to you?"

"Thankfully I'm too old for the bitch to ground me," said Odile.

Tania laughed for the first time in days.

"But I think she hired a detective," said Odile.

"She what?"

"Yeah. This very creepy-looking woman I keep seeing."

"You're being too paranoid."

"There is no such thing as being too paranoid. Not here. Even if I get cocky about it sometimes."

"Fair enough," said Tania. "Send me a picture if you can. I'll call you."

Later, as she packed for her trip, she thought about the pictures of Sig she had seen in his file. Wondered where he had been. If her instincts were right that he would come back to Minneapolis. If he could still disappear in the city like some hairless raccoon, the way he did when he was a kid.

As she picked out clothes, she wondered what it would take for her to blend in to a dissident crowd. It was like dressing for an alternate branch of her own real life. She just had to remember Dad's girlfriends, or some of her own outfits from college, back before she clarified her path. The trick was figuring out what was left in the wardrobe that fit the bill. She still had that old hand-me-down black turtleneck she wore under her suit on cold winter days, and the well-worn pair of black jeans she wore on the rare day off.

She put on the turtleneck, no makeup, and looked in the mirror. Something was still missing.

That was when she got the idea to unstraighten her hair.

When she stepped out of the shower and dried it off and let it express itself, there was a different person looking back at her. She liked what she saw, somewhat to her surprise.

Maybe the computers were better at profiling than she had thought.

She looked at the picture of Mom she kept on the dresser. Tania was pretty sure she could find Sig. What she wasn't sure was what she would do when she did.

24

THEY DROVE SOUTH AT NIGHT, ON BACK ROADS, ROADS THAT weren't even highways. The only signs were the names of little towns Sig had never heard of, some of them named after the people who lived here before, others after the people who took it away.

When first light started to seep over the eastern sky, you could see just how empty the country was. As flat as the surface of a lake, as if scraped by the hand of a god. And then Sig saw one of the giant machines that worked these fields, off in the near distance, sitting idle in the snow, big enough that you might think Paul Bunyan was the one to drive it. Paul Bunyan, the guy who killed all the trees that once grew in these fields.

"Big-ass robot, right?" said Moco. Moco was the guy they sent to take Sig to the place where they said he could safely hide, and they would give him important work to do. Moco was a little older than Sig, a scrappy little Honduran guy with a lot of tattoos. He showed up wearing a windbreaker in parka weather. Moco knows his way around, they told him, but Sig got nervous when he saw Moco's car, a beat-up old Fuji that looked like it wouldn't even be able to make it to the edge of town.

Sig looked out the car window at the robot, pink dawn light reflecting off its metal surfaces.

"They can't even grow regular crops here anymore," said Moco. "They grow corn a pig can't eat, from seeds they made in a lab, to turn it into fuel for machines. South of here, there's whole big stretches where they can't grow anything at all, no matter how they splice it. That's why they gotta go find new land in other countries."

"They just need to leave it alone," said Sig.

Moco laughed. "You can tell them that."

They drove past an old farmhouse that you could tell no one had lived in for a long time. The roof of the barn had caved in, and the silo was working on it.

Sig had slept much of the drive. The lady doctor had given him pills for the pain, but Sig didn't like the way they made him spaced out and vulnerable, so he stuck with aspirin if he needed it. He was feeling a lot better, but he couldn't help but reach under his shirt to make sure the scar was still holding together. When Sig fell asleep Moco had been listening to a tape of some lady talking, kind of like a speech, that he played through this beat-up little box that plugged into the radio. But now he was listening to a crackly signal coming in over the air. It sounded like a weather report, but after a minute Sig figured out it was somebody telling where not to drive.

"What is that?" said Sig.

"Amplitude modulation, dude. AM radio over an abandoned frequency, telling us the news."

"Who's talking?"

"I don't know, but I always think she sounds cute." Moco smiled, but he looked like he was thinking about something else.

"*Echo Delta One Six Fiver,*" said the voice on the radio. It sounded like it was coming from the other side of the planet, even though somehow you knew the source was very close. "*Walter Magic Walter.*"

Moco grabbed the map he had folded up on the center console and put it on the steering wheel where he could look at it while driving. It was an old paper road map held together with tape, marked up with extra notes in pen and pencil.

"Hold on," said Moco, handing Sig the map. "I'm gonna turn around and go back to go a different way."

Sig sat up then and took a better look at what was ahead of them, and behind. He tilted his head to look up at the gray sky, but all he saw were crows.

"It should be okay," said Moco. "They're not too bad up around here. Or I should say, there aren't too many of them. They had to move out to make room for the robots."

As Moco pulled off on the shoulder then made a hard U-turn, Sig saw the black pickup off in the distance, headed their way.

"And fortunately," said Moco, smiling but looking nervous all of a sudden, "this thing is faster than it looks."

25

"I WISH THEY'D LET ME INTERROGATE ONE OF MY PARENTS," joked the guard who escorted Tania down to the room.

Tania did not comment on that. She glanced over at his face, which had the pallor that prolonged exposure to fluorescent lighting can bring out, and briefly tried to imagine the parents that had produced this corporate constable.

Federal Annex MSP 4, aka the Box, was an almost-square five-story office building out by the airport that had been converted to the kind of cubicles where they lock you in. The perimeter of concrete barriers was the main thing that distinguished the Box from the suburban business park around it—from the outside, at least.

Tania went straight there after she got off the plane. This time she was on the list.

The heavy-duty elevator door opened into a hallway of bulletproof glass and floor-to-ceiling steel gates. You could hear the not-so-distant voices of prisoners caroming off the walls and floors, shouts and murmurs mixed in with the low-level machine noise of the building. Two other guards stood behind the main gate into the detention area. One nodded at Tania's escort, hit a button, and initiated the buzzer, so loud it startled her, when she was trying so hard to keep her cool.

They walked her back to a room with a solid metal door and a stenciled number. SB.2.223.

"You sure you don't want company?" asked the guard.

"Definitely not," said Tania. "And I don't need anybody monitoring the feed, either. Like we discussed."

"Suit yourself," said the guard as he punched in the code and let Tania enter with another buzz. "Twenty minutes is all I can give you."

Tania stepped through.

Mom was sitting there, in chains.

Tania shrieked, then swallowed it, then went in and hugged her. Mom couldn't hug back, because of the restraints. Or at least that was how Tania explained it to herself at the time.

"Have they hurt you?" asked Tania, a moment later after she had composed herself and taken the seat on the opposite side of the metal table.

"I'm okay," said Mom. "Not my first time, and others have it a lot worse than me, but I am getting too old for this shit. Maybe you had the right idea, Straight Life."

Tania let that jab go. She avoided Mom's gaze, scanning the yellow jumpsuit, wondering if it was paper or fabric, noting how the shackles threaded all four limbs and connected them to links in the floor, trying to think of where to start. She looked at Mom's hands, strong working hands, the skin still so beautiful, and so dark, darker than Tania's, in a way that sometimes they used to joke was what explained their differences in attitude.

"Look at me, Tania," said Mom.

Tania complied, wiped a tear from her cheek, and saw eyes that were angry and loving at the same time.

"How come you're the one who gets us both in trouble and I'm the one who feels guilty about it?" said Tania.

"They're listening, you know."

"I doubt it," said Tania. "But it doesn't matter if they are. Because I'm here to help you. By helping them."

"Is that right," said Mom.

"Yes, it is," said Tania. "I know you don't like me working for the government, but you and I are on the same side. I just like to take the fight inside, a little closer to the power."

"How's that working out?" said Mom.

"I got close enough to the President to scream in his face the other day."

"Seriously?"

"Seriously. It sounded like you talking."

"No, I mean you seriously just *yelled* at him? That's just stupid. You don't want to know what I would do if I got that close to him."

"Believe me, I know. But most days I do it in the back office, one case at a time. I told you how we put away that Army colonel for importing kids through the Panama Free Trade Zone."

"That even made the news. 'Guest workers.'"

"Exactly. That's what I do. At least until my contract is up."

"That's good. Maybe next you can work on the exploitation going on right here. You think what they do in the private prisons is any different? Detroit?"

"I didn't come here to argue with you, Mom. Especially not about how I do my job. I came here to make sure *you* don't go to Detroit. Or someplace worse. And to do that, I just need you to help me find Sig."

"You want to help your mother by turning in your brother."

She forgot to act surprised. That meant she definitely knew he was back.

"Jesus, now you sound like them. He's not my brother, or your son. He's not real family."

"You always were a good liar. You get it from your dad."

"Where is Sig, Mom?"

"I haven't seen that little freak since he ran away after the riot. Years."

"And you always were a bad liar. Is he still in town?"

Mom just gave her that look of extreme disapproval.

"I don't know where he is. Probably dead, if you want me to guess."

"I don't believe you."

"What else is new?"

"Mom, I just want to get you out."

"Then get me a good lawyer!" she erupted, banging her fist on the table. "Since apparently you turned out to be the other kind."

Tania growled in frustration. She stood.

"You okay in there?" said the disembodied voice of the guard, over the intercom.

"Yes!"

She looked at Mom. Mom was shaking, trying to hide it.

Tania went over, kneeled down next to her, grabbed her hand, and held it. The chains were so fucking cold.

She ran her hand through Mom's hair. Tried to calm her.

"Listen, Mom. I'm sorry you don't trust me enough to tell me what's really going on. But I'm a better lawyer than you give me credit. I can't get you out yet, but I got them to move you to Boschwitz House. You'll be a lot more comfortable, and you won't have to answer any more questions."

Boschwitz House was an old mansion named after a local politician who had once been placed under house arrest there in his own residence, back in the days of the General. Now it was run as a charity, a place where political "criminals" deemed sufficiently nonviolent were allowed to stay during detention, in the interest of keeping the peace.

Mom looked like she thought that was okay, or at least better.

"How did we get here, Mom?"

"By compromising," she said. "By letting them divide us. They know how to get all the people who should be on the same side to fight each other over differences that aren't even real. Race, religion, region, reason. And people got so poor and worn out they just gave up, at least on the idea of real change. But a new wind is coming."

"How, Mom?" She grabbed her, like an impatient kid.

"You should come home and find out. Work with us. You'll see. We could really use your skills. I know you've got the right heart."

Tania looked at her. "How deep into it are you, Mom?"

"I just provide room and board, space to meet, strong coffee, dangerous cookies, and the occasional good idea."

"I know. So help me find Sig, so you can get back to work."

She shook her head. "There's a lot to do inside, too. You should leave him be. He's been through enough."

"I know," said Tania. "But—"

Mom put her hand on Tania's head now, seeming to soften for a minute. Then she finally smiled.

"What's up with your hair, anyway?" said Mom.

"Huh?" Tania reached up there.

"I kind of like it," said Mom.

And then the door clanked open as the guards came to take Tania away, and put Mom back in her cell.

"Don't save me, Tania," said Mom, as they unchained her from the floor and let her stand. "Save yourself. Save the future."

26

SIG WOUND FRITZ'S AIRPLANE FOR FLIGHT, TWIRLING THE TINY propeller with his index finger. The rubber band twisted into knots along the length of the balsa wood fuselage. The hand-made flying machine fit in the palm of your hand and weighed no more than a book of matches.

A cloud moved overhead, and the light brightened inside the room, a sunporch at the back of the house where Fritz and Billie lived. It was sanctuary, they said, but Sig still paid attention to every movement in his periphery.

Sig looked out through the south window at the small yard leading to a creek. The house was off the old highway that connected Iowa City to Cedar Rapids. You could see the corporate parks off in the distance along the interstate, backlit by the burnt orange of the setting sun.

A big raccoon appeared out of the bushes to the left, heralding nightfall. Sig watched it look around for danger, then scamper over to the gigantic compost pile in the front corner of the yard.

"Don't overwind it," said Fritz.

Sig froze his finger. Fritz looked down over the rim of his wire-frame glasses, stroked the long gray hairs of his forked goatee, and made a sound that was not quite a word.

Fritz almost smiled, and with a subtle nod encouraged Sig to go ahead.

Sig held up the plane between thumb and forefingers, keeping the propeller still with his other hand. He tried to sense the movement of air in the room, then launched the craft with a gentle throw, imitating what he had seen Fritz do earlier.

The plane chopped through the warm air of the sunroom like a tiny trolling motor, barely enough to stay aloft. The balsa wood frame was wrapped in rice paper, with only tiny bits of metal to hold the rubber band and anchor the prop. It circled the room just below the ceiling, as it had when Fritz launched it.

Sig smiled.

"The record is fourteen minutes," said Fritz. "In the gym at Nixon High."

Fritz rolled himself a cigarette. He exhaled liquid clouds that turned into wispy vortices as the plane slowly pushed through them.

The natural dimmer switch went up another notch as the sun moved out from behind a tall pine.

The plane touched the ceiling, then fell to the ground with sudden gracelessness.

Fritz set his cigarette in the clay ashtray, next to the remains of the joint they had shared after dinner, then reached down and picked up the plane from the rug.

On top of the compost pile, the raccoon chose what it wanted from the latest tossings, moving things around with its clawed hand.

The door opened.

"Happy birthday!" said Billie, stepping through carrying a cake.

Sig nodded, still annoyed to find people who knew more about him than he'd ever told any professional interrogator, still wary of hospitality, and restless to move on before *they* found him.

Fritz poured three glasses of sherry while Billie lit the one big candle in the middle of the cake.

"We're not singing," said Billie. "But you still need to make a wish and blow out the candle."

Sig took a minute to think about that one. He had stopped celebrating birthdays when he ran. He had almost forgotten when it was. He looked out the window at the diminishing day. You could see the buds on the branches, about to pop. He concentrated on the thought that brought him, and blew.

"So now you're old enough to vote," said Fritz a moment later, as they dug in. He had a little bit of frosting in his mustache.

"Too bad there's only one candidate left to vote for," said Billie.

"Billie doesn't like the President," said Fritz.

"Billie doesn't like the whole fucking system," said Billie. "But she also didn't believe it could get this bad. Talking about Saturn devouring his children."

Billie looked up from her forkful of frosting at Sig. Her hair was silver all the way through, her eyes an intense green, more so when she got riled up.

"You don't know that story, do you?" she said.

Sig was thinking about the planet, which he had seen once through a telescope, and was always able to find in the night sky ever since, if it were there to be found.

Fritz pulled an old paperback book off the shelf. *The Banquet of the Cannibal Lords and Other Stories,* by Max Price. The cover pictured a crazy old giant eating the head and arms off a guy.

"The original king of the gods," said Fritz. "Who killed his children to keep them from taking over."

"Not the perfect analogy," said Billie, "since Thomas Mack is more like the upstart son than the tyrannical grandpa. But the basic idea is there. As your mom learned the hard way, bless her sweet soul. Never underestimate the things power and money will do to protect what they have."

Billie took another bite of cake, chewing aggressively. She looked up at Sig, watching for his reaction.

"What would she do?" asked Sig.

"Like us, I bet," said Fritz. "Keep building out better cooperative networks. Beta-testing the new systems that society will grow into once the monster runs out of food. We only have a few islands left in the network after New Orleans. This is a small one we have here, baked into county government, separate from the university and its labs whored out to the corporates. It's enough to do to build that, on its own pace."

"Don't listen to him," said Billie. "All that old punk wants to do is get high and ride his bike while his joints still work. If Erika were around she would be doing what she was doing when she died. Fighting hard for real change, using nonviolent means. Her cause is still alive, and by helping us here you are continuing her work."

Sig thought about Betty. "The people who try to do something real about it get squashed. Tricked."

"That's true," said Billie. "The state is good at co-opting revolution. Like they figured out in the eighties. If there's no work for the people, license them to go steal from our neighbors, and call it liberation."

"Blame the English," said Fritz. "They started it."

"Yeah," said Billie. "Heseltine and his royal charters. Save your broken industries by letting them do offshore business development at the point of the Sten. South Africa was the killer app. Who could argue with taking those racist jerks out? Remember watching when it started?"

Fritz nodded.

"Live footage from the raid on Robben Island," said Billie. "Who was that guy? The press secretary?"

Fritz drew on his cigarette. "McLaren," he said.

"Right," said Billie. "Fucking Neoimps."

Sig imagined midgets in kilts.

"Our guys copied them," said Billie. "Haig and his patriots and emergency powers. You ever wonder what the world would be like if the Iranians hadn't killed all the hostages?"

Fritz raised his eyebrows. "Or if that guy hadn't shot the Gipper."

"Oh, don't get me started," said Billie.

"I still want to know who shot Yoko," said Fritz.

"Her rich widower and all his peace anthems," said Billie. "Strumming away on VTV as the real revolutionaries engineer a government coup by popular demand. People think that as long as you have elections, you're free? If only they had been paying attention back then, before it was so far gone."

"*You* were paying attention," said Sig.

"Oh, yeah, I was a real 'eighties radical,'" she said. "They didn't call it torture, the things they did when they detained me, but I still have the scars."

All Sig could see was the look in her face.

Fritz reached over and held her hand.

"Billie's disobedience was less civil then," said Fritz.

"This kid knows the score," said Billie, grabbing Sig's hand with the one Fritz wasn't holding. "He just hasn't figured out the rules of the game yet. And which ones you have to break to win. I'm so glad the network found him. So we could take him in."

Sig did not really agree, but he liked his hosts. He had another slice of cake.

27

TANIA CHECKED IN TO A CORPORATE HOTEL NEAR THE AIRPORT, where no one she knew would see her, ordered some food, and got to work on the files. The room had a view of the freeway, and the mall, which had once been the biggest mall in America but was now largely abandoned. Every time she looked out the window at that big sad ruin, relic of a borrowed prosperity whose bill came due, it reminded her of the last time she saw Sig, on the day he was chasing giants.

The giants were walking through the main atrium of the mall, huge puppets brought out for the big protest. Their heads were papier-mâché, the size of small cars, with cartoon faces of capitalists, warlords, and politicians, their bodies lanky frames of stilts wrapped in fabric. When she took eleven-year-old Sig to look at them she was worried he'd be scared, but instead he was excited. He asked how the puppeteers got up inside the giants, and how they were able to walk without falling down.

There were generals holding missiles and robot airplanes in their hands, ready to launch. There were senators with money sticking out of their pockets and corporate logos sewed onto their suits. President Green was there, in chains, pulled on a leash by a general with a white mustache and five big stars on his uniform.

Tania thought it was pretty stupid white hippie stuff, and had three days' homework to do in a day and a half. But it was Saturday, Mom pleaded with her to come and help with the

114

turnout, and Tania was curious to see if they really could take over the entire mall. So far they were doing a pretty good job.

The wildest-looking puppets were the corporate raiders. They wore suits with pirate flags on the back and combat boots instead of dress shoes. They each had a gun in one hand and a wad of cash in the other. Sig said they looked cool.

One of them—the leader—wore an aviator's suit over his business clothes, a little crown on his head, and the corporate logo of Pendleton-Bolan underneath the skull and crossbones on his shoulder and back. His face wasn't an ugly caricature like the others—it was the face of a movie star.

"Who's that?" asked Sig.

"That's Senator Mack," said Tania. "The rich kid war hero CEO who's probably going to be the next President."

"But all these people—"

"Yeah, a lot of people don't like him, but a lot do. And a lot more hate the old President, who got in big trouble for stuff he did when he wasn't at work. It's complicated. Tough times produce weird politics. Hey, what are you—"

He had climbed up on the railing to look down into the atrium. Tania grabbed him by the back of his threadbare T-shirt and almost ripped it.

Peering over the edge, she could see the rainbow multitude of the mob that followed the giants. So many heads in so many colors, bobbing under banners, pickets, and flags with big slogans. It was the usual stuff—U.S. out of Panama, Honor the Treaty, Economic Justice, Ban the MMCs—but the energy was more intense this time. And there were more cameras filming them.

"There's Mom," said Sig, and Tania saw her where he pointed, two big blond braids under the Free Lakota Republic banner, mouth open to let out a chant they couldn't make out in the cacophony. Tania was pretty sure she had heard every one of the chants every different faction had, many times over.

The marchers had entered the mall without a permit, after lunch on a busy day. The crowds of shoppers were gathered around gaping at the protesters, some yelling back and even making physical threats. But the stores were still open, so Tania took Sig to the toy shop once they could no longer see his mom. Astonishingly, the kid had never in his eleven years been to a mall.

He gravitated toward the rack full of little plastic animals. They were lifelike but small enough to fit in your pocket. Black panthers, cheetahs, elephants, gorillas, wolves, foxes, lions, bears, octopuses, whales, walruses, snakes, buffalo, camels, a rhinoceros. He was holding up a platypus in the palm of his hand, smiling and asking how much it was, when Tania heard the piercing electronic horn of a police disruptor blasting through the mall.

"Hang on," she told the kid, running back out to check.

She couldn't really see. The parade of protesters had moved farther into the mall. But she heard a megaphone voice and robot tones, orders to clear out. She walked down a few storefronts to where she could get a better view. The cops were trying to corral the protesters. Looked like a standoff for the moment, but that would change.

"Hey!" she heard the clerk yell as she walked back to the entrance of the toy store. "Put that back!"

She caught only a glance as Sig bolted toward the back of the store.

"Sig!" she hollered, following the clerk as he chased the little thief.

They couldn't find him. The clerk wouldn't let her follow him into the storeroom. He claimed he even checked the common hallway, but no sign.

"Are you his babysitter or something?" asked the guy, wearing as serious a face as you could over a white shirt, red tie, and animal-patterned apron.

"Yeah, I guess."

"You guess. Well I guess you better pay a little more attention. That kid just stole a nineteen-dollar Von Streif and if you don't bring it back it's coming out of my pay."

Tania gave the clerk the finger, immediately regretted it, then spent half an hour looking for the feral kid in every nook and cranny she could find. Ten minutes in, as she heard the escalating tension, she started really freaking out. Especially when they started evacuating the mall and she had to evade cops just to keep looking.

When she finally spied him, he was perched on the branch of an artificial pine tree at the edge of the amusement park at the center of the mall, looking over the food court where the police had succeeded in corralling the protesters.

"Sig!" she hollered, just as she felt the hands on her arms from both sides, thick cop hands taking her into custody, cuffing her wrists behind her back. She argued with the cops, but they weren't listening.

Sig didn't hear her, either.

They put Tania under guard with the rest of the people they had already detained. She could see the scene, seventy or so remaining protesters backed into a corner, barricaded as best they could behind the tables and chairs of the food court.

More police came.

None of them saw the kid in the fake tree.

These cops looked more like soldiers than police. They had black uniforms instead of blue. They had helmets with bulletproof visors. Some had big plastic shields and truncheons. Others had rifles and shotguns. You could feel the trigger fingers quivering.

Tania yelled when they started to take the cameras away from the TV crews. She tried to unleash her imminent lawyer, but if anyone heard, they weren't engaging. Then this young guy in a suit came up to the cops, looking very authoritative.

"No, no, you don't get it," he said. "We *want* them to see this. Let the people see what happens when you pull shit like this. When you try to shut down commerce and ridicule your leaders."

The suit had the lapel pin, the sign of Mack's new party. The slanting *F* of "Freedom."

Erika was in the front of the protesters with four others, conferring, watching the police prepare to move. They let another dozen people surrender themselves to the police. Then they told their remaining people to gather even tighter.

The suit had the cops help the camera crews set up the positions he wanted.

The mall music was still playing in the background. You could just hear it layered beneath all the other noise.

Erika pointed at the tree, and called Sig's name.

Tania watched the way he climbed down, still blended into the background.

The police turned up their noise horns so you couldn't hear anything else. Then they moved in, a wall of men with three sides.

One of Erika's punk boyfriends came over the tabletop barricade and jumped on a cop. Another cop brought a black metal truncheon down hard on the punk, who slumped to the floor.

A hippie girl screamed, and spat at the cops.

Then one of the old guys pulled out a knife.

The volume went up. BRRRRRAAAAAAAACCCCKCK-CKKCKKKZZZKK.

Metal on metal, as weapons locked and loaded.

Gas masks on.

Thunk. Thunk thunk. Hollow projectiles arced from hydraulic guns, hit the floor, bounced, clanged, rolled, hissed.

She saw Sig back in there, T-shirt tied around his face like a gas mask.

The police started firing. Rubber bullets. You could already see them on the ground, black rubber balls. The "nonlethal" force gave the cops the excuse to fully express their yearning to unload. You could see it in their faces as they emptied their clips. As they eagerly reloaded.

The protesters cowered and yelped, trying to hide behind each other and the makeshift barricade.

"Run!" screamed Erika.

She looked around for her son, then stood, hands up.

"Stop!" she said.

Two of the men stood behind her. Another went to the felled punk curled up just in front of them.

Then Erika was down, felled like a deer, projectile to the head.

The police moved in closer.

She was not moving. Her friends were there at her side, screaming.

The police looked paused. The suit tried to egg them on.

Tania didn't see Sig until he was there on the back of a beefy cop, maybe the one that shot his mom. The cop had lost his helmet. Sig had his arms locked around the guy's neck. The cop tried to jam the kid with the business end of his rifle, but stumbled, and the kid got a grip on the barrel.

The cop dived. Tried to shake the kid off his neck. Three other cops moved in.

When they unpacked the pile-on, one of the cops was dead and one was bleeding from the gut. One cop had his knee on Sig's back; another had a boot on his face.

You could see the knife there on the floor, and the blood in the kid's face.

Tania tried to go help him, to save him from what was coming, but when she tried to push through, they shoved her to the floor and made her crawl back to the wall, and all she could do was scream, so loud it should have awakened those giants.

28

"SO YOU WANT TO COME DOWN TO THE BASEMENT WITH ME?" SAID Fritz. "See what's on that video you brought back?"

Sig made a face as he considered the invitation.

Fritz laughed. "You don't understand," he said. "There's probably money on there."

Sig made a different face. Fritz laughed again.

The basement seemed bigger than the rest of the house. It was down a flight of rickety stairs by the back door. It was dark and cold, the rooms lit with old chainpulls.

Mostly the basement was crammed with provisions. Shelves stacked floor to ceiling with bell jars full of vegetables. They looked like body parts in the bad light. Tin cans, bags of grain, and botanicals marked in a script Sig couldn't read.

There was another room with a big safe in it. Fritz unlocked it and let Sig look inside. Guns, money, ammo.

"Mostly too old to be of much use," said Fritz, putting his hand on a wooden carbine. "But Billie likes to keep them."

The door to Fritz's room was metal. It had three locks and a wooden sign over it painted in old-fashioned letters.

𝕽𝖆𝖙𝖍𝖘𝖐𝖊𝖑𝖑𝖊𝖗

Inside, the room smelled like glue and burnt silicon. There was a big workbench along the longest side, cluttered with tools and materials: wiring, wood, canvas, electronic motors, a soldering gun, camera stalks, epoxies, paint, knives, a Dremel. A yellowed book open to a page of diagrams rendered in fine black line. And in the middle of the mess, the work in progress. A big model airplane in the shape of a triangle.

"Back in the shop for improvements," said Fritz. "Vintage design. Very efficient. Trick is keeping it stable."

The space above and below the bench was packed with plastic cubbies, each labeled with its contents. To the right were deep shelves with other miniature flying machines hiding behind curtains. The other two walls were crammed with electronics. Black and silver boxes with blinking diodes, round screen monitors and television screens, big tuning knobs, and a huge microphone on a stand. Cables and wires in a half-dozen colors were cinched up in bundles and pinned to the ceiling. A couple of the machines were really old looking, with wooden cases and primitive controls.

"The listening station," said Fritz, flicking switches to turn things on.

"What do you listen to?"

"Oh, all sorts of things. News from faraway places. Information they like to make it hard for you to get. Transmits, too. It's how we stay in touch with our friends so no one can listen in."

Fritz sat at the workstation and pulled out the stool from the other bench for Sig to use.

Sig watched a blue line wiggle across a small round screen.

Fritz fiddled with tuners. Noise came from the speakers like the calls of robot birds.

"Old ways," said Fritz. "Old waves. Obsolete, increasingly hard to find, and mostly illegal. But their computers don't know how to listen to these frequencies. Don't even really know they exist. New knowledge in means old knowledge out."

A voice came into clarity, in a language Sig did not understand. He remembered the radio Betty had in her cabin.

"Here we go," said Fritz, reaching into a drawer. He pulled out the box with the videotape. The one about *Messages from Lemuria*. Whatever that was.

Fritz made a noise a lot like the sound he made when he savored the birthday cake. "Lost continents," he said, holding up the box and smiling. "Layers of secrets in this dollar store remainder. We should watch the original later, after we get your key off of here."

"There are no keys in that box," said Sig. "I looked."

"I know," said Fritz. "Here."

He put the tape into a player. He turned on one of the television sets. The screen brightened from black glass to blue snow. He opened a cover from the bottom part of the set, under the screen, revealing control knobs and jacks.

He grabbed a black handheld from a drawer. Old tablet computer, more box than screen. He plugged it into one of the jacks on the monitor. Video out.

The picture resolved. A pyramid, floating over a shimmering ocean.

"No, we don't want that just now," said Fritz. He fiddled with the knobs, until the picture flickered out of frame, replaced by scrolling black bars and white static.

"The good stuff is in the vertical blanking interval," he said. "Digital nuggets buried in analog noise. Here."

He squinted at the handheld. Entered three commands. Held down a button. "Here we go. Come here. Look at that."

Sig looked over his shoulder. The screen of the handheld was filling up with numbers and letters, scrolling faster than you could read it.

"Don't worry," said Fritz. "We're capturing it."

"What is it?" asked Sig.

"Snowflakes."

Sig raised an eyebrow.

"Because of the white noise."

Sig didn't hear any noise. He touched the screen.

"It's a key," said Fritz. "In the form of a code. That functions as a medium of exchange. To those who know how to use it."

Sig scrunched up his face.

"Money," said Fritz. "Alternate money. Money that doesn't carry its own government spies."

"Who makes it?"

"No one makes it," said Fritz. "Or everyone. Everyone who wants to. The network makes it. There's no bank, or government, or whatever. That's the whole idea. The users share the work of making it work."

"You can have it," said Sig. "If you want to give me money give me some of the stash I saw in that gun safe."

Fritz laughed. "Tell you what," he said. "I'll keep it for you."

Sig nodded.

29

IT WAS A WEIRD THING BEING SCARED TO BE BACK IN YOUR OWN
hometown. When Cousin Mell told her where they usually
had their meetings, Tania knew it was time to dress the part,
so she left her lawyer suit back at the airport hotel when she
headed into the heart of the city. She left her government-issue
sedan back there, too, and took the bus, like she used to every
day for school. But now the scenery was a little different.

She wondered if she really passed as a local among the
downbeat commuters who shared the ride. She was the only
one who looked up, and when she looked through the dirty
window in the fading light of day she knew why. The bus
rolled past a seemingly endless line outside the wholesale
grocer, people waiting to buy what overpriced essentials were
available. Being in line was no guarantee there would be anything left when it was your turn, and those who were lucky
enough to get some had to guard it from thieves all the way
home. At another intersection six beggars worked the stopped
cars, crusty kids you could tell were living outside. There were
more back behind them, silhouettes in the busted-up glass
windows of an old building.

When Tania got off the bus she almost stepped on another
pair, a hungry-looking little white girl and her zonk-eyed
mama, strung out on a threadbare blanket on the sidewalk in
the cold. The girl, maybe eight or nine, just held out a plastic
cup and looked at Tania with imploring eyes. There were only

a few chits and one coin in the bottom of the cup. Tania imagined living as a beggar in a mostly cashless economy, where even the little transactions were electronic, routed through government-monitored networks. But she had nothing to spare, and knew better than to open her wallet around here.

As she headed down Hennepin under the browning-out streetlamps at the edge of old downtown, every human profile she saw coming her way was a presumptive menace to be avoided, even if it meant crossing the street or rerouting entirely. These streets would take every opportunity to grab what was not theirs, if you gave them the chance, and the only real law and order was provided by the citizen patrols, who were often worse than the criminals—but not as bad as the militias that roamed the zones outside the big cities.

Up above the buildings, high enough that they could see it from the freeway, was one of those motivational billboards put up by the "Fellowship for a Better America," whoever the hell they were. This one was more openly political than their trademark blind joggers and puppy-saving patriotic tweens. It featured the already iconic picture of the President standing on the rubble of the White House the day after, screaming into the megaphone he held up with his remaining arm, pumping up the first of the frightened crowds he'd rallied into a vengeful national mob. The caption was in big letters at the bottom.

LEADERSHIP
To lead others, one must be ready to go forward alone

Someone had gotten up there and done a little billboard alteration—a giant robot claw where the other arm used to be.

Tania looked at the face burning through the graffiti and thought about that moment when she had looked into his eyes. She wondered what gave them that mesmeric intensity. Maybe the same qualities that brought him to power. He had a sunnier charisma back then, a youthful smile and a knack for seemingly spontaneous nuggets of oration that would lure people in like a trance and channel all their hungers and rage into his own to make him bigger on the stage of the world. But what stuck with Tania was the way, when the eyes locked on you, you could feel how they were packed with the full punitive force of the federal state ready to come down on any resistance. As if that were the only way he could get his kicks now, after all these years in office, after the attention of the crowd alone lost its juice.

It was motivating, not in a good way. You wanted to fight it, but the consequences were too grave. It made you feel alone.

Looking up at the image on the billboard, at the smoldering ruins on which he was standing, Tania thought about the victims of that day, and other days since he had taken power. People who lost their lives, people who lost their livelihoods, people who just lost their country. Or, as Tania felt, learned what their country really was when you peeled off the mask of civility. What it always had been, if you read the history books that the school boards wouldn't put on the curriculum. This city reminded her of the bad parts of her own past, the days when the fresh darkness announced its arrival and a lot of people put out the welcome mat, mistaking it for salvation. Hard times produced harder solutions.

A big black SUV rolled by slow, and as it passed under the streetlamp Tania could just make out the faces of three white dudes, out on the prowl. They looked at her, saying things she could not hear, the faces of hunters joking among each other, about the other.

She walked faster, hoping the place Mell told her about would also provide shelter, and wondering if Mell knew where she could buy a black market gun.

30

THE NEXT DAY, THEY TOOK SIG OUT TO THE EDGE OF TOWN TO burn the earth.

The place was a huge field on rolling land, covered in tall grass, the faded browns and grays of late winter, dormant plants dusted with snow. There was a leafless tree line along one edge. Sig saw a hawk perched on one of the bare branches.

"No wind today," said Billie. "It's perfect."

They were a crew of eight—Billie and a couple of the older guys from the co-op, and four others around Sig's age—two guys and two girls. They came out in a big van, loaded with gear in the back. Shovels, axes, buckets, and torches. One of the older guys followed them in a beat-up old biodiesel pickup with a huge plastic water tank set in the bed.

"Are you ready to get to work making a better future?" said Billie, grabbing Sig by the arm with a big smile.

"What are we doing?' said Sig.

"Phytoremediation!" said Billie.

Sig tried to imagine the letters in that word.

"Healing the land with plants," explained Billie. She gestured across the expanse of the field. "This is one of our test plots. Farmed for a hundred and fifty years, the last third of those enabled by chemicals that kill—kill the land, as well as the bugs and the 'weeds.' We are letting what was here before come back in, all the ancient plants, grasses and flowers and grains, to call back all the other creatures of the field."

"The Rewilding," said one of the girls, blue eyes and rosy cheeks sticking out from a wool hat tied down so you couldn't even see the color of her hair.

"Exactly, Hannah," said Billie. "In just a few weeks the wildflowers will start to come in. Then comes summer, when the hummingbirds and butterflies arrive."

Sig liked these people, but he did not plan to stay here that long.

"One of the unintended dividends of economic failure," said Billie, "is depopulation, and inattention from capital. From money, big business. It gives us room to try a different way of treating the land on which we live. People think land gone wild has nothing to give, but they are wrong. You just have to rethink how you work with it. How to take no more than you give."

"Imagine if all the empty lots in America were restored like this," said Hannah, and Sig thought that only eyes that blue could be that optimistic about what real people would do, or how little nature cares about your feelings.

"There is no such thing as an empty lot," said Sig, grabbing an axe and feeling its heft.

At that, Billie burst out laughing, a deep belly laugh, the laugh of a woman who knew.

Hannah smiled, too.

"So we're going to burn it?" said Sig.

"Yes we are," said Billie. "Like the Indians did to make the hunts better, and the Earth did before them, and our descendants will do after we teach their mothers how."

And so they did, in two burn crews, starting fires and keeping them in their bounds. And as Sig watched the flames rise up over the wide acres, and heard the sound, the quiet roar and the pops, he knew Billie was right, that this was what it took to bring back what should be.

SIG FINISHED LUNCH FAST. THE OTHERS TEASED HIM FOR IT, said he was "wolfing it," and he wondered if any of them knew what that was really like.

If they had ever known real hunger.

While they took their time, he decided to go for a walk. He was feeling healed, and strong, and ready to move.

"Hey!" said Hannah, as he stepped off. "Where are you going?"

"Into the woods," he said, nodding at the tree line. "See what I can find."

"I'm coming with you," she said, getting up without asking.

Sig kept walking and let her catch up.

"What do you think's in there?" she said, starting to sweat.

Sig looked over at her just as she pulled off her hat and the blond hair tumbled out. He remembered when he used to think that was pretty, when girls had hair like his mom, but now it made him think of the yellow of the warning lights you saw on dangerous roads.

He put his fingers to his lips, hoping Hannah would be quiet, and led her into the woods.

The snow was still thick back under the trees. They heard the scree of the hawk, and the caws of distant crows.

He showed her wild berries of winter, and acorns that you could eat, if you knew how to cook them.

He pointed to tracks in the snow. Sign of deer, fox, rabbit, and other wild rodents. He wondered if there were cougar in these woods.

They had worked long and started lunch late, and the sun was already starting to dim out. He saw deer tracks, fresh, so fresh you could still smell the musk. He looked at Hannah and smiled, and she smiled back. She could smell it, too.

They followed the trail. It went up a north-facing rise where the snow was still deep, some spots so sheltered that the crust of ice had not formed across the top. Snow this deep slowed deer down, and you could see it in these tracks.

It was when they got up close to the top of the hill that Sig first noticed the other tracks. He pulled Hannah closer to him and led her up over the edge, where the tracks were all mixed together. Then he heard the rustling, the crunching snow dance, the panicked snort of the deer, and looked to see the buck just as one of the coyotes lunging at its forefeet leapt for its neck and bit. The other coyote went for a back leg, the way dogs do with each other when they play hard. As the deer went down and the coyotes both pounced to keep it down and kill it good, Hannah screamed, and the coyotes bolted.

"Time for sharing," said Sig. "They should have wolfed it."

When they walked back out of the woods and Sig was carrying the stag over his shoulders, the animal bleeding all over his shirt, with no weapon on him but a pocket knife, the others were impressed, but Sig gave all the credit to Hannah, and let her tell the story, which was mostly true.

3

WHEN TANIA STEPPED INTO THE CLUB, IT WAS LIKE STEPPING INTO the past.

A honk band was playing, straddling the chasms between jazz and punk, dissonant blues for a fractured America. The horns led, like the calls of geese doing primal scream therapy, trading out with the electronic noise of untuned channels and interruptive bleats, a drummer banging on a spring coil, a bass like an arrhythmic beating heart. It was a beautiful groove, and for the first time since she landed Tania felt like she was home.

Her dad played this music, or the music that it came from, music that channeled the sounds of the cold midcontinental cities where it was born, cities of forgotten American diasporas hidden in the old roads and abandoned train stations. Chicago, Detroit, here in the Twin Cities. When she played it for friends back in D.C. they would just make tortured faces. You had to know the source. And feel it in person, live, the way it summoned the feelings of a moment in time, and somehow liberated you from this time, like a waking dream of astral travel.

The Ganymede Social Club had a name but no sign, just one of those fire doors that look like they have four hundred coats of paint and extra security made from found materials. There was a little purple stencil of a ringed planet, and a buzzer, and when Tania hit it and stepped through, the two dudes sitting there guarding the door looked her over and said come on in.

The crowd she found inside was mixed, mostly young, all races, working on no races. None of the faces were familiar, which made Tania realize how long she had been gone, but the expressions were—starved and sad and strong all at the same time. Many had the tattoos of overseas service in military and MMC units, while others looked like veterans of these streets. A lot of them were milling in the side room, talking away from the music, and enjoying the snack-sized previews of the hot food Mell said was the main reason a lot of people went to these events. Twenty-five percent unemployment in the states affected by the farm failures, they said, and that didn't count the people who'd stopped looking. People were hungry for more than food.

After the set they pulled the chairs in and everybody gathered to watch a short documentary about the Reagan assassination. Conspiracy theories about the fourth bullet, the double agent, and how Jodie Foster's Army was never a real cell. Provocative stuff, but presented in a way that hardly qualified as evidence, at least by the standards Tania had been taught, standards designed to lock people up or take their money away. The idea that one of the military merchant companies was behind it almost made sense until you remembered that MMCs weren't even chartered until a few years into the Haig administration. The filmmakers spun an outrageously speculative counterfactual suggesting that if Reagan hadn't been shot, his people would have broken BellNet into a bunch of mini phone companies, and all sorts of alternate interactive communications networks would have proliferated "instead of the corporate kleptonet imposed on us by Big Bell and the government it owns."

Tania wasn't buying it, but the crowd looked more persuaded. They stayed after the lights came up and the lead organizer started her real pitch. She was a white lady who introduced herself as Rook—nickname as nom de guerre. She had the diction and grooming cues of someone who grew up behind the gates but a fighter's premature stress lines that made her look twenty-nine going on forty. Tania remembered the Maxine Price joke about how fighting for real change is hard on your skin. And then Rook actually name-checked the late veep in her remarks, and the joking was over.

"'It's easier to imagine the end of the world than a change in the political system.' Maybe that was true when Dr. Price said it while she was still in office, but I don't think it's true anymore. If we don't have a change in the political system real soon, we won't have to imagine the end of the world. It's time for real democracy!"

Tania liked the slogans, but wondered if they had anything behind them. And it was democracy that got them here, by people voting Mack into office, three consecutive times. It was no guarantor of justice, or of real rule of law.

The crowd didn't share Tania's skepticism, murmuring in exclamatory mob voice like the improvised congregation at a tent revival. Which, Tania thought as she looked around, this basically was. The place was packed, standing room only, with people looking for someone to save them.

There was no sign of Sig.

"I drove up here from Chicago awhile back," Rook was saying. "On old highways where the drones don't always go and you can drive without getting stopped every hour. I saw brown wastelands where there used to be green bounty. I saw the chemical silos where the yields of fouled fields are turned into food for machines. How did we let this happen?"

"Take it back!" yelled someone in the crowd.

"Tear down the stacks!" called a woman's voice.

"Take it back is right," said Rook. "We need to reclaim the land. Tear down the pipes that suck the life from the ground. Restore the vibrant ecologies we've spoiled. Create new economies based on making, not taking. And to do that we need to be our own rulers."

Tania looked around the room again, sizing up the few in the crowd who weren't joining in the chorus, trying to guess which ones were agents of the current ruler, undercover monitors of dissidence.

. Like her. She didn't like the feeling. But the image of Mom in chains trumped all other loyalties. At least until she was free.

"There's a movement erupting all over the hemisphere," said Rook. "It's about rebooting our political operating systems. History didn't end in 1789, right?!"

"Hell no!"

"Abolish political parties!"

"That's right," said Rook. "It's about more than moving past the bogus choice between regular and decaf oligarchs. It's about direct democracy—true rule by the people instead of pretending to pick which privileged insiders we want to control our lives."

"Write a new constitution!"

Rook's compatriots handed out a pamphlet.

HOW TO MAKE YOUR OWN COUNTRY
by
The Crowdrule

Tania flipped the pages. It was full of diagrams, aphorisms, and pictures. A sociopolitical self-help manual, on a medium designed to evade surveillance. Mom had been sending her similar stuff for years. This was more ambitious. Revolutionary. Tania had seen enough signs of what it was really like when you let the people govern themselves—the worst people, usually the scariest, most aggressive men, thought they were the ones who got to make the rules. Like they always had.

Then again, she had a point about 1789. Tania never was quite persuaded about what those guys were really like. When she saw the textbook portraits of them in their wigs she saw a bunch of rich white men, slavers, who didn't want to pay their taxes. And the rules that made sense for that society, a society that had just "found" the limitless bounty of a new continent, had to be past their sell-by date.

"Take it back is right," said Rook again. "The world will only get worse until we get off our knees and kick out the klepts. If we tune the connections between our communities, build new networks that let us share, organize, and act, we can do it."

"The only One is the Everyone!"

"Utopia is a seed in a fallow field!"

"Remember November!"

"Don't get me started!" said Rook.

"They killed our farms!"

"Rogue corn and man-made drought!"

"They broke the whole heartland, from here to the Gulf!" said Rook. "Look at New Orleans. A great city turned into a toxic track mark from the martial-economic dope our leaders are hooked on. The people there took the fight to power, and no matter what you may see in the government-controlled media, they haven't given up yet. If we don't follow their example, we'll all end up like the Nicaraguans, living in the ruins while the corporate robots build a new city for our owner-masters to enjoy!"

Tania wondered if Rook would go back home to the privilege she came from, like Odile. And if she really had the stuff to deliver on what she was selling. You'd have to be a rich white daughter of "owner-masters" to believe direct rule by an unruly majority was an easy answer.

Tania looked back down at the pamphlet. There was a loose piece of paper inside. A table packed with numbers. Times of day and frequencies. AM, FM, UHF. A schedule. A handwritten code. The only explanatory text, if you could call it that, was an aphorism across the bottom.

The Network Is the People

When Tania looked back up, she finally recognized a face—one of the guys distributing the pamphlets. A skinny kid with dirty blond bangs that covered nervous eyes. One of the suspects Tania had seen in the latest file Gerson had sent her. Trace Goolsby Jr., age twenty, aka Tracer, aka G00l. A juvenile felon out of Austin who'd done two years for installing illegal surveillance devices in the federal courthouse and posting footage of sealed prosecutions onto public bulletin boards—all while still in high school. Associate of Mauricio Rojo Rivera, twenty, aka Mojo or Moco. Tracer and Moco were known smugglers, veterans of the fighting in New Orleans who now worked the underground helping outlaws, dissidents, and contraband move up and down the midcontinental corridor and across the southern border. Moco had been spotted in here in Minneapolis, with the people thought to have been harboring Sig.

On a tip two weeks earlier, regional Motherland got a warrant to bring in Tracer and Moco while they holed up in St. Louis arranging new transportation. The bust nabbed their cargo—no fugitives in the van, just old television equipment and four cases of illegal videos—but both of the smugglers evaded capture.

Tania watched Tracer work the room. She looked for signs of concealed carry. She watched him brush his scruffy hair from his eyes, and wanted to laugh and cry at how young he really was. How young most of these people were, grabbing onto a candle of naïve hope, not yet cauterized by the realities of how this country really worked.

Tracer handed out some other piece of paper to selected members of the crowd. A little red business card. Tania was not one of the recipients, but she knew what they were. Invitations to callbacks for interviews.

She wondered if she could get her own interview. If Sig wasn't going to come out, she would have to get these people to help her find him.

Just then a voice yelled from across the room.

"Hey, Tania!"

Tania looked.

"Lisbet?" said Tania.

"Oh my God!" said Lisbet. She looked older, even a little gray in the dirty blond, but she still had that thing in her nose. Of course it would be Lisbet to call her out in a crowd. Tania briefly considered pretending to try to be someone else. Then that gave her a better idea.

"Hey!" said Tania. She smiled, worked her way through the milling crowd, and hugged Lisbet. She wore some homemade midwestern scent, like ragweed and vetiver.

"I heard about your mom," said Lisbet. "What Gestapo bullshit. Like it's a crime to give people food and shelter. Is that why you're here?"

"That's the main reason," said Tania.

"Right on. How can we help?"

"I think I have a plan that will work."

If Lisbet knew about Mom, she probably knew about Sig.

"It's good to see you," said Tania.

"I heard you were in Washington," said Lisbet. Her friendly expression changed when she said the word.

Just then, a dude with a shaved head, plastic glasses, and a black T-shirt interrupted them. He whispered in Lisbet's ear, staring at Tania suspiciously over his cupped hand.

"Okay," said Lisbet, a more serious look on her face now. "Shit."

"What?" said Tania.

"Raid," said Lisbet.

Tania imagined getting caught here by Motherland. Her travel orders from work were to be in Duluth. Secret Service would disclaim her. Instead of getting Mom out she'd be locked up with her.

"You better come with me," said Lisbet.

"I gotta run," said Tania.

Just as she turned, and heard the sound of the choppers, she saw the look on Lisbet's face change.

"I knew it!" screamed Lisbet. "You fucking narc!"

Lisbet grabbed Tania's arm, fingers digging in. Tania smacked back her hand, shoved her back, and ran for the door.

"Grab her!" Lisbet shouted

Tania ran for the door. As she forced her way out through the panicked crowd, she looked back over her shoulder and saw the rage in Lisbet's face, channeled into a sharp-nailed finger of indictment pointed right at her.

Outside the police trucks were rolling up, blasting sonics.

Tania followed three dudes as they ran the other way, into the dark streets, and looked for a way to disappear.

32

SIG SNUCK OUT FROM THE BARN AGAIN THAT NIGHT AND SLEPT IN the woods by the freeway. The barn was the place where Sig and the others were supposed to stay so the people who were looking for them wouldn't find them. There were other guys about Sig's age there, and the setup seemed safe. Sig just felt safer outside, even if it exposed him to the eyes you can't see.

The woods were between the interstate and a cemetery. The cemetery was good cover for passage. Lots of trees, no surveillance, and no people, at least at night. The new section by the highway was huge, filled with the fresh white head-stones of fighters fallen in foreign wars. Some from wars closer to home. There was a big monument to the martyrs down in one of the low spots of the field, made of black stone. On a clear night with a new moon it looked like it was filled with stars.

Sig's spot was past that, back through the weird old tombs of people from centuries before. One was a woman with out-stretched wings, taking off. Her long hair reminded Sig of when his mom would let her braids out.

Sig liked to climb the old oak trees. The crooks of the branches were so big you could sleep in them. To the west you could see the corporate parks they built after all the farms died. There was the Quaker Biofuels research facility, the Data-Feed monitoring center, and the Greyrock Aerospace Special Projects Division, where they came up with new designs for unmanned craft. Fritz said his grandfather had worked there, after they captured him at the end of the war. Fritz said the building was big enough that they could fly planes inside it. Sig wished he could see that.

It still wouldn't be as big as the open sky beyond the big boxes, the endless acres of sick fields trying to dry their way back to wild, or kept on chemical life support to grow more fuel for the machine.

Sig could feel the spring weather having second thoughts, especially when he got up in the tree, and wondered whether they might wake up to a blanket of white. The seasons got harder to predict every year. He put on his gift from Billie and Fritz, a black hoodie of thick material that Billie said came from old plastic bottles. It felt good. It would give him a way to remember when he moved on.

The snow didn't come in the morning. It felt warmer. He walked down to the river at sunup and went duck hunting before breakfast. He'd found a lagoon where they pumped warm water out of the plant and the ducks liked to hang out and get cozy. The way Sig hunted them was to strip down, get in the river, and sneak up on the ducks from underneath, where he could grab their feet and pull them under. He got two nice ones. He was hoping the gift of fresh game would make Billie less mad when he told her it was his last day.

33

GERSON GAVE TANIA CREDIT FOR THE RAID ON GANYMEDE, EVEN
though that was not what Tania had in mind.

When Gerson called to say so, Tania bitched her out.

Running into Lisbet, there at the meeting, was a huge
break. Lisbet could have helped Tania find Sig. She was
plugged into the underground, the people who had been
harboring Sig. Instead Tania had been outed before she even
got to ask the first question.

At least now Tania knew for sure that Gerson and her
people were tracking her.

She wished she could explain it to Lisbet. If they had
enough time and space to share, she could get her to understand.

Instead of talking to her old friend, Tania would have to
play the interrogator she never wanted to be. Gerson had it all
set up. Almost as if she took pleasure in getting Tania to do
things she did not want to do.

It turned out the raid was not a well-planned operation.
Three Motherland field agents and local police took it on short
notice and deployed as the meeting was already dispersing.
They got Tracer, two other members of Rook's cell, and four of
the recruits. Tania was kind of sorry Rook got away, mainly
because she seemed like such a high-level source, and also
because her privileged demeanor just bugged her. Tania was
happy that Lisbet was not on the list, even though that meant
Lisbet might now be on the hunt for Tania.

So much for the plan to get some of Cousin Mell's pie.

Instead, Tania found herself back at the Box.

Mom was already gone, transferred to Boschwitz House.

The guard, who told her that, congratulated her on her connections, for being able to secure such cush treatment. And told her this guy's not so lucky.

When she sat down with Tracer, Tania could see what the guard meant, in the prisoner's face.

"I'm sorry you're here," said Tania. She meant it. She'd read the file. The things that first got this kid into trouble were almost admirable. He got on the wrong track early, and once he had a record there wasn't really any other path.

Tracer just looked at her with a skeptical face.

"I mean it. It's my fault. I didn't mean for it to happen."

"Are you fucking kidding me?" he said. He had a stoner voice, like a southern surfer.

"No," said Tania. "And if you help me out, they said I can get you the same deal as the recruits you seduced."

"What's that?" asked Tracer. He had a fresh bruise on his cheek. Tania wondered what other bruises might be hidden under the yellow jumpsuit.

"Avoid prosecution if you volunteer for eighteen months of military service, or agree to six weeks of reconditioning therapy."

"I'll take my chance on prosecution. You can't put us in jail for talking to people."

"You watch too many old TV shows," said Tania. "They can put you in jail for whatever they want, just about. I don't like it, either. I want change, too, just by different means. That's why I want to help you get the best outcome."

"The least shitty outcome. What bullshit."

"What if I told you they have a whole file on you. And Moco."

His expression changed.

"Enough for seven counts of felony violations of the Secure Travel Act."

He got whiter.

"And what if I said all I want is for you to help me find some people who will never know I talked to you," said Tania.

He stared at her through his bangs.

"Where is Moco?"

He kept staring.

"He's here in Minneapolis, too, right?" said Tania.

"I want a lawyer."

"Not with your charges," said Tania. "Emergency powers. How do you think you got to this building?"

"The permanent emergency," said Tracer.

"I don't like them, either, but those are the rules. You're lucky they let me talk to you. I might be able to help with this predicament you find yourself in."

Tracer pushed back his bangs. Looked at the picture of the President on the wall. Sighed.

"How about this guy?" said Tania, showing Tracer the mug shot of Sig. "Where would I find him if I wanted to ask him a few questions?"

"Never seen him," said Tracer. "Looks like an asshole though."

"He can be," said Tania. "Why don't you tell me the truth? I know he was here."

Tracer shrugged. Tania watched him look away again.

"Where do the underground broadcasts come from?" said Tania.

"From TV."

"Where's the station? They know you guys work the sneakernet. Move packages that the gangs bring across the Canadian border. Like that load of tapes you took to St. Louis."

"We didn't take any tapes to St. Louis."

"Then where did you take them?"

"Shit."

"St. Louis is where they caught you."

"That was you?"

"Colleagues. I just got on the case."

"Fuck!"

"It's okay," said Tania. "Work with me. I know you don't want to go back."

"What are you gonna do to help me?"

"Get you into reprogramming. It's that or Detroit, if you're lucky. It's a good deal."

"Fucking sucks."

Tania waited.

"Where will it be?" asked Tracer.

"There's a sanctioned clinic in San Antonio, attached to the Army hospital. Close to home."

He snorted a chuckle.

"Or wherever you want," she said. "Here's the list." She turned the tablet to him so he could read it. "Page two of the form, right after the signature. You know it has to be consensual."

He looked, fiddled, and squirmed.

"It's not supposed to hurt," said Tania, trying to convince herself as well. "I hear it's like rehab."

"Rehab sucks," said Tracer. "Rehab with brain machines is worse."

"Just fMRI," said Tania. "Dreaming." It almost sounded pleasant, the way she said it.

"Dream hacking."

"It's the best I can do. Sign it or we're done and you can fend for yourself."

He made his mark with an angry thumbnail.

Tania reclaimed the tablet.

"So where's the station?" she asked.

"I don't know," said Tracer. "I wasn't on that run."

"Who was?"

"Moco."

"And where's Moco?"

"Iowa City."

"You make deliveries there? A station?"

"There's all kinds of stuff there. People like us run the whole town. It's sanctuary."

That can change. "Can you show me where in Iowa City? On a map?"

"No, wouldn't do any good, they move around all the time. But that other guy's there, too."

Tania pointed.

"Yeah, the guy in the picture. He was here, like you said, and they wanted to get him to a safer place. Guess they were right."

Tania tried to keep her cool.

"You think he's still there?"

"I guess. I mean, I don't know, I don't even know his real name."

I do.

34

BILLIE GAVE HIM CRAP FOR GOING OUT AFTER CURFEW AGAIN, but she smiled about the ducks. Great gift for a vegetarian, she said. He decided to wait until after lunch to tell her, or maybe just take off without telling her at all.

They had Sig working with Billie at the New Democracy Co-op Fulfillment Center, which was in an abandoned Sears by the old mall. Billie was the manager. She put Sig to work there shortly after he arrived at their secret shelter.

His job at the Fulfillment Center was to put stuff in boxes. "Care packages," Billie called them. Shipments of material aid to New Orleans, St. Louis, El Centro, Tijuana, Managua, and other nodes in the network. No weapons, no matter how many times the young guys suggested. Mostly just things to help people communicate—net kits, little handheld televisions with the transmit boxes built in, memory, pop-up antennas, gear to power the networks with energy from sun, wind, and water. There were purification systems, packets of pure seeds, and tons of books and pamphlets.

When Sig was sitting there working, Moco walked up.

"What's up, killer?" he said.

"I didn't know you were still here," said Sig.

"Gone and back," he said. "Had to make a run to St. Louis with a buddy, but we almost got busted. Lost our packages, but got away, and I made it back here to lie low."

"Where's your friend?"

Moco shook his head. "I don't know, man. No word, getting a little worried."

"What happens if they catch him?"

"Nothing good," said Moco.

Sig imagined the possibilities.

"Definitely nicer to lay low here in hippietown," said Moco. "For a while, at least. You bored yet?"

Sig nodded.

"Me, too," said Moco.

"Hunting's not too bad, though," said Sig.

"Yeah, dude, I saw those ducks. Are you like those guys that hide in shacks by the side of the lake or whatever?"

"Kind of," said Sig. "But no guns. Never hunted ducks?"

"No, man," said Moco. "I'm from the big city. We hunt different stuff."

"I thought you were from Honduras," said Sig.

"No, dude, I'm from New Orleans. I mean I was born in Honduras, but my mom fled with me and my brother when I was a little shit. So where I'm really from is the biggest refugee camp you've ever seen. So big we got our own government."

"How did you get up here?"

"I got really fucking lost."

Sig laughed.

"They sent me all the way just to get you, dude," said Moco, smiling. "Glad to see they already got you healthy enough to put you to work. Feeling strong?"

Sig nodded. "I feel good. I like it better when they let me work outside."

"I hear you on that," said Moco. "Stuffing boxes is not my thing."

"You like driving," said Sig.

"I like moving, not sitting around. Drive a car, take a boat, walk, you name it."

"Best way not to get caught is not to stop moving."

"Exactly," said Moco. "So I'll move whatever they need delivered, wherever it needs to go, whatever way is best. Used to mostly move people. I started out working for these guys back home, getting people out of the country, into Mexico, Nicaragua, Costa Rica, whatever. Sometimes smuggle stuff back in. Sometimes people, the kind trying to get back in and help fix things. Got good enough they trust me with more important things, like the information they're afraid to send any other way."

"Information more important than people?"

"Some information, some people," said Moco.

"I had some friends who did stuff like that."

"Yeah? Where?"

"Up north."

"Like borderzone north?" said Moco, looking at Sig more closely.

Sig nodded.

"So that's where you got fucked up," said Moco. "I heard something about what went down. I'm sorry, dude. I guess you lost some people."

Sig was quiet. Thinking about what happened reminded him what he needed to do.

"You know how to get to New Orleans?" said Sig.

"I know lots of ways," said Moco. "You want to get in on the shit?"

"Check it out, at least."

"Now that is a great fucking idea," said Moco. "Let's hit the road, dude. Go to New Orleans. I'm bored out of my freaking mind."

Sig nodded, taping the box closed.

"I mean these people are nice but stuffing boxes is not my

kind of work," said Moco. "Let's go have some fun. We can see if Big Mama and her council of abuelos need us to make any deliveries, there or along the way. Spot us some walking-around money. I kind of take the scenic route, as you know. Got some secret spots along the way you are going to love."

Sig looked at Moco's huge smile, which revealed his messed-up teeth. Sig laughed, and smiled back.

"Let's go tonight," said Sig.

Moco gave him thumbs up. "First thing tomorrow, how about. Early morning's the best time to move."

Sig put his box on the ready-to-ship stack and stepped out the back door to get some air.

THE BACKSIDE OF THE CO-OP WAS NEXT TO A LITTLE RAVINE. Sig sat in one of the beat-up old chairs they had out there and took in the weather. He whistled toward the ravine, which was full of scrubby trees. Out came the mangy mutt the other workers called Mr. Johnson. Sig tossed Mr. Johnson a fresh bone from the icebox. Mr. Johnson stepped back at first, scared, then decided it was probably okay, nervously grabbed the bone, and disappeared back into the brush.

Sig heard a siren in the distance. Like a police car or a fire truck, but a different tone. It was getting closer.

Then there were more than one, and they got a lot closer. Sig thought about joining Mr. Johnson in the ravine.

Mr. Johnson howled back at the sirens.

Five trucks came roaring down the street from the north. Only one had flashers, and none were police cars. They were pickups and SUVs, red, white, black, and yellow. One pulled a big trailer, the kind they hauled animals in.

The yellow SUV had a megaphone mounted to the roof. It blasted dark metal riffs that sounded like machine death.

Three of the vehicles came straight for the loading area where Sig was, while the others pulled up in front of the store and blocked the entrance.

Then the music went off, and a machine-filtered voice spoke over the noise as the vehicles came to a hard stop.

"THIS IS THE HAWKEYE SELF-DEFENSE MILITIA. WE HAVE PROBABLE CAUSE TO BELIEVE YOU ARE ENGAGED IN INFORMATION TERRORISM AND HARBORING FUGITIVE ENEMIES OF THE STATE. WE ARE DEPUTIZED BY THE FEDERAL GRAND JURY AND THE AUTHORITY OF THE GOVERNOR UNDER THE LIBERTY ACT TO SEARCH THE PREMISES. EVERYONE COME OUT NOW WITH YOUR HANDS UP."

The vehicles ejected armed men, and a few women, scrambling for the doors. Must have been a dozen of them, beefy locals acting like police or border patrol even though they were neither. Which made them more dangerous. They dressed like farmer-cops, Carhartts and overalls mixed with Kevlar and tactical gear. Their trucks, hats, and tops flashed images of sharp-beaked hawks with weapon wings, omniscient eyes, and a little bit of bling.

They swarmed one of the big front doors. Got to work on busting it open.

The dog Mr. Johnson came up out of the woods, barking like crazy and making a pretty good impersonation of someone closely related to a wolf. Not good enough. One of the Hawkeyes aimed and fired, killing Mr. Johnson with a round to the head and another to the torso.

Sig grabbed the hatchet from the woodpile and hurled it at Mr. Johnson's killer. It missed.

Sig saw the guy aim, heard the crack, and went down, like he'd been tackled right in the middle.

The guy and his comrades kept on coming.

Sig saw the rubber bullet there in the gravel in front of him, and felt the spot in his chest where it had hit.

Moco came out with the other guys from the back building, looking to see if they could run for it.

Up in the front, Sig could see Billie come out to argue with the militia, inciting a gun butt to the head that knocked her out of sight.

"Go!" yelled Sig. He got up and charged the approaching trio, hoping to give Moco and their coworkers a chance to make a break for their escape route down along the creek bed.

The Hawkeyes stopped him in his tracks with a barrage of rubber bullets.

Sig could hear the screams of the guys behind him. The nonlethal rounds almost caused more pain than the real kind, even if they didn't pierce the skin. Maybe because the guys shooting them felt no need to restrain themselves.

Sig tried to curl up and shield his soft parts with his back. He could see his buddies behind him. Looked like a couple had gotten away. The rest were on the ground, a few behind the dumpster. Moco looked pretty fucked up.

When the firing paused, Sig sucked in a fresh lungful, jumped up, and rushed the guy in front. He got him, low, right through the knees. The guy fell hard. You could hear his head crack on the pavement. Then they shot him some more, not quite point blank. One of the guys got his boot onto Sig's neck, and he and his partner managed to hold Sig down until they could get him hog-tied tight like they wanted it.

Sig saw the work boot coming, but they were holding him so he couldn't move. That was the first kick. There were a lot more to come.

35

WHEN TANIA WENT TO TRY TO FREE SIG FROM HOSPITAL CUSTODY
the day after the mall riot, he had already freed himself.

She wasn't surprised.

They let her see the room. It was weird to see a bed with
straps like that, imagine them used on a kid, no matter what
he did. Not that they worked in this case.

"He tricked a social worker," said the policewoman who
escorted her. Officer Beckmann. "Choked her, made her free
his restraints. Gagged her with medical tape and strapped her
in where he was supposed to be. Poor lady."

Tania looked out the open window, took in the cold sun.
Yesterday's April snow was already starting to melt. Three
floors down you could still see where he had landed in the
drift blown up against the building. She followed an imagined path out across the parking lot and into the stand of
pines.

"He won't get far," said Beckmann. "All he had on was a
hospital gown."

"I wouldn't be so sure."

The platypus was there on the bedside table. Tania picked
it up and put it in her pocket. The cop didn't notice.

When she got home she put the platypus on her dresser,
next to one of the only pictures she had of Sig, with a dead
flower and a very old coin that Sig had once given her. It gave

her something to cry to, and motivate her continued searching, but it didn't make him come back. In time, it became more than a way to remember Sig. It was like a memorial to their dreams of a future they would want to live in.

Until she moved on, and forgot about it.

36

SIG CAME TO WHEN HE VOMITED, BLOOD AND HUEVOS.

He was gagged, so he had to swallow it all back down or suffocate.

He tried to get up, but he couldn't. His wrists were bound to his ankles. He wasn't sure his body would have stood up anyway.

He could feel the spots where they kicked him, but the muscles cramped up from the hog-tie hurt worse.

He was on the floor of the pen car with the others they had rounded up. He saw Jed, Buzzy, Hannah, Angie, Beto, and two others he didn't know. No Moco.

The trailer smelled like pigs and gunpowder.

The sides of the trailer were narrow slats. Enough to see through, except at the front, where it was solid. They were on the highway north, headed toward Cedar Rapids. They said militia were worse than feds. They made up their own rules. Personal, tribal, primitive. If they got you, your best hope was to get sent to a real jail.

He could see the welts from the rubber bullets on the gagged faces of his friends.

He remembered the time when he learned how rubber bullets can kill, if they hit the right spot. It hurt, thinking about Mom, and it made him angry.

Sig looked at the convoy behind them. A pickup, an SUV, and a motorcycle. There were three big guys crowded in the cab of the pickup. The driver was looking right back at Sig, with a messed-up smile on his face. One of the other guys was sticking some kind of pole through the back window hatch. The guy riding shotgun was talking on the radio, and then suddenly all three vehicles accelerated to pass. That was when Sig saw what was in the bed of the pickup.

A cage.

A cage for humans.

Moco was in the cage, like an animal, cowering, trying to get away from the guy in the back.

The thing the guy had was a cattle prod.

Sig watched as the guy poked Moco and delivered the volts.

Moco screamed.

The guy laughed.

Then the guy saw Sig looking through the slats, and pointed right at Sig, and smiled.

Sig tried to call out through the gag, his grunts lost in the noise of the wind, and then they were gone, pulled ahead.

Sig looked at his binds, and decided he would break them.

He wriggled, working his ankles and wrists to where the joints of the zip ties were centered. Then he kicked, flailing, three times, putting all the body motion he could into it, until the ankle cuff popped. Panting, he stood up, stretched his bound wrists up over his head, then whipped them down to his bellybutton as hard as he could, throwing his elbows out to the side.

The zip tie snapped.

He tore the gag off.

Two of the others, whose legs weren't tied, copied Sig's example.

Sig found a metal splinter on the floorboards that he could use to open the pins on the other zips, by poking the pin into the joint and popping it, a trick he'd learned from an old poacher he got locked up with up north.

While they finished freeing each other Sig tried to get the back door loose. It was barred and chained. He kicked at one of the metal side panels with his sneakered feet until it busted out. It clanged onto the highway.

"Come on," he said.

He was worried the noise might have alerted some of the Hawkeyes. He poked his head out. All clear. He nudged himself out, crouched just through the opening, got his nerve up, and jumped for the green roadside, trying his best to land into a roll.

When he sat up at the bottom of the ditch, his left arm looked like a bent fork and screamed to the touch. The rest of his body felt like it had been backed over by a bus. But he could walk, and the woods were right there.

PART FOUR

The Hand Made Drones

37

TANIA WAS EXCITED WHEN SHE HEARD THEY HAD NABBED MOCO.
When she learned they had used local militia to do it, she was
scared.

She went anyway.

It was only a few hours' drive, so she took the car from
Fleet.

She logged her movement with the travel office, to make
sure her credentials preceded her. There would be checkpoints.

As she drove through the bleached-out flatlands where
Minnesota dissolved into Iowa, she was reminded again of
why she left.

Back east they called it the "Tropic of Kansas." It wasn't a
specific place you could draw on a map, and Kansas wasn't
really even a part of it, but you knew when you were in it
and you knew just what they meant. Which wasn't a compliment. The parts of the Midwest that had somehow turned
third world. They tried to return the Louisiana Purchase to
the French, the joke went, but it was too damaged.

They were still arguing about what caused it. Entire political movements had grown around different theories, but the
truth was no one really knew.

What they did know was that big swaths of the corn belt
had turned sick, from bad splices, failed economics, burnt
climate, broken politics, or divine retribution. Tania voted
for all of the above. It was happening around her when she

was in school, from adolescence through law school, and she had tried out every one of the theories along the way. Since graduation her default mode had been resignation tempered by sparks of optimistic hope quickly extinguished by stark reality.

The bad behavior started in the deep countryside. Out on old roads past the evacuated seats of whole counties depopulated by disappearing futures. The people left behind to tend what was left got the idea they would do better with autonomy and local control of land and law. The sickness, and the politics it bred, soon spread to the nearby cities.

The recolonization took longer. They called it healing, the way they refit the prairies for fresh extraction, but driving through it, watching the new machines bring down their giant proboscises to pierce the crust, you had to wonder.

Cedar Rapids was one of the regional centers from where the recolonization was managed. When you approached it from the north it looked like you had arrived at some industrial ruin of the twentieth century. Weathered concrete towers of grain elevators and food factories rose up over the wide expanse of the railyards, tattooed with the fading logos of dead corporations. Some were retrofitted with new infrastructure—the chromed pipes, black sealants, and aluminum glands of the new biofuels processes. Even with the windows closed, the town smelled, like cotton candy burning into some toxic gas.

You could see the river from the overpass as you came into the old downtown, and you could see it was dead. Something about the color, like chemical mud, the gelatinous texture of the current, the way all the banks were devoid of flora and even the adjacent urban blocks appeared to have been cleared out.

Along the highway was a billboard with the image of the President, back when he had both arms, out in a green field with a group of farmers in their biotech logo ball caps and scientists in their company lab coats watching the new corn come up, corn so big it looked sci-fi. The governor was there, too, his hand on the shoulders of one of the farmers. They called him governor for life, which used to be a joke, until the dominant factions made it real.

THE MILITIA BASE WHERE THEY HAD MOCO WAS A GATED compound out on the east end of the town, the home of one of the local owner class families who relied on the militia to protect their property and keep the other locals under control.

The militia were mostly white, generally stupid, and all scary. The kind of men you would avoid if you saw them on the street, especially if you were black and a woman. The midwestern ones were extra dangerous, because most of them seemed kind of nice when you first talked to them. Nice like the guy at church who smiles at you and offers you a brownie before he tells you how he is going to regulate your life. It helped if you remembered that they were as miserable as the people they were policing. Guys, and a few gals, who had grown up in these blighted quarters neglected by capital and had no ticket out. The kind of people who believed it when the politicians who worked for the businessmen—or were the businessmen, using their fortunes to buy another flavor of power—told them that the source of their suffering was other people living among them, the people who had even less than them and were trying to cut in line.

Having a black woman in a big-city suit show up at their door was not quite as exciting for these guys as having aliens land, but Tania tried to use the shock to her advantage, and to make herself feel as alpha as she could manage among this predatory gang.

The welcome party were a big ruddy guy in bulletproof brown overalls with built-in ammo pouches and the smell of cigarettes, and a little red-bearded guy dressed more like a run-down pastor than a militiaman, complete with a wooden cross hanging from his neck—and a big pistol on his belt. Turned out he was the doctor, Dr. Craven, and the big guy was the commander. Patrol Leader Koenig was the way the commander introduced himself, but then he said just call me Bob.

"Where's my prisoner, Bob?" asked Tania.

"So which agency are you with again?" asked Bob.

"OSI," she said, showing him her ID badge. "Seconded to Secret Service for now. You can cross-check my credentials on the govnet."

"Okay, they don't give us access to that, but they called and said you'd be coming. We got him down here in the basement."

"We've been giving him the special treatment, just like you guys asked," said Dr. Craven.

"I'll be the judge of whether you've been following the protocols," said Tania, asserting status she didn't have, and hoping it would work. Seemed like it did, from the look they gave each other.

The house was huge, on a big acreage, a suburban home converted to paramilitary command center. The walls were covered with big maps of the area, annotated in black grease pencil and red marker. Tania saw photos of targets, some of them mug shots, others surveillance photos. Radios and computers and all manner of gear. Styrofoam cups and a big pile of beer cans in a corner. More guys who looked like Bob, other guys who were leaner and harder looking, and one Asian woman who looked toughest of all, even though she couldn't have been much taller than five feet. More guns than Tania had ever seen in one place outside of an armory. And tons of motivational posters, the banners of identity.

Out on the porch were dog kennels holding two German shepherds and a pair of pit bulls. One of the dogs, a tiger-striped pit with scars across his snout, stared right at Tania as she walked by.

"Come on down here," said Bob, unlocking a triple-bolted metal door that led to the basement.

The light down there flickered, the barely perceptible strobe of cheap fluorescents.

Bob led and Dr. Craven shuffled behind her as they walked into a hallway of cinder-block walls and cell doors made from the material of chain-link yard fences. The cells were empty, except for the one at the end, which had a solid door with a tiny glass window. Tania had to stand on her tiptoes to look.

Inside was a naked little brown kid, strapped to a cot, freshly shaved head propped up with a bunch of cheap pillows.

"What the hell?" said Tania.

"He had a concussion," said Dr. Craven. "We needed to keep him elevated."

It was cold down here, winter basement cold, and you could see it was even colder in the cell. Opposite the bed was a small portable toilet, overdue for a cleaning.

"This is a total violation of protocol. A violation of human rights."

"Don't come in here talking about 'human rights,' girl," said Bob, turning nasty fast. "We're fighting terror, you understand, and this is how your own people showed us to do it. We're keeping him safe and healthy until you all come get him."

"Don't call me 'girl,' big Bob," said Tania, looking up and jabbing her finger at him without actually touching him. "And don't tell me what the rules are. I know all the rules. I can quote them to you. Like the rules that authorize me to suspend your militia privileges pending review the minute I see something I consider a violation. Just because no one ever has the guts to yank it doesn't mean people like you aren't on a short leash. Jesus."

You could see that Bob had never been bossed around by a black woman. He was back on his heels for the moment, but Tania knew that particular spell wouldn't last long. As soon as he got out of her sight he would be scheming how to get the pecking order back the way he liked it.

Tania looked over at Dr. Craven—his eyes, his weird little beard, his wooden cross—and gave him new orders. "Unbind that boy. Get him some clothes. Bring me some water. Better yet, some hot coffee. And a space heater."

"Suit yourself," said Bob, turning away. "You do it, Doc."

"WHO ARE YOU?" SAID MOCO.

"My name is Tania. I work in Washington, for an office you've never heard of, investigating rich crooks."

Moco rubbed his face, then rubbed his arms. He had his clothes back now, and the sweatshirt she made them give him. He felt the hoodie, looked at it, like he couldn't remember where it came from, and then leaned forward, looked right at her, pulled back his sleeve to expose his left forearm.

"What the fuck is this?" he asked.

His arm was fresh and irritated in a red tender spot just above the wrist. In the middle of the spot was a cluster of black bars and dots, but it didn't look like it was made of tattoo ink.

"I think it's an ID," said Tania.

"Thought so," said Moco, looking down at it, looking pissed, then pulling his sleeve back down.

"I'm sorry," said Tania.

"Fuck you, too," said Moco.

"Who did that to you?"

"That creepy-ass doctor," said Moco. "Him and two other dudes. Woke me up in the middle of the night last night."

"I'll find out what it is. He is creepy."

"Comes in here with sugary treats and talks to me about Jesus in bad Spanish and tells me in his soft voice how I can get better treatment if I just rat on everyone I care about. How my tattoos, the ones I came here with, are going to send me to hell and that he could take them off if I want to be 'clean.'"

"What else did they do? I can make a report."

"A report? You must think I'm as stupid as them."

"Tell me. I can tell you want to."

He looked down, then looked at her.

"Fuck with me every way they can think of. Stand there and watch me while I'm taking a shit. Punch me around."

"Let's talk about something else," said Tania. She wanted to hold the kid. She started thinking in the back of her mind how she could get him out.

They brought the coffee, and Tania helped Moco feel better, or at least more comfortable.

They talked for a long time, and as he drank more coffee he became more chatty, even if he seemed to know very little about the subjects Tania wanted to cover. Which was part of her plan—the technique where you ask questions you know the subject can't answer, questions so hard they make his brain hurt, so that when you get around to the questions you really want answered, the subject is keen to display his knowledge. It didn't always work, but it worked more times than not.

She asked him about senior leadership in the underground, what they were planning, what their beliefs and ideals were. She asked him the same kind of questions about the movement in New Orleans, who had survived the Repo, where they hid. She asked him about antennas and secret frequencies and pirate TV, even quizzing him on codes. She got more from him than she expected. About safe houses he'd worked in Chicago, down south, and around here. About holes in the border. About the autonomous cooperative in Iowa City, and the supplies they provided to others. That was when she showed him the picture of Sig.

"Where was this guy during the raid?" she asked.

"Gone," said Moco. "He was gone like three days before that."

"Where did he go?" Tania watched for the tells, trying to assess whether Moco was lying.

"I don't know," he said. "Where would you go?"

"Where he would go is keep moving. Maybe New Orleans. Sounds like there's sanctuary there."

"Not anymore. Unless you count the camps."

"Not what I heard. Where else would you go if you were him?"

"South. All the way, across the border."

"Nicaragua?"

"Nicaragua's over. You could see it even before the merger."

"How many 'business trips' have you made to Nicaragua?"

"A couple."

"Land?"

"Yeah, first time. That sucked. So I introduced my team-mates to some guys I know that have boats that work the coast."

"Is that where you took the Minnesotan?"

"I didn't take him nowhere. I picked that other lady up to go to Houston. Real top secret stuff."

"What lady?"

"The burned lady. Traveled all covered up."

Tania tried to imagine the scene. Made a list in her head of underground leaders. Ones who would match that weird description.

"Name?" she asked.

"They never said, and I didn't ask."

"Was it Maxine Price?"

He paused. Tania tried not to hold her breath at the implausibility of her question, and the possibility of his answer.

"If you want me to take you away from these marshmallow crackers you need to tell me it all, Mauricio."

"I didn't even know who she was. They said she didn't used to look like that, and I never even knew what she looked like the first time."

"She was the Vice President of the United States."

"Yeah, I heard, but I didn't know. I was like a little fucking kid back then."

"Did you know she was supposed to be dead?"

"She looked pretty worn out."

"Who was with her?"

"Nobody. Some people brought her to the boat when we picked her up but she was the only one who got on."

"Hard to believe a VIP fugitive like her would travel solo. Crazy."

"She was a real nice lady. Real smart. I didn't understand half the shit she said but when I did it was pretty cool. Don't you think we should all be more like how they were doing it in New Orleans before the Repo? You should have seen it. Crazy. They were like people from the future. Only like a future that came from a totally different past."

"Now it's just the past. And a lot of us might like the ideas, but not think it's okay to blow up the White House to make them real."

"You don't think someone should blow up that asshole?"

"You know that's another federal felony you just committed?"

He shivered and stared at her.

"Where is Maxine Price now?"

"I don't know."

"Where did you leave her?"

"I told you already, didn't I? New Orleans. We got tracked, fucking submarine drones, who knows. Diverted in time. Delivered her to safe friends. Then we split up and burned the boat."

"I have some more questions about the Minnesotan."

"I need a break," said Moco.

WHILE SHE LEFT MOCO ALONE IN THE ROOM, TANIA'S MIND reeled with the implications of what she had just learned. The idea that Maxine Price was still alive, and in hiding.

It made her suddenly very confused about what she was doing. She thought about Mom, and what she said to her when they parted.

Maybe Tania could take Moco with her. Turn him into an ally.

She asked the redneck on guard where to find Bob, and the guy said he was just looking for you.

When Tania got to the top of the stairs, Bob was standing there waiting, with half his crew, all armed.

"Time's up," said Bob. The short woman Tania had seen earlier was cozied right up next to him, looking even meaner than before.

"I need to take the prisoner back with me," said Tania.

"Not without some official Motherlanders with you. I think you're fishy. Joyce here just made some calls and we're starting to get a little confused."

Joyce stared hard at Tania.

"That's because you are a little bit slow," said Tania. "And you are calling the wrong people. But I don't have time to teach you how to do it. Get out of my way."

And then she straightened up her suit and walked right through them, and they let her.

As she drove away, south instead of north, looking back every few seconds for them to come roaring after her with the full crew, she thought about Moco, and how she could free him. About Mom, and how she could free her. About all the other people like them.

Things were starting to clarify, except that she didn't really know where she was going.

Maybe Sig could help, if she could find him.

She drove faster.

38

"This is not a regular meeting," said Billie to the seventeen people she had called together. "It's a crisis council."

Sig looked around the room. It was all gray hair except for his.

"Let's have a war!" joked one of the old guys. He had a long silver beard and a shaved head.

"Cut the shit, Rich, or leave," said Billie.

Billie, it turned out, really was a terrorist. Fritz was the one who finally told Sig about it. She'd been a member of the Blackhawk Army, a midwestern student revolutionary group from back in the eighties. She was arrested after the BellNet Regional Headquarters bombing in 1986 but skipped bail and went underground. Fritz said her real name was Catherine. Even he didn't know her real last name.

Sig flexed his hand in the strap-on cast. They had taken him to a bone doctor who was a friend of the cause. The doctor set it as best he could and told him to take it easy if he wanted to get his full range of motion back.

Sig listened to Billie make her case to the group. She wanted them to free Moco. The militia had announced he was a high-value denaturalized terrorist they planned to turn over to the feds for transfer to the Corn Islands.

"That's the extraterritorial prison," said Billie. "Worse than Detroit. The one where the Constitution doesn't even apply— unlike here, where it's just suspended. One-way trip, guys."

There were a lot of incredulous groans. All of the others who didn't escape with Sig had been freed, through a combination of good lawyering and payoffs from the community kitty. Fritz told Sig that was the real deal with the militias in those parts—most of their so-called law enforcement was really just kidnapping and protection for money.

"We need to stop harboring these little militia bait pets of yours," said one old guy who looked like a bad Santa. The guy pointed his thumb at Sig as he said it. "Or we'll lose everything we've built here."

"The ones who are hot are going to leave, Tom," said Billie. "After we free the last one."

"By going back to the ways that failed the first time," said one of the women in the group.

"There's real change brewing, Mary," said Billie. "Yes, we may need to help get the fire going again. Right now, the deal is we told these kids we would give them sanctuary, and we failed, because we had the naïve idea that if we did it peacefully no one would mess with us. We need to fix that. Now. We cannot let anyone be sent to that place."

"So you want to blow up a bunch of militia?"

"I don't want to kill *anyone*," said Billie. "I just want to start fighting back again. It's more like psychological warfare— playing the media game. Hopefully better than they do."

"Psychological warfare with guns?" said one of the women in the group.

"Hear me out," said Billie. She laid out her basic plan. It took a while, with all the discussions and digressions. Billie had explained to them at the Co-op how she did not believe in the idea of management hierarchy—of people telling other people what to do. She believed, she said, in "pure autonomous cooperation."

This time, though, no one was cooperating with her. She lost the vote.

"I'm sorry, Sig," she said when he argued for his friend afterward. "But I can't second-guess the wisdom of the group. It's for the best."

39

FRITZ OFFERED TO HELP SIG. IT GAVE HIM A CHANCE TO USE HIS homemade drones.

Of course, Fritz didn't call them drones. He called them models.

They used the big one first. It barely fit in Fritz's rusty old Mercedes wagon. It was one Sig had seen in the basement, shaped like a stuffed triangle. Turned out the nose was a lens. A thick antenna swept back from behind the lens, not quite flush with the fuselage. The pusher prop blade was at the back, powered by a gas engine.

Sig wondered if a thing like that could fly.

It turned out it could fly really well. The trick was getting it into the air.

The season's last snow came the night before they drove up to Cedar Rapids. It was bigger than expected. But not big enough to block the roads. Or to mask the stench of Cedar Rapids, where the biofuels plants filled the air most days with the odor of a sugarcoated slaughterhouse.

They set up in the parking lot behind an abandoned office building. The pavement was wet and slick from snowmelt, but plowed clear. Fritz fiddled around with the engine of the plane while Sig watched for patrols. The engine sputtered and kicked in. It was pretty loud.

"Okay, clear!" said Fritz over the engine noise.

The plane accelerated as it moved. The engine throttled

up. It sounded kind of like a leaf blower. And then it lifted, as if pulled by an invisible string.

Sig drove the car while Fritz drove the drone. Fritz had the backseat set up as a cockpit. He had a TV, a bunch of computers and radios, and a video game controller. It was so packed with gear that Fritz had to slide down through the sunroof to get in and out.

Fritz knew where the militia base was. It was a house in the rich part of town. The home of some guy who had sold his family's factory to one of the big biofuels companies and now spent most of his time in New York. The guy was one of the main sponsors of the militia and gave them the run of the house.

They drove closer to the house and parked on a quiet street a couple of blocks away. Sig moved to the back and watched the grainy black-and-white footage that came in from the drone. The house was huge. It looked like it probably had ten bedrooms. The lot was bigger, maybe three acres. There was a big garage, a shed, an empty swimming pool, and a boarded-up cabana.

The yard was full of trucks, the snow packed down from the weight of the vehicles driving all over it.

Six prisoners in sweatsuits stood in the bottom of the empty swimming pool, milling about under the watch of two armed guards.

Fritz circled overhead for twenty minutes, while Sig made a map in his head. Then they landed the drone and took a lunch break when it was almost time for dinner.

IT WAS DARK WHEN THEY FINISHED EATING, AND A LOT colder. Fritz said those were perfect conditions to fly the copter.

176

The copter did not look like a helicopter. It looked like a flying ball made out of toothpicks. It was smaller than a basketball but bigger than a baseball. The balsa wood lattice was dotted with little fiber eyes all attached to a controller the size of a pack of gum. It had six small rotors inside the superstructure. It made no more noise than a fan. Like the plane, it did not look like it could fly. And it didn't. More like it floated.

It had a short range, so they had to park down the street to launch it, which made Fritz nervous. But it worked. They flew in and bobbed around the outside of the house, peeking through the windows and seeing what was going on inside, until they found the room where they kept Moco.

Fritz was very pleased with this, until Sig said he wanted to go in that same night.

40

TANIA DROVE TO THE OUTSKIRTS OF IOWA CITY, LOOKING FOR A safe place to hide and figure out next steps. She kept waiting for a militia truck to appear in her rearview mirror, but there were hardly any vehicles coming from either direction, just big transports moving cross-country loads. The only passenger car she noticed was a bright yellow Benz wagon that looked like it was older than Tania, headed in the direction Tania was coming from, spewing old-school diesel fumes.

She called Bert, but he didn't answer. She left a reckless message, asking if Bert had any idea how she could arrange a prisoner transfer. She wanted to help Moco, but to do that she first had to protect herself, and save Mom. A task that now seemed a lot harder, after learning from Moco that she had just missed Sig. First Lisbet, now this. She needed to regroup.

Tania scoped out the corporate hotels along the interstate, out by the big plants. At the truck center, she nearly maxed out her credit card buying prepaid cards off the rack, to use as anonymous cash equivalents. Gift cards, mostly, one of which the clerk showed her could have its limits altered at the register.

She pulled up to the lobby of a corporate clean M-Class hotel on a big berm along the frontage road, but got a dangerous vibe watching two business-casual guests stumble in from the bar. So she drove closer into town and decided to try the River Inn, a place that looked clean but on the empty side, with the kind of old cars in the lot that people drove when they wanted to stay off the satellite, or couldn't afford to be on it.

The night clerk looked like a hippie mortician, which in this case was a good thing. Tania prepaid a week with her new Bux card and gave the guy a fake name. Have a nice stay, Ms. Rourke.

She persuaded him to give her a corner room on the second floor, far from the elevator and close to an exterior exit, with a view of the highway and the field behind.

Before she unloaded the car, she found a beat-up old cash machine and took out her limit. Then she picked up provisions at the cooperative convenience store—bottled water, noodle packs, night snacks, a prepack sandwich, and Iowa wine. It calmed her to see she was in a town that had figured out how to take over an abandoned corporate outpost like Kwik Stop and turn it into a trading post well stocked with local goods.

She parked the car around in the back, behind a shed, where it wouldn't be seen unless someone was looking really hard.

She sent an incomplete update to Gerson and then spent three hours trying to figure out how to disable the tracking devices in her gear, including the uplink in her car. She told Mike she was on the move, without telling him more. She sent an encrypted message to Todd, asking if he'd had any luck getting access to the DdB, and if he could get her a tap into the security feed of this motel.

She called Odile, but no answer, not even a voicemail prompt.

She looked at pictures of her mom, and of Sig.

She looked out the window, looking for danger, and noticed an old antenna off to the south.

The Feed box was on, in the background, tuned for news, with the sound off. It wasn't until she decided she was probably safe for the night and needed to rest that she bothered to try to change the channel, saw that the same show was on every channel, and remembered what night it was.

The anniversary. The Day of Memory. Another day since they killed the hostages.

Flags and dirges and photos of the dead. The national pain that can never be fully avenged.

Tania wasn't even born when it happened, but they made it the centerpiece of the patriotic narrative starting in grade school. Maybe that was why it still worked so well to get people worked up into a nationalistic fervor.

Remember the Martyrs

Before every commercial break, they showed a one-minute life of one of the sixty-six. Newton Towns narrated the sequences about the military response, with documentary voice-over solemnity.

Tania felt the programmed feeling coming on. Empathy for this long-dead young woman's life cut short. Felt the cry coming up inside, even though she knew she was being manipulated. She wasn't just crying for this dead American diplomat with feathered hair. She cried for her own dead future, in sudden recognition that her entire career was a misguided emulation of these childhood icons of nationalist virtue, noble public servants whose own innocence masks the sins of their master. She cried for Mom, the soul-tired in her eyes from fighting her whole life against a leviathan she could not even scratch. She cried for Moco, the spirited kid learning the ugly lessons about what they did to those who tried to freely move, especially if they came from one of the camps. She cried for Tracer, the teen who had the foolish courage to challenge his own family's privilege. She cried for Sig, out there roaming Lord knows where, surviving like an animal, alone. She even cried for untouchable Odile. And for America, her country gone cannibal.

Her radical white school friends used to say Martyrs Day was the event that broke the American heart and turned it black. When she repeated that to Mom over dinner, Mom said it just gave them permission to be more honest about it.

Tania turned off the set and stood. She looked at her reflection in the black screen. She went to the window again. Saw two blinking lights on the mast in the distance, one red and one white. Maybe it was time to watch a different kind of TV. Time to figure out a way to find Sig, and free Mom, without having to rat anyone out, or lie, or exploit old friends. If she played it right, and got a little lucky, she might be able to keep them all free.

Tania went to her laptop bag and dug out the portable set Todd had loaned her. She set it up on the coffee table. She grabbed the sheet they handed out at Ganymede, with the frequencies. She plugged in the power. Then she got to work on tuning it in.

She got a dot in the center of the screen, and then it grew into a blizzard of electronic noise.

She flipped the channels. Each one, variations on the same thing.

She fiddled with the focal knobs. Thought for a second she saw the contours of human faces in the dissonant dots, then laughed at herself for thinking there would be answers in that noise.

And then the phone rang.

Tania didn't recognize the number, but when she saw the time, she knew who it was, and what she needed to do.

451

FRITZ SAID THEY COULD RUN BACK DOWN TO IOWA CITY AND GET
a gun from the safe, but Sig said he didn't want one. He didn't
like guns and he didn't think he'd need one.

Fritz said Sig's idea to put spikes in his cast so it would
work like a mace was goofy. But he helped him anyway. They
made the new outer layer from long carpet nails and duct tape
they bought at the Stone City Maker Co-op.

They got most of the materials for the bomb in the garden
department.

Fritz gave Sig a headlamp to use if he needed it. He put
one of his little drone cameras on there, too. They didn't have a
radio, but at least Fritz could watch and know when they were
coming back. He didn't say if.

It was a little after three in the morning when they got
started for real. They parked in the same spot a block away, and
Sig set out on foot. He cut through the backyards to the house
he'd seen that came right up to the back of the militia mansion
fence. Even with one hand, he was able to climb up the drain-
pipe on the garage, then work his way up two stories onto the
roof. From there, it was an easy jump down into the snow.

He could hear the whine of Fritz's big drone.

He jogged across the yard, using what tree cover he could,
and came around behind the poolhouse. The pool was empty
of prisoners now. There was one big militiaman standing back
there walking patrol and smoking a cigarette. Sig went back to
the fence and around the long way to the east side of the house.

It was clear. He ran up to the basement window. It was partly covered with snow, but you could still see down into the room. The lights were on. So was the radio, playing some kind of loud rock that sounded like power tools. Same as the SUV that had delivered the militia to the Co-op. Moco was curled up naked on the floor. He looked like shit.

"Hey!" said a voice behind Sig.

Sig looked around. Guard, with flashlight on Sig.

BLAMF BLAMF BLAMF. The sound of bullets penetrating snow. Sig dove into the snow, and swam.

He came up away from the window and ran toward the front of the house.

An alarm went off, blasting a klaxon inside and outside.

BLAM BLAM BLAM BLAM BLAM BLAM.

He ran like a wild animal. He was used to it. He had been hunted before.

He heard the whine of the drone coming in. He stepped into a drift too deep, and fell flat on his face in the snow.

When Sig turned over, the fat Hawkeye stood over him, staring with the third eye of a headlamp. You could see the sweat on his face and the metal of the barrel glowing blue in the weird light of the LED blended with the moon and the crystals of the snow.

Drone whine, like the sound of a tiny dive bomber coming in. You could see the blur of the shape as it crashed into a second-floor window.

KRRRRABOOOMM!

Fritz's biofuel-compost payload detonated. You could feel the blast before you saw the fireball. You could even see it passing over the face of the Hawkeye as he turned to look.

Sig got up on his feet and planted his mace fist in the side of the guard's head, just below the ear. You could hear the sound of the nails going in. The guy screamed. Sig brought his knife up under the guy's sternum and went all the way in.

It took a second before Sig realized how much his wrist hurt. He had to cut the duct tape and nails loose from the cast to separate them.

There was a lot of blood in the snow.

He took the gun with him as he ran back to Moco.

There were other militia running around outside now. You could hear a woman and a man barking commands out by the main entrance. It didn't seem to matter. Whatever paramilitary order they had was broken by the surprise.

Moco was not in his cell. The door was open. The music was still on.

Sig smashed the window with the rifle. He climbed down into the room, bringing snow with him. Someone had ripped a poster from the wall. Sig stepped into the hallway, bracing the rifle as best he could with his clumsy left hand.

Moco was on the hallway floor, pounding away at a guard he had pinned, using the guard's metal club. You could hear the crunch. Moco looked back at Sig with a crazy face, that look that no other type of animal ever showed.

Sig waved at him to come on.

Moco's expression changed, and he flashed his messed-up teeth.

They helped each other get back up out through the window.

They ran through the chaos outside. They saw militiamen attending to the explosion. They got to the spot Sig had seen from the drone eye, where the snow was blown up against the fence in a low spot at the bottom of the hill. They struggled a bit in the layer of fresh, unpacked stuff but managed to clamber up and over the top.

42

"YOU'RE LATE," SAID BERT. EXCEPT BERT WASN'T REALLY BERT,
not in this place. Here Bert was Jasmine, a Yemeni spy with
the world's most insane eyelashes. And when he/she talked, it
came through as text messages at the bottom of Tania's screen.

"Sorry," texted Tania, typing on the keyboard side of the
remote that operated the hotel room Feed box. "Researching,
lost track of time."

"Thought you might be watching the special."

"Making my own."

The speakers filled with the sound of jets, and then the
image shook. In the background behind Bert/Jasmine, you
could see the pyramids were burning.

"Sunday nights in Cairo" was what Bert called it, this way
to secretly communicate when they were both in the field. The
game was *Call of Freedom*, a multiplayer military shooter set
in an alternate universe where the Iran War never happened,
the General never happened, and America was in a religious
war with Arab guerrillas who hid in mountain complexes and
urban tunnel forts. Bert liked it because it was so unpopular,
buried in the deep back channels of the Feed where the bots
rarely roamed, and because it was almost exclusively popu-
lated with buzz-cut special forces guys, frequently shirtless
and often grunting. Tania found it grim as hell, from the opening title shot of terrorists flying a plane into the Empire State
Building to the way the rules allowed players to torture each
other, but Bert was right that it worked well as a clandestine

hangout, if you didn't mind getting virtually shot at all the time.

"How's Duluth?" asked Bert.

Tania did not want to answer that one, so she answered with a question.

"Ever wonder what happened to Maxine Price?"

"Not really," answered Bert. "She was the first American suicide bomber. I just wonder why the bitch couldn't pull it off. But she always did choke when opportunity struck. Talk is easier than real action."

"Maybe. You don't wonder about the official story?"

Jasmine shrugged. You could see the pixel Sphinx behind her.

"They had a body?" said Tania.

"They had some kind of crispy toast on the Feed," said Bert. "They always show a body, even when they don't have one."

"Burial at sea," said Tania.

"Exactly," said Bert. "You know I know you're not where you're supposed to be, right?"

Shit.

"I can't help you unless you tell me," typed Bert. "Especially not with this insane prisoner transfer thing you burned on my vmail."

"Iowa," typed Tania.

"Iowa? You're supposed to be in Minnesota. The part of Minnesota that's farthest from Iowa."

"I got different orders," typed Tania.

"You what?" typed Bert. Jasmine's inkbrush eyebrows wiggled.

Tania trusted Bert. She needed help. She told him the whole deal. Most of it.

When she was done typing, Bert told her she'd been played.

"Don't you get it? They're using you, and entrapping you, all at the same time."

Tania processed that.

"I've seen them do it before," said Bert. "To other informants. You're going to help them make a bunch of arrests, and then they are going to say you were part of the conspiracy. You told me before you feel like you're on one of the lists, and they're just waiting for you to make a big enough mistake."

"I have a deal with them. In writing."

"Wishful thinking. You know those things are unenforceable."

Maybe he was right. Bert had been around a long time, and usually knew.

"You're only going to make it worse for your mom," he added.

"What would you do?"

"Run. Bug out. Go under."

"Can you help me?"

Bert didn't answer.

Tania would have run right then, but she was afraid to go outside. Afraid to even leave the room.

I can't do this anymore. Tania said that out loud, but did not type it for Bert to read.

"Best I can do is try to cover for you at work," blurted Bert. "Gotta go now bye."

Tania stared at the suddenly lifeless figure of Jasmine, and the flickering cursor waiting for her to tell it her next move. She could hear the wind hitting the building as the isolation started to burrow its way in, and wondered where she could find friends out there in the dark.

43

WHEN THEY GOT IN THE CAR, SIG HELPED MOCO CUT THE NEW TAT-
too from his flesh. When they were pretty sure they had gotten
whatever tags were in there, they threw them out the window.

They heard the choppers and sirens as they drove, saw
the searchlights, wondered about the things they couldn't see.

Fritz had extra clothes for Moco, a flask of brandy, a bagel,
a bottle of water, and some vitamins. He had a first aid kit that
Moco and Sig both used.

Fritz knew some pretty good back roads from bicycling.
He got them out of town and drove them an hour south to the
Missouri state line.

He dropped them off behind an abandoned motel where
they could crash until they were ready to move on. Fritz
gave Sig a piece of paper with his and Billie's contact info, the
names of some other Subway conductors between here and
New Orleans, and the code he said would let him access his
snowflakes. The code was a crazy long string of numbers and
letters that took up one whole side of the page. Then he gave
him another piece of paper sealed in an envelope that he said
he wanted him to deliver to the people in New Orleans, the
people Moco would know how to find.

Fritz held Sig's arm for a long time when he was telling
him about all that.

They never got to see Fritz's videos on the news, at least
not until a long time later.

PART FIVE

Movie Nights

44

IN THE DREAM, TANIA WAS IN THE CAGE, SHIVERING AND NAKED.
Moco was standing right there on the other side, sneering at her, holding a fire hose. Mom was behind him, smiling.

Mom said something. Again? Moco went for the nozzle.

BOOM BOOM BOOM.

Someone pounding on a door.

Tania opened her eyes. It took her a minute to remember where she was. That ugly wallpaper.

More knocking, harder.

Tania got up, looked through the peephole. It was the hotel night man. He looked worried.

Tania cracked the door, leaving the chain on.

"Hey, Ms. Rourke," he said, looking down the hallway both ways as he talked. "I wanted to tell you some people just came around here and I think they were looking for you."

"What are you talking about?"

"Militia, with a couple of state troopers. They didn't have a picture and they said a different name but they gave a description that sure sounded like you. They said they needed to ask you some questions, maybe something to do with that raid that just went down."

"Are they still here?"

"I got rid of them," he said. "But you can bet they'll be back. I don't think they liked the way I blew them off."

"What time is it?" said Tania.

"Half past five."

A good time to make an arrest.

"Thank you," said Tania. She grabbed her purse and handed the clerk a hundred-dollar bill, so old and dog-eared that it was hard to believe it came out of a machine, but that was how almost all of them were these days.

"You betcha," said the clerk.

"There's more where that came from," said Tania.

Tania closed the door back up and looked at the den she had made. The room was littered with her stuff. Suitcase open and half-unpacked, wires and cords, files, snack food remnants, boxes of takeout, half-drunk bottles of water and soda and one mostly drunk bottle of wine. It hadn't been that long, but the days stretched out when you locked yourself up in a room like this, more so when you used it as a portal to disappear into your screens, hunting in the clouds.

It was time to move on, before they came by looking for her again, before Sig got too far.

As she thought about packing up, and where she would go, Tania looked at Todd's portable TV there on the desk, her open notebook full of scrawls on one side, sleeping laptop on the other. She remembered how she had stayed up most of the night experimenting with different tuning strategies and interpretations of the Ganymede codes in search of a clear transmission. She gave up in frustration sometime around three, but left it on just in case.

It had finally worked. The screen was filled with a test pattern, made from a cartoon of a robot armadillo, its plates painted in the colors of the rainbow, standing on a logo.

CHANNEL ZERO
Please Stand By

She turned up the volume, which she had muted in the night, tired of hearing the white noise. The static was still there, but she heard a voice. Not the same voice as she heard in Todd's lab, but saying the same kind of thing, reading numbers and codes aloud.

She couldn't move now, or even turn off the set, and risk never getting the signal back—for all she knew it was tied to this spot, and the current transmission was definitely tied to this moment in time. Just a couple of hours, at least, she thought.

Tania started taking notes, and tried to listen for hope in the coded transmissions instead of the danger lurking in the sounds outside.

45

ON THE TELEVISION, THEY WERE TORTURING THE PRESIDENT OF the United States. The crowd in the bar cheered them on.

It wasn't actually President Mack. It was an actor playing the role of the President—before he actually became President. In the movie he's a freshman senator from New York who takes leave to reactivate his Navy wings and help liberate the South Koreans, only to get shot down and captured on the wrong side of the DMZ.

On-screen, Mack struggled against his bindings. He was tied to a chair bolted to the floor of a windowless room. Shirt ripped off, toned torso spritzed with fake sweat and blood, face pulled into a tight grimace.

"Pinche rich boy," yelled a lady at the next table, laughing.

"¡Mátalo!" hollered a guy in the front.

"Newton Towns," said Moco to Sig, drawing out the sound in ridicule. "This actor is such a ball-licking pendejo. Look how he has the hair waxed off his chest! I think he is one of those Furmanólogos."

Sig drank his Sandino and scanned the room. The bar was windowless, too, except for the slider on the door that the armed bouncers looked through when you knocked to get in. From the outside, the place looked like a concrete bunker, marked with a painting by the door of a cheesecake Aztec princess remotely piloting a giant flying snake with a fleshy joystick. The spot was remote, at the end of a gravel road back behind the big drone plants in East St. Louis. Sig still didn't feel safe, but they had been running long and hard enough that Moco talked him into sitting still while they waited for Moco's contacts to show up and close the deal. It helped that the place had the biggest television Sig had ever seen.

Crazy eyes stared from the screen. Close-up on a wide-faced woman with thick black hair piled up in a beehive, Mao jacket unbuttoned to reveal a jade skull necklace and telenovela cleavage. The woman smiled and held up the exposed end of an electrical cable, sparking blue.

The crowd in the bar whooped and yelled like they were watching a boxing match.

"¡MAGA MAGA MAGA!" they yelled. "¡Ya se armó!"

Moco looked at Sig and laughed. "This lady is like the godmother of Mexican crime movies," he explained. "She ain't no Korean. She's Guatemalan. Margareta Ana García. 'Doña Maga.' Before she moved to Hollywood to be devil dictator daughter and shit she was a big diva in Mexico City, pop singer who started playing the queen of crime."

Newton Towns as President Mack gritted his porcelain teeth as the electricity ran through his body. Techno tuba notes pumped out of the jukebox on the other side of the room, competing with the hoots of the crowd and the crackling sound of the President being fried.

Sig looked around at the other patrons. They were mostly women—Mexican armorers and assemblers who spent their fat paychecks from the flybot factories on the flavors of home and TLC procured from hungry locals.

"Why do they need to hire these people from so far away?"

"Do the math," said the woman seated at the table behind Moco. "The locals can't." She patted the blond hair of the skinny white boy who was giving her a neck rub. "Es la verdad, right, Bobby?"

The boy laughed, pulled up the collar of the woman's coveralls, and poked the embroidered robot on her shoulder.

"Everybody knows the maquilas produce the best drone techs," said Bobby. "And the best of the best are the ladies of Juárez."

The torturer was asking the President a question, but you couldn't hear it over the noise.

The name on the door of the bar was "El Agasajo," which meant something like "the royal treatment." Of which, according to Moco, the staff offered several variations. But few people ever used that name, he said. Mostly they just called it the Embassy. For obvious reasons, and not so obvious, like the fact that the walls were lined with lead to provide total privacy from prying electronic eyes. And as if that weren't enough, he claimed some of the factory workers were gradually reprogramming all the machines they worked on to read the place as a blank spot on the map.

Smoky vapor came off the heaving pecs of Newton Towns as Thomas Mack.

"This isn't personal," said Mack, busting his right arm free from its bindings. The camera went in close. "It's business," he said, eyes twinkling.

Plink. Plonk. The sound of metal bolts snapping.

The President ripped the chair from the floor and shoved it at his tormentor, producing a mix of laughs and boos from the ladies in the bar.

"It's business," said Moco, raising a can of Huckleberry Lite.

Sig nodded. He had a dollar and change in his pocket. They were running up a tab on the come. Parked outside was an ugly red Mercury they jacked from an abandoned farm when they were moving cross-country two nights earlier. The trunk was filled with fourteen guns they stole the day before from the storm cellar of a small-town VFW hall outside Kirksville. Home-modified assault rifles from old wars and a dusty crate of grenades that someone else would have to test. Moco said they needed money to travel right, and this was a way to score and help the cause at the same time. He "borrowed" Sig's last fifty to buy their way across the bridge, thanks to a fat-ass militiaman guard whose name he knew. The guard told them a pair of hunters had come through an hour earlier showing pictures of Moco and talking about a hundred-K bounty. Now Moco's contacts, the ones who were going to "buy the car," were working on an hour late. And the President was escaping.

He had a stolen machine gun of his own now and was blasting his way through the inside of a military prison packed with guards.

"Bulletproof," said Sig.

"In real life he probably bought his way out," said Moco. "I heard a story he left his copilot behind. They say the dude's still rotting in a prison over there, all deformed and shit from crash burns."

"Se llama el Elefante," said the woman behind Moco.

The bartender came up to Moco. Butch redhead with a pit bull made out of sequins smiling across her bosom. She whispered in Moco's ear.

"They're here," said Moco, thumbs up. "Right outside, in back."

"Shouldn't we meet them inside?"

"Juana won't let us," he said. "No business in the club. Keeps her out of trouble."

Moco stood, and Sig followed him.

As they walked toward the back door, down the hallway where the private rooms were, Sig took one look back. One dude who did not look at all like a droner was standing up now, looking back at Sig, talking on his phone. Dark skin, green eyes, blue ball cap.

On the television behind him, President Mack ran across the roof of the prison, looking for a helicopter to steal.

46

THAT NIGHT, WHILE HER MACHINE RAN A ROUTINE TO PING THE dark nets, Tania made a run for provisions.

The militia hadn't come back looking for her. Tania guessed they wouldn't. At least not without a fresh tip.

She had thought the town would be safe. It was supposed to be sanctuary, an island of self-determination, regulated by authentic community instead of external authority, instead of guns and machine eyes.

But when she went back to the cooperative store with all its fresh local foods and goods, she realized everyone else in town was white. Or if they weren't, they were hiding. Like maybe she should be, she thought, after seeing how some of them looked at her, and wondering which might be the ones who tipped off the militia, or worse. Surveillance didn't need to be electronic.

She stocked up enough to not have to go out for a while.

She sent Gerson an update, saying she thought she was close but needed more time, and asking for a confirm on her mom's status. Gerson hadn't replied, to that message or the one before, and Tania wondered if Bert was right, and it was time to go totally dark.

She decided the best way to disappear was to stay in the hotel room, and figure out ways to act like she wasn't.

She stayed off the securenet, using the generic address of the Feed box for open-source intelligence on one screen while she tuned the analog signals of the other.

She asked the night manager if he knew someone who would drive her car to Minneapolis, or at least Cedar Rapids. He got all shifty when she asked, until she said a price.

Tania plied the night man for ideas on where someone like Sig might hide in this secretive little burg, but she could tell those questions set off his narc radar. She would focus on finding him—and the network that was moving him and the others—through her screens. If she could just crack the codes and learn what they were saying to each other over this bizarro alternet.

As she worked to find a way in, she kept thinking about what Moco had said about Maxine Price, and what it would mean if it was really true.

She was trolling conspiracy theory sites on the back pages of the boards, reading theories of the outlaw veep's secret life in exile, when the alert came through. It came in the form of a video, or something close to it, a series of sequential stills taken by the camera dot she had affixed to the ceiling over the door before she left for Cedar Rapids.

The angle, and the frame delay, made it look like a screen grab from some old phone game.

The footage showed three big men in suits, coming to see her, at the extended stay in Minneapolis where she was still registered as a guest. They knocked. They did not know she was already four hours south of there. They announced themselves as private security. She wondered if they were friends of Lisbet, even if they didn't look the part. Or "friends" of Gerson, doing no fingerprints work, in line with Bert's warning. They might even be corporate bagmen, employer unknown, working for a company she had ticked off with one of her cases—or for Odile's vengeful mother. Tania knew they were not people she wanted to meet.

They tried the door, but they did not pick the lock.

Tania tried to remember if she had left anything behind in that room that she couldn't do without. And then she wished she could do more to make it look like she was still there, as misdirection, like that movie she once saw.

I want room service, she thought, and when she called she told them to please leave it in the room. She'd be right back.

And when the scruffy kid came around to take her car keys, Tania gave him the room key as well, and told him to take his girlfriend, stay a few nights, and be sure to run up the tab.

47

THAT AFTERNOON WHEN MOCO WAS DRIVING, SIG HAD LOOKED AT
the brittle paper map Fritz had given him.

Pioneer Trails of the Prairie States

It showed how the modern highways tracked the old un-
paved routes. The pioneers got the trails from Indians, who got
them from the animals. Up north, some of the trails were so
old they were said to have been the trackways of mastodons,
the hippie-haired giant elephants that the first peoples followed over here from Siberia.

In St. Louis, Sig had seen a sign for the old highway
his great-uncle had told him about a long time ago, the one
grandpa took back from California with his new Mexican
wife after he finished his Army tour fighting their wars. He
remembered Uncle Borg said the place where Route 66 started
in St. Louis had once been a great city of some tribe that built
gigantic midwestern pyramids.

Sig looked at the big red line that cut through the middle
of Missouri and into Kansas, which was like a ghost on the
map. Out there the trails branched off and turned in unexpected directions. Sig tried to imagine sailing through oceans
of grass, beyond the old border of the United States, before
they wasted it all.

He wondered how many different nations this place had
been before.

He wondered if there was a spot on the map where he could stop without worrying about them catching him. If New Orleans really still had some pockets of sanctuary left.

He looked out the window for signs of lost pyramids, but only saw factories, fuel silos, and a railyard so big you couldn't count the cars.

The railyard, it turned out, was where they closed their deal.

48

THE TRANSMISSIONS WERE MOSTLY ON AT NIGHT. AT LEAST THAT'S when Tania was able to tune them. Usually late at night. Something to do with atmospheric conditions.

There was more than one channel.

Channel Zero was the numbers station. It usually came in on Channel 17 or Channel 64, running codes at dawn and dusk, sometimes by voice, but mostly as graphics—bleeding chyrons flashed in rapid sequence, too fast to record by hand.

Channel 13, which ran most nights on Channel 23, was mostly videos from amateur contributors. They ran the ads every few minutes soliciting people to send stuff in. Payment by cash or snowflake, whatever that was, for the good stuff. Footage from soldiers of combat and its aftermath. Money shots from wild game hunts. Corporate raiders showing off their treasure. Trophy videos from drug turf battles. Scenes from inside the Superdome, Detroit, sometimes one of the smaller detention camps. Matches in underground fighting rings. And all the amateur pornography.

They would mix in some politics with all this stuff, like they went together. Sometimes they ran recruiting ads for the underground network, usually localized, sometimes not.

After dark Channel Zero ran the straight-up propaganda. Chalk talks and shaky video of people speaking at underground rallies. Jerky footage from the other end of government raids. A family watching TV when Motherland boots come through the living room wall. Injured children being tended to in improvised hospitals, allegedly after an RPV strike. It was hard to watch, but Tania couldn't stop. It was hard to call it propaganda, when the footage was real, sent in by citizen journalists.

It was like a reality network where people watch each other destroy their own country.

The third night, Tania got the special feature. The one that made her start to see a whole different movie.

She heard it before she saw it, and the words reminded her of words she had heard before.

"The rising race is all rhizomatic," crackled the voice inside the machine. "Grown strong from underground roots that connect us with each other, across socially constructed divisions, in ways our oppressors cannot see."

Tania adjusted the antenna and fiddled with the tuning. The image resolved, crazy colors, like a transmission from out of the past.

The words came from a living wax bust of Thomas Jefferson, wearing a black T-shirt. His hair was made of fire. The strands of flame burned a network map into the background.

"The more you look around, the more you realize that we are all indentured servants, even those lucky remaining few with middle-class privileges. A home mortgage is the ultimate payday loan. Every owner is someone else's debtor. And debt makes us its slaves."

Thomas Jefferson morphed into a black woman. Maxine Price, bad cartoon likeness notwithstanding. The writer turned politician who almost pulled it off. The woman who took the literary utopias of her early years and turned them into the basis of a new politics, a seemingly workable vision for a better world, in that brief window when she was supposed to be in charge, and before they disappeared her. The woman whom Moco said he had transported to New Orleans, after she was supposed to be dead.

"The warlords are the real masters," said the voice. It sounded computer-generated, androgynous, untraceable. "And the real owners. And the ultimate owner-master is the warlord in chief."

Maxine Price turned and pointed to a city on a hill. Zoom on the President sitting atop a mountain of skulls and treasure. People in the opposition claimed the President had personal profit interests in many of his policies, but they could never find hard proof. Mack had been a businessman before he got elected, heavily invested in MMCs, oil and gas, and global real estate, riding the General's wake. It's not like he needed the money.

"Maybe you gave up on voting when you decided your choices were illusory, or after you got so fed up with your misery that you intentionally voted for the worst candidate. Maybe you can't remember back when you actually had choices."

The President said that, and winked.

The first candidate Tania wanted to vote for got impeached and removed from office before she got her chance. His Vice President, Maxine Price, resigned rather than take the job. She proposed delegating the powers of the office back to the people. Then blew the whistle on the whole thing. Tried to, at least.

"Before you give up on trying to change the world you live in," said Maxine Price, sitting up out of her unmarked grave, "remember this: the ground you are standing on is liberated territory."

Tania was not persuaded that applied to this run-down motel, but she got the idea.

"Rhizomatic space is all about creating a new world in the interstices of the old one."

Tania thought about all the people who literally lived in the empty spaces of the cities, outside, under the overpasses and in the little pockets of woods behind the factories and warehouses.

On the screen, a child in a cardboard box on a sidewalk was talking.

"We can only change others by example. Especially people infected by the unquenchable appetites of greed, consumerism, and narcissism."

Suddenly the concrete was liquid, and the kid started paddling upstream.

"Better to recognize there are others who want to live differently, and carve out your own autonomous space where and when you can."

The cardboard raft landed on an island in the middle of the city, where a group of people were building a tree house inside the ruins of a high-rise.

"Build networks of authentic community invisible to the state, and to capital. It's not that hard. You don't need leaders. You need what comes after leaders."

An antenna, radiating waves.

"The old pyramids will collapse, sooner than you think, under their own weight. It's already happening. The planet is past its carrying capacity."

Zoom back, to see the city swallowed by the sea.

Tania thought about all her friends who had lost their jobs as their companies failed. She remembered when the currency crashed, and the banks tumbled. Her mom feeding people whose pensions disappeared, putting up people who got evicted. She thought about Vice President Price, and the collapse of the government she was part of, the hope that disappeared with it. Remembered her voice, and heard its cadences in the voice coming from the television.

"The ground you are standing on is liberated territory. And when everything else collapses, what we build will be there standing ready to welcome a better future."

It had to be true. The official stories were lies. It was her, communicating through this weird outlaw medium. Old technology to seed new politics. It wasn't a coherent argument, the way her speeches used to be. More like a series of aphorisms, like someone was writing down her musings and putting them together in this mashed-up animated gospel. But they were her words.

The screen went black, and then a test pattern came on, a rainbow flag this time. The numbers ran in a bar across the bottom.

Watching the codes, and thinking about the words she had heard, Tania wondered if this thing might work the way the mesh network did, back in the Blocks.

How to win the Rat Race.

She opened the back of the set and looked for I/O jacks.

Maybe this would prove a faster way to find Sig.

Or maybe, even better, it would lead her to Maxine Price, alive.

If she found her, Tania could negotiate an even better deal with her handlers. If she could pull that off, it would be a much safer move than Bert's advice to run and hide. And what she had already might be enough to entice Gerson and her colleagues.

But as she thought about Mom, Tania remembered her parting words, and wondered whether the real prize in finding Maxine would be negotiating a better deal for the whole damn country.

49

SIG KEPT WATCH FROM ATOP THE RAILCARS WHILE MOCO WAITED
for his contacts. Up on the empty freight cars at the far edge of
the yard, this side of the secured area.

From up there he could see all the way across the layout.
He'd never seen so many tracks laid out in one place. Most
were lined up with cars ready to load or ready to roll. Land
drones stacked up three-high like new cars, flybots folded up
into their prefab containers, tanker cars that oozed the poison
molasses of fresh biofuels. One train looked like it was designed for people, which gave Sig the creeps.

He could hear the racket of workmen and moving trains,
but it was at the far side of the yard, over by the Burroughs
fab where they built the motherboards for the bot assemblies
down the road. Farther on he could see the fuel depot, and the
control tower of the commercial field.

Off to the left was the red Mercury, parked where the road
dissolved into the gravel of the railyard. And that's where they
came from, a man and a woman on bicycles, looking for the
car tagged with the coyote in sneakers. That was the car Moco
was in, next to the car on which Sig was perched.

Bikes were not what Sig expected, but it made sense. Bikes
and old cars were the only wheels you could move around
in that were off network. These bikes looked hard, minimal,
black and bare metal. Their riders were close to the same,
black dude with a big vest and a felt brimmed hat, white chick

in overalls and a ball cap. They gave Moco the sign as they walked up.

No trace of the guy from the bar, or anyone else.

Sig moved over to Moco's car as the pair stepped up into it. He had a partial view through the latticed hatch in the roof and could hear everything they said.

"Where's your partner?" said the guy.

"Keeping watch," said Moco.

"Didn't see anyone," said the guy.

"That's the idea."

"You trust him?" said the woman.

"Totally," said Moco. "Dude's been running from them for a long time."

"You heard about Tracer?" said the woman.

"What?" said Moco.

"They got him," said the woman.

"Raid," said the guy. "Minneapolis."

"Fuck," said Moco.

"Somebody blabbed their safe place," said the woman.

"Maybe it was you," said the guy. "Heard they got you, too."

"Bullshit, dude, I'm standing right here. Where is Tracer now?"

"Shipped for reprogramming," said the woman.

"Fuck!" said Moco.

"What did you tell them?" said the guy.

"What the fuck are you talking about?" said Moco. "And what do you care, anyway? I don't work for you."

"You know a lot about our network," said the guy.

"It's true," said the woman. "Like you know how to bait us out with a lethal sales pitch. Wondering when they're gonna show up."

"Let's get our business done and you can split," said Moco. "I don't like working with this kind of material anyway."

"Where is it?" said the guy.

"In the car over there," said Moco. "Ready for you to drive it off without having to unload."

"We need to see it," said the woman.

"I sent you pictures. You can check it out before you leave. We'll wait. Money. Five K like we talked."

"That's what you proposed. We're paying two K. That's market. For all we know the grenades are duds."

Movement in Sig's periphery. He turned. Listened. Looked for shadow.

"Forget it," said Moco.

Blue ball cap, then the full torso, moving between cars. The guy from the bar.

"Come on, Moco," said the woman. "Help us in our fight. Do it for Tracer."

"I need serious travel money," said Moco. "Going back to where the real fight is. You guys have the craziest faction around. Should have known you'd pull this shit."

Sig crawled along the top of the cars.

"Maybe we just need to take it," said the woman. "You're probably alone."

Sig jumped to the roof of the next car, and out of hearing range. His landing echoed as the metal roof vibrated under his feet.

He ran for the other end of the car. The dude in the blue cap was there, pistol drawn, looking up, but in the wrong direction.

Sig dropped on him. Took him down. The guy yelled.

Sig started pounding. Kidneys, back of the guy's neck, side of his head.

"Hey!" yelled the woman.

Sig looked. The woman, her partner, and Moco, running toward him. The guy's gun was there, in the dirt.

WHAM. Rock to Sig's head. Then a fistful of ice and ballast in his face.

"He's with us!" yelled the woman.

Sig blinked stars. Saw the truth in the guy's eyes. Took the next punch, grabbed the arm that delivered it, tried to pin the guy.

Moco and the other guy pulled him off.

"Motherfucker," said the guy.

Sound of radio crackle, nearby. Security dispatch.

"Come on," said Moco. "Crazy ass. Let's go. We're done."

"Money?" said Sig.

"Yes," said Moco. "We're taking the bikes."

Sig shook his head. He couldn't ride. Never learned.

"You can catch up." He grabbed the black bike. "Nice doing business as always, guys, good luck."

Moco rode back toward the bar. Sig jogged behind, looked for a better route, realized he didn't know where they were going next.

They didn't hear it. Not really. Maybe a faint whistle, maybe a sound a dog could hear. But they knew that's what it was. Or at least Moco insisted he did, the signature sound of that particular explosion.

"Hellfire." A missile, air-to-ground, launched by a robot.

Sig couldn't really hear Moco when he said that. The blast was all he could hear, even though the sound had passed.

They looked back. One of the dudes was crawling from the wreckage. Orange flames crowned by black smoke framed the silhouette of the scorched car. Second explosion, something detonated by the flames.

"Come on!" said Moco.

Sig looked up at the clear winter sky. He couldn't see the drone.

50

"THE VISITORS CAME TO OUR WORLD ALL IN DRAG, DOUBLE-X SOL-
diers and preachers, cops and chauffeurs, linemen and lawyers.
They came on a Sunday, when no one was paying attention,
in a place, New Orleans, where you could be whoever you
wanted to be as long as you stayed in your place. They came
through a portal, the Earth end of which was an abandoned
concrete bunker at the back of an empty lot overgrown with
weeds. They never left."

Tania found the old paperback in the lobby, on a small
bookshelf with other seditious tracts. Someone had left it with
the cover facing out, its figures watching her walk by. Those
seven mysterious androgynes painted in vintage pulp fiction
brushstrokes, standing under the wrought iron curlicue decay
of some French Quarter side street.

Her mom had given her that book. For a birthday, she
couldn't remember which one. She read it with a flashlight.
Like four times. Then she read the others in the series. All
seven of them. And the short stories, which were even weirder.

The Visitors were people from another dimension. A
mirror Earth. One where the dominant culture was rooted in
matriarchy. Their politics was based on the idea of governance
by "the Everyone," the whole multitude of the population acting as some kind of cooperative hive mind.

The author was a black woman. They first published it under the name Max Price. They must have thought it sounded

like a white man. This copy was a later printing, under Maxine Price. But still no picture of her on the back.

The books were not written for kids, but that was how they were marketed, and the strategy worked. Maybe because the books did best with people who had open minds. For a while, even as the country was going crazy, it seemed like half the kids in America were reading those books. When they grew up, the deep-planted seeds had germinated. And the author had morphed from bookish recluse to public figure, royalties funding her run for office, the zeitgeist taking her to the next level.

Maybe it was because the books were suppressed by the current regime that they had turned into their own ideology. The multivolume bible of a disenfranchised political movement that had developed the character of a utopian religious sect. A well-armed one, with a dead prophet who was now sending fresh messages from beyond.

THE NIGHT SHE FOUND THAT BOOK, TANIA SAW ANOTHER face she recognized, this one on Channel 13.

The guy on the screen even had an old-fashioned nameplate on his desk.

WARD WALKER
Chairman

Chairman of what, the plaque didn't say.

He had that mustache, and those old-school glasses.

Walker was the guy the President had singled out for slander in the installment of *Hello America* Tania had seen the night before she and Odile went to the White House.

Tania turned up the volume.

It was like when you turn on the news and the anchors don't know you're watching them yet. Walker sat at the metal desk, staring, shuffling paper. He wore a red tie and a blue button-down with the sleeves rolled up. He sipped from a tumbler of brown liquor over ice. He tapped the microphone. He cleared his throat and stared at some point behind you.

Behind him was a green wall. And then the green wall turned into blue photons. Then a weather map. An old whiteboard-and-magnets weather map.

It was snowing.

You could hear people laughing and talking intermittently in the background.

Walker held up some shiny sheets of paper, stapled and folded. He waved it at the camera.

"Yes, you all, this is a fax," he said. "My team makes fun of me for still using a fax machine."

He looked shifty and stressed out. He was sweaty under the lights. The video yellowed his skin and reddened his eyes.

"The people who tell me this seriously want me to believe their BellMail accounts are secure from prying eyes. I trust my fax. Especially *this* fax, which is still warm from the machine that was nice enough to bring it to me."

He looked at the paper as if to read from it, then caught himself.

"Yes. This is live. We are transmitting from a secure undisclosed location. There is beer here."

He unfolded the paper again.

"This is the decision of Judge Parker of the U.S. District Court for the District of Columbia in the case of, and I am reading this now, 'the United States of America versus One-Hundred Shares of Zapata Communications Limited, Real Property located on Farm-to-Market Road 669, Presidio

County, Texas, One Autographed 1991 John Lennon Black Album Master, One Smith & Wesson Model 10 Snub Nose Revolver, One Silver 1966 Cadillac Calais, et al.'"

That was the DOJ's case, part of a suite of suits they were pushing for Zapata's Panama and Nicaragua frauds. Tania knew the case. Mike had worked a piece of it, which involved offshore MMC contracts, and he had Tania help with the memo.

"Like me you may be wondering how it is that the government can sue a ranch, the cars in the garage, the collectibles on the mantel, and the stock certificates in the safe. My lawyers say it's another part of the inheritance from our cousins across the pond, but I don't buy it."

Walker waved the papers.

"It's because they killed the Constitution. Because they outlawed free speech. Because they fear nothing more than an independent media, and they will do anything they can to crush it."

Walker ran his hand across his bald head.

"They call me a thief! When I spent years helping lay data pipes through jungles and under mountains, under fire and underpaid."

The evidence, as Tania recalled, was that Walker's outfit had reaped around seven million in undisclosed markups, stolen four million in surplus equipment through well-arranged payoffs, and charged at least two million for work not completed.

"So today, they lost!"

He shook the paper like a sword now.

"He lost! Seems there's at least one judge left who isn't on El Presidente's choke chain. That judge has dismissed their forfeiture case. Summarily!"

Walker raised his glass.

"Thank you, Donny Kimoe, and all those seven-hundred-dollar-an-hour poindexters you hired in Washington to help make this happen."

Tania looked up the name. Donald Kimoe, Esq., criminal defense and personal injury, Houston.

"Now it's time we start giving back. They want to demonize us on their state-controlled networks? Take the hard-earned assets of the people who made them rich? Guess what." The backdrop changed to the image of a transmission antenna. Walker pointed his thumb back at it. "We got our hands on the means of motherfucking production!"

The image of the antenna looked live, too. Grainy, static surveillance camera shot, backlit by the evening sun and the silhouettes of buildings Tania did not recognize.

"I'm talking border blaster! A hundred thousand watts of cathode ray freedom blasting out from our secret spot into the heart of the USA."

The backdrop dissolved to a map of the country, with cartoon radio waves pulsing across it.

"So keep an eye on this channel. Ask your friends about the schedule, or if you already have it, pass it on. To people you trust. Because we are going to be making some important announcements and special offers. Starting with this one."

Walker held up an official photo of the President, and smiled.

A pair of hands came on-screen and deposited a huge stack of cash on the desk in front of Walker.

"That is one million dollars. And I am going to pay it to the first person who brings me information that leads to the arrest of this man."

He pointed at the President.

"I'm talking video. Footage so incriminating it can destroy a dictator. Yes, that's what I said. Footage people will pay to watch. That's how you monetize revolution, see."

He wiped his brow.

"And if you can't do that, I'm sure you can come close. I want your material. Your illegal content. The stuff they can't show. The stuff people really want, because they can't have it. I don't decide what goes on my network. You do."

He fanned the cash and smiled.

"It's got your name on it."

Maybe Tania had a bead on Bert's video smugglers after all.

"You know it's out there. Here's the number."

It wasn't a phone number. It was some other kind of code.

Tania wrote it down.

5

MOCO HAD THE MONEY. TWENTY-FIVE HUNDRED.

"Twice what we need to get there," he said.

Money attracted friends.

"This is my girlfriend," said Moco, pointing at the ancient black Honda parked at their meeting point a couple of blocks from the bar. "My St. Louis girlfriend."

Sig panted as they caught up, still chasing Moco on the bike. He looked back in the direction they came from, and up at the sky.

The car had tinted windows and a bad stencil of a black panther face on the hood, same color as the paint job. They couldn't see the people inside until they crammed in the back.

"Hey baby," said the driver. She was a Latina with a mohawk and earrings that looked like they could cut you. "What the fuck was that explosion?"

"That was almost us!" said Moco.

"We should go back," said Sig. "Those guys."

"They looked okay to me," said Moco. "Didn't you see?"

Sig looked at Moco and could tell he was trying to believe that was true.

"We need to go," said the driver, starting the car. "Hey, Sheila, thanks for picking us up, baby," said Moco, reaching over the seat to "hug" her.

Sheila peeled out, throwing Moco back onto Sig's lap. Sig pushed him over against the door.

There were three other girls in the car. One in front and

two in back. The black girl in front with the big black hair was called Wooly. The two Sig was crammed up next to were a dark-haired white girl with a gold tooth called Bianca and an Asian girl named Tran who had ponytails, a little face tattoo, and a big pistol on her lap.

"This is Sid," said Moco.

"Cute," said Wooly, looking back and smiling.

"Hey, Sid," said Bianca.

Inside the car smelled like a cocktail of homemade perfumes, gunpowder, and gasoline.

"Good thing I drove," said Sheila, scanning four points. "Bet you guys are ready for a little R-and-R."

She held up a purple velvet bag with gold drawstrings, the kind they sold Royal Sceptre whiskey in. She shook the bag. It sounded like it was filled with candy.

"You like to party, Sid?" said Sheila.

"He totally likes to party," said Tran. "He was born to party."

"We should keep moving," said Sig.

"We need rest!" said Moco. "Night's coming. It's safer."

Sig grumbled.

"Don't forget to smile, Sid," said Sheila. "They won't let you into the hotel if you don't smile."

Sheila drove too fast and got away with it. She drove on the part of the old highway that was under the elevated freeway, to hide from eyes in the sky. She drove back to the Missouri side, past the downtown towers of the Blue Zone where the owners lived and the corporates worked, around the armories on the south side, through the washed-out neighborhoods of the bottoms, to the big interchange where all the freeways came together in a crazy ribbon of giant-sized concrete.

It took them three tries to find a hotel that would take

them and their cash. They stopped for burgers along the way, drive-through.

The room was a suite, the kind traveling salesmen lived in. It had a separate bedroom with a door you could close, and more couches than your living room. It had a refrigerator they put the beer in.

They got right to work retraining it for loco.

They unplugged the Feed box from the TV and the power. They unplugged all the lamps, wrapped them in the bedspread, and put the bundle in the closet. They closed all the blinds. They had their own music, a little box that ran on batteries and was crammed full of thumping Fezcore. They had beer, and smoky clear liquor from New Mexico. They had crazy energy, light and dark at the same time. They had little candles they used instead of the lights in the room. And they had the Royal Sceptre bag, which Sheila put in the middle of the coffee table, arranging the drawstrings just right.

"Sid, baby," said Sheila. "Bianca's gonna run you a bath. And not just 'cause you need it. Which you do."

Bianca smiled. You could see the bathroom from where they sat, glowing with the candlelight.

Sig drank his fourth can of beer. It tasted like cold white bread. He could feel the chill wash over the folds of his brain.

Then Sheila pulled open the mouth of her bag.

"You like Purple Maxx, Sid?" asked Tran.

Sig shrugged.

Moco laughed. When he smiled that big you could see all his fucked-up teeth, even the molars.

"Sid's a country boy," said Wooly. "Probably never had anything stronger than ditch weed."

Sheila pulled out a waxy cookie the color of congealed blood.

"That's what I'm talking about," said Bianca.

"You even know what this is?" said Wooly, smiling.

Sig shook his head.

"Maxximol," said Bianca. "The stimulant."

"Performance enhancer," said Wooly. "Developed for war-fighters."

"Cut with Lafferty powder and sassafras oil," said Bianca. "To amp up the feelings. Open the doors."

"Gonna turn you into a motherfucking superhero," said Wooly.

"He already is," said Sheila. She had the cake on a thin metal platter that she held up with a little clamp. She pulled out a metal lighter that made a big flame she used to heat the bottom of the plate.

The smell was like Sterno and cherry candy.

Sheila cut the cake into six little slices. They passed the plate around like it was sacrament. Sig was fourth in the line.

"It's cool," said Moco. Bianca and Wooly were on either side, encouraging him with friendly touch, pulling off his hoody.

It tasted like liver and cough syrup. He washed it down with another beer.

The music sounded better.

Moco was all over Sheila. He liked the bald parts of her head. Ran his hands through the mohawk. She led him to the bedroom and closed the door.

It was like someone turned up the candles. They shined through skin like you could see the bones of people's faces.

Wooly stood up, stretched, and flexed. She looked strong.

"Can you feel it?" she said.

He nodded.

"Take your shirt off," she said.

He did. It felt great. He spread his arms out like an eagle. He felt like he could throw a car.

It seemed like a long time until he found himself in the bathroom with Bianca, helping each other get the rest of their clothes off. The door was open and they could see Wooly and Tran messing around on the couch and vice versa but no one cared. Time got slippery. It was like the moon slowed down and watched.

Bianca had the saddest scars he had ever seen.

When they were in the bath and he saw them so close and exposed, the sadness settled into a spot in his chest like it had little claws.

Then he was looking up at Bianca, and for a minute it was like she wasn't there. Like she was traveling through some other space.

Then Wooly and Tran were standing there. Bianca, too, in a towel. Wooly saluted him like a soldier, except she was laughing.

He tried to get up but he couldn't. He tried to talk but nothing came out.

He started to seriously freak out.

The women left him there.

He felt the water over his whole body trying to pull him in.

He felt sleep pulling him in like a fish on a reel.

He thought about that girl who babysat him that time when his mom left him with her black friends in Minneapolis. He could almost hear them saying her name but he only got part of it.

52

THE NAME ON THE DOOR WAS MR. WIZARD.

The shop was at the far end of a run-down strip mall on the other side of town, across the street from the repurposed big box where they had arrested Moco and the others. Tania had left the hotel looking for this place, after seeing an ad on Channel Zero, just a name and address that flashed on one of the test patterns. She hated to go out, especially in daylight, but the possibility of getting help in cracking those codes and accessing the deeper net was worth the risk.

There was an old TV in the window, playing a yellow oscillating wave against a blue background, almost like installation art.

Through the glass, she saw other old sets inside, running test patterns. The floor was crammed with boxes, filled with what looked to be old tapes and discs.

The door was locked. But she could see there was someone in there. A door behind the counter, slightly ajar, incandescent light seeping through.

She banged on the door. Then she saw the doorbell. The chime was a tune from a long time ago. Back when everything was on a different trajectory.

The storekeeper looked about the same age. Gray goatee grown into little horns. Mr. Wizard was right.

"We're closed," he said.

"Oh, sorry, it looked open."

He scrunched up his face. That's when Tania noticed the fresh cut on his brow, sutured with a pair of gauze butterflies.

"I saw the light on in the back," said Tania.

"Appointment only."

"How do I make an appointment?"

Mr. Wizard harrumphed. Hand to goatee, like he was pulling the thoughts out of his chin.

Tania looked at the open door to the back room. A workshop, crammed full of TV sets, radios, keyboards, and other devices all connected with spaghetti bundles of cabling. There was a vintage microphone by one of the radios, with the logo of a station that must have found its second life. It reminded her of the old mesh network, but much more advanced. She wished she could take a picture.

"I'm afraid we're not really open to the public anymore," said Mr. Wizard. "Not since the latest troubles. Kind of a membership club. Hobbyists. Old geezers like me. Terribly boring really."

"It's a hobby of mine, too," said Tania. "I just got my first set. Amazing what you can find on-air these days. I saw your clip last night. I was looking for some help learning how to really tap all the capabilities. Like how to use this code I got on Channel 13." She held up the notebook page on which it was written. "There's not exactly a user's manual, you know?"

Mr. Wizard raised his eyebrows and made a quiet grunt. He looked at the code, looked her in the eyes, then looked away.

"Why don't you leave me your name," he said. "I will call you when we schedule the next meeting."

He seemed nervous all of a sudden, even as he was blowing her off.

"Great," said Tania. She wrote down a made-up name and the number of her prepaid phone. "When will it be?"

"Depends," said Mr. Wizard, looking right at her. "Have I seen you before?"

"I don't think so," said Tania. "I just got to town. Staying out west."

"What brought you here?"

"Freelance data mining contract. Exciting stuff. Working one of the corporate parks up north there, but thought it would be nicer to stay here. Kind of reminds me of where I grew up."

"I see," he said.

"So I guess you're Mr. Wizard?"

"Mr. Wizard is dead. I'm Fritz."

53

SIG DREAMED AN ANIMAL HOLOCAUST. WHOLE HERDS OF GIANT beasts, dinosaur buffalo dogs, hooked up to machines that sucked the fluids from their bodies and pumped out white mushy food at the other end.

He woke up splashing in water, coughing it out.

The high was gone. He could move.

His head felt like someone had been playing basketball with it all night.

Their shit was gone, too. Sig found his pants, but the wad of money that was his share was no longer in the pocket. No sign of the three guns they had kept, or of Moco's stuff. Maybe worst of all, Sig couldn't find the paper Fritz had given him with the contacts.

Maybe he could remember some of them.

The door to the room was wide open.

He ran down the hall, looking for Moco. Through the window by the elevators he could see the sun fully risen, nine o'clock at least.

There were two police cars parked out there, by the entrance.

Adrenaline jolt. Time to run. Time to find his own way.

He ran down the stairs, exited the lower level. Looked— *empty*—headed down the corridor toward the exit sign.

He stopped when he saw the indoor pool. There was Moco in one of the reclining chairs, passed out in his underwear. There were beer bottles floating in the pool.

For a minute, he considered leaving him there. Then he heard them coming.

54

TANIA BOUGHT A TRUCKER'S ROAD MAP OF THE CENTRAL UNITED States, taped it to the wall, and annotated it in grease pencil, string, pushpins, and paper notes, trying to reverse-engineer the network by mapping it.

There were no topo lines on the map, but you could infer their broad outlines from the ways the river flowed. And when you spent enough time looking at the region that spanned from Minnesota to the Gulf, you realized it started with the river.

The river system, when you drew it over in thicker blue, looked like a tree, the way its many branches fanned out across the northern plains. Like the capillaries and veins of the heart of the continent. Like a network.

On another network, she found a database of the communications infrastructure that predated the MOFUC. She marked each transmitter with red pins. She drew dotted line circles to mark transmitter ranges. She flagged three she suspected could be the live station Walker claimed.

One was in North Dakota. The tallest TV antenna on the continent, apparently.

One was in Mexico. An actual border blaster whose specs she found on a page about those old high-wattage stations.

One was in New Orleans. That seemed least likely, given the conditions on the ground there. Maybe that's why it made the most sense.

It was right before the last presidential elections that the people in New Orleans took back their city. The storm that drowned half the wards made it possible, driving an evacuation of the MMCs who had made the city their principal staging area for operations in the near South. The city had been granted an independent corporate charter by the feds, reasoned the committee that replaced the board of managers, and this was just a change in ownership.

They lasted almost two years. Then came the Repo. And the Purge.

There was still fighting going on. People hadn't given up. She saw the hero clips every night around eleven on Channel Zero. Scenes of resistance sent in from New Orleans and all over the Tropic. Vehicles on fire. Grainy zooms of primitive bombs detonating at the gates of storage depots and biorefineries. Shaky fragments of unlawful arrests and citizen roundups at the end of electric truncheons. Morale videos of disabled veterans making their own machined prosthetics as they prepared for what was coming. Combat-ready DIY cyborgs.

The clips were curated. Some nights by Walker himself, but mostly by others when he was "in the field." When the sound was bad, or the shot didn't speak for itself, they added voice-over narration.

At the end of each segment they flashed a long code across the screen. An address, Tania gathered. The direction to transmit your own footage for inclusion.

Maybe it was her set. Maybe Todd got the wrong kind of box. Or maybe she was missing some essential hardware you needed to make the thing interactive. Watching the broadcasts, and the messages from the other viewers that flashed on the screen, she got so frustrated with the primitive controls of the idiot box that she wanted to smash it.

Then she saw Sig there, fighting in the snow. It was an aerial shot, ethereal, the scene bathed in ambient light pollution and blue moonlight off the crust of ice crystals.

Blood on the ground. Then fire in the building.

She tried to capture the footage, but was too slow.

She wondered how old the video was.

Then she recognized where it was.

A brief glimpse of Sig, in bad light, hauling Moco through the snow.

No wonder the militia came around looking for her.

He was right here, under her nose, and she had blown it.

Blown her best shot at getting Mom out, sitting in a hotel room trying to decode answers over the airwaves when she should have been out working the streets.

She took a chance. Logged into the securenet, looked for reports. Militia hadn't even logged the loss of their prisoner, or the assault on their "facility." She tried to remember exactly how long ago it had been that she was there at that place, interviewing Moco. Did the math. Looked at the map, and imagined how far they might have gone.

It was a big circle. Partly because she didn't yet know that Sig preferred to walk.

She needed to get moving. Just as soon as she could get that antenna outside the window to show her the way.

SHE HAD GIVEN UP AND STARTED PACKING WHEN THEY BE-gan running shots of old pay phones on Channel 13. They didn't explain why. But the images included text that gave the exact location.

Tania looked at the old dial-tone phone in the room and got the idea to plug it into the analog receiver Todd had given her.

She had glimpsed a similar setup at Mr. Wizard's. The revelation took a while to percolate.

The trick was figuring out how to make the TV set work as a transmitter, as well as a receiver.

The phone worked as a keyboard. Primitive, and excruciatingly slow, but it worked.

The handout from the Minneapolis rally, the one with all the program frequencies, was the key. One of the frequencies was an access code. She learned this through trial and error. When she finally typed it in, it opened up a new window on the screen.

It was like a community bulletin board, newsletter, post office, bank branch, and draft board all rolled into one. With some work you could find bridges between different rooms.

She found the Minneapolis boards and got an update on her Mom.

She posted a note, with her reply code, asking for leads on the whereabouts of Sig.

She made inquiries about safe transport to New Orleans.

She asked about Moco. Maybe a bad idea.

She found Lisbet, and sent her a message, a coded explanation. Definitely a bad idea.

She eventually found the way to contact Todd, inside the network. The way the net worked was like a refer-a-friend system. She could leave him a message that showed him the door in, packed with his code for opening it.

She would come to regret that the most.

55

PERCHED IN A BIG HACKBERRY AT THE EDGE OF A NORTH DALLAS
office park, Sig waited for breakfast.

He could smell them coming. They were upwind, close by,
but not close enough to hear, at least not over the noise of the
air conditioners cooling empty buildings.

An owl called from the woods behind him. Sig and Moco
had spent the night back in there, a thin strip of forest sand-
wiched between the office park and the freeway.

They were broke. In Oklahoma they tried to pick up some
day labor, until they heard the rumors about outlaw cops
rounding up vagrants and putting them in work camps. One
of the guys said the "work" was fighting with each other for
gamblers. They sold videos you could buy under the counter
at the right C-stores. He'd seen one in the hostel. "The kind of
fights where the loser never gets up."

By the time they crossed into Texas, people hunters were
tracking them. Moco was convinced he was still giving off a
signal. He'd been digging at the wound where they cut out the
tattoo, and now his whole arm was infected. They had stayed
ahead by keeping to the woods, moving at night. It was getting
harder, especially as Moco got slower.

A jumbo jet flew over from the west, on approach, blinking lights and churning air.

The lamps over the parking lot crackled. You could hear
the bugs crashing into the plastic covers. First light was just
starting to seep over the treetops.

Sig looked for his reflection in the dark glass of the nearest building. He wondered what was on the other side.

He saw the deer. Four does, loitering on the manicured grass around the machine-made lake in front of the office park.

Sig waited.

The first car of the morning, a delivery guy in a beat-up old Ford, spooked the deer. Three of them broke for the woods as he approached. The fourth followed when the plastic-wrapped junk mail flew from the car window.

It worked. One of the does stopped on the trail beneath Sig for a moment, smelling but not seeing. It wasn't much bigger than a big dog.

Sig readied his knife and dropped on the deer.

The doe tried to bolt as Sig locked on to its back. Sig sunk in the knife as the deer bounded. It leapt off balance and landed on its side with Sig underneath.

The doe flailed, but did not get up.

Sig cleaned the animal there, just inside the tree line. Through the trees, the people were arriving for work in their cars. None of them even looked his way.

The vultures saw.

Sig dragged the cleaned carcass back into the woods to their spot, a shelter made of canvas he had pulled from a dumpster and camouflaged with cut branches from the nearby scrub trees.

Moco was really sick now. Sig thought the fresh game would help. It didn't. Moco had lost his appetite. He was burning up. His arm looked like it was mostly made of pus.

If they didn't keep moving, they would get caught.

That afternoon they went to an emergency hospital by the freeway. Moco went in alone. Sig gave him all the money they had left, which wasn't much. When Sig went back later to check on him, they wouldn't let him have any information because he couldn't prove his relation. He tried again the next day, and he found out that Moco had been taken to a detainee clinic.

They were not successful in detaining Sig.

56

THE JARRING RINGTONE OF THE LAND LINE JOLTED TANIA FROM her fidgety slumber. She opened her eyes to the frantic red pulse, and only then remembered that the phone was plugged into the alternet.

She picked it up anyway, and listened.

"Tania," said the voice at the other end. Crackly, scrambled and reassembled, but identifiable.

"Lisbet," she said. "How did you find me?"

"How did I *not* find you. You plugged this damn BellNet line into the network, a major security breach. And they've been watching you since you got there. You think we don't talk to each other? Now you're lighting up every node, sending out crazy notes, including to me, notes that have them wondering if I'm some kind of informer."

"It's not what you think."

"You need to stop. You need to go back to Washington."

"What are you talking about?"

"I can't believe you tricked me like that. Tricked us."

"That wasn't me, Lisbet. They were tracking me. I had no idea."

"What the fuck happened to you?"

It's complicated.

"I shouldn't even be calling you," continued Lisbet. "These people are almost as crazy about their security as your people."

"I'm just trying to find my brother," said Tania.

"That's what you say. So why aren't you out looking for him? Did you really think we wouldn't find out?"

"Find out what?"

"If you keep snooping around they are going to disappear you, you stupid bitch. And I won't grieve. You ratted out my friends. I—"

The signal wavered. A high-pitched electronic scream shuddered over the line. Tania pulled the handset away from her head.

"Hello?" she said. Nothing.

She grabbed her mobile to try to hack the open line, but when she picked the house phone back up there was a beeping dial tone.

She turned on the lights. Daylight was seeping through from behind the drapes.

The room was a disaster. She had mostly packed her stuff, but hadn't touched the crazy network configuration, which sprawled from the window to the desk to the TV counter to the coffee table, barely leaving room to walk.

She was staring at it and thinking how she could break it down for travel when there was a knock at the door.

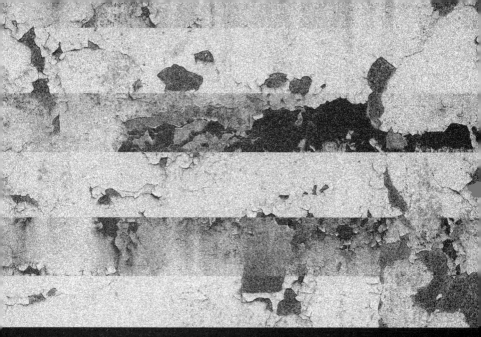

PART SIX
The Edgeland Hunters

57

SIG CAME TO HOUSTON TRACKING MOCO, BUT HE LOST THE TRAIL.

It took him two and a half days to get there from Dallas, walking and hitching, finding his own food along the way.

He roamed all over Houston looking for the detainee clinic, but either no one knew where it was, or they didn't want to say. One old black guy outside the street hospital told him they keep that stuff secret, unmarked, no signs. "Hidden in plain sight." He told him where he thought it might be.

What Sig found there was a refugee camp made out of an old parking garage and the empty lot next to it where a building used to be. He had never seen that many tents. One tent was big and white, with a red cross on it, but when he went in there all he saw were sick kids and old people. The refugees were all from New Orleans, mostly escapees from the fighting, some from the disasters that came before. Nobody there had any useful information, except for some ladies doing laundry in a repurposed feed trough who told him they thought the place where they kept sick prisoners was near the bayou, east of downtown.

They were wrong, too.

But Sig did find a good place to hide down there. An abandoned shed right on the banks of the boggy river that ran through town, behind an old junkyard. He could hear people talking in the building by the junkyard, but they wouldn't hear him. As the sun went down, Sig ate the bag of beef jerky he had stolen from the gas station, and watched a nutria walk right out between him and the bayou, big whiskered snout sniffing in the turf along the bank. He thought about trying to catch it, but then, as if it knew what he was thinking, it got in the water and started swimming around like some oversized, oily water rat.

Sig fell asleep early that night, on a sheet of Tyvek he pulled out of a tree by the river, with his mostly empty little duffel for a pillow. It was a dark spot back there, dark enough to be out of the city lights but not enough to see the stars. He listened to the bugs and the frogs and slept hard, until he woke to the sound of some man's voice, and opened his eyes to see a big silhouette behind a flashlight and a gun.

When he tackled the guy and took his gun, the last thing he would have thought was that he was making a new friend. One who could get him where he really wanted to go.

58

THE OLD PUNKS AT THE DOOR LET THEMSELVES IN.

"We want to talk to you," said Mr. Wizard, aka Fritz. He had a key to her room. They probably had keys to all the rooms.

He had a short little lady with him. She had a hard face. Something in her eyes. The other three were dudes. One really old but fit-looking fellow with a silver buzz cut, and two younger guys in work clothes, one with a big lumberpunk beard and one with a corn-fed baby face looking down from the height of a three-pointer.

Lumberpunk and baby face crowded Tania at the door while the others looked around the suite.

Her gun was in her bag, on the other side of the room.

"Interesting collage," said the woman, looking at Tania's wall file.

"Why don't you sit down," said Fritz, looking over her improvised networking setup. It wasn't a question.

Tania looked up at baby face. She pushed him back.

"Why don't you leave me alone," said Tania, sitting down. The two guys stood over her, ignoring her plea. The lady pulled up a chair and sat across from her. Mr. Wizard kept looking over her stuff.

"Because you won't leave us alone," said the woman.

"What are you talking about?"

"Who invited you?" said the woman.

"I invited myself."

"That's not how it works."

"It's a free country," said Tania, and as soon as the words blurted out she knew how stupid that was, since it really wasn't.

The woman just gave her a look that said try again.

"You want to keep your hands off my stuff, Mr. Wizard?" said Tania.

"Something to hide?" said the woman.

"We all have lots to hide, don't we?" said Tania.

The woman smiled.

"I guess," she said. "But this is a small town. Strangers who show up in our private places tend to attract attention."

Fritz was holding up the phone, looking at how Tania had connected it to the television. He unplugged the line from the wall, severing the dial tone.

"I thought you had an open community," said Tania.

"We do," said the woman. "To people who are on our side."

"So what's the problem?" said Tania.

"I think you know," said the woman. "I don't know if you're a Motherlanderfucker or a lost little dilettante, but you smell like trouble, and we've had enough of that lately."

"What if I'm neither?" said Tania.

"Look, dear," said the woman. "We don't detain people. We're not like them. We don't have any secret prisons."

"Saving that for later?" said Tania.

"See?" she said, looking at the guys and pointing at Tania.

"I'm just saying," said Tania. "If we're about the Everyone, doesn't that apply to everyone?"

The woman threw up her arms.

"Yes and no," she said. "What I'm saying is you are free to go. But you *need* to go."

"Get out of town," said the lumberpunk.

"Go back wherever you came from," said the woman.

"East," said the lumberpunk.

"I bet he's right," said the woman.

"And like I'm saying," said Tania, "what if I told you I wasn't on either side? If I were just looking for a loved one. One who got lost in the mess we all made."

The woman looked at her.

Tania got up. Pushed lumberpunk back. Grabbed the file. Pulled out the best picture of Sig she had. Showed it to the woman.

Tania could see it on her face.

The woman shook her head. "Nope."

The tell was in the eyes.

She wondered if this woman might know her mom, or know of her, through the network. But instead she tried a different tactic. It didn't work. At least not right away.

"What if I gave you something you could use?" said Tania. "What would it take in a trade?"

"Fritz here is going to help you pack your shit," said the woman. She stood up. "And then he is going to help you find your way out of town. You have nothing I could ever want, because everything you have is infected with all of the compromises you have made."

That stung, especially when Tania thought about it later. Odile had said something like that to her once, but when this lady said it, it felt true.

"Don't come back," said the lumberpunk.

59

SIG WIPED A DAUB OF SALSA FROM HIS CHEEK, THEN LICKED IT off his finger and took another bite of the taco. It was as spicy as the food Kong used to make, so spicy it made him sweat, but he couldn't stop. It was the first real food he had had in a while.

Next to Sig at the picnic table was Dallas, the security guard who had tried to roust Sig from his squat and ended up chatting Sig up, and even talking him into giving him his gun back—with a promise of a hot meal and cold beer. Across the table were Dallas's aunt and uncle, who provided the food, after a long drive over the biggest bridge Sig had ever seen.

The picnic table was on a patch of dirt outside the office of Patriot Bay Self Storage, at the end of a rough Baytown street that ran along the ship channel. Out there beyond the chain link, a massive tanker lumbered home in the burnt orange light of dusk, blowing its horn.

They could hear bullfrogs and diesel engines, herons and hydraulics, cargo jets cutting through air so thick it slowed down the mosquitoes that swarmed in overfed clouds.

Behind them were the rows of numbered lockers, a thin stand of pine trees, and the miles of refineries they had seen from the bridge. Acres of giant structures made of plumbing, mud, and the worms of the earth, venting the inferno below.

"Why are they on fire?" asked Sig.

"Flareoffs," said Clint, the uncle, smacking a mosquito on his neck. "Burning up the excess so they don't blow up." Clint was an urban cowboy—wiry, strong and rangy, but with a left arm that came to a cinched-up stump just below the elbow. He owned the storage locker with his wife. Dallas lived on-site and helped with security. His mom was Clint's older sister.

"Candles on the cake of the gods," said Xelina, the aunt, standing up to fetch more food. She was a dark, skinny Tejana in her late twenties, a few years younger than Clint. "They're having a party to celebrate the end of nature."

"Thanks for that, bruja," said Clint. "You be sure to tell us when you figure out how to make your own energy."

"That one makes weed killer," said Xelina, pointing at one of the plants. "The one next to it makes liquid polyester. Polypropylene, polyethylene, polyvinyl, all the stuff you can't even pronounce, sweetie, that only powers this fucked-up imperial consumer society you claim to dissent from but make your living off."

"Hey now," said Clint. "We store a lot more important stuff than people's household junk."

"Careful what you talk about in mixed company," said Xelina.

Sig stared at the jewelry of bone and gold Xelina wore, some woven into her hair, some pierced through her skin. He had never seen anything like it.

"She makes most of it herself," said Clint, busting him. "Looks pretty fucking good, right?"

Sig nodded. He thought of Betty. She would like this lady.

Xelina struck a pose, stretching her arms out. There were words in Spanish tattooed in cursive on her left forearm. When her pearl snap shirt spread out like black wings, you could see the image stenciled on her tank top. An antenna made of human bones, radiating waves. You could also see the pistol holstered in the waistband of her jeans.

"Did you grab the beers?" said Clint.

"Forgot," said Xelina. "Sorry, too busy trying to finish the new video." Sig had seen her from behind when they first arrived, through the door to the room behind the front office, bent over a computer in a room full of TVs.

"I gotcha hooked up," said Dallas. He pulled four Alamo Martyrs from the cooler. Dallas was one of those guys who made being fat seem healthy and natural. Maybe it was the fisherman's tan.

"All right," said Clint. He took two beers, popped the tops on the edge of his belt buckle, and handed one to Xelina. Dallas opened the other two and gave one to Sig.

"You like that?" said Dallas, nodding at Clint's buckle trick. The buckle was brass, engraved with the picture of a cowboy throwing a lasso. "He won that thing."

"In a rodeo where the other ropers all had two whole arms," said Xelina.

"Long time ago," said Clint.

Sig sucked down half the beer, and burped. The beer was so cold you could hardly tell how bad it tasted.

Dallas took a pill bottle, cracked the top, shook two shiny black capsules out, and swallowed them down with the beer.

"When are you gonna wise up and get off that shit?" said Clint.

"Dude, this Maxximol makes me feel like a superhero," said Dallas.

"Yeah," said Clint. "Like a mutant. Your fucking skin is turning orange."

"Team colors," smiled Dallas, making horns with his hand.

"Don't let him push that poison on you, Sig," said Xelina. "Supposed to improve your performance and mood, but the real reason is to make you more docile."

"So your masters in the glass buildings can get you to do whatever they tell you," said Clint.

"I'll stick with this," said Sig, holding up his beer.

"Wise man," said Clint.

"I'm the one who just got a promotion," said Dallas.

Sig held the can close to his face and looked at the label. A big 3-D star rising out of the ruins of an old fort.

"So this really was another country?" asked Sig.

"Hell, yes," said Dallas. "This ain't Minnesota."

"We invaded New Mexico once," said Clint, with a sly smile.

"Where you got your asses kicked by Indians and then surrendered to Mexicans," said Xelina.

"I guess every place was another country once," said Sig. "And will be again."

"Sooner than you think," said Xelina, tipping her bottle to Sig and smiling.

"I'm gonna have to get you one of those 'Secede!' bumper stickers," said Dallas. "Just as soon as you get a car."

"I like to walk," said Sig.

"California will secede before Texas ever even gives it any serious thought," said Xelina. "Too hooked on the MMC business."

"Nothin' wrong with that," said Dallas. "Couple buddies of mine been with Kodiak since the Greek thing, and they make good dough helpin' freedom fighters turn their projects into moneymakers for everybody. Told me they're hirin' like crazy for Nicaragua and the Tribal Areas. Like seventy grand a year, housing and food paid for, plus combat bounties. I might check it out."

"I thought you were on our side, son," said Clint. "What the fuck are you talking about?"

"Just about wantin' to make some better money and see cool shit," said Dallas. "They keep showing those recruiting ads when I can't sleep late at night. What's not to like about raisin' hell on commission?"

"I'm gonna have to break this bottle over your head to knock some sense into you," said Clint. "How cool would that look?"

"Give him a break, Clint," said Xelina. "It's a good thing to want to see the world. Maybe he can meet our new investor."

Dallas perked up at the word. Clint squinched up his face.

"He's the one buying our videos," said Xelina. "And helping us fill up more lockers with more important stuff. He was telling us the other day how he needs some out-of-town help. Security work, like you do, with travel overseas."

"Hell, yes," said Dallas. "I want to meet this guy."

"We'll talk about it," said Clint, looking at Xelina. "But in the meantime we need your help. Got a new site you can help me access with all them fancy codes they put on your phone. So tell me again where you scouted teen Tarzan here?"

Sig took a deep bite into a juicy piece of white meat.

"Another one of my patrols," said Dallas. "This old junk-yard on the bayou that got took over by museum people for some project. Found him squattin' back there. He kicked my ass halfway to the road before I calmed him down. Offered him a job on the spot."

Clint laughed.

"Dallas said you could get me into New Orleans," said Sig.

"Did he," said Clint. "Dallas talks a lot, you might have noticed. What do you want to go into the middle of that mess for?"

"I promised a friend," said Sig.

"Is that right," said Clint.

"I told him you knew how to get into the emergency zone," said Dallas. "He was sayin' how he was just gonna walk and I told him that's a bad idea."

"You might say that," said Clint. "How old are you, anyway, Sigurd?"

"Nineteen," said Sig, grabbing another taco.

"Got no ID," said Dallas. "Not in the system at all. Least I couldn't find him on our office net, and we get the main Motherland database updated every day."

"Huh," said Clint. He and Xelina were staring at Sig now, both with curious smiles.

"And he's tougher than a mean dog," said Dallas. "So I thought maybe he could help with these screwy projects y'all are doin'."

"Why aren't you in the Army, son?" said Clint. "You sure look plenty fit enough."

"Why aren't you?" said Sig.

"I did my mandatory service," said Clint, shaking the phantom fist at the end of his stump. "Eighteen months in bugfuck Panama with the Rangers after those dumb shits blew up the canal and fucked up our already fucked-up economy. Hunting Cubans in the swamps and building pontoon highways with a bunch of crazy-ass Malaysians."

Sig drank more beer. He wondered what a Malaysian was.

"I told you," said Dallas. "He ain't in the system. No ID, no plastic, nothin'. Not registered. Not in a single dang database. I checked 'em all."

"Well that is pretty awesomely convenient," said Clint. "Let's hang out, Sigurd. How do you feel about hunting some pigs with us?"

Sig thought about cowboys chasing cops. About hunting all the law that had ever hurt him or taken someone from him.

"He doesn't mean that kind," said Xelina, putting her hand on Sig's shoulder. He pulled away.

"Not just yet, anyways," said Clint.

"Oh," said Sig. "What's the pay?"

Clint laughed. "All you can eat, son. This is about food, not money. Especially since having money doesn't guarantee a full pantry no more. Half these lockers are stockpiles, for when it gets even worse."

"Okay," said Sig. He understood hunger, and was happy to help get food for the group.

"We can give you a better place to sleep, too," said Xelina, smiling.

Sig looked around and tried to see if this place looked safe enough to stay in.

"Come on," said Dallas, and they drank the rest of the beer while they loaded the guns in the truck.

60

"THE SECOND MOON WAS NOT A MOON. IT WAS NOT EVEN A PLACE. It was the infinite connections between all places. The threads that tie all beings to each other. The one that is the absence of one. You might call it a network, if it were not imbued with the divine, and devoid of line."

Tania took the Maxine Price paperback she found in the hotel on the road. Mr. Wizard packed it for her, not knowing it wasn't hers. Maybe it had answers to questions she didn't know to ask. She gave up when she realized she had read the same page about seven different times. Some people claimed the books worked that way, that any random passage encoded the full message. As if the words rewired your brain the more you read them, in whatever order you wanted.

Through the window of the train car, she could see the networks that were imbued with something other than the divine. The lattices of aboveground pipelines that carried the fuel. The telephone pole bulbs that transmitted the Feed. The rutted tracks that guided the dumb generation of old drones that patrolled the back forties.

She looked up at the sky. The flybots didn't even leave any contrails, but sometimes you could see them, when the light and the baffling were right. The bombings had given them the green light to choose their own patrols based on the latest predictive analytics that churned the available data about suspicious people and patterns. Now they were talking about letting them choose their own targets. Maybe they already had.

The train was a single passenger car attached to a short freight. The after-crash railroad version of a tramp steamer, with a handful of motley stragglers along for the ride wherever the cargo was going. St. Louis, in this case.

Tania looked at the other five passengers sitting on the metal bench and tried to figure out which ones might be there to keep an eye on her. And which side they were looking at her from. She had two inbound and unanswered messages from Gerson, after days of silence, and had to assume they would try new ways of tracking her.

Then she took another look at her bookmark. The name and number Mr. Wizard had given her to call when she arrived in St. Louis. Tania had taken a chance, and told him why she was looking for Sig. Told him about Mom, about how they were using her, about how she was ready to switch sides. When she said it, it felt true.

Either it worked, and he believed it, or she was walking into a bigger trap.

Fritz said he would make some calls about Mom. He knew the name, and knew people up there who could help.

She asked him which faction they were with.

"There are no more factions," he said. "Only nodes. The network pulls people together, through deep connectors built by the people who came before."

She asked him what the hell that meant. He said you have to find out for yourself, and pointed at the contact codes.

She wondered if it was really possible. That Maxine Price could unite the factions around a single cause.

She heard a loud noise in the far distance. She looked, and saw a burning silo on the horizon, spewing plasma fire like a gelatinous smokestack.

ST. LOUIS WAS THE INDUSTRIAL HEART OF THE TROPIC. BRO-
ken infrastructure had made the river relevant again, and
the big railyards pointed east. The biggest bots came out
of the assemblies here and floated down to their customers
in New Orleans for deployment in green territories farther
south.

Tania got in at dusk, to a shipping depot near the docks.
She asked around, and found a place where the guest workers from Tecate and Juarez stayed, outside of the secure
zone. An old business hotel that had changed hands and
still had the Marriott sign on the side, short an *r*. It was
known among the locals as El Mar Blanco. A little expensive
for Tania, but she didn't plan to stay long, and the network
reception was solid. She had figured it out on the train. She
was going where those barges loaded with bots, batteries,
and raw fuel were going. She was going to New Orleans.

Just as soon as she could figure out how to get a ticket that
wouldn't generate an alert.

And get her handlers off her back.

Gerson called shortly after Tania got to her room. Tania
needed to pick up this time.

"I don't like it when my sources blow me off," said Gerson.

"Sorry," said Tania. "I don't want to bust my cover when
I'm getting so close."

"You've been in a hotel room watching TV. Do you think
we are that stupid?"

"Do you think I'm that stupid? Do you have any idea what
I have uncovered?"

"I would if you gave me complete reports instead of misdirection and bullshit."

"I have the keys to the whole network. Which actually is a

network. One that all the supercomputers in Crystal City have completely missed. It's huge."

"Nice try, but you are not going to distract me from the fact that your target, your baby brother, is a thousand miles from you."

"How do you know that?"

"We picked up one of his fellow travelers. Said they were together until they split up in Dallas."

"Dallas?"

"I thought you were going to be much better at this than you turned out to be. Just shows you how the tests can lie. Very disappointing."

To Tania's surprise, the put-down stung, even though the idea of earning Gerson's approval made her sick.

"I need you to come in," said Gerson. "You can report to local Motherland there, and they will arrange your transportation home."

Home. D.C. That wasn't really home. Never had been.

"What about my mom?"

"If you really have something as good as you claim, then maybe we can keep our deal. But if you are not in my office day after tomorrow with the real shit, we are going to find you and lock you up and transfer your mother, and you can see if you can lawyer up good enough to get a cell to share in Detroit."

"Give me five days," said Tania.

Gerson was silent.

"Three," said Tania.

"I can do that," said Gerson. "Make it worth it."

Tania put down the phone and tried to collect herself.

She washed her face with cold water and tried to see who it really was looking back in the mirror.

She went to the window and looked at the city. The room was on the ninth floor. To the west she could see the fortified section of old homes where the managers stayed. The owners lived a lot farther away. To the east were the factories, and beyond that, to the south and east, sprawled the blocks where everybody else lived. The big river hid in all that, somehow, as if all the life of the whole continent had drained out where it used to be.

She closed the blinds, opened her bag, and got to work rebuilding her network connection. Fritz had given her a small peripheral that made it easier to log in from anywhere with a signal.

When that was done, she contacted the address Mr. Wizard had given her and told them where to find her.

And then she went to the pay phone in the lobby and called Odile.

61

THEY DRANK MORE BEER AND WAITED UNTIL IT WAS TIME. SIG
watched for animal sign in the overgrown grasses of the abandoned golf course. Dallas showed Xelina his arsenal of pawnshop pistols while Clint wrapped the dogs in Kevlar.

The dogs knew what the vests meant. Clint could barely
hold them still. East Texas fighting dogs, they looked like pit
bulls crossed with bulldozers. The black one was Loco, the
white one Watermelon Head. You could tell the names fit.

"They smell the pigs," said Sig.

"Yup," said Clint. "They've been having fun with no greens-
keepers around." He pointed his chin toward the shaggy fairway. You could see the giant ruts. "Looks like some drunk's
been tearing around in a jeep."

Dallas brought more guns than he had hands, and seeing
him pound beers while he loaded them made Sig wish they'd
brought extra Kevlar.

Clint mumbled at the dogs and they jumped up into the
bed of his old Cheyenne. Sig joined them and helped Dallas up
to where he could sit on the cooler. Xelina took shotgun.

Clint drove slow, lights off, rolling over the fairway. He
cut past a water hazard and the edge of a big sand trap, back
to the spot he had baited earlier. A flat green with a flagpole.
The pennant was going back to thread but still showed part of
the number 9.

Clint slowed down as they approached the green from a

higher grade. He cut the engine, put it in neutral, and rolled down closer.

The bait was dried corncobs covered in cherry Kool-Aid powder. It worked. Sig smelled the musk, heard the snorts, and saw the movement in the dark.

Clint flipped the lights—brights and rooftop. Sig blinked away the flash and counted again. Nine wild hogs, pigging out. Snort snort snorting in chorus while they ate. Six big ones, two juveniles, and one monster.

"Holy shit," said Clint. "That hoss must be five hundred pounds."

Dallas opened up first, action movie style—all spray and no aim. Sig pushed the dogs out of the bed with him.

Sig kneeled by the front wheel on the driver's side, while Xelina joined in. Clint said she was a deadeye who'd grown up hunting with her dad, before they took him.

The hogs squealed when the rounds hit. Xelina nailed the giant hog in the haunch, which only made it look mad. The tusks almost glowed in the weird light of the city sky.

Sig held the quivering dogs back with two fistfuls of Kevlar, making them watch the hogs scamper off into the rough, toward the tree line. When they had a good enough head start, he unleashed them.

"Git 'em," ordered Clint.

Loco was faster, back legs overtaking the front with crazy gusto, chasing the juveniles through the tall grass. Watermelon Head went after the big boy. Clint signaled Sig and Dallas to follow.

Sig nodded at Dallas and started running. The big hog had gone through tall thick grass between fairways, but left a trail to follow, downhill toward a man-manipulated little stream.

Sig heard Watermelon Head bounding down the water, chasing after an animal smart enough to try to lose his scent. Sig looked back up the path for Dallas, who walked to the lip of the hill clanking gunmetal. He waved at Sig, then leaned over to catch his breath.

Sig took in the surroundings. A gentle breeze wafted through the trees. Downstream, he could see Watermelon Head's white ears bounding above the grass. Sig smelled the hog in the wind and realized Watermelon Head had lost him. Sig followed the stream a bit farther, trying to follow the scent, and saw the bent grass where the pig had tracked out of the stream. A little blood, too. He heard a snort, looked right down a long fairway, and saw the beast standing a hundred yards away. It turned and snorted again. Sig knew hogs couldn't see much, but it looked like the boar was staring right at him.

Sig ran after it.

62

TANIA'S INTERVIEW WAS IN THE BASEMENT OF AN OLD INDUSTRIAL building along the riverfront.

"What's that noise?" asked Tania. It sounded like a giant robot doing an Irish clog dance.

"The makers," said the interviewer. "Playing with the metal stamper they just got working."

"What are they making?"

"We can talk about that later," said the interviewer. She was a tired-looking white lady with black hair going gray. She said to call her Davis. "I already have a question pending. Why should I tell you where this guy is? Assuming we even know."

"He's family."

"Not much of a resemblance."

There was a big mirror behind Davis. Probably two-way. Tania looked at her hair. It was growing out. She wondered if she should cut it close. Retro-radical. Maybe too late to worry about faking it. Especially since she wasn't entirely sure that was what she was doing anymore.

"Can you find him?"

"What's in it for us if we can?"

"I have a clearance."

"Really."

Tania nodded. "And I know how to use it. Do a lot of free-lance data mining."

"You must have a nice box."

"I built it myself," said Tania. "From salvaged parts. Couldn't afford it otherwise."

"That's illegal," said Davis. "Or at least violates the terms of service. BellNet owns all the hardware and we can't touch it."

"Things you find in the trash are fair game," said Tania. "Even if it's the virtual trash."

"That's what cops say."

Tania skipped a beat. Wondered if this lady could see her blush. Then figured they already knew. Were past that, into a different kind of bargaining phase.

"Yeah, maybe, but that's not the kind of data mining I do," said Tania. "Commercial, not political."

"Who said there's a difference?"

"There's a difference."

Davis laughed, not like anything was funny. She made some notes, then looked up.

"So does that mean your access is clean?" she asked. "Like anonymous. Off-issue."

"Kind of. I have a clean account I use. They think I'm some guy in Sacramento that died."

"Huh," said Davis. "Could you bring it in? Show us how."

"No."

Davis grumbled. She looked at Tania from a different angle.

"I have a question," said Tania. "Is it true about Maxine Price?"

"Is what true?"

"She's alive."

Davis waved that off with both hands.

"It's loud but not loud enough for that," she said. "You're

worse than I heard. Why don't you go look that up with your magic box."

"Maybe I will," said Tania. This lady was getting under her skin. "If I find proof of that, will you tell me where my guy is?"

"If you want us to trust you, why don't you find some of their secrets instead of ours," said Davis. "Stuff we can use. You look smart enough to know what that might be. Stuff that needs sunshine. Work on that and wait to hear from us. I'll give you a dropbox code you can use to send us anything you find. I mean anything good."

"On who exactly?"

"Who do you think? Them. The generals. The MMCs. *Him.*"

Tania wondered if Davis might be like her. Undercover. It was harder to tell than she would have thought.

"I'll think about it," said Tania. "But I still have my own work to do."

"Not anymore, if you check out," said Davis. "Prove your intentions. We can help you disappear if that's what you want. Maybe with your bro there. Give you places to stay. We're making a new world. It's invisible to the people who live in the other one."

"I saw that show already."

Davis nodded. "Then we're going to have a merger."

"Reminded me of a book I read."

"Put it this way," said Davis. "Maxine's words are definitely not dead. Even if she is."

"You should reread them."

"Maybe I've lived them. Learned to turn the words into actions. Maybe *you* should write your own version. In your own real life."

WHEN TANIA WENT BACK TO THE BUILDING TWO DAYS LATER, there was no sign of the people. She wondered how they moved the machines. Or maybe they didn't.

It was a while before they contacted her again. In the meantime, she did her research, only it was a little different than she said.

63

SIG CAUGHT UP WITH THE HOG JUST IN TIME TO SEE IT DISAPPEAR
at the edge of the course.

This was a lot of fence for an abandoned golf course.
Twelve-foot deer-proof running ten thousand live volts. Another twenty yards in, another layer, this one with razor
wire.

Fluorescent light seeped through from the other side, illuminating the tops of glass and stucco cubes, one of which
was adorned with a neon-backlit sign. The sign had a blue
logo that looked like a cross between a church bell and a pad-
lock, and a name:

BARBICAN SECURESOFT
A BellNet Company

The electronic hum of outdoor floodlights competed with
the rumbling of air-conditioning compressors, drowning the
sounds of nature other than the swarms of flying insects buzz-
ing around the lamps. And the snort of the pig, when it appeared on the other side of the far fence. It trotted across the
turf, between two stands of trees, and disappeared into a wide
expanse of asphalt.

Sig backtracked, and on the second try found the spot, a
deep washout where the rain had carved a fresh culvert then
pooled up like an accidental pond. More mud than water,
really, as he found when he followed the pig through it.

Clint had told him to come back when he found it, but Sig figured better to check it out for himself first.

He came up into the smell of lawn chemicals, pine sap, and pollution, but no more musk. He heard crickets and cicadas singing to the machines. More distant but still close, he heard the whining roar of jet engines, the sounds of Charlie Wilson International Airport, which they passed on the way up. And he heard a loud metal bang from inside the office complex, like the sound of a dumpster slamming shut.

He walked through the eerie landscape of the corporate campus, past the loading docks at the rear, along the edge of the parking lots, around the silently humming office monoliths.

Around the other side Sig found a clearing where the buildings formed a three-sided courtyard around a large pond. The turf was the uniform unnatural green of grass fed by manmade chemicals. Sprinklers spurted on the other side. Sig noticed all the hidden security cameras surveilling the site, and imagined a fat man sitting in a cubicle somewhere inside one of the buildings watching a monitor that showed twenty simultaneous feeds.

And then Sig wondered if the fat security guard was watching the monster hog as it walked casually out of the shadows and down to the pond for a drink.

Sig had crawled halfway after the pig before he realized what a stupid idea it was to come out of the shadows.

And then he heard the guy yell freeze. When he turned to look, the guy wasn't fat at all, but his shotgun was.

64

"THIS IS AMAZING," SAID TODD. HIS FACE LOOKED LIKE IT WAS coming from forty years in the past, saturated with the colors of a richer time.

Tania adjusted the vertical hold to check the datastream.

"Amazing how much they can cram into the blanking interval over these crappy bandwidths, right?" she said, looking at the peripheral camera she had added to the rig.

"I'm impressed," said Todd. "I couldn't figure this out."

"I had help," said Tania. "Sort of."

"So what do you need me for?"

"I need a clean access profile. You never delivered."

"No wonder you contacted me this way."

"I'm so close to breaking through."

"They're telling me you already came out the other side, Tania."

"They don't know. Those Pennsylvania Avenue ramrods have no appreciation of ambiguity. The fact that they think that just shows how well I've infiltrated."

It was hard to really judge his expression over this weird vidstream, but it looked like maybe that one got through.

"I've done such a good job I need to cut off all my access so they don't catch me," said Tania.

He let out a groan.

"Don't forget about the Calibration," said Tania. "I haven't."

He looked around, off-screen.

"Let me see what I can do," he said.

"Make it high level," said Tania. "I need to see what they have on the people I'm working."

"I bet."

"So you've been watching the shows?"

His eyes opened wider. Pulled down a lid so you could see the red.

"Did I tell you?" he asked.

"Tell me what."

"Oh, cripes. I've been watching them so much I was finally able to decode the source. Triangulate the origin."

"Mexico."

"New Orleans."

Of course.

"How precise?"

"Working on it," he said.

Todd looked off-screen again.

"What do you hear from Mike?" he asked.

Tania shook her head. "I've been out of contact."

"Nothing?"

"Nope. Why?"

"He said he was trying to find out. Asked me to help. Where should I tell him you're staying?"

Tania always knew Todd was the kind of colleague whose main concern was protecting himself. But this was the first time she seriously wondered if his interoffice contacts were more dangerous. And as soon as she had the idea, she cursed herself for not seeing it earlier.

"I can't tell you that, Todd. And I need to go."

65

WHEN SIG STOOD UP FOR THE GUARD, THE HOG CHARGED, AND SIG
ran for the dark.

Now, hidden behind the edge of one of the buildings, Sig
watched the guard inspect the dead boar.

"You better come out, you homeless freak!" yelled the
guard. "This ain't a safe place for you to camp."

Sig moved on, looking for a different path out. He should
have minded Clint's instructions.

He heard the sound of the jet engine again. This time it
was closer. He could tell from the way the sound bounced.
And then he heard the sound of trucks, and men talking.

"Shhhh," said an even closer voice. It was Dallas, in
shadow.

"You stink," whispered Dallas. "I've been trying to find you."

"Looks to me like you got lost," said Sig.

"Go fuck yerself then," said Dallas. "Maybe I didn't grow
up catching birds with my hands and shit. Come on."

Sig followed Dallas down an unlit path past the office
buildings and through another thick stand of trees. Xelina
was there, her skinny frame prone on the grass between two
trees, looking through a pair of hunting binoculars. Clint
stood back in the darker shadow, holding a home-modified
military carbine. He had gotten pretty good at bracing it with
his stump.

"Nice tracking," Clint said quietly. "I knew this was here,
but I didn't know there was a back door."

Sig looked through the gap in the trees. The landscaping graded down to a big blacktop parking lot, striped but cleared of cars other than three Chevy Raiders parked in front of a windowless garage that looked big enough to be a warehouse. A small military cargo jet painted with civilian markings was parked nearby, engines warming up. Bright lights like a football field shined down from the perimeter of the parking lot, enabling its dual use as an airstrip. A dozen people bustled around the scene, some in business attire, some in coveralls, and a couple in matching white windbreakers embroidered with a red corporate logo on the back.

"MMCs," said Dallas.

"Corporates," said Clint, nodding. "These boys work for the President's pet company."

Ground crew were loading shrink-wrapped white metal boxes the size of refrigerators into the back bay of the jet.

"What are those things?" asked Dallas.

"Beats me," said Clint. "Maybe some kind of office computers?"

"They're voting machines," said Xelina. "Offshore-modified, special order. Bringing them in for the midterms. Time to elect a new Congress."

"How about that," said Clint. "I thought he had it all locked up good enough without having to hack it. I suppose those are the candidates?"

The MMCs helped the suits pull two captives in yellow bodysuits from the back of the truck. Their hands were cuffed behind their backs, and black hoods clamped to their heads with white headphones. Sig looked at Clint, who raised his eyebrows.

"Extraordinary extradition," said Xelina. "Members of the opposition being brought back in from exile. Without the permission of the government that had granted them asylum. Wait—"

One of the suits lifted up the hood of one of the captives, like he was checking to make sure he was still there.

"Holy shit, I think that's Robert Luca," said Xelina. "Used to be a congressman from Chicago. I need my camera."

Xelina handed Sig the binoculars.

He didn't recognize the man, but he recognized the pain on his face as they pulled the hood back down over it.

Sig did recognize the other cargo.

There were three loading pallets.

Two were stacked with shrink-wrapped bundles of cash. It looked like foreign currency.

The other pallet had a stack of gold bars, embossed with words Sig could not read.

"We can't let those guys get away with this," said Xelina.

"And we can't let them keep that loot," said Clint. "Probably stolen. We need to put it to better use." *

"I got a few ideas," said Dallas.

Sig put down the binoculars. Xelina was filming with her phone, and nodded. Clint was smiling and shaking his head at the same time. Dallas made a weird face and flashed two thumbs up.

"Don't gimme that 'what the fuck?' look, Sigurd," said Clint. "We use one of the dogs to distract these guys, pin 'em down from cover, and then it's a simple grab and nab."

"Git and go," said Dallas.

"Imagine what we could do with better video of this," said Xelina.

"There's cameras all over," said Clint. "Call Walker. He has people that can grab it."

Xelina looked and nodded. She stopped filming, started

looking for the number, and walked back around the other side of the building.

"How do we get away?" said Sig.

"We take one of their vehicles," said Clint. "I don't think they're gonna call 9-1-1. That's strictly off-the-books pirate shit they got going."

Sig watched the gold flash as the headlights of one of the Raiders passed over it. "Even shares," he said.

"All right," said Dallas, almost dancing. "This is gonna be better than Friday Night Strikes."

66

INSTEAD OF HIDING THAT NIGHT, OR RUNNING, TANIA WENT RIGHT into the Blue Zone, hunting for credentials.

The Blue Zone was the secure sector of downtown, the office towers and urban malls protected by corporate security and government law. There were no checkpoints per se, but you could see the patrols when you crossed in, and the eyes on the poles.

One of the Quantico shrinks once told them in a training lecture that police officers and juvenile delinquents tend to have more or less the same psychological profile. When Tania heard that, she knew it was true. She'd always wondered if they'd found out during her background checks about the times she'd been arrested before she started high school—like maybe it was one of the "talents" they wanted, even though it was supposed to be a disqualification. Part gypsy, her mom said the third time she got caught for pickpocketing business men downtown. Some of the older kids had identified her talent early. They taught her some of their social engineering tricks to distract the marks—have you seen my mommy, bus fare to Chicago, there's bird poop on your shoulder, look at the gold ring I found—and how to make the lift. Tania never thought she would need to see if she still had the touch.

The fact that she tried it in a noisy bar helped.

The bar was a restaurant, but no one seemed to be eating. Colonel Starr's was the club inside the Federal Tower where the St. Louis Restoration Corporation had its management offices along with many of its vendors. Tania got there when happy hour was turning into the other thing it sometimes becomes, and the tongues and hands of people who work together get loose, especially if they are far from home.

As it turned out, she didn't need to trick anyone. She just needed to be looking when the dude dropped his badge as he stood to go pee. The colleagues with whom he had been loudly trading interoffice conspiracy theories didn't notice, too busy imagining each other's secret agendas.

And when she got far enough away and saw just what kind of access it was, she couldn't believe her luck.

THAT WAS HOW SHE FOUND HERSELF STANDING ON A STREET corner thirty minutes before curfew staring up at the concrete box where they cage the cloud. There were a lot of people on the streets despite the hour, which made her feel a bit safer, even as it seemed odd, especially in the business district after hours.

The BellNet Midcontinental Long Lines Building was in the heart of the Blue Zone. You might mistake it for another office tower, if it had any windows. To Tania, its abstracted vertical lines looked like a giant alien cenotaph, marked by a single sign—an illuminated blue bell spreading threads across the planet.

It was a place for robots, not people, especially not people who weren't supposed to be there. But she had to try it. The badge would be remotely disabled by morning, and it was a sure thing she would never have a chance like this again.

Not to suggest she knew what she was looking for. Data fishing, sneakernet style.

She did not bother with a disguise, figuring there was no

way she could pass for Scott Dombrowski from Network Engineering, but she did pull her hair back.

She got farther than she expected before she wished she had stayed outside.

Right through the main door, into the lobby. Good evening to the guard, who barely looked up from his screen.

The nearest elevator opened, like it had been waiting for her. She stepped in, swiped the access card again, and tried the top floor. It didn't work, nor did number nine. She settled for SB3, a subbasement.

She wondered how many bad entries it took to lock it up.

There was a TV screen above the control panel, scrolling war commercials.

When the doors opened, a lidless white eye floated into the cab, airborne on six tiny rotors.

Tania stared back.

The hall monitor hovered, bobbing gently, processing.

Tania grabbed at it, but it pulled away before she could touch it.

It came back in to continue watching her. Then it made a plastic click inside and moved on before Tania could think of a way to trick it.

Too far, and too photographed, to turn back now.

Tania stepped out into the hallway, bathed in the sound of a thousand fans. The ceilings were more than twice normal height, covered in thick bundles of telecom cable. Red, yellow, orange, and white. The walls were concrete and blue painted steel.

The hall monitor continued bobbing along the ceiling, popping down to look through the windows and exchange information with the security panels on the doors.

Tania followed it, down the hall and around the corner,

273

through a blast door stenciled with alphanumeric codes. The little orb hovered at the door, which emitted a loud electronic hum, then opened with a metallic knock.

Tania stepped through, into a library of sleek black boxes racked floor to ceiling in lateral stacks. The only light came from the hundreds of diodes blinking on the exterior of the servers, like a sad disco for tiny robots.

Using her phone as a light, Tania inspected the servers, looking for a sign that would lead her to something she could use.

Some of the servers had names, printed on small white stickers taped to the front. A lot of the names were the same.

leviathan 187.65.747.2.421
leviathan 187.65.747.2.422
leviathan 187.65.747.2.423

And so on.

She took pictures.

She tried grabbing one of the little leviathans, using the handles on the front, but it was secured to the rack. She tried to jimmy it, but it gave off a shock that made her hair try to stick up straight.

"Hello!" said a voice from somewhere else in the room.

Tania turned off her light and crouched against the server rack behind her.

Muted tones of someone inputting information into a keypad.

The whirs of all the cooling fans.

Metal on metal. The sound of the vault door closing.

The light from the hallway extinguished.

Fuck.

Tania peered around, stood up into a crouch, and worked her way into the labyrinth, a different route from the one she had navigated in.

She turned around one rack and saw a faint blue light. It was coming from the floor.

She heard soft scrunching, not far. The smell of dandruff, coffee, and cheap men's deodorant. Then she saw the flashlight beam.

Tania moved, trying to find a different way out. She followed the blue light, which came from a stairwell down to the next floor. There was a faint odor in the stairwell, like burning silicon. It looked like the opposite of an exit.

"Hello!" said the flashlight. "Who's there?"

Tania walked down two long flights, as quietly as she could.

A glass enclosure was there a few feet away, a transparent room within a bigger vault of shadows. The light emitted from thick knots of translucent cables strung across the ceiling. There were computer monitors stacked three high along one wall, displaying different data trajectories—graphs and numbers and network maps. A skinny young guy in a black shirt sat at one of the monitors, typing, squinting, and tuning knobs on a control panel that looked like a piece of future technology made from obsolete parts.

In the middle of the room was a medium-sized television set on a small table, fed by the bundle of glowing cables coming down from the ceiling into the back of the set.

The image on the screen was the face of a man, in snowy black and white. A bald man with gray hair and glasses, speaking words Tania could not hear. The image was so blurred

Tania wondered if it was a projection of her own mind, false pattern recognition. For some reason she felt the urge to smash it. But instead she just took a picture.

When the technician looked around, sensing someone over his shoulder, he saw only the little white drone.

67

DALLAS HAD THREE GUNS, SO HE GAVE SIG ONE, A BIG REVOLVER
that was easiest to use. Xelina pulled a long hunting rifle out
of the truck. Sig wondered if there were more guns in Texas
than Texans.

Sig crouched behind Dallas as they surveilled the scene
from the backside of the garage. They had just helped Clint get
up onto the roof, where he planned to take a position with his
carbine behind a big HVAC unit. Clint told him it was a custom job from one of his underground gunsmith buddies, full
auto on hardware store metal and homemade pins.

He seemed disappointed Sig wasn't impressed.

Sig could see Xelina at her position in the trees, looking
down from the perch provided by the grade, video logging
through her rifle scope. Xelina was the one who persuaded
Sig to accompany Dallas into the lair, and take Loco with him.

The dog was right at Sig's side, at the end of a short leash.
It was muzzled for noise, good enough that you couldn't hear
it over the sound of the jets.

Sig nudged Dallas to move in closer, sneaking along the
side of the big garage. Watching his chubby comrade emerge
from the edge of shadow with unexpected stealth, Sig thought
of the nutria, and how they moved through twilight, staying
invisible in plain sight.

Sig checked his revolver. It was old, with a screaming red
eagle embossed on the grip, but it looked like it worked.

Dallas pointed at the plane. One man was visible inside the cockpit, wearing big headphones and talking into a mic. The rear windows framed two of the suits attending to one of the sensory-deprived prisoners. A man in a windbreaker walked around the fuselage, checking every little part. Two men in coveralls worked to unhook a thick fuel hose from the wing and reel it back into their truck. Underneath them, the door was open to a cargo hold. One of the suits watched a younger suit, a ball-capped contractor, and the other two workmen load the pallets into the hold.

The engines were getting louder, but Sig and Dallas were close enough to hear it when the windbreaker pilot yelled at the head suit, the one with salt-and-pepper hair.

"Hey, Horvath, you still want us to stop in New Orleans first? Before we take these traitors to their family reunion? I'm about to file the new flight plan."

The head suit, Horvath, had his hand to his ear, then moved it to signal thumbs down.

"No no no!" he yelled back. "Listen. First stop is New Orleans. We need to pick up Holt, and we might pick up some more passengers there—transfers from the Dome. Then Jacksonville, drop off the freedom machines. Then Quantico, deliver the stray politicians and the treasure. Holt says the Prez himself wants to be there to greet our passengers and receive our tribute. Got it?"

The pilot gave him the finger, then turned it into a thumbs-up.

Holt. Sig remembered that name. From the rez.

The cargo was almost fully loaded. Horvath grabbed the unloaded gold and handed a bar to each of the workmen, securing silence. The contractors put the rest of the gold in the hold.

Sig took off the muzzle and unleashed Loco with the attack word Clint gave him.

The monster dog charged out into the light.

The pilot did a double take.

Firecracker pop. One of the big arc lights exploded.

Horvath pulled a handgun from behind his back and fired three rounds at the dog. One hit, but Loco kept coming.

Bulletproof dogs are scary.

Men scurried. Guns appeared from inside coats and pant legs. Horvath signaled the two contractors to go after the source of the gunfire and the two other suits to secure the perimeter.

Rat a tat tat from the roof. A fast line of bursts along the blacktop. Horvath and his escort sought cover.

Another light popped.

Horvath's men fired in the direction of Xelina. One held his hand to his ear like he was talking on the phone.

Sig saw Horvath crouch behind the fuel truck. Horvath pointed at the pilot to get his attention, then made little circles in the air with his finger.

Xelina hit one of the contractors in the arm. He dropped his weapon and howled.

A workman emerged from inside the garage hangar. Sig and Dallas both shot at him, and both missed, but scared him back inside.

Sig saw Xelina emerge from her shadowed perch, rifle up, firing. Then truck lights behind her.

Clint fired at the truck. Xelina went out of sight. They heard gunfire up there that wasn't Xelina's.

Horvath and his crew ducked under the fuselage and up the ramp into the plane. One of the linemen followed them.

Dallas looked back at Sig. Sig nodded.

The engine got louder.

Dallas made a break for the open cargo hold. Sig went right up over the hood of the fuel truck and jumped the remaining lineman. He was unarmed.

Clint sprayed the side of the aircraft with three bursts.

Dallas was all the way inside the cargo hold now, tossing gold bars out onto the tarmac.

The plane lurched forward abruptly, then started rolling and turning.

Sig ran for the plane. Dallas tossed more gold. Then he smiled and closed the cargo door from inside. Sig frowned.

The plane turned. Full throttle for the fence.

Up, up, and away.

68

WHEN SHE STEPPED OUT OF THE STAIRWELL INTO THE UNDER-
ground garage, Tania could hear the riots in the streets. She
jogged up the ramp and into the crowd that mobbed the avenue. No little hoverbots followed her that she could see, and if
they did, they had their work cut out for them.

It was a human swarm. Two hundred people moving as a
group. Mostly young, but not all. Some beautiful, some not, all
races, all angry. Many carried torches. A few held homemade
weapons, some of them vicious looking. Tania remembered
the sound of the stamper.

She could hear sirens from every direction. Megaphones
and rotors, explosions and gunfire. They passed a corporate
sedan that was on fire, black frame silhouetted by viscous orange flame. A gang smashed the plate glass front of an office
tower. Another lobbed computers from the high windows of
a skyscraper, to smash on the pavement below. The chants of
the crowd were cacophonous and out of sync, but she could
understand them. Demands for the release of political prisoners, relief from the emergency administration, local autonomy.
The energy was viral, the call of a living collective, a call to
self-liberation.

They came into the plaza, where a much bigger mob was
gathered in front of the Federal Tower, facing off with the local
police and corporate cops that guarded the entrance.

Tania saw the burning cocktail of bottled fuel arcing
through the air before it exploded on some cop's helmet, and

she felt her feet lift up off the pavement as the crowd surged, pressing through the line. When the gunshots started, she fought her way out, at the moment the crowd logic broke and panic set in.

WHEN SHE GOT BACK TO HER HOTEL, THERE WAS A MESSAGE waiting. Finally.

"Where are you?" said Odile.

"Tropic of Kansas," said Tania. She used the lobby phone, prepaid chit, two minutes.

"Oh, that sucks," said Odile.

"Remember I'm from around here."

"That doesn't make it any better, does it?"

"I guess not," said Tania. "Very illuminating, though, about the state of things."

"Glad you're starting to see more clearly."

"Glad you're happy with me. Maybe that means you will help me with this huge favor."

"Oh, Tania, it's been so hard. My own mother has people following me."

"They may be following me, too. Or trying, at least."

"It wouldn't surprise me. Things are getting even scarier back here. I have to really watch everything I do. The bitch says I've had my three strikes, and I think she means it. I shouldn't even be talking to you."

"Please just this one thing. I need credentials. MMC, middle management, second- or third-tier company. Enough to get me into New Orleans."

"Can't you just use your badge?"

"Undercover," said Tania. "Way undercover."

"Do you know the risk you're asking me to take?"

"It will be okay, I promise. It's a risk worth taking. If you get me what I'm asking for, I think I can change the whole game, to where none of us have to worry anymore about what we say or do."

"You sound crazy, Tania. Are you really okay?"

"The only reason I'm not in detention right now is that I hid in a riot. I saw drones on fire and an old lady run over by a bulldozer. My picture is probably lighting up the net now. I don't have long."

"What have you gotten into?"

"Oh, baby, I went down into the hole, and the only way I can get out is to go deeper."

There was a dude staring at her from across the lobby, talking to his hand.

"This is so scary," said Odile. "I wish I could hold you."

"Just help me."

"Okay, I will make it happen. I still have a few favors left to cash in. Including with her. Watch your phone."

"You're the best. Personal account."

"It just goes to the number. Tied to the device."

"Sure. One more thing before they cut me off. If you really wanted a piece of information that would turn over the tables, what would it be?"

"Easy," said Odile. "I've thought about it a lot."

"And?"

As Tania listened to Odile's very excellent idea, she looked at the dude and wondered what he would think.

69

THEY COLLECTED FOURTEEN GOLD BARS. THEY GAVE TWO TO THE remaining crew to keep them quiet when they tied them up in the warehouse.

Sig was pretty edgy. All the close-in gunfire gave him bad flashbacks.

Clint was wounded, with shrapnel in his thigh and a chunk of his left ear sliced out by a round.

Xelina was gone. They found her rifle, with the camera still running. They found her messenger bag. And they found one of her boots.

The dogs were in their crates in the back of the truck. Loco was whining and Watermelon Head was barking. Clint told them both to shut up.

There were truck tracks, and tons of footprints. Sig was the one who noticed the blood.

"Probably one of them," he said. "Looks like she stood her ground."

Clint didn't talk. He just had a freaked-out look on his face.

They heard sirens in the distance.

"All right, fuck," said Clint.

"You need a doctor?" said Sig.

"No, I need to get my wife back. This was fucking stupid. What I get for letting that dimwit nephew of mine git in my ear."

"What do you think he—?"

"Maybe he just wanted a Florida beach vacation. I can't worry about him just yet. Let's get going."

"Let's go try to find her," said Sig.

Clint's phone emitted a siren peal and vibrated wildly. The sound seemed too loud to come from such a small device.

"We need to split up," said Clint. "They're gonna be looking for you."

Clint showed Sig his phone. There was a picture of Sig zoomed from security camera footage. It looked altered.

FUGITIVE ALERT—TERRORIST
Male-20s-Prob Hispanic
Armed and Dangerous
$5,000 for Info Leading to Detention

"Citizen emergency alert," said Clint. "Probably pinging on every phone within a hundred miles."

Sig did not like seeing his picture like that.

"But I have a feeling they won't have a lot of luck if you just stay off the map or whatever it is you do. I'll find you if I need you. I know some guys that might be able to help me."

"Can the dogs help?" asked Sig.

Clint ignored him.

Sig loaded the gold in the bed of the truck with the dogs and put his share of four into a canvas bag he found under one of the seats.

Sig rode with Clint until they got to the freeway on-ramp, where he jumped out and walked, carrying a package that Clint told him was probably worth fifty thousand bucks.

"Don't worry," said Clint. "Be cool. I'll come find you if you're still around once I get a bead. I appreciate what you did."

Sig nodded, and Clint drove off.

Sig walked down the frontage road for a while, in the shadows, until he tired and the heavy load finally caught up with him. Then he walked back into the woodsy area he saw behind a Royal Petroleum station, found a dark spot behind a pile of concrete rubble, and dropped his load.

WHEN HE WOKE JUST BEFORE THE SUN BROKE, THE FIRST thing he saw was the gas station sign on top of its tall pole, illuminated from within. A big yellow crown like a king would wear, glowing against a field of mellow green.

There still were kings in the world. Some were elected.

The red and blue lights of a police car flashed nearby.

He hefted the bag over his shoulder and walked farther into the woods, away from the road. The woods were bigger than he expected, piney and sprawling. Good cover but easy to walk through. He worked his way south.

After a while he saw houses off through the trees to his right. There might be food there, too, or other stuff for the taking. He followed a trail that meandered most of the way, but when he got to the development it was behind a tall fence of painted steel.

It was late morning, warm, sunny. He stood in the shade of the trees and looked through the fence at a huge swimming pool in the backyard of a three-story house that could have a hundred rooms. The house looked like it was made out of pieces borrowed from a dozen famous houses of lots of different countries. Like something a kid would make up, but real, and perfect.

Moco told him Texas was like this. It was where the pipelines ended, pumping from every part of the Tropic they could suck it out of. And when it got to here, it came out as money that flowed into the rich people's bank like water comes out of a faucet.

There was a lady swimming in the pool with sunglasses on. When she got out, she dried herself in the sun, wiping off the water beaded over her skin. She was tan, blond, and enhanced. Her man was sitting at a table on the patio, reading on a tablet and talking on his invisible phone.

Sig wondered how many gold bars they had.

A servant came out from inside the house to check on them. Then a bigger guy walked around from the front yard, wearing a loose-fitting resort shirt. He looked around, then looked right at Sig.

The bodyguard tapped his ear and started talking to his thumb.

The dogs ran around the other side of the house.

The woman covered herself. Her man looked up from his work.

Sig ran, as best as he could without dropping his gold.

Five minutes later he could hear the sirens.

He found a man-made creek that ran for a quarter mile, then hid in a culvert until it was quiet.

He got really hungry that day.

70

WHILE SHE HID IN HER ROOM AND WAITED FOR ODILE, AFTER SHE gave up looking for network coverage of the riot she had just witnessed, Tania looked for gold inside the screen of her government-issue laptop, seeing what she could find before they cut off her access, while the weird programming on Channel 11 of Mr. Wizard TV played in the background.

Every command she typed, she half-expected to get a lock out alert.

What she was looking for wasn't in any of the places you would expect it to be. She looked to see if she could read into the records of the Federal Emergency Detention Facility—South Central Region, formerly known as the Superdome. The other screen, the analog box, kept distracting her.

The program on Channel 11 was grainy color video. Footage from inside some shipyard of guys unloading a freighter, at night, under lamplight. MMCs, from the look of it. You could tell whoever had the camera wasn't supposed to be there.

The Dome was in a bit of an information lockdown. Contractors ran the inside, behind the perimeter maintained by the Army. It still amazed her that they let them use corporate security protocols without providing private keys to federal investigators. She could try to route a fix, but then she'd have to explain why she was following this thread.

They said the President still maintained ties to his old company and used them as one of the instruments of the Ex-

ecutive. The guys running the Dome were probably some sub-
sidiary of P-B.

The corporates were unloading people now, herding them
off the boat like livestock. They were brown people, Central
Americans probably, what Bert sometimes called involuntary
refugees, and the law sometimes called guest workers—like in
Tania's Reinbeck case. They looked tired, terrified, and hungry.

Tania wondered if Odile would come through. And if she
did, if that would be a ticket that could get her in.

A couple of the men being herded off the boat tried to
break for it. One of the corporates blew an air horn, like you'd
use to scare off dogs, and then a gun went off. That spooked
the whole group and started the stampede. And then a lot
more guns went off.

After the last lingering shot of blood on the dock, the screen
went to a test pattern and then to a primitive animation. A robot armadillo waddled into view, stood up, and peeled back
an armored hatch in his belly, revealing a television screen.
Rabbit ear antennae came out from behind his ears.

"Change the channel!" he said in a cartoon voice.

Then he popped into little dots that dissolved into
whiteout.

Really.

And then the channel changed itself. Blinking message in
the middle of the screen.

>>>>>FRESH FOOTAGE<<<<<

Cut to lightpost surveillance camera view of men loading a plane. MMCs, by the look of it. The footage infrared enhanced, weird glow.

What the image showed would make a very good start on a very serious case, were Tania still in a position to open new files. She tried to see where exactly they were. Made notes. Tail number. Signage.

And then it went really crazy.

A giant dog.

A fat man.

Guns guns guns.

And . . .

Sig.

The little fucker. He was turning into a damn TV star. Reality bandit. That it was rebel pirate video only made it worse.

She could yell at him after she saved him.

75

THE DAY AFTER, SIG WALKED FROM HIS SQUAT DOWN TO THE OLD railroad bridge by the water treatment plant, still carrying his heavy load.

He followed the tracks over the bayou and north past the back sides of factories and warehouses and a baseball field to where there was another bridge, this one over the East Freeway. Sig stood up there for a minute, watching the ten lanes of cars and trucks going both directions, toward Florida one way and California the other. He thought of big fat Dallas relaxing on a beach. Then he imagined him in a cage.

Then he imagined him dead.

On the north side of the freeway was a big Siesta Mart, the grocery store where they also sold sombreros and cheap work boots. The Siesta anchored a run-down strip mall and a little retail business district, with a store where you could buy clothes on layaway, an AutoShack for folks who fixed their own cars, a chicken joint, a pawnshop, and a martial arts school.

What caught Sig's eye, though, was what was next to the Siesta. A shop with a big sign in the window that read:

We Buy Gold

Sig went inside. The place was small, basically a counter with one window. The window was made of bulletproof glass. Behind the window was a skinny white guy with cigarette smoke skin and smudged glasses. The guy was haggling with a middle-aged black woman who was trying to sell him a handful of gold chains. The chains were balled up in the space between the window and the counter. The lady was upset.

"What kind of country is it where you gotta work for forty years only to have to sell the things your dead husband gave you just to pay for the goddamn pills you need to keep walking," she said, taking the hundred-dollar bill the man had slid in front of her.

She walked out, giving Sig a mean look on the way.

"Fuck you, too, Chief," she said. "What are you looking at?"

The door closed hard. The clerk took the chains and put them in a drawer.

Sig set his duffel on the counter. The evident weight had the clerk's full attention. And then Sig pulled the zipper across and revealed the contents.

The clerk leaned forward, hands on the counter.

"Can I see one of those?" he asked.

Sig slid one of the bars through the slot.

The clerk lifted the bar up to the light and smiled.

"I've worked here for a year and a half and I've never seen one of these," he said. "These are Good Delivery bars. Fort Knox stuff."

The clerk turned the bar and inspected the inscriptions.

"Is that Chinese or something?" asked the clerk.

Sig shrugged.

"Where the hell did you get these?" asked the clerk.

"I earned them," said Sig.

"Right," said the clerk.

The clerk weighed the bar. "Jesus," he said. "That's like four hundred ounces."

"How much money?" said Sig.

"Oh, man," said the guy. "I wish, pal. We don't buy hot property. We buy people's jewelry, basically. Look around. This ain't exactly PetroBank."

"How much," said Sig.

The clerk stroked his chin.

"I could do five," he said.

"They're worth fifty thousand," said Sig.

"Maybe to a legitimate owner, with provenance and a bank or broker to sell it."

Sig scratched his head.

"Pay me that for just one of them," said Sig. "I'll save the rest."

"Twenty-five hundred for that," said the clerk.

Sig nodded. They settled up.

72

WATCHING TV THAT NIGHT ENDED UP BEING THE WAY TANIA FI-
nally found the Classified List of Banned and Suspicious Persons. Sort of.

Limousine liberator Odile had been bugging her to look
for it for years. But skeptical Tania had mostly believed her
bosses when they told her it was an urban legend. An invention of the radical opposition designed to discredit the efforts
of the Executive to keep the people safe. Maybe they were
suckers, too. The security clamps on the file were insane. It
would only be a matter of time before the autonomous audi-
tors would find her trail.

But once she got the idea that it could be real, she had to
try. Todd had shown her some tricks awhile back, plus she had
a few of her own.

The real trick to finding the Enemies List, it turned out,
was kind of simple. You had to be doing work inside the system on someone who was already on it.

It started with trawling the property tax records of Orleans
Parish, Louisiana. Which were kind of a mess after the years
of disaster recovery, rebellion, expropriation, occupation, and
corporate piracy, but they still managed to make sure they
knew who to collect from on commercial properties like the
broadcasting facility on the east side of New Orleans that Todd
had pinpointed as the strongest source of the transmissions—
radio as well as TV signals, with signal strength somehow
amped up even further.

Nine months earlier the property had changed hands, sold off by a holding company owned by the members of some old family who'd all run for Houston before the hurricane with the rest of the city's owners, and given up after Maxine and the Colonel led the uprising and gave their powers to the people. The buyer was a Nevada company called CARMA-NET Inc. An hour and a half on the Nevada secretary of state's database through a labyrinth of a dozen companies ultimately led to Zapata Communications Ltd.

Walker.

Walker was such a sleazeball Tania could almost forgive the Executive for tagging him like this. Then she found the portal, through the Leviathan server, that took her to the full Enemies List. The codes she had collected inside BellNet were the extra keys she needed to open the vault.

After she found Lisbet's name on there, she spent an hour looking for other people she loved.

Mom, surprisingly, was not on it.

Then she looked at everyone else.

Tania had the young lawyer's idea that the rule of law restrained the exercise of executive power. But the truth she now understood was that law merely served power, like the devil's butler. Sampling the hundreds of thousands of entries, she saw how they had lawyered the thing up to make it look legit, even as its arbitrary and political character was evident on its face. The standard for inclusion was low—reasonable suspicion. Of what, exactly, the law was no longer terribly worried about making clear. Suspicion of whatever qualities the people in charge of eliminating seditious threats during the twenty-plus-year state of emergency thought made it worth a tag.

"Enforcing the Constitution," they called it.

Once you were tagged, they pulled in all your history, from

all the private data mines that had been tracking you as a unit of commerce and labor since you went through puberty, and sometimes before. They layered it over the more sober history maintained by the state in its official records, and your life was mapped from a thousand points of data—things bought, calls logged, trips made, content consumed—and a plausible narrative written to support your categorization. The ending of which might be enhanced surveillance, "temporary" detention, or extraordinary deportation.

The Enemies List wasn't the only thing she found. Walker's files also led her into the classified MMC ledgers, the ones even her office couldn't normally access, which showed the flow of funds from offshore plunder into the masked accounts of the President and his cronies, again under specious color of law. She felt like she had stumbled upon the hidden door in the wall of the library, where they keep the books she had always thought imaginary. It was probably a snow day glitch that she had access, something that would be corrected, maybe in a few minutes.

All the more reason to act while she could.

Tomorrow was her deadline to go back in. Gerson was waiting, and ready to come get her.

Tania knew what to do. It would require her to violate all of her oaths, three confidentiality agreements, and a half-dozen federal criminal statutes. It was what her pre–law school self would have done. It was the thing the spirit of the law compelled, even as the letter of the law made it treason punishable by a life locked up in the Supermax (if you were able to stay off death row). She had worked with a lot of whistleblowers, but she never thought she would become one.

If she took the list, she'd be added to it. Probably pretty close to the top. It might take them a few weeks to figure it out, or maybe a few minutes. The idea was horrifying and liberating at the same time. If she pulled it off—really pulled it off—there wouldn't be any more list.

It didn't really feel like a choice.

So she took the first step into oblivion. She shared all the files with herself, renamed the copies, put them all in a pocket drive, and packed them in her bag.

She made a tiny excerpt for Davis the insurgent HR lady, the page that had her on the list, hashed it with the key, and put it in her dropbox. She had her Subway ticket for sure now.

If Gerson and company came knocking before she could cross over, Tania would tell them she was trying to penetrate the network. Which had the benefit of being true.

She wanted to avoid that, though. She sent Gerson a note, saying she found the good stuff and was ready to come in. That made her imagine being back in detention, without a way out for her or any of the people she loved. Just to be safe, she moved to a different hotel in the middle of the night that night. One that was even dumpier, in another state, and accepted cash and fake names.

And on her way there she threw the phone, the one Gerson gave her, into the Mississippi.

Maybe it would get there before her, to the sanctuary city at river's end.

73

THERE WAS A LITTLE BENCH OUTSIDE THE SIESTA. SIG SAT THERE
quietly with an old Mexican man, watching the cars and people
come and go, all trying to make it to the next day.

Sig noticed a sign stapled to a nearby pole. Bold letters on
bright yellow paper.

CA$H
FOR YOUR
GUN$
TOP DOLLAR
1-866-437-9912

Sig reached into the right front pocket of his blue jeans
and pulled out the contents: some pocket change, the coin he
had extracted from the boar, and a crumpled-up classified ad
Dallas had ripped out of the paper and given to Sig.

Adventurers wanted.
Paladin Global. Security personnel.
Travel. No background checks.

Up on top of the Siesta was a big billboard with the face of
a white guy with a suit and tie and dreadlocks. Donald Kimoe,
Esq. The lawyer the law is afraid of. Free initial consultation.
Toll-free number.

A few feet away was an old pay phone, the handset dangling by a sectioned metal cord.

He was finishing his call when Clint pulled up. Clint was driving a different vehicle—an old Volkswagen Amok with New Mexico plates. The thirty-year-old SUV was a sunbaked yellow. So was Clint's face, even as he tried to look in charge of the situation.

"What the fuck you sittin' there starin' at," he said. "Let's go. New Orleans is a long drive."

74

THE NEW HOTEL ROOM WAS PRETTY CRAPPY. NOT NICE ENOUGH for a business traveler, but not nasty enough to have been taken over by Maxxheads. It was in East St. Louis, on the river, with a view of barges in sludge. Those were the nice rooms. Tania's was on the second floor, door to the exterior, situated such that when you stepped out it was almost like you could take one more long step and be in the middle of the elevated freeway, dancing with the high-speed trucks.

Tania couldn't sleep, agitated by the noise and anxiously awaiting the reply to her latest inquiry. So she watched TV. Not the analog set. The Feed box in the hotel room.

There was Newton Towns again. One of those celebrity interviews about an upcoming movie he was working on—*Jupiter Under Siege*—about New Orleans and the White House. Tania got creeped out watching his crazy smile as he talked about the challenges of the new project, the research he planned to do visiting the affected areas, the challenges facing the country, whether there would be a fourth movie, the duty to make art that makes your country better. She wondered who they would get to play Maxine Price, and how she would play it.

That got Tania wondering what the Maxine Price version of the movie would look like.

She looked out the window, at the run-down city. A zone of colonization. You could never purge it of its original sins, of which there were many. Change would not come without

300

strife, and a change in power would hardly guarantee an end to corruption. But you had to fight for something better. Accepting the world in the condition you found it was no longer an option.

Especially when you saw the country as it really was, far from the secure comforts of the capital.

Suddenly the risks that had seemed so horrifying felt like the opportunity for liberation. Even if you didn't know if you were leaping onto the cloud floating by, or about to splat onto the hard pavement underneath it.

Tania had an idea that she knew how to get to the cloud.

She checked the pocket drive again, to make sure it was still there.

She read more of the files, as the shock of the information grew into righteous anger.

She thought about Mom, the things she said, the life she led, the life of futile struggle Tania thought she had escaped.

She called Cousin Mell. It was late, but she answered. Mell always answered.

"What are you doing?" asked Tania.

"Watching the news, instead of my own nightmares."

Tania laughed, a gallows laugh, and Mell laughed with her.

"Can you get a message to my mom?"

"Sure, honey, I was going to go over there tomorrow anyway and take her some books."

"Just tell her I decided to take her advice."

A little while later, after they hung up and Tania got to work in the dark of night, her computer pinged with the secure reply from her contacts.

WHEN SHE CALLED THE NUMBER THEY GAVE HER, IT RANG TO a series of clicks, and then a voice came on. It sounded like another revolutionary white lady, but it was hard to tell because they were using some kind of filter.

"We read what you sent us," said the voice. "We want the rest."

"That's a lot to ask for," said Tania. "I'm already taking a huge risk even talking to you."

"We appreciate that. We know you can be trusted now. We can protect you. You must trust us or you wouldn't have reached out."

"It's not like there are any actual journalists left who could do anything with it that wouldn't get them prosecuted."

"We can do what needs to be done with your information. We want to meet you. Tonight. We will send a car."

Tania laughed.

"You're making me feel less safe," said Tania. "Not more."

"We are so much more safe you have no idea."

"I want to go to New Orleans."

"That is very hard right now. Do you want to fight?"

"I want to help."

"Yes, you say you do."

"And I think I've already proved I do. But like I told you people, I have family issues I need to deal with first."

Quiet on the line. You could hear the crackles when no one talked.

"I understand."

"How can you get me to New Orleans?"

"Call us again in twenty minutes. We will send you a new code. We need you to stay where you are."

TANIA PULLED ON THE OLD TURTLENECK IN FRONT OF THE mirror and watched her hair spring out as her head popped through. True hair, and true self, maybe. Whether she would stick with that version remained to be seen. Once you got your head around the idea of spending some serious time in jail, your fears became very different. It was like the first time you figured out that to do your job right you needed to kill your fear of getting fired.

IT WAS TIME TO PLAY HARD TO GET. TANIA CLOSED THE LAP-top before the new code came in and walked down to the river.

PART SEVEN

The Tchoupitoulas
Autonomous Zone

75

THEY DROVE EAST THROUGH THE SWAMPS, OVER HIGHWAYS ON stilts.

At dusk you could see the alligators out there, and the big wild birds that looked like little dinosaurs. Old houses with legs and boats for cars. And the petrochemical extraction machines shoved into the biome like giant robot mosquitoes.

That was after they went to the storage lockers, where Sig got to see some of the special things Clint was keeping for folks, and for himself.

Dallas had told him Clint had an arsenal in there. He wasn't kidding.

They loaded up the Amok with foot lockers and wooden crates packed with heavy metal. They left Loco and Watermelon Head to watch the yard. Clint said his brother-in-law Luis would look after them.

Clint played a tape while they drove. Country twang about pickups and Kalashnikovs.

Something about the song got Clint to talking about how Luis and his buddy Jerry in Tomball were working on a special project for Clint and "the Investors." Jerry was a tinkerer, Clint called him, an electrician who worked at NASA until he got fired for telling the truth in the comments pages of the news Feed. The thing they were building now was called "the flashlight."

When Sig asked what's so special about a flashlight, Clint said it's not really a flashlight.

"It's the kind of superweapon you can build in a garage," he said.

Sig still didn't understand, but didn't want to sound stupid, so he didn't ask anymore.

The land between Houston and New Orleans was a cyborg swamp. The lattices of pipeline traversed all terrain, whether woodland or bayou, flooded forest or open gulf. They drove with the windows open to the mug, and the sweet toxic smell of the gas filled the cabin. In the darkness you could see the silhouettes of the big storage tanks under the flame of the flareoffs and the pulse of the warning lights, and whenever they slowed down enough to kill the wind whipping through the windows, you could hear the machines beating the earth with loud hammering knocks.

"Vulcan works for Mars." That's what Xelina said.

Sig remembered the northern swamps of his childhood. *Clean* wasn't the word, but *healthy*. Alive. Mostly left alone. Room for all the other species. You could take what you needed, and know the space that was left would be quickly filled.

"You really think we can fix it?" said Sig, looking out at the creepy landscape. "All this? Like Xelina says."

"My queen of the Anthropocene," said Clint. "Gotta start somewhere. I look around and figure we're just setting ourselves up for the big die-off. Mother Nature'll take care of that. But doesn't hurt to try. It's like the Jesus freaks say. 'It's comin'. Look busy.'"

Sig saw a night heron out there sitting on a half-submerged pipeline. Maybe it was the things Clint said, or just the weird moon, but for a minute he could see the future, when the wet earth takes back all the metal and feeds on our remains.

"FUCK," SAID CLINT, LOOKING AT THE REARVIEW MIRROR.

Sig turned to look.

White and red flashers, approaching fast.

"Be cool," said Clint.

He pulled the car over to the side of the road.

"Glove compartment," he said.

Sig opened it and reached in. DIY pistol of steel and PVC, like the bad dream of some loco plumber.

"Just hide it under yer hoodie or something," said Clint.

Clint had his own pistol already out of sight, between the side of his seat and the center console.

Sig looked out into the swamp.

"We should just run," he said.

"You can bail if you want, but I'm gonna get this cargo to its destination. Most of these guys are happy to have you pay the unofficial fee if you know how to talk to 'em."

Sig watched the lights approach in the rearview mirror. And then they drove right by, followed by a convoy of six armored tanker trucks with a corporate personnel carrier as the caboose.

On the back of the CPC was a guy sitting in the turret, wearing his night-vision helm. He was so close that you could see the ghosts of the green screen inside his visor.

"He just took our picture," said Sig.

"Yup," said Clint. "Asshole. Better change our route."

AT 2 A.M. CLINT PULLED OFF THE ROAD AND TUNED THE RADIO to a station way over to the left of the dial. The sound of some lady talking, reading numbers out loud. Clint kept an eye on his wristwatch and waited until the lady paused. When she started again Clint wrote down all the numbers on a piece of paper. Then he looked them up in a little pad he had in his shirt pocket.

"Message?" asked Sig.

Clint shushed him and kept writing.

"Money," Clint said when he was done.

"I thought you needed the video for that."

"Yeah, it helps, but if you have to you can do it this way, too. Radio tunes the video frequencies pretty good, but it's a pain when you wait for 'em to actually read your new number over the air. Some people trade 'em for cash money, but I like to stick with the codes. No hyperinflation, no pictures of fascists, and no trace."

"What did you sell?" asked Sig, as Clint pulled back out.

"Everything inside one of those lockers I showed you. One of the ones that's mine, not the ones I'm keeping for this guy we're goin' to see. Dude in California paid me forty. Might be enough to get whoever's got my wife to sell her back without us having to go to war over it."

"I had some snowflakes, but I just gave my keys to a lawyer," said Sig. "Maybe he hasn't collected them yet. I can check if it would help."

"I'm good," said Clint. "And good luck gettin' money back from a lawyer."

"He seems okay."

"What do you need a lawyer for anyway?"

"Trying to spring a friend."

"Okay, long as you're not wasting money on that dumb-ass nephew of mine."

Sig shook his head.

SIG OPENED HIS EYES A FEW HOURS LATER TO DEAD TREES sticking out of gray water, crisscrossed by weathered pipeline, as far as he could see.

Clint was quiet. He was hauling ass. The truck was vibrating pretty hard. Sounded like something might pop.

The road passed back under living treetops, wound through the phantom topography of a forest that had been clear-cut for pharma harvest, and then widened and slowed into something like a town. A very messed-up town. Signs of damage from extreme storms. Broken trees and demolished buildings. Flooded-out cars decaying in the ditches. People salvaging from wood and drywall ruins. Sometimes with Bobcats, sometimes with their bare hands.

There were military vehicles there, too. And paramilitary. Corporates. Some local militia. Typical wildlife of the emergency zone.

At one intersection there was a pickup parked in front of a bombed-out Kwiky Mart, tanking up from broken pumps. The truck was custom-painted matte black with a big white stripe, jacked way up on a crazy off-road suspension and monster tires. Mud was spattered all over the fenders, a wet, black dirt the color of old blood. One dude was sitting up on the cab in ballistic overalls, smoking a cigarette. He wore a necklace of animal tails and strips of hairy leather. An assault rifle half-covered in duct tape hung down along his thigh on a low-slung shoulder strap. He caught Sig looking at him and pointed at Sig with a finger gun and a fucked-up smile.

"Skunk hunters," said Clint. "They do the jobs the federal law can't, or won't. Not even official militia—just kinda who's-gonna-stop-us types. Homegrown versions of the death squads they use to keep people 'liberated' south of the border. Hire 'em out to the corporates for special projects. Couple guys I grew up with in Pasadena run with those dirtbags. Hopefully I won't have to kill 'em this trip."

SIG LOOKED AT THE MAP AS THEY DROVE ON. IT WAS AN OLD paper map, half worn through at the creases, hand annotated with secret routes and scribbled encryptions of landmarks no regular map revealed. Double red lines encircled the areas under federal control, the biggest of which was around New Orleans. Other areas were marked off in orange hatch marks to indicate toxic no-man's-lands. That's all there was where the town they drove through should have been.

The flip side of the map was a detail of the city. Clint pointed to the spot that was their destination. It was already marked on the printed map, with an icon for a big antenna.

When Sig looked up, they were crossing through the imaginary red line at the outskirts of the city. They came in from the southwest and tracked onto an old road that followed the river. The Mississippi, twice as wide as when Sig saw it in St. Louis, wider than any river he'd ever seen. In the distance you could see a big bridge that had been blown out, the whole midsection gone, dropped into the muddy river.

There were more military vehicles on the road and along the side. Engineers and disaster response troops, and a few tacticals.

The sky was rumbling, filled up with churning clouds that blocked out the morning sun.

Clint pulled off the road before the bridge, joining a line of civilian vehicles queued up at the riverbank.

"Wait here," he said, and got out of the car.

Sig got out, too. He grabbed the map and sat on the hood. He watched the river and surveilled the scene on the other side, looking for landmarks he could match to the map. There was a barge working its way toward them, loaded with a half-dozen cars and trucks. More cars were lined up on the opposite landing, next to a squadron of soldiers tending a fortified checkpoint they had built at an intersection. Sandbags and razor wire protected the parking lot of a roofless fast-food joint, with two heavy machine gun nests and a cannon pointed at the sky. The sign rising from behind one of the nests announced the change of use in black interchangeable letters crammed into the available space once used to advertise special promotions.

LOUISIANA EMERGENCY ZONE
RESTRICTED ENTRY
ALL VEHICLES AND PERSONS SUBJECT TO SEARCH

Sig looked for Clint in the mob of people down by the water but couldn't see him. He looked around at the cars lining up behind them. That's when he saw the black pickup.

He slid off the hood. The skunk truck was parked six cars back. Fully loaded, with three heads inside the cab and two standing up in the bed. Sig recognized the scalps before he recognized the faces. Until the guy saw Sig checking him out, and gave him that fucked-up smile again.

Sig folded up the map and shoved it in his pocket.

The guy elbowed his partner peering over the top of the cab and pointed at Sig.

The pair jumped out of the bed and started walking Sig's way.

Sig started walking, away from the truck, toward the water.

The rain started. Hard.

Sig looked around for Clint. All he saw were soldiers pulling up in a convoy of roofless SUVs, cutting to the head of the line, crowding out any view of the action down at the dock.

"Hey, you!" hollered the guy from behind him. "Hold up there! We need to talk to you!"

Sig started jogging.

"Motherfucker," he heard the guy say.

He heard metal rattle.

He heard men holler.

He heard thunder.

He heard his sneakers squishing into the muddy ground with each step.

He heard the overtuned engine of the skunk truck rumble into action.

He looked back and saw the truck skidding his way.

He sprinted for the water.

"Stop!" yelled another voice, amplified, from a speaker embedded in the trunk.

BANG.

A single warning shot.

Sig felt his right foot as it hit the ground wrong, then felt all his momentum teeter off balance as his right shoulder went for the dirt and his hand reflexively went out in the lead. He ate it, bad.

He spit dirt, looked forward, saw the water.

He scrambled, looked back under his legs, saw the guys on foot, running too fast to aim, and getting too close to miss.

He rolled, came back up running, slipping.

RATATATARATATATARAT.

He heard the whip whine of lead cutting air.

He dove for the water, leaping to clear the concrete bank.

He half made it. His shins hit the edge hard, slamming him into the business side of the river wall. Then he tumbled on over and hit the water even harder, a big slap up his left side.

The water tasted like rusting pipe and insecticide.

He swam deeper into it, as hard as he could.

He saw nothing but brown-gray blur that burned his eyes.

He couldn't tell if he was swimming up or down.

He inhaled a gulp of the rank. Then he found the air.

CRACK TTSSCCHHIIIIING.

He saw where he was and went back under.

He swam like a turtle evading a dog, popping up only when he had to. He intuited misdirection, and was more than halfway across when he saw them standing there on the bank he'd left with their truck and their guns, unable to see him emerge.

He couldn't see Clint, or Clint's truck.

76

TANIA SECURED PASSAGE ON ONE OF THE BIG BARGES HEADED
south.

She had been out there for four hours in the dark, carrying her shit around on the river wall like some crazy bag lady, waiting for daybreak, watching for danger. She got a feel for the water traffic, watching and listening as the leviathans trudged along. On some the cargo looked bigger than the boat.

When the sun came up she had walked down to the dockmasters and asked around, looking for passage to New Orleans on account.

She had the credentials Odile had gotten her. JoAnne Martinez, Contracts Administrator, Cavalier Robotics.

Her fraudulent employer, it turned out, was the developer of the system that ran the ship on which she got a berth. Kentucky computers were the new kings of the river. She wondered if this one would check her cousin's personnel files. Who knew where Odile got this from.

The human captain, who really just assisted the robot brain, was a porky smiling fellow named Herman. He was excited to have a woman on the ship, and said that means you get your own room. His crew were two, a burly black mate named Leathers and a skinny white engineer named Edwin.

The *Roger Kozlovsky* was an old river barge retrofitted for semiautonomous operation by its current owners, Choctaw Logistics. Two hundred forty feet long, deck and quarters at the rear, long fore loaded with big containers stacked three high.

Captain Herman hadn't been lying—Tania was the only woman on the boat. The other two dozen passengers were employees of Choctaw in charge of parts of the cargo, a few lone travelers from other companies, and a big contingent of Royal Petroleum roughnecks heading back to base. All the kind of corporates who rarely warranted airfare.

They looked as excited as Captain Herman to see Tania on board for the cruise. Tania wished she had a gun, but was stuck inventing nonlethal strategies for safe passage.

At lunch after they put out, Captain Herman sat with her and two of the Choctaws and asked Tania a lot of weird questions about her work and background. Tania wondered if the Captain was asking or the Kentucky Cavalier he reported to. Tania left half of her barely edible turkey sandwich and chips and said she wasn't feeling that great.

She decided she would hide in her cabin as much as she could. Claim she was sick, which always worked with guys, especially stupid ones. The cabin was made for two. Still small, but comfortable enough. The light was crappy, but enough to read by. And there was a power outlet.

The problem was there wasn't any way to lock the door.

She tried to chill, see if she could take a nap, but the noises outside prevented her. So she looked out the very tiny window, watched the river roll by, and wondered what it looked like before all the big concrete, and all the foam in the water.

71

THE CURRENT WAS STRONG. IT WAS A BIG RIVER. IT TOOK SIG A long time to cross, and a lot of energy.

He followed the channel of a small boat moving across with a single truck tied down on its deck, up a canal that cut into the city on the north side of the river. He swam out when he saw the burnt-out hulk of an old military truck sitting in shallow water off to the right. He crawled up into the cab of the truck and lay out on the bare rusty seat springs, catching his breath while his clothes dried a bit and he thought about what was next.

He pulled out the map, and it fell apart in his hands.

He tried to find the pieces he needed, but all Clint's marks had washed out.

He looked around, listened, tried to remember what he had seen before.

He stood up on the roof of the truck but couldn't see the antenna anywhere he looked.

So he guessed, and set back out in what he thought was the general direction. Maybe he would find some food along the way.

He waded through the fetid shallows of the canal, then clambered up the concrete wall onto the beat-up old road that ran parallel. There was a big tank farm off to the right. He heard the sounds of machines working but saw no people, just a couple of boats working their way up and down the canal.

To the west, across the canal, he could see the high-rises of the business district.

He found an improvised trail that ran along the fence line of the tank farm, through cover of scrub trees. He followed that until it opened up on the right of way for a row of power line towers that cut between the industrial estates. The way was overgrown with tall grass, and you could see the fresh paths of small mammals who used it as their freeway.

A wild dog was there, staring at him before he noticed it. Mottled coat like a tiger that had been through the wash, burly lean, with a face like a pit mix and the eyes of a coyote. It was wary but followed him a few beats behind as he set out down the long weedy avenue under the big tower frames that looked like lanky robots marching off to fight.

A pair of dark green helicopters flew over low, headed toward the central city, staying clear of the power lines. The second chopper had its cargo door open. Sig saw a soldier sitting there manning a big pivot-mounted machine gun, staring down at him through a mirrored helmet visor.

The dog was right on his heel now. Maybe it could tell Sig was looking for food. Maybe it thought Sig already had food.

Sig walked east, looking for landmarks, trying to intuit his way. At one point the path was blocked by a new section of fence, but the dog showed him a spot where the chain link had been pushed through along the bottom by animals, drifters, or kids, and he was able to squeeze under.

They came out onto a flat old road that ran along the edge of an industrial bayou. They followed the overgrown edge of the road, past piles of demolition debris and abandoned shipping containers marked with the stencils of faraway lands.

Sig heard more helicopters and wondered if they were circling back around.

A big green truck approached from down the road, rumbling on the wobbly waterlogged pavement.

There was a bombed-out old house off to the right. Sig ran for the shelter. The dog chased after him. They ducked under past the stilts that held the building up above the ground. The staircase was gone but Sig was able to jump and grab the lip of a hole in the floor and pull himself up into the inside.

The dog looked up at him with a sad, puzzled face.

He was in an old kitchen. There were newspapers all over the floor. A ratty mattress in the corner cluttered with cheap blankets and a bedsheet printed with some cartoon character. A stove that looked older than the house, with the oven door open and signs of rats inside.

He looked out through the haze of a broken window and watched the truck bounce on toward its destination.

Then the building started shaking with the sound of the helicopters coming in close. They chopped up the wind and threw it hard against the rickety wood-frame structure. Sig could see the shadows of giant metal bumblebees passing across the floor through the holes in the roof. The building throbbed with the premonitory rhythm of imminent machine death.

The dog was out in the open field in front of the house, barking its brains out at the choppers.

Sig imagined the gunner looking at him through whatever enhanced feed displayed on the inside of his helmet visor. Seeing Sig as a red ghost against a blue background, and waiting for a good shot.

He heard an explosion. Far away, but still loud. A faint blast echo washed over the building, mixing with the rotor throbs.

The choppers pulled away.

Out the window, Sig could see them flying off toward the west, in the direction of a column of thick black and orange fire rising up over the roofline a mile away.

Watching the plume, he finally saw the antenna. It was two antennae, one a lot shorter than the other, way north of where he was. He hadn't gone entirely the wrong way, but close enough.

He kept moving.

SIG AND THE DOG WERE BOTH EXHAUSTED BY THE TIME THEY reached the antenna site. There was no sign of Clint. Just a quartet of armed guards at the front gate, a sliding metal slab built into the masonry wall that encircled the installation, which took up the entire block. There was no sign, not even a number.

Sig decided to keep clear of the guards. Across the street from the north wall was an empty lot with more stacks of abandoned shipping containers. The dog found a satisfactory puddle in the dimpled pavement, and Sig found a container with an open door where he could get out of the sun and keep an eye on the main gate from the safety of shadow.

The main antenna was incredibly tall, supported by long metal guylines. The wall that wrapped around the base was ten feet high, with barbed wire along the top, the exterior surface covered with layers of old posters advertising beer, to-bacco, forgotten bands, and failed revolutions.

Sig planted his butt on the beat-up wood floor of the con-tainer, leaned his back up against the cool metal wall, and watched the shadow of the antennae slowly work its way across the street.

The container smelled like the sea.

HE DRIFTED INTO A DREAM OF WATER. THE BIG COLD LAKE of the north, surface like glass, as still in the morning as a block of ice about to form. The loons were there, and the ship from that song Merle used to sing after dinner when he was a kid and they'd all go camping at the protest sites. He remembered the lament of that song, about workingmen losing their lives out in the elements far from home.

He swam in the dark, and came up on a different shore. He smelled rich fresh food, spices, fruit, and fried meat. He heard festive music with drums and horns. He heard people talking in upbeat voices, doors opening and closing, birds singing in the trees.

He dreamed he was a raccoon, sneaking around the human city, feasting on the bounty of bottomless dumpsters full of the half-eaten meals from expensive restaurants.

He heard the dog barking its brains out again.

78

THE FIRST NIGHT ON THE BARGE THEY HAD A PARTY.

They told Tania she had to come.

They made a pig for dinner. Beer and bourbon flowed, releasing stories about big machines, fierce rivers, the broken people of battle zones, the dangers lurking in the earth, and the sort of women who cavorted with men like these.

After dinner the party moved outside onto the forecastle, and the fights began.

The first fight was between the captain's little dog and three big rats, inside a wooden box. It was a close one. The sound the rats made, in fighting and in dying, stuck with Tania.

The next fight was between two pipefitters. They were friends. Colleagues, at least. She had seen them together at dinner. They took off their shirts and revealed their tattoos, arcane annotations of the hard, wandering lives of combat-ready wage laborers. The taller one had a buzz cut and robot bulldog on his breast. The shorter, harder one had a kind of mullet and a big letter Z on his shoulder.

Another of their colleagues explained that Bulldog had borrowed Z's pocket music player in the field, and when it was returned, it no longer functioned.

We have our own way of settling stuff, said the colleague.

Z threw the first punch, and they were quickly on the deck, ringed in by the crowd of others, who threw beer and spit and expletives on the fighters.

Tania had never heard sounds like the slaps, blows, and grunts of two big men fighting up close like that.

Then Bulldog was on his feet, with a knife. A weird-looking knife, DIY. Foot-long, single-edged, fat at the back, and tapered into a spiky point. Held like a sword, or a meat chopper.

Z produced his own knife, smaller, a folder.

The crowd of rowdies got rowdier.

Captain Herman stepped in and bellowed, like he was going to stop them, then quickly dodged Bulldog's swinging rebuff and backed out. Wise move—it was like stepping between two trucks about to crash.

Tania could see every move, but she couldn't follow all the motions—no one could. These guys were so fast, and so practiced. It was beautiful, in a sick way, like a savage dance.

It couldn't have lasted a minute, though it seemed a half hour. Bulldog faked like he was going for Z's head, then changed directions as he stepped in, aiming a big chop at the left side.

Z parried with a downward stroke. Tania swore she saw sparks. Then he swung his arm around into a weird backhanded slash at Bulldog's jugular. Bulldog deflected it, but instead drove the point to where it peeled off a big slice of his salty scalp.

That's when Herman and the others grabbed the guys and stopped the fight, just as the pair had broken each other's guards and were ready to kill.

It turned into scrum for a minute, and Tania was ready to run, but then Herman fired off his pistol in lieu of a whistle.

The colleague who told Tania the scoop earlier called the fight for Z, and they made Bulldog pay out a hundred bucks in reload chits.

Later, as they sat drinking beer, Tania caught the captain and two of the Choctaw managers talking and staring at her from the other side of the deck.

The thing Tania always hated about parties on boats was you could never leave when you wanted.

79

SIG OPENED HIS EYES. A FIGURE STOOD FRAMED BY THE HATCH and backlit by the afternoon sun. The dog was behind her, hollering as she ignored it and walked on by.

"Hey, buddy." A woman's voice. "You need to come with me."

She stepped into the container. Blond, thirties, athletic build, dressed for the office.

Sig shushed the dog.

"I'm Paula," said the woman. "From across the street. Nice nap?"

There were two men with guns standing behind her. They weren't the guys from before, the skunk hunters. They looked more corporate.

"My client says he knows you. Wants to have you over. And your buddy the armorer is here, too. Just showed up twenty minutes ago."

Sig stood slowly, sizing up the trio.

"Relax, bud," said one of the gunmen. "You're cool. Boss is having a party. Come on."

"Nice dog," said Paula. She squatted down and ran her hand over the mutt's crazy cranium. She made a weird smile. She looked up at Sig.

"Oh my God," she said. "Now I recognize you! You're that guy."

Sig grumbled.

"Come on, I've seen your clips! On the network. It's totally you. What are you doing here? Come on."

Sig followed them, hoping there would be food.

THE GUARDS WERE STILL THERE BUT THE FRONT GATE WAS
open now. There were a bunch of cars parked along the street, and more lined up to pull inside, clearing security one by one.

The guards waved Paula and Sig through. The dog followed them in.

Inside, they were indeed having a party. There was music, food, and a bunch of people standing around chatting and drinking under the shadow of the antennae. There were a dozen cars parked just inside the fence, expensive cars—big English Rovers, German luxury jeeps, and tricked-out shiny Detroit pickups. Clint's beat-up VW truck was there, too, kind of off by itself.

Sig looked for Clint but didn't see him.

The setup looked even bigger than Sig had imagined from the outside. Like a secret ranch, out of time, here in the middle of the half-ruined port city.

The base of the antennae was on a pad next to a two-story house of painted cinder block. Flat roof, walls faded to fungus, windows filled with old fog. There was a weathered sign by the door.

X-WFL
CHANNEL 13

There was an old camping trailer parked on the side of the station.

Back behind that was a metal prefab building, almost as tall, that looked like it ran to the back wall.

The weirdest thing was the big crater in front of the buildings, right there inside the gate. It was full of water, and on one side they had dumped a truckload of sand. Some beach. The partiers were clustered around there.

327

The crowd was a weird mix of suits and street fighters, including a few street fighters in suits. Bullets and bling. Cowboys and insurgents. And lawyers. Even the suits were carrying. There were women dressed for urban combat and young dudes not much older than Sig holding the keys to all those exotic cars. There was a guy going around taking pictures, and another one with a video camera, like it was some kind of fashion shoot from the end of the world.

There was a DJ over by the house playing upbeat music, not far from the table full of food they were grilling on the steps. And there was Clint, looking stressed and worn out, talking to one of the suits. Sig was wondering who the hell would wear a necktie in a place like this, when the guy turned and looked at Sig.

The guy was bald, with sunglasses, a mustache, and a cigarette dangling from the same hand as the glass he raised to Sig. Then he said something to Clint, and Clint looked over shaking his head.

"That's Walker," said Paula. "The boss. Come on, you look thirsty."

"Hungry," said Sig. "What is this?"

Paula handed Sig a beer from the cooler. "Kind of a combination meeting and celebration," she said. "Those guys can fill you in. Grab a burger if you want, I'll be back in a minute."

Sig was washing down the last bite with a swig of his second beer when Clint walked up with a bottle of his own tucked under his stump.

"Where the hell did you go?" he asked.

"Swam," said Sig.

"I figured those fuckers popped you. Guess the nephew was right about you."

"Any word?"

"On him? No. Waiting to talk to the man about Xelina."

"So this guy is your investor?"

"Yeah. He's out of Houston, or was. Into all kinds of weird shit. Calls it investing in the future. Talks a lot, but mostly delivers. Says he knows you?"

"I don't know him," said Sig.

"Uh huh," said Clint. "Come on, help me unload."

THEY PULLED CLINT'S TRUCK AROUND BACK TO THE BARN. The Barn was an armory, but it was still loud with the noise of generators and big fabricators running jobs. There were rows of vehicles on the floor, a small aircraft, and racks of light artillery under production. The fabbers were along the far wall—laser cutters, water jets, and 3-D printers, all cranking. There was an open mezzanine packed with computer work-stations. There was just one guy working up there, in a black T-shirt and glasses, watching jobs on three monitors. The rest were at the party.

They unpacked Clint's lockers—shoulder launchers, the missiles to go with them, and a hundred rifles—and put them back behind the cage with the previous shipments.

Clint showed him the cars. A Toyota Timbuktu pickup with an M-60 installed into the bed. An old Land Cruiser being bulletproofed with sheets of scrap. A vintage Nova sanded down to gray putty-colored primer and outfitted with an off-road suspension.

"It's like a whole factory," said Clint. "Not much of a match for the war machine, but it will come in handy when the shit starts to really go down. And they come up with some pretty cool stuff. They get all these nerds from all over the country, smuggle 'em in, put 'em to work, give 'em a place to crash and a reason to go on and all the beer they can drink. Engineers, industrial designers, architects, welders, grease monkeys, gunsmiths, plumbers, you name it."

"So he's the leader of the underground?"

"No. The network doesn't really have leaders. Not like you're thinking at least. He's like I said. An investor. He's in it for money. Raises money from even richer guys, big business types who have had enough with the way El Presidente plays favorites and are ready for a change of management. Phase one was building out the communications networks, finding programming to put on 'em. Now he's branching out into guns and stuff."

"You trust him?"

"Hell no," said Clint. "But I've been doing good business with him. And he has done some pretty cool shit. Right now I just got one big-ass problem and I gotta trust or hope that he can help me fix it."

WHEN THEY WENT TO MEET WITH WALKER HE WAS IN HIS OF-fice, sitting at a gray metal desk, talking into a red plastic phone. It was an old phone, the kind that plugged into the wall.

On the desk by the phone were a revolver, a daily diary, an unlabeled bottle of liquor, and a Rolodex. Four monitors behind the desk screened surveillance camera feeds, with toggles for sound. The walls were decorated with photos of Walker hanging out with other suits and celebrities, a map of North America with different countries drawn in, a trophy redfish, and a framed handgun.

"Yeah?" said Walker. "Fuck you, too." He banged the handset on the desk and smiled at his guests.

Paula was there, sitting in an armchair by the desk.

There was another guy sitting on the couch on the other side of the room. Big blond guy with button-down shirt and fancy cowboy boots. Boots looked up for a second, then turned his gaze back to the battle in progress on the old color television set against the wall.

"Holy shit," said Clint, looking at the screen. "That's you!"

Sig watched the scene. A house exploding. Drone's-eye view. Zoom in on two guys fighting in deep snow.

"You still there?" said Walker, still on the phone. "Tell you what. How about if I up it to five? Plus the motherboards. Yeah? Seven tonight? Deal."

The video was surprisingly clear.

"Jesus, what the fuck is that?" said Boots. Clint was gaping, too. "Are those nails sticking out of your hand? No you can't have—fuuuuck."

There was no sound on the video.

"Ouch," said Walker, hanging up the phone. "Trey here just got that footage awhile back from our sources up north, friends of our seditious neighbors in Bywater. Maybe we can get a sequel now that we found out Clint's been the one hiding Kid Spartacus here all this time."

Sig wasn't sure what that meant.

"So, kid," said Walker, "you ever consider the business implications of the idea of redemption through gladiatory death?"

Trey and Paula laughed.

"No?" said Walker. "We should talk some more. The death part is strictly optional. You've got raw talent, kid. Real charisma. Not a lot of people can shine through a surveillance camera like I've seen in your clips. I'm glad Clint brought you here."

"You want to update Clint?" asked Paula. "His shipment checked out."

"Yeah?" said Walker. "What a guy. Goddamn one-armed roper. Well we're doing our part, too, my friend. I found your lady."

"Where?" said Clint.

"She's on her way here," said Walker. "Those P-B boys are selling her to the feds. Turns out she's on the Enemies List. Which kind of makes me nervous to hear, since the reason I use you all for so much stuff is because I thought you were below the radar. Very messy."

"Taking her here? To the Dome?" asked Clint. "I'll show you messy."

"Relax, cowboy," said Walker. "I just made a deal. I may be on page one of the Enemies List myself, but I still have some friends at Pendleton-Bolan, and I've done enough deals with those guys to know they'll always change their minds for a little more money."

"How much?" said Clint.

"Five hundred K," said Walker. "Plus some extra goodies I threw in to close it. And all the footage we've got of whatever it was they were up to. They sounded like they wanted that more than anything."

"Footage fine—I seen you already ran some of it anyway—but I ain't got five hundred thousand goddamn dollars," said Clint. "Just tell me where and when and I'll get her back for free. Sig'll help me."

"'Sig,'" said Walker. "Love it. Love you, Clint, when you get crazy like this. But you need to chill the fuck out. I know you don't have that kind of cash on hand, and I can tell you these guys don't take snowflakes and I don't even want to tell them those things exist because I'm not sure they've figured it out yet. I am going to give you credit for your shipment, and loan you the rest."

"You're gonna loan me four hundred grand?" said Clint. "I already owe you three."

"I know, and you've been a great investment, so I insist. I'm gonna let you pay me back in services. There's plenty to do. You just gotta get your buddy here to work for me, too."

"Yeah, he's good," said Clint. "Right?" He looked at Sig.

"He doesn't look so sure about all this," said Paula.

"That's 'cause he hasn't heard the part yet about how I'm going to make him a TV star," said Walker. "Just what our underground network needs to win hearts and minds."

80

CAPTAIN HERMAN AND HIS MATE CAME TO ARREST TANIA EARLY
morning on the third day, before sunup. Three of the Choctaw
managers were with them.

She was already up, waiting for them.

Captain Herman said the ship told him that JoAnne Martinez was no longer with Cavalier Robotics. That Tania matched
the profile of a woman who had just come up on the alert list
for a security breach. "Detain if possible."

Tania told them you're right and you're wrong. Said her
real name and her real job. Said she was undercover, investigating Cavalier Robotics and Choctaw Logistics for violations
of Reg MM under the National Security Act and the rules
governing demilitarized autonomous vessels. Specifically,
she said, she was documenting how the ship was failing to
enforce the cargo reporting and health and safety rules with
which it was supposed to be inflexibly programmed.

She asked Captain Herman if that was an alteration made
by him, or by corporate.

He said he didn't have the access and didn't know how
to code his own desk lamp, let alone the specialized intelli-
gent computer running the ship. Which he called a fucking
bitch.

Tania knew the ship was listening. She had never negotiated with an autonomous marine vessel before, especially one
that talked through a fat white man.

She said they had forty-five days to remedy the violations before she came back. Documentation would come after she got back to the office.

Tania told the computer to drop her off in Memphis, thirty minutes downriver.

And it did.

81

SIG WENT TO THE HANDOFF WITH CLINT. IT WAS OUT WEST, BY THE airport, down at the end of an industrial road past the international cargo warehouses.

It was basically a dead end, which made them both uncomfortable. Sig suggested he hide in the woods to jump these guys if they pulled anything, but Clint wanted to follow the instructions they were given.

While they waited they talked about Dallas and their theories of where he might be.

When the P-B guys pulled up in their big black Chevy Shiprock, Sig had a flashback to that night in the northern borderzone, when he lost Betty and Merle and almost himself. It seemed so long ago now.

"Keep your cool, wild boy," said Clint as he got out of the car.

Sig waited in the backseat of the Amok with the side door open, Clint's old Mini-14 in his arms but below the seats, chamber loaded and the safety off.

The MMCs were predatory-looking motherfuckers. Three big white boys with the eyes of people hunters and an Asian guy who looked like the finisher. They carried their grisliest souvenirs around their necks, and the tools to collect new ones hung from their belts.

They brought Xelina out and stood her up in the middle of the road. She had a black bag over her head. Her hands were tied behind her back with zip cuffs and her legs shackled with duct tape. All she was wearing were her radical tank top, her tattoos, and someone else's sweatpants. She was very dirty.

Sig wondered if the tattoos protected her the way he thought they were supposed to.

He watched, ready, for a long, tense minute.

But the MMCs wanted the money, so it worked out okay. Just a transaction.

Sig drove while Clint held Xelina in the rear seat. Even cowboys and revolutionaries cry. They drove to the safe house Walker's people hooked them up with, an abandoned shotgun on Mandeville that had a second story in the back. The pair disappeared into the bedroom that night. Clint only came out once, to get Sig to help him heat up enough water with the propane stove to make a hot bath, which meant they would need to find more water in the morning, but who was going to argue with what she needed.

Clint said she's okay, they just fucked with her, nothing really bad. Sig wondered what the truth was, and what they were going to do about it.

AFTER DARK SIG WENT UP ON THE ROOF AND WATCHED THE skies for dronesign. He knew the skies well. Even had his own secret names for the stars he had made up during his long wander. The best way to "see" a drone at night was by the stars it blocked out. That also meant it was pretty low. He wondered what it would take to take one down from the ground.

There was a surplus of drones around here. Not just aerial. Marine and terrestrial, too. For twenty years New Orleans had been colonized by the war machine, the base of operations for the never-ending fighting in Central America. The insurgencies and political experiments of the South had provoked a predictable response, which had the unexpected consequence of turning an old city that had flown ten different flags into a domesticated colony. Sig had heard people talk about it for years—people like his mom, Betty, Billie, Moco, Clint—but it was crazy to see it in person.

The roof was high enough and the town flat enough that you could see pretty far in most directions. To the north was the tent city Moco had called home—Camp Zulu, the sprawl of improvised shelter for tens of thousands of refugees, boat people who escaped the wars in Central America and locals displaced by the violence of several years of civil unrest. The Dome was due west, lit up with its prison floodlights that attracted helicopters like flies to a streetlamp.

South of the Dome you could see the remaining towers of the business district, and the federal quarters, where the MMCs based their operations.

To the east was Echo Sector, the neighborhood that had been abandoned after the toxic event they had blamed on terrorists before Sig was born. The MMCs had cleared and leveled most of the buildings of Echo Sector after the federal occupation of the city a year earlier, and it was weird to see it from this vantage. Like someone had just erased most of a twenty-block-square section of the city.

They hadn't erased it all. There were shells of a few old buildings left, and one stubby high-rise over in the northeast corner of Echo Sector, standing intact, lost in time and place. It looked like the kind of building you might see in downtown Duluth, but surrounded by the ruins of an ancient colonial port.

Echo Sector was still contaminated, they said, off-limits. Maybe they sent robots in, or guys in special suits. But Sig could see a couple of fires in there, inside the shells of the old buildings. Maybe the stories were true, that the zone was the real refuge of the revolutionaries.

IT WASN'T UNTIL LATE THE NEXT MORNING THAT CLINT AND Xelina came out. They looked tired, and scarred, but like they were working on getting ready to do something about it. Sig had an idea to pitch. Something he had brewed in the night air.

82

TANIA FLEW CORPORATE TO NEW ORLEANS, ON HER OWN DIME, almost depleting her remaining funds. You couldn't get a domestic passenger flight to N.O. You had to go to Baton Rouge and drive, charter a private flight, or get Air America'd on official business. Tania paid cash to charter a small prop from Memphis to Houston, where JoAnne Martinez was able to talk her way onto an AmLog cargo drop out of Charlie Wilson International.

When they were leaving Memphis, banking over the river, she was pretty sure she saw a Motherland chopper landing on the deck of the *Robert Kozlovsky* as it fueled up at the docks.

There were a few other tramps crammed in the jump seats with her staring at the crates of food and ammo strapped into the bay of the big Boeing G-42, aka the Flying Clydesdale. MMCs flashing corporate swag and gunmetal from under their tactical two-pieces. One of them had a lapel pin that spelled out ZOMBIE HUNTER in gold plate. He stared at Tania most of the flight while his buddies traded stories about the most outrageous things they'd seen guys do to score a big lithium deposit. Tania tried to put on her best cop face and plan her next moves.

When they banked in for final approach, out the little porthole you could see the pipelines and refineries, and the big swaths of swamp converted into farms harvesting weirdwood for the Maxximol plants up north. She wondered if there were any alligators left.

Tania had kept her shoulder bag on her lap, her overnighter under her feet, and the pocket drive in a safer place. She felt it when she coughed. That was when she realized she hadn't thought to pull back her hair before she got on the plane. She corrected that before they deplaned and walked into the air arrivals checkpoint.

Tania flashed JoAnne again at the checkpoint and pretended to herself that her secret cargo was a special message from the President to General Butler at his Metairie command center. The soldiers standing behind the kiosks with their tightly harnessed assault rifles looked her over through the eye slits in their balaclavas, but it felt more prurient than policing. She caught the eye of one of the supervisors after they waved her on and was scared she would get stopped. She didn't.

She tried very hard to walk like she wasn't in a hurry, when the opposite was true.

On the other side of the checkpoint, the soldiers were replaced by paramilitary private security guards who looked more eager for a reason to demonstrate the capability of their business-class firearms. They monitored the long lines of tired people in line at the single remaining ticket counter, all trying to negotiate passage on one of the daily charters out. Two dozen European aid workers hogged the middle of the hall with their big strapped suitcases, meeting up to check in as a group for their flight home to Geneva.

A big photo banner hung from the high ceilings over the crowd. The Commander in Chief standing in heroic profile on the prow of the presidential yacht *Miramar* as it passed through the breach in the Mississippi River Bridge. His shining new prosthesis pointed forward, directing a low-flying escort of five fighter-bombers in close formation.

COMMITMENT
Energy, power, and will:
This is the mix that demolishes the barriers to success

The gift shop was shuttered, the newspaper boxes were empty, and the Queequeg Coffee was dry.

She felt eyes watching her, but looking around she couldn't see who. Maybe it was the ubiquitous surveillance.

Maybe it was everyone.

She walked past the little mob of armed chauffeurs holding up their nameplates and went outside into the muggy air. She caught a whiff of cordite and knew she was in the right place. Like existential smelling salts that broke the brain haze and sharpened your political senses.

The only taxis were people powered. Three knobby-tired pedicabs operated by young men with big legs.

Tania told her driver the name of the lodging she had called from the road. He headed that way, down the old Airline Highway past the motels repurposed as barracks, car lots, and suburban strips converted into military staging areas packed with diesel armor, gas stations running out of gas, and fast-food joints running out of food. He told her how this was the best way to get into New Orleans if that's where you wanted to go, because the freeways were closed to most civilian traffic, when they weren't bombed out. He pointed at the roof of the old Sheraton that had been taken over by General Butler as his field HQ, where a black helicopter was landing.

Tania asked him if he knew where she could pick up some transportation, a car, and the pedicabbie laughed. She said how about a gun, and he said that we can do.

Tania watched behind them, and above, scouting for tails.

The pedicabbie, who said his name was Alfonso, took her to a mechanic's shop off the main road and introduced her to a big fat guy inside named Lou. Lou asked if she had snowflakes she could pay with. She wasn't even sure what that was, but she had enough cash for an unbranded "government surplus" 9 mm automatic pistol and two boxes of ammunition. It cost her $1,275, but she was happy to pay it.

She paid Alfonso a couple hundred as well, hoping it would buy his discretion.

It was when they were headed down to where Alfonso said her hotel was that she noticed they were being followed. She told Alfonso to keep going past the hotel, and by the time she thought they had lost the gray Lincoln, Alfonso looked like he was tired of pedaling.

83

"I KNEW THIS KID HAD A SQUARE HEAD ON HIS SHOULDERS," SAID Walker. "Finally someone else who gets it. The way to make this revolution succeed is to give it a profitable business plan. Tell me more, Sigster. How much do you need? Bearing in mind they froze most of my assets."

"You forgive that loan you gave Clint," said Sig.

"How about I let you help him pay it off interest-free," laughed Walker. "You ought to be able to make that in a month."

"Can you help us fence what we get?" asked Clint.

"Sarge, matching buyers and sellers of goods and services of dubious title and/or uncertain legality is how I cut my teeth," said Walker. "My first programming was the illegal classifieds. Just remember my commission varies depending on the particulars of each deal."

They were seated outside the station, drinking beer in the shade of Walker's new craterside cabana. The cabana was made of lead plate Walker harvested from one of the salvage lots.

"You can float your commissions if you get us good information about where to hit," said Sig.

"Yeah, they don't always put dollar signs on the shipping containers that matter, do they," said Walker. "Information is not a problem, boys. My network is good. We just need to be careful about not rubbing the rhubarb in a way that provokes too much heat from the Prez. The status quo is pretty good here right now."

344

"We don't need a political editor," said Xelina. "We need a peddler. And we need to get these scumbags out of New Orleans. Bring back the TAZ."

"Is that your victory condition, honey?" said Walker. "Restore the Tchoupitoulas Autonomous Zone? Those nutjobs fucked things up so bad, people couldn't even get a roll of toilet paper at the corner store, to say nothing of a decent steak."

"A new political system based on self-determination and real democracy doesn't happen overnight," said Xelina. "And a correction of predatory mercantilist monopolies takes even longer. The people are ready for free networks without bosses and rulers and the men with guns who serve them. The TAZ isn't dead. It just went underground. And viral. With your help, by the way."

"The victory condition is to make the whole country the TAZ," said Sig. "We feed the people by liberating the food, and fuel, and money and property your friends stole from us."

"Ex-friends," said Walker. "How do you think you pull that off? March on Washington?"

"Cut off the head," said Sig.

Walker knocked three times on the lead roof of the cabana. "You didn't just say that," he said.

"Why not," said Sig. "She showed me your commercial offering to pay for it."

"That was a joke!" said Walker. "I mean not a 'ha ha' joke. A provocation. A rhetorical prod. A psyop. A contribution to the national conversation."

"It's a good idea," said Sig. "We want to make you pay for it."

"It's a real good idea," said Clint.

"If you say so," said Walker. "Maybe we can get you your own alternative MMC charter. In the meantime, kids, let's talk about which trains you might want to rob."

84

"THE WORLDS MERGED ON A DAY WHEN THE DIMENSIONAL BONES of a glass gate on a country road on the Southern Continent of the place you can call Everywhere (but really is just part of it) synced perfectly with those of a trellis behind a shotgun shack on Prytania Street that belonged to a lady named Bernadette Duval. No one could tell when it was happening, except for the Visitors, who were the emissaries from Everywhere that came for the express reason of watching it happen (and taking great notes). But when it was over, maybe a few days after, people could tell. It was something in the light."

Tania found the re-bound old book in the common hallway, on a small bookshelf with other banned tracts. *The Monsters Parade* was the last volume in the series. A book so important to some that it caused sectarian arguments over whether the author meant for it to have an apostrophe in the title, and if so, where exactly it was supposed to go.

This was Maxine Price's hometown. The principal setting of her books. Looking out the window of her second-floor room to measure the light against the paragraph she'd just read, Tania wondered if maybe her hero's old house was in view. But all she could see were the tents and pop-up sheds of Forward Operating Camp Byrd, which started in the empty space under the elevated freeway and sprawled north along Tulane for twelve blocks.

It was crazy that this dump she had found on Rampart was so close to the base, when you could tell it was like a hostel for the kind of people the soldiers hunted, with its cryptic sign over the front door, the old TV in the lobby tuned to Channel Zero, and the portrait of the Colonel hanging on the wall and the book she held in her hand. But Tania was learning that hiding in plain sight often worked a lot better than you would think.

She looked at the picture of the Colonel, posed in the insurrectionary edition of her National Guard uniform, tough dark eyes and the brown skin of the global South. She was the force that really made Maxine Price's TAZ possible, the one who saved the city after the flood and grabbed the power in the process, the face the streets loved the most, but who let Price do most of the talking in public. She had gone underground after the Purge, the one the feds said was leading the last pockets of guerrilla resistance to their new order.

The people she was about to contact probably knew her.

Maybe they *were* her.

Tania used the house phone to call the number they had given her. No clicks on this line. Just static and a series of tones that sounded like a cross between a food processor and an old fax machine.

To Tania's surprise, the number worked.

As the voice at the other end said hello through its creepy machine filter, Tania suddenly thought of the possibility that the people she was calling were the ones who had been following her since she got off the plane.

She cleaned her sidearm before she went out that night.

IN THE BAR ON CARONDELET, AN OLD MAN IN AN ELECTRIC kufi hat played the blues for his dead city on a huge baritone saxophone that looked older than the crumbling warehouse they were in. The crowd was sparse among the mixed-up collection of tables and chairs in the vaulted room, and half of them looked like the kind of folks who'd wandered in off the streets with no place else to go. The bar seemed to welcome them, asking nothing in return.

The horn was loud, an improvisation on the sound of the civil defense alarms. Just the kind of sonic background these people liked to conduct their meetings in.

Tania sat on the side, with her back against the wall so she could see the entrance, which was close to the table she picked. But when the couple came to sit with her, they came from behind the stage.

They were a burly, olive-skinned white lady and a short little white guy with a black goatee going gray. They said to call them Rhoda and Cinder. They could just hear each other over the noise.

"What are you doing here?" said Rhoda. "You were told to meet our cousins up north."

"I saw your recruiting ads on TV," said Tania. "Your comrade the pirate Ward Walker is especially persuasive."

"He's not our comrade," said Rhoda.

"He's a parasite," said Cinder. "A convenient one."

"He's a pornographer," said Tania.

Cinder nodded. He looked like a grad student gone astray.

"He makes you pay for the airtime?"

"He accepts our protection so he can occupy the people's property that he claims to own. He gives us our own channel to program. He uses our energy and helps us obtain new tools to restore our sovereignty."

"What kind of tools?"

"Use your imagination," said Rhoda. "Let's talk about what you brought to exchange."

"Information," said Tania. "Whether it's a tool depends on what you do with it. It's a lot more powerful than anything you can get from Walker."

"We don't know that unless we see the whole thing. And this special edition you won't even let us peek at."

"You probably want to see if you're on it," said Tania.

"I think she's a cop," said Rhoda.

Cinder looked a little freaked out.

Tania kept an eye on their hands.

"I'm here alone," said Tania. "I'm here to make a deal."

"What do you propose?" said Rhoda.

"I want agreed terms on how we get the information in these files out to the world."

"We can talk about that," said Cinder.

"Maybe," said Rhoda. "So long as you agree with our plans."

"And I want you to get me to my brother so I can get him out of here."

"Who's your brother?" said Rhoda.

Tania showed them a picture. "He goes by different names."

Rhoda and Cinder looked at each other.

"You don't watch a lot of Channel 13, do you," said Cinder, looking at Tania.

"I've watched so much of it my brain is burned and my eyes are rotting," said Tania. "So yeah, I took a break."

"Why don't you come with us," said Rhoda, standing.

"Why don't you go fuck yourself," said Tania, drawing her pistol and training it on Rhoda.

The music stopped. Twenty pairs of eyes on Tania. Probably all in on the secret.

"Hey hey hey," said Cinder. "Let's work this out. We're on the same side."

"I don't know about that," said Rhoda.

Neither did Tania.

She backed out the front entrance, not as slowly as it felt. And she ran, down the alley she had scoped out earlier, into the darkness of the city about to get a lot darker as curfew arrived.

85

SIG HEARD THE EXPLOSION BLOW OPEN THE NIGHT SKY AS HE RAN down Arabella for Annunciation and the rendezvous.

The oil-train railyard was too well guarded to B-and-E, but it turned out to be pretty easy to sneak onto a moving train out in the country and ride it in to Mom's house. Sig had hopped enough trains to know the good places to hide, though it wasn't as easy now as when he was a scrawny teenager.

Walker was the one who gave them the idea. He told them how much of the oil to feed the war machine moved on trains now. Most of the crude came from the deepwater rigs in the Gulf and the occupied Caribbean or the Canadian excavations, and almost all the stuff from the Gulf moved through the depots in and around New Orleans for processing and distribution. The pipelines out had been mostly destroyed by the TAZ as an act of sovereign assertion—it made it easier to control the stuff that had been expropriated as a resource to be controlled by the people.

And inevitable that they would come and take it back.

Fully loaded, the train ran almost three-quarters of a mile. A hundred black tank cars, some shiny and new in the ambient light, others buried under a palimpsest of graffiti, all topped up with petrochemicals.

Sig wore Xelina's new camera rig, the one Walker hooked her up with. It tucked behind his ear so slick he almost forgot it was there.

They had other cameras, too. The high-end one Xelina carried, and a micro mounted in the nose of a little RPV.

It was weird how if you remembered the cameras were there, your mind kept trying to look through the camera eye while you were doing stuff. So he tried to put them out of mind.

Sig ran along the tops of the train as it hauled ass through the open country, empty and hungry to reload, headed for the big tit.

He put the parcels from his pack on the cars, right in the spots Clint told him would work best. The Army taught Clint all about how to blow things up.

The packages felt like energy bars. Solid goop inside foil soft enough that you could bend it into place.

The explosions lit up the night sky with a fireball they could see in Baton Rouge. It looked more solid than fire. Like a towering geyser of some infernal lava. It burned until morning.

"It's the kind of fire you can't put out," said Clint, while they drank beer and watched from the roof of the safe house. "You can try, but mostly you just gotta wait for it to run out of fuel."

Sig wondered how much fuel they would have to burn to break the machine.

THAT WAS ABOUT THE TIME MOCO TURNED BACK UP. THE lawyer Sig hired actually managed to get him out—turned out he was Walker's lawyer, too. They found Moco when they went to Camp Zulu looking for recruits.

Camp Zulu was Moco's hometown hood. More or less. He definitely knew a lot of people in there. Especially the kids.

They started their crew with twelve other teenagers, mostly a little younger than Sig and Moco. Seven boys and five girls. Kat, Alé, Rudy, Sonya, Eric, Mongoose, Pancha, Slider, Wyn, Martin, Freddy, and Don. Walker set them up in a beat-up house behind the station, next to the windowless old brick building they used as the armory. The neighborhood was pretty well cleared from crash, disaster, and fighting, and the folks who were left paid them little mind. Sig put up a tent in the backyard, since he slept better outside.

Clint taught the kids how to shoot, using an abandoned bowling alley on St. Claude as their range. Moco let them in on how to steal, break locks, pick pockets—knowledge several of them already had. Sig showed them a few dirty fighting tricks he'd tested, survival 101, and how to start looking at the world through the eyes of a tracker. Xelina gave them history lessons. And once in a while Walker would come by and give his own version, stories about business and "how the world really works." Eric, Mongoose, and Kat said that was their favorite part.

When they started going on their raids, Xelina brought along another lady. A lady who wore a black scarf around her head and had even nicer cameras than Xelina. Nassra was a stringer for an Emirati news network who sometimes sold stories to New York, Oslo, Paris, or Santiago. An Omani girl who had gotten herself into Columbia only to graduate to the emergency zone with an expensive degree, a word processor, two video cameras, and three credit cards, looking for the story that would be her big break. It turned out she had good timing.

The first week, they stole four government cars and one truck full of drone parts, and held up the casino for six hundred thousand. Xelina told them they should do more political operations, and Walker agreed. They hijacked an oil tanker truck and set it on fire in Jackson Square. They started dumpster diving for secrets, planting vidbugs on cars and land drones, and breaking into poorly guarded offices of MMCs, government functionaries, and the oil and pharma operations. They kidnapped corporates from whorehouses and underground Maxx bars and sold them back to their employers. When they got the vice president of surveillance operations, they put him out to sea in a barge with a handheld camera and told him to send pictures.

They mostly worked at night and slept in the day. Moco taught the kids how to let off steam, and some nights they partied pretty hard. If Xelina got drunk sometimes she would get pretty crazy sad and Clint would get rowdy mad. One night Sig woke up with Nassra in his tent, his face buried in the mop of thick black curls she otherwise kept tightly under wraps. She smelled faintly of some faraway sea, of strange fish seasoned with stranger spices.

Not long after that they went out in the middle of the day. Sig had the crazy idea they could bait an air drone. He did it by leaping from an overpass onto a passing Motherland Humvee, dropping a smoke grenade through the open turret, and jumping off the front hood onto the street so they could get a good look at him before he ran off down behind the houses, and before the smoke evicted them from the cab. He'd gotten four blocks through backyards and over fences when they first heard the whine of a tri-rotor coming down into audible range, tracking him almost faster than he could get to the ambush point. Sig jumped through the window of the nearest house when the RPV started firing its dual cannons. The fusillade ripped through the rotted wood siding. Clint was the one who got to fire the rocket from the church steeple down the street, and his seat-of-the-pants one-armed targeting system worked out just fine.

They split up that night. The kids took pieces of the dead drone back to Camp Zulu and gave them out as souvenirs. Clint and Xelina made a run back to Houston to check up on things. And Sig moved in with Nassra for the time being, in her walk-up on Magazine Street. She cooked in that night, after he watched her file her story about the day, and later while they lay in bed she showed him how it got picked up all over the Feed and all over the world on other networks. Then she showed him other television that featured his adventures, and the bulletin boards where people traded their theories about who he was and the movement he must be part of.

NASSRA WAS THERE FILMING TWO WEEKS LATER WHEN THEY got ambushed. They'd gone to the East Bank at sunup with the plan to hijack a truck en route to the naval yard in Algiers. Walker told them it was carrying a special weapon to be taken to sea for the fighting in Central America.

Walker did not tell them that he had ratted them out.

They didn't figure it out until four of the gang were already out in the middle of General Meyer Avenue, playing their gypsy trick where one of them acted like she'd been hit by a car and the others were flagging down help. That's when Sig saw the first recon RPVs. Eight Motherland patrols followed, with five NOPD police interceptors, two SWAT trucks, one militia pickup, and a Marine platoon with forty-two rifles and one squad pushing an AMC "Alligator Snapper" amphibious assault vehicle stenciled with trophies of prior kills.

"I knew it was a stupid fuckin' idea to cross the river," said Clint. "Walker probably sold us out to cut some deal with his prosecutors."

"Or make better TV," said Sig.

Xelina had stayed behind that day, leaving Alé in charge of the on-site footage.

Clint hollered into the radio, telling the crew to disperse. That wasn't soon enough. It rained hot metal.

Three of the kids died that morning. Six were captured. Moco ran south with Slider, while Sig led Pancha and Mongoose into a storm sewer, which they followed all the way to the spill-off where it drained into the river. They huddled in the bay of an empty barge for an hour, until the sounds of their hunters dissipated. Then they split up and searched for sanctuary.

PART EIGHT

The Colonel and the Mastodon Queen

86

NEON LIGHTS CRACKLED AND GLOWED IN THE ALLEY OF POP-UP
bars along the wharf, where the adventure capitalists cele-
brated another prosperous day. The improvised street had no
name, but everyone knew where it was: in the labyrinth of
converted shipping containers beyond the Quarter, where the
official city disappeared in the contaminated ruins they said
even the robots feared.

When the searchlights of a low-flying helicopter patrol
passed over, Tania glimpsed the bombed-out buildings of the
Vieux Carré looming in the shadows. It was an apparition out
of time, a beacon across two decades of natural disaster, exploitation, insurrection, and invasion.

The crowd of ruggedized network administrators and
Kevlar-suited middle managers were too busy staggering
through the Mardi Gras before the end of the world to notice.
Tania almost stepped on one guy sacrificing the contents of his
stomach to a dead president stenciled on the painted cinder-
block wall.

The revelers did not look like pirates. They had great teeth,
dressed in tactical variations on business casual, and brought
their lawyers with them. The military merchant companies
always lawyered up on deployment, to make sure they didn't
violate the heavily negotiated terms of engagement chartered
by Washington and end up blowing their corporate liability
shield. Depending on who your direct report was, that could
be worse than getting fragged by the local insurgents.

New Orleans was one of the first major MMC hubs, the launching point for excursions into Central America. They all got evicted when Maxine and the Colonel's improvised army took over the city with the support of the streets and declared independence from the Motherland, setting in motion a series of events that resulted in MMCs being deployed stateside in support of the federal troops who now occupied the city pursuant to the special emergency authority.

Tania thought a retreat to the MMC sector would be a safe sanctuary from the people who wanted her files, but being a black woman in this drunk mob of off-duty capitalist conquerors made her feel almost as vulnerable as she had on the boat.

Tania ducked into the most crowded-looking joint. She elbowed her way through and into a space at the end of the counter.

There must have been fifty people crammed into this little metal box. Bigfoot's little brother stood behind her, a tall, still white guy with a big brown beard, weather-worn bibs, and a ball cap embroidered with the logo of Deadhorse Conflict Truckers. He looked like he was working off a few thousand miles of bad road with whatever that was in his plastic bottle.

A brunette in a T-shirt for Alpharetta Tactical Informatics was at the bar next to Tania, a wad of fresh renminbi next to her glass, trying to blow off the predatory-looking suit talking in her ear. The dudes playing stud at the tables by the door wore their PKX and Zapata colors—the crews who built data pipelines through jungles and next-generation prisons out of banana plantations. The loudest of all was the woman next to them, a PR flack from Fairfax Unmanned showing a highly entertained trio of Alabama cargo agents her capacity for shots of Roq.

On a television over the bar, Ashton Brightwell was on Freedom Network News reporting the breaking headline from New Orleans: federal forces' daring interception of an attempted hijacking by known terrorists of a truck carrying a nuclear device for delivery to Naval Drone Station Algiers.

"The terrorists used children as bait," explained Brightwell, "while they lurked in safe positions. Sadly, three of the children died, but most of the rest of the gang were captured. Only three are thought to remain at large, including this man, who federal authorities say has been one of the principal actors in a string of kidnappings and attacks on federal and contractor facilities over recent weeks."

The screen showed grainy footage of a lean guy with long dark hair running through a backyard and vaulting a fence. It looked like a scopecam outtake from one of those Sunday morning hunting shows, the way they filmed the guy. As he landed, the guy looked back over his shoulder and up at the camera. Freeze frame and zoom, but too pixelated to really make out the face.

Tania tried to look closer, but they cut back to the anchor. She wondered.

"Motherland reports that they have been unable to identify this perpetrator by name, but ask that any leads be reported immediately. The suspect should be considered armed and dangerous."

"Turn on the game, will ya!" hollered a voice from one of the tables. "Blockbusters are playing!"

"Hang on," said the bartender, turning up the volume and watching the report. Another face came on the screen, one Tania recognized.

"We now go live to New Orleans," said Brightwell, "where none other than actor Newton Towns was actually there at the scene this morning, while researching for his newest role. Newton, what an amazing story! How did this happen?"

Towns smiled, revealing his 70 mm teeth. He wore a fancy waxed field jacket. Behind him were a trio of armed paramilitaries in their swamp dungarees, watching from the tailgate of a battle-armored Ford pickup.

"It's crazy, Ashton—the most amazing thing I've ever seen in person. We're here scouting locations for *Jupiter Under Siege,* and I came along to ride with these guys on some of their patrols into the areas still being purged. It's all so surreal, and then today—wow!"

"Straight out of one of your movies," said Brightwell.

"Totally," said Towns. "What an incredible show of force by our guys. Can you imagine if those people had gotten their hands on a functioning nuclear device?"

"Turn on the fucking game, man!" yelled the Blockbusters fan. A Californian, to Tania's ears.

"Hold on, buddy," said one of the guys at the bar, watching rapt. "That's the Newtron Bomb talking. I saw him out there yesterday riding with Skunks, headed for Bywater. Let's hear what he's got to say."

"Who gives a shit?" said the Californian.

"Did you have an active role in the operation, Newton?"

"Well, I was ready, Ashton, but I didn't need to fire my weapon. I was out with the Nacogdoches Militia, and we helped in the search for the bad guys who fled the scene. These Texans are great guys and I've learned a lot working with them as they help the feds clean up the outlaw holdback neighborhoods."

The guys behind the actor grinned and flashed hand horns at the camera. One held up a weird-looking modified shotgun.

"That's amazing, Newton, I wonder—"

The bartender clicked to the Blockbusters game.

"Thank you!" said the Californian. Tania looked over at him, sitting at a table to her left. He was a good-looking blond guy in an expensive blue suit and open collar, surrounded by an entourage of other combat preppies.

The game quickly cut to commercial. The bartender muted the sound. The crowd had quieted watching the news flash.

"In any event," smiled the Californian, drawing his audience back in, "these idiots have no idea what they've got." He stopped to pour a fresh glass of Kentucky Hunters from the bottle making its way around. "Like a hundred acres of Louisiana weirdwood growing right there in the hillsides around Lake Nicaragua. Meaning: *Artemisia auduboniana*, the essential, and increasingly impossible to find, ingredient in Maxximol. Worth maybe a hundred million to those pharmers in New Jersey—enough to support at least a decade of production at current levels."

Right, crazy, amazing, nodded his crew.

"You know what those stupid fucking Nicaraguans have been doing with it?" said the Californian. "Making chairs!"

Laughs all around.

"Okay, I know," laughed the Californian. "Weirdwood is a weedy shrub with nice thick branches, and you kind of have to know how to *read* before you can practice ethnobotanical entrepreneurialism." The last part came out a little sloppy and slurred, but he made up for it with enthusiasm. "So I won't blame the chumpesinos for being who they are. But that doesn't mean I have to tell them what they've got, right?"

Snorts and guffaws at that. The guilty group laugh of a privileged high school gang. Tania wondered if any of them would have jobs after she figured out how to get her files out there.

Behind the Californian was a dog-eared motivational poster pinned to the wall near the jukebox. This one had the President walking in the mountains with his dogs, hand pointing toward the horizon.

THE POWER OF THE LEADER
Real leaders don't fight to be first, but are first to fight, and are first to risk the ultimate sacrifice to win.

The Californian held up an instructional hand.

"They think they have the deal of a lifetime," he said. "It helps that the mayor of the little town is also the notary I'm using to paper the deal—with a nice little piece of the action thrown in for good measure. We close in the morning for less cash than I spent on my MBA. Then I turn around and call Philly and tell them what I've got."

He puckered his lips.

"Those pencil-necked lab rats will have their bankers wiring me more money than the Colonel has stashed in the Wexbank Tower!"

The Californian turned suddenly, an annoyed look on his face. A figure stood behind him, tapping on his shoulder. A young guy, long black hair, sinewy arms stretching out of a weathered black T-shirt. He looked out of place in this crowd—scruffy, weird, and unwashed, almost like a homeless guy.

Since the night she downloaded the files, it was almost like Tania had forgotten.

"I thought they captured the Colonel a year ago," said the man, in familiar northern vowels. "Burned her out of her refuge on the oil rig and buried her at sea."

He looked so different. Not as big as she expected, even on the short side, but somehow looked bigger. Maybe it was the way the light revealed fine scars on his face and forearm. Tania tried to imagine.

"You believe that propaganda?" said the Californian, playing the gathering crowd. "Anybody with half a clue knows the corpse they showed on TV was someone else. Like, the face was burned off? How convenient. The Colonel is a survivor. You don't carve out a major American city, however trashed, and turn it into an independent republic or people's state or whatever without being a seriously formidable negotiator. Maybe you didn't get the memo, dude, but trust me. The Colonel cut some deal. She's chilling right now, right over here in the heart of Echo Sector, in her secret bachelorette pad inside the old Wexbank Building, with all her favorite stuff and enough money to buy another sweet little fiefdom to run."

Tania looked at Sig. She wanted to call out his name. She held back. He looked drunk. She would get him outside, alone, when no one was watching.

"If everybody knows it," said Sig, "why hasn't somebody ratted her out to the Authority? Send in the people hunters and collect the bounty that's still posted. I didn't think masters of the universe like you guys let revolutionaries walk freely through the heart of your cities."

The Californian's eyes popped with astonishment, before his mouth opened with a roar of laughter and his companions joined in.

"Listen to this fucking Canadian mullet! He's going to capture the lady even the government couldn't kill. You watch too many movies, dude."

"I'm from Minnesota."

"Well, listen to me, Minne*sota*," said the Californian, stabbing the air with a confident finger, "here in post-Purge New Orleans, there are more dangerous, competitive, savvy motherfuckers hanging out than you can imagine. If there were a way to extract the Colonel from her hideout, or steal her treasure, it would have happened a long fucking time ago. Her refuge is in the middle of the contaminated heart of the ruins, for fuck's sake, where the toxic residues are so bad they have to scrub the land drones when they come out. Just 'cause it's a bank building doesn't mean you can just like check in with the lady up front."

Chuckles from around the table.

"If you got through the front door you'd have to navigate a maze of booby traps and armed enforcers. And if you got through that you'd have to deal with the meanest bitch in the Western Hemisphere. Redneck juvie hardcase with twenty years in the SEA Eagles before she got stationed back here and went rogue. She'd probably cut you into pieces and feed you to her pets."

Sig scowled. "Tall tales. I've seen the building you're talking about. The only guards are water rats."

"Listen to this guy!" shouted the Californian, hands raised like he was summoning the gods of the Pacific surf. "Maybe he's one of those freaks helping Newton Towns, master of kung fu, doing his cinematic portrait of the President as a pose-able action hero. Come on, dude, show us the flying round-house you used to fight off the North Korean ninja guards!"

Tania chuckled at that one. Sig looked at the Californian with a gaze Tania didn't recognize, while the Californian soaked up the reactions of his buddies and the other patrons who had leaned in on the debate.

"Come on, dude!" shouted the Californian. "Tell us how you're going to steal the Colonel from the fortified penthouse of her private skyscraper!"

The lights dimmed for a moment, then tried to come back up. Brownout wheeze of a wounded city.

"Maybe it takes skills they don't teach in business school," said Sig.

"Fuck you!" shouted the Californian, knocking his chair to the floor as he stood. He had the physique of a class A gym rat, and his suit was cut to show it.

Tania checked her sidearm.

"You think we don't know how to eat what we kill?" said the Californian, roostering. "We own the world, fuckface!"

Sig turned to leave.

"That's right!" mocked the Californian, pushing Sig from behind and brandishing a small pistol. "Get out of my bar!"

The lights flickered again, then disappeared completely.

Tania ducked, readied her pistol, and crouched under the edge of the bar.

She saw shadows collide, and heard the sounds of breaking glass, rips, kicks, punches, screams, grunts, expletives, cracks, and four gunshots. When the lights came back on, the center of the room was cleared except for the body of the Californian, a broken bottle of Falstaff jammed into his neck, blood pooling on the floor underneath him.

Sig was nowhere to be seen.

Tania ran for the door, and finally called out his name.

If he heard, he didn't stop.

87

SIG WOKE UP THE NEXT MORNING IN THE MUD, BY THE WATER. THE empty bottle of Kentucky Hunters that was not empty when he left the bar told him why it was he couldn't remember how he ended up here.

He looked up. He was on the banks of the Industrial Canal, close to where it meets the Mississippi. There was an old bridge that once crossed the canal but now just dropped off the first trestle into the water, a rusting ruin covered in graffiti. It was when he looked at the bridge, and the other bank it used to reach, that he realized he was on the wrong side.

A little jolt of adrenaline shocked him into alert. This was the contaminated zone. Echo Sector. Too toxic for humans or animals.

He cursed the bottle for his not knowing whether he'd been dumped here by yahoos or walked over under his own drunken power.

He sniffed the air. He looked around. He looked at the water. The mud around him was full of the tracks of raccoons that had come down to the water at night. Three egrets and a big heron worked a shallow patch around the old bridge pilings.

Behind him was a garden of rebar. The cab of a fifty-year-old pickup sunk into the soil and aimed at the sky. A beat-up old warning sign whose letters were mostly chipped off or obscured by mold.

DANGER
Biohazard Quarantine Zone
Keep Out

Beyond that, weeds and volunteer trees as far as you could see, interrupted only occasionally with the profile of an old building.

He wondered if there was anything more toxic around there than what he'd drunk out of the bottle. The plants looked like they were thriving.

Sig felt the headache come on pretty strong as he stood up. He also felt the emptiness in his stomach.

He looked at the canal. He thought about the season. He walked down to the bridge, took off his boots and T-shirt, stepped into the water, and started to look for holes.

88

TANIA SAW A GLIMPSE OF SIG OUTSIDE THE BAR AFTER THE FIGHT but lost his trail quickly as he disappeared through the maze of identical metal boxes along the wharf. It was only after she had given up, walking along the river an hour later, that she heard him singing, some awful weird ballad about guys dying on a Canadian lake or something.

She couldn't see him. She called his name, three times, which was two times more than was probably safe. He kept singing. She could hear he was moving. She followed the sound, down the riverbank, then up along the canal.

When she finally spotted him, he was across the canal, in the western edge of Echo Sector.

She could see the path. Past the warning sign through a gap in the chain link, then down into the drained concrete bottom above the watergate and back up onto the other side.

She called again. He looked, but in the wrong direction, then stumbled out of view.

She looked at the warnings of death, disfigurement, and genetic damage that marked the entrance to the forbidden zone. The signs were old, battered, and effective. She thought about the files she carried in the thumb drive she could feel still hanging from her neck. She turned around, back the way they came.

It was twenty minutes before, remembering all the things she had done and risked and given up to find him, that she decided to turn around again. Maybe he could help her.

She waited until daybreak, then followed his path through the same well-used hole in the fence.

Looking out across the unclaimed scar on the other side, she saw no path at all. Tall grass grown over old concrete. The shells of a few buildings here and there. Like one of the ghost cities you could still find in parts of the Tropic.

One building stood out at the eastern edge of the zone, backlit by the morning sun. It was a stubby high-rise, maybe fifteen stories sticking up out of the ruins. An old office building, late twentieth century. A brutalist concrete fortification that would probably still be standing after the next apocalypse.

There was no sign on the building, but she knew what it would have said if there were. Wexbank Tower.

She walked to the closest building. It looked like an old storefront—two-story brick with one side completely blown out. The original interior stairs were gone, but someone had left a wooden ladder you could get up despite the two missing rungs.

From that vantage, she could see the ruin sprawled for at least twenty blocks. She looked around, until she saw movement inside one of the relics. An old church, with its steeple only partly severed. The motion was slow smoke from a fire inside.

Then he stepped into view. Eating. Corn on the cob, it looked like, from the way he was holding it, until he took a big bite and she realized it was a whole fish. With whiskers.

89

SIG DREW LINES ON HIS FACE WITH ONE OF THE COOL CHARCOALS from the edge of his fire. He had that feeling of machine surveillance, and a long open field to cross. The pattern was equal parts digital raccoon and pixel-hacking war paint. Xelina told him you could frustrate the facial recognition that way, a temporary version of the tattoos some guys got. "Neoprimitive augment," she called it. "Improvise. Keep it irregular."

He found a ratty old brown blanket left behind by someone who had camped in the shelter of the church.

He stood in the doorway and looked east at the tower. If it really was true that the Colonel was there, then she might be able to help him and his friends. He wanted to get them out of jail. Then he would deal with Walker.

He stepped out and into a crouch under the blanket, morphing into a blob that moved out of pattern through the vegetation grown up between the expanses of old paving stones and foundation remnants. A few doves flushed out as the man-thing interrupted their feeding in the tall grass.

The ground was littered with mismatched detritus. Broken glass, bits of electrical cable, shards of brick, parts of old signs, shreds of paper, a shoe, a ball, the teeth of an animal. The glistening brass of spent rifle cartridges that might have been there an hour, or a decade.

The sun burned away at the flat green paint of a marooned old military tank. The gun barrel was broken off, the head covered with a hundred spray-painted eyes.

Fast shadows glided over the ground just ahead. Sig pulled back the blanket and looked up. A trio of turkey vultures, riding the thermals.

It was already hot, and never stopped being muggy. He dripped sweat under the wool, soaking through his clothes.

In the shadowed interior of an old office building, Sig saw the silhouettes of four people standing around the flame burning in the base of an old oil drum. A wary, wily street dog lurked outside.

The sounds of the city seemed banished.

Sig clambered up the remains of a demolished building across from the tower, grabbing a spot on the roofless second floor where he could study the tower from behind the frame of an old window.

The tower rose up out of dense scrub trees, brambles, and bushes. You could see bits of a rusting old fence, sidewalk fragments, and crumbled roadbed. There was no sign of gate or guard.

A few yellow songbirds pecked around on the ground under one of the trees, foraging in the gravel and grass. A big tomcat leapt out through the bars of the fence, pounced on one of the birds, and snuck back into its weedy little jungle.

Sig's eyes followed the long concrete spines that ran up the sides of the building, worn from weather and the collateral damage of warfare. Sunlight shimmered off the glass of the tower, revealing cavities where the windows were knocked out. Sig thought he could see a figure looking out through one of the tall windows on the top floor, but then it was gone.

That's when he saw the lady walking up, out in the open where she was sure to be seen by the vehicles he heard coming from the north.

90

TANIA WATCHED SIG WALK OUT OF THE CHURCH AND DISAPPEAR right in front of her eyes. He ducked into the grass like a wild dog. Every time she thought she saw him, it was just the wind.

She climbed down and tried to follow his path. She walked, out in the open, anxious at being exposed to eyes in the sky and who knows what else. Or maybe they didn't bother watching an area that had been emptied of people for a generation.

She remembered the story, sort of. Something about a barge with toxic cargo. Tropical disease, strain unknown, carried in the trash. An accident. Thousands dead. Unsafe for fifty years. Quarantine.

Then the deluge. Deluges.

A smaller city they would have just cleared out the whole town, but this place was too important, especially after Maxximol really took off. Oil and human performance stimulants. Food for the machines and fuel for the workers. Draw a hundred-mile circle around the city and you could really see its economic necessity to the Zeitgeist. The military-industrial orifice through which they extracted what was left of the Tropic of Kansas and staged their way south looking for fresh meat.

She looked out over the ruined landscape. Maybe the end of the world already happened and nobody noticed.

Tania freaked when a shadow rushed over her, but then realized it was just a passing cloud.

She walked down what had once been a street. There was no sign of Sig, so she headed for the tower, where she was sure he was headed.

She saw an old billboard off to the left. The face of an elegant woman with a retro blond haircut and a long white cigarette gazed through the peeled-back remains of a vintage Pepsi logo, watching over the empty quarter.

Tania stopped for a moment in the stillness. She looked up at the tower, only half a block away now.

She heard gunfire. Close.

She looked north, down the overgrown old boulevard, toward the source of the noise.

A battered little white Toyota pickup hauled ass down the roadbed. A screaming guy in a red ball cap manned a machine gun mounted in the bed. The driver was screaming, too, spitting through a thick black mustache, while the front seat passenger leaned out of the doorless cab with a stolen M4 in her arms, aiming as best she could between the suspension-busting bounces.

Tania hid behind a crumbling wall nearby, peering around the corner to watch.

They fired at the armored jeep that chased them. The jeep had no driver or windshield—just gun barrels and the painted nodes of eyeless avionics. It looked like one of the aftermarket land drones the Mexican custom riggers put together, usually on old VW suspensions. What body there was had the color of primer and scorch, with a morale slogan stenciled in red and black caps across the battered hood:

En Este Futuro, Hay Reglas

"In this future, there are rules."

The insurgents pounded the unmanned interceptor with armor rounds, but that did not deter. She could hear the ricochets bouncing off the armor, and the hot thunks as the guns of the drone tore up the fuselage of the old truck.

Tania drew her pistol.

She heard the insurgents yelling. They veered left, accelerated over the grassy curb, and drove head-on into the wall she hid behind, launching the gunner from the bed and the passenger through what was left of the front windshield.

Tania crawled into the grass, got on her stomach, and fired at the robot. She wasn't trained for this.

Her bullets bounced off the armor. She wondered if it could image her in the grass. Of course it could. She knew— she'd looked through these things from the other side. Your best hope was that the server would process your face as a Do-Not-Kill.

The drone pulled up to the side of the demolished truck and stopped. Machine rotors whined and snapped as they turned and adjusted. The ejected gunner tried to crawl through the grass toward Tania. The jeep shot him with five evenly timed single taps, until he stopped moving.

Tania stood, angered, unloading her clip on the murder machine, trying to find a weak spot.

BANG.

Sig appeared from above, jumped onto the back of the truck, a big chunk of concrete debris in his hands.

BANG BANG *CRUNCH*.

Sig tried to crack the armor open.

The drone bathed the truck and the other two occupants in automatic bursts. Flames flickered up from the engine block.

The drone swiveled its main turret toward Tania.

Her cartridge was empty.

She dove again, behind the wall, crawled, and ran for the dense foliage at the base of the tower.

91

THE BRICK WAS NOT A VERY EFFECTIVE WEAPON AGAINST THE AR-
mor of the drone. There wasn't even a good handhold on the
streamlined hull. Sig pounded against the black glass eyelid.
Not even a crack. The guns swiveled, turning their attention
from the woman to him.

Sig glimpsed the woman running for cover. She was
black—that's all that registered. He rolled off the jeep, evading
the cannon fire that tore up the wall on which he had been
perched moments before.

The jeep shredded the wall, trying to shred Sig.

He dove into the dirt.

When he looked up, the drone was close enough to punch.

92

HEART POUNDING, TANIA RAN FOR COVER WHERE SHE COULD RE-load and help Sig.

She could hear her own heaving breaths between the machine fire of the drone.

She stepped over the broken curb and onto the dirt. Saw the old concrete barriers.

It was like slow motion. The third step . . . and then the ground wasn't there. Or it was, but it gave like thin paper.

She fell, into darkness.

She hit the bottom hard.

93

AS THE JEEP LURCHED TOWARD HIM, SIG ROLLED UNDER THE ELE-vated suspension. There were no guns underneath, nor any easier handholds. It was armored for ground ordnance and rough terrain. But there was a hatch. An access port that popped open with the back of his knife and a strong hand.

The robot was a lot easier to kill from the inside out.

Sig climbed up into the empty cockpit, ripping and cutting, tearing wires, panels, and plumbing, until the life seemed to have drained out of the machine. He punched his way through the main eye, reeking of gasoline and burnt silicon.

The rebel pickup was still burning.

He read the slogan on the front of the drone again while he caught his breath. He wondered what it meant.

He looked at the scorched bodies of the fighters.

He turned to the tower. What radiated danger an hour earlier now looked like sanctuary.

94

TANIA SAT UP, WINDED AND BROKEN.

She looked up at the light. The hole was big enough for a car.

She had fallen on concrete. Maybe fifteen feet. She could feel the smack all along her right side.

She looked for her gun. She saw a dimly lit tunnel. A hallway.

There was a man standing there, in an apron and a gas mask.

He was holding her gun.

95

THE TOWER HAD NO LOCKS. THE SPACES FOR DOORS WERE FILLED with the dense invasive vegetation that had moved in from the courtyard. The barbed vines and weedy shrubs thrived in these conditions of young ruin.

Sig worked his way through the bramble, past the remains of a Chevy Impala with waxy grasses shoving up out of the engine block. The tarnished brass skeleton of an old revolving door moved just enough to open a slit he could squeeze through into the dark cavern of the old lobby.

The weed jungle continued inside until it came to a big pile of debris. Sig clambered up the side, above the volunteer shrub line, into the ambient light of a gigantic cave made by collaboration between man and natural disaster.

The tower had no interior floors. He stood on what remained—big chunks of concrete and twisted rebar. From the ruins, new structures had been built up inside the super-structure. Honeycombs of scaffolding and found materials rose up out of the vegetation along the interior, all the way to the roof in some spots. It looked almost organic, as if the whole thing had grown from the ruins of the old city on the fertilizer of a sick future. At the top, the improvised edifice spread back toward the center, clamped on to the ceiling. At the very center, a big fan blade spun in an aperture open to the sky, chopping the long shaft of hot sun that flickered on Sig's scratched-up face.

Looking back, he could see how the vegetation thickened in lush green clumps where the water and light came down. And the idea grabbed him that this is what the future looks like. All the wild green things that survive our big binge will move in to tear down what we leave behind after we're gone, and in a generation the concrete and steel will be covered in new life.

Scanning the scaffold spans for routes of ascent, Sig could see what the augments were made of. Pieces of chain link, timbers from old buildings, netting, pallets, ornate woodwork from demolished homes, painted metal signs, cardboard boxes, pipes, stained glass from some forgotten church, giant sheets of technical fabric, rusty cables. Sig wondered who the builders were, and where they were now.

A quartet of foraging feral parakeets skreeted in a nearby treetop, then flew past Sig, finding their way through the scaffolding to a broken window and the open air beyond.

In front of the broken window, Sig saw the woman he had saved. It looked like she was working her way up to the top of the tower, limping.

Then, for the first time, he saw her face. And realized it was a face he had seen before.

He tried to remember her name. It started with a T. He knew her so well once. She was his babysitter. He had a lot of babysitters, until he had none.

Then he saw the people behind her, with guns, pushing her. It came to him.

Tania.

96

"KEEP WALKING," SAID THE MAN. "DON'T LOOK BACK."

Maybe because, as she could hear, he had taken the gas mask off.

He prodded her up an old cast concrete staircase they had somehow lifted six stories up.

Her ankle was twisted and her elbow banged up from her fall, but she could walk. She didn't know if he had reloaded the pistol, but she wasn't ready to find out.

They pushed her through rooms filled with signs of human habitation—bedding, clothing, water bottles, cooking equipment, cans of food.

They crossed a metal deck with no railing. The floor was a battered old sign with a smiling minstrel figure.

"Stop," said the man.

Tania tried to look over her shoulder.

"Hey," said the man.

Too late. She saw him holding his phone, showing something to the other figure she had sensed. A woman.

Tania looked down onto the carpet of thick green weeds six floors below, all gathered up like hungry supplicants in the space where the light and water landed from the aperture in the roof, and wondered if they would catch her if she jumped.

She looked to the right, through a broken window from the original construction. A view to the east—temporary housing, maybe barracks. Beyond that the sprawling refineries, depots, and tank farms, where the pipelines ran out to sea and north

to the cold country. There were a few shiny new office buildings in the foreground, part of the new tax-free zone they were
trying to build in the ruins of Chalmette, launching point for
the next leg of the PanAmerican Data Pipeline.

They pushed her on, through a door plastered with the
campaign poster of a dead politician, then another door inlaid with hand-carved images of swamp birds swimming in
curlicued air, into a room walled with a mosaic of recycled
bits of wood and plastic. There was a cot, and a radio on at low
volume, playing a broadcast from Nicaragua that came in and
out of signal.

The next door was metal. With a lock. Her captors held
her while one of them used the key to open it.

She heard other voices inside, as her nose filled with the
smell of chemicals.

97

SIG LIKED TO CLIMB. CLIMBING HAD SAVED HIS LIFE. DURING HIS years outside in the north, he had learned from animals how useful climbing could be—to be able to sleep in a safe place, see predator or prey from the bird's eye, or reach sources of food for which there was little competition. It was also fun. He had climbed mountains and power line towers, churches and malls, cliffs and dams, sandy embankments and crumbling glaciers. Once, in North Dakota, he had climbed a radio antenna so tall that you almost thought you could see the top of the world.

He tried to track Tania, but there was no sign, and he kept getting lost in the maze. So he thought the better idea would be to beat them to wherever they were taking her. Which he guessed, from what he saw and heard, was the top.

He found a spot where the window glass was mostly gone, hung his sneakers from his back belt loop by tying the laces together, and stepped out into the clear air ten stories up.

It was not an easy climb. The face of the building was completely vertical. But the concrete superstructure was speckled with chips worn in by weather and war, and it was only ten feet between the horizontal forms. He rested when he had the chance to step through another broken window. As the sun reached early afternoon in a sky interrupted with only a few scattered puffy clouds, he finally climbed over the top onto the roof of the building.

The roof was covered in solar panels. Sig navigated through the spaces between the panels to the center, where he found the big fan he had seen from the lobby. He looked down the shaft and saw the green of the foliage and the gray of the rubble.

On the other side of the fan someone had hauled barrels of dirt all the way up here to make a raised bed. The garden grew long rows of leafy greens. One end had a small patch of unmowed grass, with two cheap plastic chairs and a small cooler on which someone had left a book. Nearby stood a rain barrel with three hoses running from the base, and a small compost pile.

On the other side of the barrel was a hatch. It was open, with a ship's ladder leading down into the interior.

Sig put his shoes back on, took out his knife, and descended.

He came into a quiet apartment filled with the indirect light of northern exposure. The floors were covered in carpet remnants laid over flimsy floors that gave a little bit with every step. There were signs of people, but their smells were masked by incense and candles.

The apartment was open along the length of the north wall. A couple of the windows had been ventilated with small screens cut into the top. The opposite wall was a patchwork of mismatched pieces of painted and unpainted wood, plastic, and plaster. There were five doors built into the wall. A small plastic sign hung from the door on the right.

NO MOLESTAR
Hôtel Colon
Managua

In the center of the wall was a kitchenette made of found objects. The counter was a piece of green freeway sign on slats of lumber atop cinder-block stacks. A hose with a trigger spigot dangled from the ceiling over a metal basin cut into the table. A mini fridge hummed on the floor, plugged into a long orange extension cord. To the left of the counter was a big propane camp stove. There were wooden bowls of fresh fruits and vegetables, stacks of canned goods, pots and pans, a coffee can full of knives and utensils, and thick candles, some in glass cases with skeletons and saints.

Two of the candles were lit.

A machete leaned up against the wall. The handle was hand-carved. Colored leather fringes and feathers dangled from the hilt.

In front of the kitchen was another table made from a pair of inlaid wooden doors. One door had the image of the sun in the form of a beardless masculine face. The other had the face of the moon as a goddess. There was a teapot on the table, cold to the touch, and an empty but recently used clay cup. Loose papers were spread across the table, held down with small toys and plastic dice in bright colors and unusual shapes. In the center was a map drawn in pencil on a big sheet of graph paper. The map looked like part of the United States, detailed with drawings of castles, rivers, mountains, forests, and roads. A thick hardbound book held down one side of the map.

WIZARDS OF THE CATACOMBS
The Creature Compendium

There were plastic soldiers and tanks on the map, tiny figures from gumball machines. Sig picked up one of the figurines—a painted tin rider. The rider was a woman with long yellow braids and a jeweled golden headband, wearing a steel bikini and a flowing white cape, riding on the back of a wooly mammoth with huge tusks and an armored helm. The rider held the reins of the mammoth in one hand and held a sword over the head with the other, as if preparing to lead a charge.

The sword was bent. Sig straightened it.

There were chairs at the table, around the room, and along the windows. Boxes and crates served as footstools and coffee tables. More than anything there were books—stacked against the wall, piled on the floor, shelved inside the crates.

An automatic pistol lay on top of the stacks of books. Sig removed the clip and pocketed it.

He found a door ajar on the other side of the apartment. It was a big room, dark, illuminated only by the green diodes of a rack of stereo equipment stacked on a small table near the door. An incense cone burned in a small metal dish atop the stereo. The unit was an old tape player like Sig's mom had, but with a small microphone attached. Tapes were stacked up all over the table in their plastic cases. Some were factory-labeled recordings of music Sig recognized. Old bands his great-uncles listened to like Crimson Lloyd, Alfred & Sibyl, Electric Hephaestus. But most of them were homemade, labeled in old-lady script.

5/3—Network as Polity
11/1—The General in the Mall
3/2—Crossing the Concrete Hellespont
7/4—How to Arm an Infobomb

There was a magazine photograph that had been cut out and taped to the wall. It showed a woman in a suit coat standing before a gigantic crowd, one hand gripping the podium while the other stretched out at the end of a strong arm in an oratorical gesture, with a skyscraper-sized obelisk behind her.

As his eyes adjusted, Sig looked into the darkness and saw a figure recumbent in the shadows. He could hear the slow breathing. It was a woman, curled up under layers of blankets on a daybed at the very back of the room. Her face was badly scarred. In the dim light, the flesh looked almost like a putty you could mold, the nose a bulbous, misshapen mess.

The woman rumbled from deep within, then exhaled with an impatient, growling plea.

98

HER CAPTORS WORE PURPLE BERETS. OR AT LEAST THE THREE
young ones did. The older black woman didn't look like she
needed a uniform for anyone to know who she was.

Bywater Masques. In the early days of the fighting, the
news reports used to show them in actual masks, but Tania
always figured that was some kind of psyop. By which side,
she didn't know.

Everything else they wore was improvised. The Creole boy
had brown Carhartt bibs over a worn button-down, the shells
for his long-barreled .308 shining from his front pockets. The
dirty-blond white girl had faded indigo jeans, a green T-shirt,
and a pair of mismatched pistols holstered in two separate
belts slung low. The burly Asian girl had a purple ball cap for
her beret, a lightweight gray technical jacket, and cutoff cargo
pants that told the story of her war in tattoos that covered
most of her legs above her tropical boots. And a shop-built
twelve-gauge aimed at Tania's head.

"What are you doing here?" said the black woman. She
had tight salt-and-pepper hair, a black T-shirt, black dungarees fading to gray, and scuffed black boots. No gun. A lot of
red in her eyes. Tania noticed the ring on her right hand, a big
black onyx set in gold.

"Trying to make a deal. And looking for someone."

The room smelled like a photo lab. A gas-powered generator vibrated loudly in the corner. There were other machines,
big white boxes with blinking lights, some with electrical

motors running. Buckets, reams of paper, cardboard boxes stacked on top of each other. Each box was stamped with the image of a black pineapple crossed with a hand grenade.

"What is this place?" asked Tania.

"It's a freedom factory," said the blonde. "Your trespassing interrupted our work."

"Don't you know it's not safe here?" said the Creole boy.

"The pigeons don't seem to mind," said Tania.

"They're immune," said the boy.

"You people lie," said Tania. "Just like your comrades."

She saw the job coming off one of the printers. The front side of a stack of two-hundred-dollar bills. The ones the government had introduced the year before in the face of hyperinflation and an eroding dollar. They tried to make up for their intrinsic weakness with the taciturn face of President Haig, wearing the military commander in chief uniform he used for public appearances during his second term, after he crushed the Ayatollah and fought the Soviets into submission across three proxy fronts. Even across the room you could see how the six stars on his lapel stood out in the green and black etched ink.

"That's not for us," said the blonde, almost guiltily. "It's for people who really need it."

"Making care packages," said Tania. She could see the stacks of pamphlets, shrink-wrapped electronics, plastic jewel cases. "What's that thing making?" she said, pointing her head at the 3-D printer.

The Creole boy handed her a little plastic box.

"Check it out," he said.

The thing sprang open into branches like a broken umbrella. Right in her face.

"Fuck!" yelled Tania, throwing it back at the laughing kid.

While the berets harassed her, the lady was looking through Tania's bag.

"Which one of these identities are you wearing today?" she asked.

"My own," said Tania.

"You sure you know which one that is?"

"Yes," said Tania. "And maybe we're on the same side. Can I show you something?"

Tania lifted out the thumb drive.

"Keep talking," said the woman.

99

"I'm not Tony," said Sig.

The woman opened her eyes. Dark orbs reflected the green lights of the stereo.

"The uninvited guest," she said. "What a pleasant surprise. It's so rare that you come to visit."

She sat up and turned on a table lamp. The effort set her to a fit of coughing. She drank from a glass of water on the table next to the lamp and collected herself, observing Sig as she did so.

"I see you found the Mastodon Queen," she said, looking at Sig's hand.

Sig looked down. He was still holding the figure he had found in the main room. He looked at the tiny rider, and back at the woman.

"One of the few things that ended up in my bug-out bag the night I wiped the contents of my desk into the duffel and fled for exile," she said. "A souvenir of another time. Or maybe now it's just a dream."

"What is it?" asked Sig.

"Of course, you are too young. It's a miniature. Meant to represent a character in a role-playing game. In this case it's me. The persona I adopted over a series of long Saturdays in college, before you were born, aided by good tea, fertile young imaginations, and amazing California grass. We repurposed the game, made it our laboratory for the invention of new politics, new polities, new natures."

"I don't understand," said Sig.

"That's okay," she said. "It's really just a silly war game, if terribly fun. Very low footprint, you know, since it's basically all in your head. And you can use it to think through pretty much any scenario you want—and change the rules as you see fit. I've been teaching it to Toni, and she's been teaching me her own game theories, and helping me make up new rules. Thinking through scenarios for reversing our current situation. I have strategy, she has tactics."

Sig thought about what he saw in the other room. The map, with tanks and airplanes and armed mounted riders.

"We have such long days up here in our fortress of solitude for two, you see. We need to stay busy." Sig could see her eyes sizing him up. "Are you an assassin?" she asked. "You look like some kind of redneck ninja. And I mean that as a compliment. I wondered how long it would take them."

"I don't even know who you are," said Sig.

"You can call me Max," she said.

"You're not who I'm looking for," said Sig.

"You're looking for Toni," she said. "Of course. You are a bounty hunter. I never was very keen on westerns. The worst part of the American memescape. All about deluded loners fighting over chunks of land to isolate themselves from each other. Nothing about community building. Nothing about the land as part of the community. Just phallocentric dominion and lots of horns."

"You talk a lot," said Sig.

"What do you expect?" said Max. "I'm a politician, and before that I was a writer." She looked at Sig. "You really don't know, do you?"

Sig shook his head. He put down the miniature on the desk and picked up one of the homemade tapes.

"Amazing. We hear about these Americans who live in a news bubble, but I'd never actually met one."

"There are many worlds to see," said Sig. "Not just the babbling realms of politicians and professors. Ask the animals that live in your walls."

Max coughed out a chuckle. "I like you," she said. "How wonderful to talk with someone who never read one of my books, or saw one of my campaign ads. Though you missed some magnificent debates, the kind television culture rarely allows. Anomalous, really, that things got so bad, the pendulum swung so far, that a ticket like ours could come to power in our country. Of course, they didn't let it last long. Not even three years. We got too ambitious, and they took us out with a bloodless coup of invented scandal and misinformation."

Sig looked at the magazine photo taped to the wall. The speaker looked intense. She was also beautiful.

"That was after I was back in the loyal opposition," she said. "The jabbering politica formerly known as the presidential understudy. Suited me better than governing, truth told. Before the burns, at least."

Sig looked at Max's melted face. He saw that her hands were burned, too, many of the fingers mere stumps. He remembered the stories, about the bombing.

"I know who you are," said Sig.

"Oh, well," she said.

"Did you do it?"

She looked at Sig, through keen eyes.

"Of course I did it," she said. "After finally deciding it was the only way to secure a better future. But unfortunately I bungled it. Left him in power and me in this degraded state, when I meant to kill us both."

Sig watched her take in a long, labored breath.

"You can't give up," he said.

"You have no idea how long I have been fighting them, or at what cost," she answered.

"Where is the Colonel?" asked Sig.

"I'm surprised you didn't hear her snoring over there," said Max. "She works at night and sleeps most of the day. Speak of the devil."

Sig turned around.

A tall woman with brown skin and long gray hair stood in the doorway, wearing a green tank top and black gym shorts. A gold animal skull pendant hung from her neck. The fringed machete was in her right hand, over her head, about to cleave Sig.

100

TANIA SHOWED THEM THE KILL LIST ON HER PHONE. THE ENEMIES List, too.

They looked up the names of friends and colleagues. They kind of freaked out at all they found.

Dot started crying. That was the name the white girl went by. Her colleagues were Tommy and Bao. The lady in charge was Claude. A name Tania had come across before.

Bao told her to stop, that they knew what they were getting into when they signed up, that this just proved things they always suspected.

Claude told Tania this information needed to be free. Tania said that's what I'm trying to do. Claude said then what the hell are you doing in here. Tania explained. It kind of made sense, but she could see the WTF look on Claude's face.

Claude said we need to go upstairs.

Tania asked who's upstairs. Claude said come on. You, too, Bao.

Tommy gave Tania a copy of their manifesto, the one about how to build your own country. Tania said she'd already read it, but she didn't mention her counterarguments.

Can you imagine, said Tommy, eyes lit up like a little boy describing a new fort he is going to build.

Tania didn't want to say what she imagined.

101

SIG SIDESTEPPED THE MACHETE WITH ANIMAL INSTINCT.

But the Colonel had better training. Government training, the kind that makes it so you don't have to think.

She knocked his knife from his hand on the first move.

She fought like whatever you did, you were replaying some fight she had practiced a hundred times. She caught every punch, and when he landed one she could take it.

She grunted a lot.

The floor bounced under their feet, like they might bust right through it.

And within a minute she had Sig on the ground. Her pin wasn't that strong, but she had the point of the machete poking right up under the soft tissue under his jaw, ready to shove.

He was evaluating whether to try to wiggle out of it when the look came over her face.

"I know this guy," she said, not releasing him. "He's all over Channel 13. And now all over the real news. A fugitive."

Sig felt like a free animal must feel when it's caught, alive.

"One of ours?" asked Max.

"No, not a Masque," said the Colonel. "Not even a political, really. Part of that gang. Does it for money."

"Oh, right," said Max. "The bandits. Social bandits, right? Local heroes? Give the money to the people et cetera?"

"Maybe some of it," said the Colonel.

Sig tried to nod but the machete point broke the skin when he did.

"He's tied up with Walker," said the Colonel.

"Oh, I see," said Max. "Maybe we could get him on the right path."

"Or sell him to the Authority," said the Colonel. "He's a high-value fugitive. We could probably trade him for ten people in the Dome."

"Why don't we talk to him about it?" said Max.

"How did I know you would say that," muttered the Colonel. She twisted the hold a little tighter for punctuation, then released it, keeping the machete on him. "Sit up, outlaw. Sit on your hands."

Sig did as they said. He sat on the rug on the floor, Max sat up in her bed, and the Colonel sat in the chair, holding the pistol—now with the clip she had repossessed from Sig.

Then Tania walked in, with an old black lady and a tough short girl that made Sig think of old Kong.

102

"OH MY GOD," SAID TANIA. SHE KNEW WHO IT HAD TO BE. SHE HAD suspected it when Claude led them up here. But she had no idea.

"What are you staring at?" said the Colonel.

"Sorry," said Tania. "I used to idolize you. Both of you."

"Sorry to disappoint you," said the Colonel.

"You did that a long time ago," said Tania. "When you fucked it all up."

"Who is this bitch, Claude?" said the Colonel. "And why is she not hooded?"

"She's with me," said Sig.

"Who are you?" said Claude.

"Stray dog," said Max.

"Exactly," said Tania.

She looked at Sig. Those unfathomable eyes. Almost feral, except you could sometimes see the feeling.

"You have to see what she brought," said Claude.

Tania looked at the eyes of Maxine Price, which were the only part that looked the way she remembered.

"Show me," said Max.

"What's that smell?" said Bao.

Tania looked at Sig. He smelled it, too.

"Those motherfuckers," said the Colonel, moving toward the metal door behind her. "We had a deal."

Then Tania heard a click, and the floor exploded.

103

THE TRAPDOOR IN THE FAR CORNER BLEW INTO THE AIR WITH A single subterranean boom. The blast knocked them all down, except for Bao. Smoke filled the room.

The Colonel and Max crawled away.

"Safe room!" yelled the Colonel.

Two gunmetal eggs arced from the hole and clattered on the ground. They popped as they rolled, blasting the area with intense flashes of bright light.

Sig covered his eyes before the flash. He looked back up to see three black figures crawling up out of the hole. Men in combat coveralls, faces hidden behind gas masks, eyes looking down the red beams of laser targeting scopes.

SEA Eagles, coming at them, for kill or capture.

"Wall Walkers!" yelled Bao. She pumped the first one, shot to the neck. He fell back in the hole.

The other two had good firing positions, halfway out, arms on floor. They unloaded.

Sig and Bao dove behind furniture.

Everything shredded.

Tania was down. Claude was with her. She tossed Sig a pistol, then dragged Tania back to the safe room.

"Lock it!" yelled Bao.

Tommy and Dot were at the front door now, leaning around, pushing back the invaders.

Sig put a bullet in the side of the second guy's face. It was armored, but he buckled.

That was the last bullet in the gun. Sig tossed it.

Helicopter chop pierced through the noise and blast-muffled eardrums. Sig looked out the window. Saw nothing. So he ran up onto the roof.

A black-green twin-rotor Mohawk came around the corner of the building, same level as the apartment, cannons scanning, hunter-killer.

Sig jumped.

He hit hard, but with a good grip on the left skid, and was able to pull himself up before they saw him.

The chopper was full of fuel.

People would watch the films of the burning high-rise for years to come. Especially after they found out who lived there.

PART NINE
The Auteur Theory
of the Hostage Video

104

SIG WAS SITTING NAKED ON THE FLOOR OF HIS CELL WHEN HE heard the guard and another man approaching.

"Ten minutes, strict," said the guard. "I'm gonna lock you in there with your client so I hope you know what you're doing."

"Thanks, Sarge. Enjoy the care package—you boys deserve it!"

The guard opened the cell door and Sig watched as Ward Walker stepped through, wearing an "I hope you're happy to see me" smile.

"About time you got a haircut!" said Walker.

They had shaved his head before they hosed him down with chemicals. SOP.

Sig tripped Walker with an ankle lock. Walker fell hard— old man hard. Then Sig grabbed him with his left hand on Walker's right ear and his right hand around Walker's necktie, picked him up, and shoved him against the wall so hard it almost seemed like it would give.

"Hey!" grimaced Walker. "That's no way to treat your lawyer."

"Lawyers don't lie as much as you," said Sig.

"It worked to get me in here to see you," said Walker. "That and some well-placed bribes of cash and contraband."

"I should call them down here and rat you out and get you the special cell they're saving for you."

"I came here to help you," said Walker.

"Snake," said Sig. "They call me a thief, but I don't steal other people's liberty. I should crack your windpipe. Spare others the tricks that sneak through your lips."

"What are you talking about, swamp thing?" said Walker, pushing back. "Capitalism is not a crime. And if it weren't for me nobody would know what a star you are. I'm here to get you out of confinement again. I even talked to your actual lawyer."

"I don't have a lawyer," said Sig, releasing Walker.

"That's not what he says," said Walker, straightening his glasses. "Donny Kimoe. Moco made the connection. Great guy. I use him, too—go figure."

"Okay," said Sig. "What did he say?"

"Not much good yet, unfortunately," said Walker. "But he has a conference call with the judge tomorrow morning to see if he can get bail set. And if he does, I'll help pay for it."

"You'll pay all of it, with the blood money."

"Look, it's not like you think."

Sig scratched himself. Walker lit a Churchill from the crumpled pack in his jacket pocket.

"Do you suppose if I ask where they put your clothes, that guy screaming down the hall will answer?"

"They burned," said Sig.

"Yeah, that was pretty intense," said Walker. "I could see the fires from the station. Wish Xelina had been there with her camera."

"Where is she?"

"They haven't come back from Houston," said Walker. "Might not at all. You're all I've got left. Moco's still all freaked about those poor goddamn kids, and the Masques have cut me from the pack. Say I'm a parasite on the body of the people."

"They're right," said Sig.

"I absolutely give more than I take, financially and in-kind," said Walker.

Sig grumbled. He thought about the dead kids. He thought about who was most at fault.

Walker took a long drag on his cigarette. He acted cocky but looked almost as yellow as the lenses of his glasses. And if you looked through the lenses at his eyes you could glimpse the real story.

"Look," said Walker. "I know how you feel. But we're all on the same side, and we're getting our asses kicked. I want to turn that around. I want to live in a free country again. We need a goddamn reboot."

Sig took the cigarette from Walker and listened.

Walker pulled out the black antenna tablet he called his office. "Recognize this guy?"

The screen showed photos of Newton Towns. Flashing his porcelain canines in a headshot, playing the President on TV, and touring New Orleans with paramilitaries the day before.

"This fucking guy has seriously lost the ability to distin-guish between Hollywood spectacle and dark American real-ity," said Walker. "He's driving around with these loco yahoos rounding up 'bad actors.' In the Ninth Ward. With a camera crew following him around. You see where I'm going?"

Sig looked at Walker. Watched his eyes, and hands, and wondered what his real agenda was. Someone had something on him and he was trying to turn the tables. Or maybe he just saw an opportunity to create a transaction that would replen-ish his coffers.

"But that's not what I really came to talk to you about. Here's my problem. The goddamn Masques have evicted me from my own house. They took over the station. Said it's an es-sential resource of the people or some bullshit like that. It's an essential asset on my personal balance sheet is what it is. And I thought the current regime was bad about respecting property rights. Now I'm getting it from both ends! It sucks! You gotta help me take it back. They can still have their channel."

Sig grumbled.

"I'll cut you in," said Walker. "Equity stake. Like maybe five percent."

Sig smiled.

"Seriously, you have no idea. This thing is really just getting going and there's a nice hockey stick coming. The eyeballs are growing exponentially. Viral. The content's all *free*. We make money off advertising, DVDs, snowflake transaction fees, product placement. And now that the shit's starting to fly, look out. There is no one better positioned to make money off this revolution than yours fucking truly."

"Except that you don't have a station," said Sig.

"Exactly," said Walker. "I knew I could count on you."

"Look—" grumbled Sig.

They heard the guard coming.

"Tomorrow," said Walker. "I believe in Donny Kimoe. Say that to yourself when you're going to sleep tonight. And when you get out, you know what to do."

Sig wasn't so sure.

105

TANIA WOKE UP IN A SUNNY ROOM. AN OLD ROOM. LIKE GRAND-
ma's house, except it smelled more like a hospital. There was a
picture of flowers on the wall.

She was in a bed, with heavy blankets over her legs. Something else was wrapped around her legs, something wet, and
they kind of hurt. There was a tube in her arm.

Through the window, she had a view of a tall broadcast
antenna. All metal, painted red and white in sections, with big
boxes and dishes clustered toward the top. There must have
been forty vultures perched up there, watching over the city,
already satiated from the day before but ready to go out for
more.

The morning light was clean. Her legs burned, but her
mind was clarified.

"Hello?" she said.

"Hey, sweetie," said a voice to her side, a familiar voice.

She felt a hand on her arm and turned to see if it was real.

Mom was sitting there, right next to her. Tania sat up and
reached.

"Lie back down now," said Mom, hand on her shoulder.
"You need to rest."

"How did you get here?" said Tania.

"You got me here," she answered. "Those friends of yours
from Iowa. They got me out of Boschwitz House, me and
two other detainees, and drove us all the way here, two days
straight."

"My friends? But I thought—"

"They said they tried to reach you after your story checked out, but they didn't know how. Said we all needed to get to New Orleans to get ready for the big day."

Tania lost it as the feelings started to pour out. She grabbed Mom's hand and pulled it close, laughing through the tears at the bright purple nail polish Mom was wearing. Mom leaned in over the IV tubes and hugged her tight for a long time.

A few minutes later another woman came in to check on Tania. She dressed more like a biker than a doctor, but said she was the medic. She smiled at the reunion.

"How's she doing?" said the medic.

"She's amazing," said Mom. "But she may want to stick with long pants in the future."

Mom pulled back her covers, and Tania saw the scars herself as the medic changed her dressing. She thought about making a liposuction joke, but didn't.

"We do field surgery here," said the medic. "Functional stuff. For plastics you have to travel. How's your pain?"

"Where am I?" said Tania.

"Bywater," said the nurse. "Inside the DMZ. They leave us alone here."

"Right," said Tania. "Part of the cease-fire."

"That's the deal," said the nurse. "But based on what happened to you, it sounds like the deal may be off."

Mom nodded, and looked worried.

"It's my fault," said Tania, seeing it with fresh clarity as she remembered where the scars came from. "They probably followed me all the way, right to the ones they really wanted."

"It's okay," said Mom, in the way parents lovingly lie.

"What happened to the others?" asked Tania.

"We don't know yet, sweetie," said Mom. "Still waiting for word."

CLAUDE SHOWED UP ABOUT FORTY-FIVE MINUTES LATER.

"You're doing all right," she said. "And you did right."

"Glad you think so," said Tania. "Because there's no going back."

"I know all about that," said Claude. "The only way out of this life is forward. To a renewed reality."

Tania looked at the flowers on the wall, and thought about the ruins outside.

"It doesn't seem possible," said Tania.

"It's inevitable," said Mom.

"It's just a matter of when," agreed Claude. "That's the way of these kinds of changes. You can wait for evolution to happen at its natural pace. Or you can help it along. And you definitely have given it a kick in the ass. We can't believe the trove you secreted out. It's exactly what we've needed to turn the situation around."

"Yeah?"

"Oh yeah. Andrei's already working it. Three editors he trusts. Paris, Berlin, Delhi. We're going to release it in digestible morsels. And make plenty of copies."

"Okay."

"I can't promise people will pay attention."

"It doesn't matter," said Tania. "They just need to know."

"And they will. It's so clarifying how things really stand between the President and the people. That ledger, those details, really shows the extent of the corruption. And when the main course is served, the Kill List—that's prosecutable stuff."

"I don't know," said Tania. "His judges have neutered the Constitution pretty good. You need prosecutors to prosecute someone."

"The people still make the law," said Claude. "In the final reckoning. Even if it has to be natural law."

"There's a reason they don't teach the Declaration of Independence in law school," said Tania. "Or make clear it doesn't count."

"Yeah, well, thankfully most people don't give a shit what they teach in law school," said Mom. "They just know what seems right and what seems wrong. What's fair."

"The people are crazy," said Tania. "Manipulated by political marketers into a rabid toddler mob that feeds the President and his oligarchs."

"That's true, too," said Claude. "But what if we implanted our own virus? Watch and see."

Tania looked out the window at the broadcast antenna.

"Is that—"

"Channel Zero."

"Yours?"

"*Ours*," said Claude. "That means you, too. And really ours, now. We just expropriated it."

"Good," said Tania. "Maybe you can cancel all the porn."

"Uh huh," said Mom.

"What happened to the kid?" asked Tania.

"Which kid?" said Claude.

"Sig."

Claude looked at Mom. When Mom nodded, with a sad face, Tania already knew.

106

SLEEPLESS, SIG WATCHED OUT HIS CAGE DOOR AND TRIED TO
parse the hundred disparate conversations that filled the huge
atrium of the enclosed stadium, muffled by rushing blasts of
forced air. It was always loud, and always light.

His cell was in the lower deck, where they had ripped out
whole sections of seats from the bleachers and replaced them
with temporary cells made from cubicle walls and chain link.
More cages were under construction on the upper decks. The
cells ringed the old arena, looking down on the unsegregated
detainees milling about the fenced-in AstroTurf pitch. A guard
tower had been erected on the fifty-yard line out of five shipping containers stacked on top of each other and wrapped in
scaffolding, creating a pedestal from which every single cell
could be visually monitored. The old scoreboard dangled over
the tower from the ceiling, its four Jumbotron panels screen-
ing reprogramming videos that really started to get into your
head when you had been awake for thirty-six hours.

Sig's stomach growled for his attention, just as one of the
guards showed up with a bag of takeout and another bag con-
taining's Sig's new clothes. Walker had kept one of his promises.

"It's your lucky night, big boy," said the guard, sliding the
bags through. "Extra spicy. Sorry I can't let you have the plastic cutlery, but I'm sure you understand."

After he dressed, Sig devoured the fried chicken, until
there was nothing left but bone.

That was about the time the nightly horror show started.

It started with a siren peal, then a strobe, then a series of booms. The jailers had figured out how to use the full array of light and sound equipment left behind by the previous management. A postapocalyptic halftime show.

The noise from the speakers sounded like Sig imagined a big earthquake would be. It shook the cages.

There was music that sounded like power tools grinding on sheet metal, inside your head.

There were more videos on the Jumbotron, designed to more aggressively demoralize. Live feeds.

Of interrogations in progress in other parts of the building. Of a grown man, naked, shackled in a back-bending yoga pose, screaming on the floor. Of a man trying to evade a pair of guard dogs straining at their leashes to eat his face off.

A woman strapped to a metal chair in a dirty hospital gown, watching in horror as an unknown chemical is delivered by a syringe into the thickened veins of her arm.

A man shoved inside a three-foot by three-foot box, naked with a spider.

Close-up on the eye of a woman as she watches the torture of her son.

All the ways to break mind and body they had developed fighting people on the other side of the world, they now used on their own people, justifying it by saying their treason had forfeited their citizenship. Made them stateless aliens, without real rights.

Sig wondered about Donald Kimoe, Esq.

While the videos played, some of the prisoners were let out onto the fenced-in football field. Groups of jailers walked the rows of cells, with electric truncheons in their hands and rubber masks hiding their faces, selecting revelers for the floor show.

The Jumbotron showed more feeds. From the helmet cams of counterinsurgency squads purging Bywater. Blasting through a wall and into a living room, where a family were watching TV, shooting the father as he goes for his gun and separating the mother and children for processing. Going down the stairs into an old brick basement, LED headlamps illuminating the way through the metal door and into the vault where the fighters who are still alive writhe on the ground, maimed by the grenades that have just been detonated. Infrared eye of a remotely piloted interceptor as it inventories the faces seen entering a warehouse in an industrial neighborhood, then obliterates the western half of the building with an air-to-ground missile.

The camera eye lingered on the flames.

The guards got the parade under way on the floor. A halftime show of dehumanizing subjugation. Human caterpillars and man-dogs. Real dogs teaching primitive submission. Dances induced by localized delivery of electrical current.

The Jumbotron screened another atrocity exhibition—long, lingering shots of the collateral victims of war, superimposed titles crediting the insurgents for the maimed children and dead elders.

The guards came Sig's way, telegraphing with obscene exhortations and the sound of a metal baton dragging across the cages. There were two of them—a man and a woman.

"Your early release got canceled, traitor, so you get to stay for the show," said the man, thick mustache visible under the sliced-off nose of a half-zombie mask.

Zombie man tucked his prod under his arm. He unholstered his Taser and handed it to the woman, who wore a red, white, and black harlequin mask. Harlequin aimed the Taser at Sig while zombie face pulled out shackles and unlocked the cell door.

Sig sprang on the man as soon as the door was open. His hand held a chicken bone sharpened into a caveman shiv against the concrete floors. Sig shoved the bone up between the mustache and the beak and grabbed for the prod.

Holding the weapon with both hands, the woman fired the Taser at Sig. One cable attached to his shoulder. The other stuck in the chest of the man. Current jolted Sig's arm, igniting spastic twitches that ran through his body and the man's and back again. Not enough to incapacitate him. Sig shoved the man back onto the ceiling of the cell below and yanked on the cable, pulling the weapon from the woman's hands and pulling her forward, off balance. Sig planted a big fist right in the center of her face. She went down.

Sig took the prod from the man, and his keys, and started unlocking the other cells in his section. He gave the woman's gun to one of his fellow inmates and the man's gun to another.

Sig didn't need to tell them what to do.

By the time the guards in the tower turned their heads from the carnival, the riot had already moved into the hallway and three more weapons had been seized.

107

THE SUPERDOME BURNED THAT NIGHT, THOUGH YOU COULDN'T see the flames from outside. There were twice as many detainees as there were guards, and they had a lot to get even for. When they found the fuel storage for the emergency generators, it didn't take long.

The Army guard numbered twenty-four on the graveyard shift. They were able to retake control of the interior once another platoon showed up to help, followed by the fire department. But that was after Bravo Gate had already been breached and seventy-two detainees escaped onto Girod Street and the city beyond.

Those who didn't get out in the ten-minute gap when four gates were open at once found themselves trapped when the G level collapsed. In the rush to find a secure place to detain combatants and the people brought in after the roundups, they had worried a lot more about keeping people in under any circumstances than letting people out in case of a fire emergency.

Tania watched the reports on the official news, and wondered about Sig, and all the others who were in there.

108

SIG AND THREE ESCAPEES MOVED THROUGH THE SHADOWS OF
Mid-City, sneaking down alleys and the dark lanes between
the shotgun shacks, jumping fences when they needed to.
They heard the sirens and the barking dogs. They saw the
helicopters and heard the low drones. When they heard the
screams and gunshots as some others got cornered what
sounded like a block away, they hid in a dumpster for an hour,
huddled together in trash and listening for danger.

They got lucky. They entered Camp Zulu just after dawn,
tired, hungry, and filthy. They would blend right in. One of
the group, a Guatemalan named Alvaro, knew a spot on the
north fence where you could get through without having to
deal with the guards. They snuck in and disappeared into the
multitude.

They navigated the labyrinth of narrow pathways between
tents, converted storage containers, and shanties and shelters
made from trash and salvage. There were a few temporary
disaster relief houses in the mix, most of which had grown
improvised additions. The sounds of freestanding power generators thrummed in the background, behind the sounds of
daily life of the settlement.

The shantytown bustled with activity. People were busy
making food, building improvements, fixing things, running errands, carrying messages, making deliveries, tending
wounds, nursing maladies, buying and selling and otherwise
negotiating. They saw adults playing cards and dominoes, and

kids running through the gauntlet acting out games of war and insurrection. Two other kids were passing free handouts, alerts of the day printed on the clean side of old paper. There were radio and TV antennae rising up over the rooftops, and in some of the shelters you could see people meeting and planning like something big was coming.

When they found Moco, he told them they were just in time to go to the meeting.

109

THEY GOT TANIA A WHEELCHAIR TO GO TO THE GATHERING AT THE Church. They drove her in an armored trailer pulled by two bicycles.

They told her they might find out what happened to her brother.

They went the long way. The north barricade had been breached, but the line was holding. For now.

The Church was a command center in the heart of Bywater. Bundles of cable, banks of telephones and computers, big maps on the wall overwritten in layers of scrawl that told the story of quarters won and lost and lost again. There were lines that marked secret pathways, codes that denoted the distribution of cells, dots to mark the opposition by color and capability, hatch marks for the dead—there were too many of those.

The Colonel was there, up on the platform with Claude, Andrei, and others, jabbing her finger at one of the maps. Tania asked about Maxine Price, but no one would tell her. Maybe she had gone back underground.

The Colonel was telling her colleagues how the liberation of the Dome was the last opportunity they would have to turn the tables before they were all hunted down and terminated. Written out of history. Time to strike, with chaos, and break the machine.

Some of the escaped detainees were there in the big room, eating food and resting, knowing they would soon have their chance to head back out. Mom was there, helping. Tania looked, but didn't see Sig, and Mom hadn't heard word, either.

Tania was talking to the returnees, asking if they knew, when Andrei walked up to her and pulled her aside.

"How's it going?" she said.

"Not so good," he said.

"What do you mean?"

"I mean the files. We can't get them out."

"But the Germans. You said."

"She said," said Andrei. "She was right. But to send the files we had to embed them in a broadcast. And we're having trouble."

"Can't you get past the firewalls?"

"Well, no, not anymore," said Andrei. "They are just too powerful. Since the MOFUC they are crazy. We don't have the machines to do that kind of math. Only military can."

"So how can you put the files on TV?"

"There's a space in the transmission for it. The blanking interval. We have this old guy who knows all that stuff. But they captured him."

"Who?"

"Militia. Texans maybe. Repo. Captured the whole station. It's off the air. We're jammed."

"You have to—"

"They're working on it," said Andrei, pointing at the Colonel, Claude, and their crew.

"Let me talk to them."

"Yes, okay, but there's one other thing I have to tell you."

She could see the change in the look on his face.

"We don't know for sure, but it sounds like your, uh, brother—" Andrei put his hand on her shoulder. "They're claiming him as a casualty. There are pictures, but too hard to tell."

"I'll believe it when I see it," said Tania. And even then she wouldn't be sure. "Can you get me a console to work?"

110

SIG KNEW THE INFORMATION WAS GOOD WHEN HE SAW THE THREE
bodies stacked up outside the main gate of the station and the
American flag rippling off one of the crossbars of the antenna.

"Surprised they didn't put their heads on poles," said
Slider, as they watched from the brush across the street.

"Didn't have time," said Moco.

"Even left the door open," said Mongoose.

The metal gate had been breached with the big pickup
that was now parked inside the yard, front end crunched but
probably semifunctional, glass shattered, side armor heavily
pocked.

"You're not going through it," said Sig. "No more dead
kids."

"We're all kids, dumb-ass," said Moco. "You and me only
got a couple years on these guys, and they're both crazier than
the two of us added up. I've seen it."

"We're all going to die," said Mongoose.

"See?" said Moco.

"Maybe, but I'm going in first. Scout it. You guys keep the
circle."

He went around to the back, over the wall, and up to the
small door at the rear of the building. Walker had shown him
the trick to open the door, and it still worked.

The main hallway was dimly lit. There was a militiaman
standing down at the far end of the hall by the main entrance.
He wore combat bibs embroidered with the morale logo of

the Skunk Hunters. A hand-tooled Mexican assault rifle hung from his back.

Sig flashed memories of skunks he had seen in the wild. The way they disappeared into the field, sticking their huge tails up out of the tall grass to warn off any predator they sensed. It usually worked.

It did this time. Sig snuck along the wall the other way, toward the stairwell.

Upstairs he found the door to the office suite unlocked. The carpet was rank with mildew and tracked with the indentations of recent entries and exits. He heard no noise inside, so he stepped through, hoping to find the panel of surveillance and studio monitors Walker kept in his office.

He smelled men. Heard a muffled cough.

The light was weird in the room. The windows had been covered with brown paper.

Sig went to the floor in front of the old secretary's desk, then crawled around along the wall to where he could see through the half-open door into Walker's office.

Walker was there, bound to a metal chair with electrical cord and duct tape, lying sideways on the floor. He was gagged, his necktie balled up, shoved into his mouth, and taped over. His white shirt collar was speckled with blood. His glasses were on the floor nearby, crunched.

Walker got excited when he saw Sig, making noises and wriggling around.

Sig looked at the monitors behind the desk, running live feeds from multiple cameras.

He saw Moco and Mongoose in the yard, under guard by another Skunk Hunter. They had been hog-tied and thrown in the bed of the pickup. It looked like Moco had been shot.

On another screen he saw three other men being held hostage in the studio. Two were hooded. The other was an older guy with gray hair and a beard—Fritz! He must have come down here to help with the network. The skunks were asking him questions and slapping him around when he didn't answer.

Sig cut Walker loose from the chair. He didn't bother with the gag. Then he went to work on the window.

Walker tried to rip the duct tape from his face but there was too much and no time.

Walker grunted at the chair when he saw Sig messing with the window. Then he rummaged around in his desk, looking for something.

"Guard the door," said Sig. He grabbed the metal chair Walker had been tied to and shoved the legs through the window glass. The plates popped more than shattered.

Walker had an old revolver in his hand. He stepped around.

Sig worked to clear out the metal latticework from the window so they could get out.

BANG. A single shot.

"Get down!" screamed a man's voice from the hallway.

Walker struggled with his pistol.

BOOM. Shotgun. Walker flew back, knocking the back of his head on the desk as he came to the ground.

"Get the fuck back in yer hole," said a voice.

"You! Get away from the goddamn window," said another voice.

Sig dropped the chair and dove behind the desk.

CRACK CRACK CRACK.

"Little motherfucker!"

Walker screamed into his gag as the guy kicked him.

"Check on Dallas, you idiot!" the guy yelled at his colleague.

Sig got a glimpse. It was a burly bald guy, more corporate than cowboy, wearing black Kevlar technicals. He aimed a combat shotgun. He had lost the earring, but Sig still recognized him. That face was burned into his memory, and he remembered the name from the tarmac in Houston.

"Holt," said Sig, stepping out with his hands up.

Holt eyeballed Sig with wary eyes and barrel aimed. There was another militiaman behind him in a balaclava, attending to their downed man. Sig looked and recognized the big guy bleeding out on the floor, as well. Dallas.

That made for another friend lost due to Holt, even if in Dallas's case he had it coming.

"You copied my hairdo," said Holt, cracking the beginnings of a smile as he put his gun barrel to Sig's fresh-shaved head. "Smart change. We've been looking to catch you for a long time. Fat boy over there said he thought he could help us get you to come out of whatever hole you've been hiding in lately. Guess he was right."

"Looks like he picked the wrong team," said Sig.

Holt glanced at Dallas. "A little too eager, that one, but we needed the extra hand and there was literally nothing he wouldn't do."

Sig caught Dallas's eyes. Dallas tried to say something, but all that came out was a gurgle.

The other man was bent over Dallas, trying to apply first aid without knowing the first thing about how to do it.

"Help me out, Holt," said the guy, in an emotional voice. "He's bad."

"Hang on," said Holt.

Sig looked at Walker. Blood was seeping into his white shirt in a tight pattern. He was breathing, slowly, eyes open, glassy.

"Don't die on me yet, porno king," said Holt. "You need to make one last live television appearance. Just as soon as I get the message to the big boss to tune it in. This particular double feature offering in tribute is going to get me a hell of a bonus."

"Your big boss is the one who hides in a hole," said Sig. "But it won't be deep enough when we get to it."

"Dream big, little chief," said Holt. "Those kind of endings don't happen in real life. Ask your buddies back on the rez, if any are left."

Sig leapt at Holt. Holt was fast, trained, and experienced, like the Colonel. He met Sig's tackle with a gun butt to his head, then brought a knee up hard into Sig's balls. Sig crumpled.

"Stay down," said Holt.

"Dallas is dead, Holt!" said the other militiaman.

The militiaman bent over Dallas's body pulled off his balaclava. He was crying.

"Jesus Christ," said Holt, quietly before he turned to yell. "Can't you see I have my hands full?"

The crying man was Newton Towns. The movie star, in person. He did not look like he was acting.

"Fine" said Holt. "Hold on."

He grabbed Sig by the ear, lifted him up with one hand, then smacked him across the face with the other.

"Look at me, bitch," said Holt.

Sig reached for Holt, hoping to tackle him, but the gun butt had better reach, and when it connected with his face, everything went black.

TANIA WAS IN THE CHURCH WHEN THE MISSILE HIT.

The explosion was so loud that your ears failed immediately and you couldn't hear the rest of the blast.

It was not in slow motion like in the movies. It was instant. The speed of military physics. Everything suddenly flying, exploding outward. Bricks, glass, paper, nails, flesh, dirt, pieces of clothing.

She was up by the front when it hit somewhere in the back. The part where the priest's office had been or whatever.

She crawled over rubble, oblivious to her new injuries, and to what happened to her clothes.

There was a finger there in front of her. The nail was painted. Purple.

The world was silent, even as everyone was screaming.

Tania was screaming the loudest, as she looked for the rest of Mom.

112

SIG WOKE TO THE FEELING OF BEING HANDLED. BRIGHT LIGHTS blinded him as he opened his eyes. He felt his legs bent back against some object, and tried to resist but he was already bound.

As his eyes adjusted, he saw the cameras, and the silhouettes of men, and the red illuminated sign on the wall.

ON AIR

He was lying on the floor of the television stage, bound. His bent knees poked out of a truck tire, secured with a broomstick pinion behind the joints. His hands were tied behind his back with cable. His mouth was gagged with a ball of fabric made from the T-shirt they had cut off his body.

"Look at how he squiggles like a rat in a trap," said Holt, a silhouette.

Laughter from other shadows. One of the shadows stepped into the light. A masked policeman, carrying a flexible metal club. He kicked Sig, then whipped the club across the bottoms of Sig's exposed feet. Twin jolts of sharpened pain shot up to the crown of his head.

"Welcome to the counterrevolution!" said Holt. "We are going to show your viewers at home what you weak-minded freaks are really made of."

Sig rolled over and looked around. Moco was bound up and gagged the same way as Sig just a few feet away. Mongoose was offstage, hog-tied on the floor, next to the body of Dallas. Fritz was working in the booth at the barrel of a gun. Walker was behind Sig, trussed up to a swivel chair, with his arms tied behind the seat back and his legs tucked up under the seat. His shirt was drenched now, his skin chalky.

Behind Walker, the bodies of two young men, the Masques who had been with Fritz when the studio was captured, hung from the metal rafters by their legs, dripping blood on the floor as their bodies slowly swung in front of the American flag draped over the backdrop map.

"These skunks are real sneaky," said Holt, walking between Sig and Moco. "But you can still smell them a mile away. Especially this one, who wandered in off the street, after he snuck across the border."

Holt kicked Sig in the stomach. Sig swallowed back the bile that couldn't get out through the gag.

"His buddy here," said Holt, stepping over Moco, "is one of these little illegal gangbangers we found hiding in the bushes with a little boy.

"These terrorist runts came here to rescue their master, this suit who's been stealing from the people. And who even had the nerve to take a wild shot at the national treasure who's been helping us clean up this city of traitors. Come on out, Newton!"

Towns stumbled out of the shadows, pushed from behind. He wore olive coveralls and held a military pistol in his unsteady hand. He flashed his million-dollar smile when he saw the camera eye, but his eyes told the truth.

"Newton already cut two scalps today, and he's just getting started," said Holt.

Towns looked at the dangling bodies, and back at Holt.

"Ward Walker here," said Holt, "is wanted for other crimes, too many to count—fraud, treason, money laundering, aiding the enemy, and even stealing from the enemy. He's the one who's been putting all the propaganda and filth out there out of this lawless zone, poisoning the minds of patriots, of our kids. So we're going to make some new TV here. Let Newton Towns show you how he dispatches the bad guys in real life."

Towns chambered his pistol and stepped over to Walker.

Sig heard a noise in the rafters. He looked up and saw Slider, crawling on the rails from which the TV lights and mics hung.

"Make him confess!" said Holt. "Just be careful if you take that gag off. His mouth is dangerous."

"Yeah," Towns said. He ripped the tape from Walker's face, then used the barrel of his gun to draw out the necktie ball. Towns was crying again.

"Don't," Walker coughed, barely audible.

Holt smacked Walker in the side of the head.

"Give the people your admission," said Holt.

Walker muttered. Sig heard the words *love, hate,* and *America.*

"He's guilty," said Holt. "A traitor. Dangerous. Deliver the verdict."

You could see in his face how Towns coexisted with the camera. Inhabited its gaze.

Sig felt the broomstick start to give.

Towns lifted the gun up and looked at it. It looked polished and oiled under the lights. You could see the blue in the metal.

Towns pointed the pistol at Holt and shot him in the face.

CRACK.

Sig snapped the broomstick, just as Slider dropped from the ceiling onto Towns.

Holt staggered. Sig scrambled up and tackled him, low, in the knees. Holt couldn't see but he was still fighting.

The ball gag came loose as they wrestled. Holt was stronger than Sig, but fading.

Slider came up with Towns's pistol, aimed at Towns's head.

"You rednecks better back the fuck off!" said Slider. "El Presidente won't like it if we get to kill his pet movie star 'cause you guys couldn't secure the building."

The masked policeman backed away and signaled the guys in the booth with Fritz to follow him. They tried to take Fritz with them, but Sig, standing with Holt's gun now, negotiated a better deal.

When they had the room under control, the camera was on Sig as he smelled the blood on his hands.

PART TEN
Tropic of Kansas

113

THE TROOPS PULLED BACK WHEN THEY FOUND OUT ABOUT THE rebels' new hostage. Tania was in charge of interrogating the prisoner while they negotiated ransom and other terms.

They moved their headquarters to Walker's station facility, which was between Bywater and Echo Sector. Tania survived the strike on the Church. Claude did not. Mom was going to be okay, and Tania was there when they took her away in one of the vans headed to the hospitals in Baton Rouge. The Colonel's injuries were worse, and she would probably not be okay. Maxine Price was alive, at her side. She went on camera. Delivered a message. It lit it up.

They pulled the foreign news reports down off the satellite after Andrei went ahead and released the rest of the material to his contacts. Even the British were shocked.

The Kill List wasn't just Americans, it turned out.

Nor were the beneficiaries of the movements of money recorded on the secret ledgers.

The firewall tightened up like a fisherman's knot, but it was too late—the word was out there.

None of the techniques the wizards had taught Tania were necessary to get a movie actor to talk on camera. It was more about conventional deposition techniques, the kind of stuff you learned as a young lawyer. Ways to get self-impressed people to let out their glib.

That, and a little bit of Stockholm syndrome.

She used Socratic dialogue, clips from his movies, and material Andrei and the others pulled together to lead Newton through his on-screen reeducation. It wasn't hard. While he wasn't terribly bright, he had a particular gift for sensing the feelings behind the eyes watching him through the screen.

Newton's father was an actor, too. A serious actor, and a serious radical, who had been a supporter of the prior regime. Newton let the parts he played dictate his politics, such as they were, and the deconstruction was weirdly pleasurable. For both him and Tania, you could tell. Except when she played the dissonant daddy clips and it looked like something was going to snap.

The truce talks broke down while the interviews continued. You could hear the gunfire while they talked on camera. Booms of artillery uncomfortably close. Newton looked kind of jumpy at times, which made it even better.

Then they got the idea to get him to read names out loud, off the Enemies List and the Kill List.

It wasn't long after that they had to flee for the swamps.

114.

THE FEDERAL RAID ON CAMP ZULU CAME ON A SATURDAY NIGHT.

They came in armored cars and emerged in full riot gear. Boots on the ground, with masks on their faces.

One of the trucks was a corporate, loaded with killers who followed their own rules of engagement.

They came looking for terrorists.

They came to the right place.

A large number of the people they wanted were there that night, partying into the wee hours at the wedding of two of their number.

The boots and the trucks were not welcomed.

A group of teenagers started the fire when they dropped a homemade napalm bomb on one of the trucks.

The troops called it in and the rotor drones were there in two minutes, dropping gas canisters. The canisters made *that* noise when they hit the ground. Sounded hollow.

Clink. Clinkety-tink.

It was a new gas, designed to be nonlethal. It wasn't. At least not in the peculiar atmospheric conditions of Camp Zulu and the Crescent City.

There were news cameras there that night. Nassra brought a bunch of French documentarians from TV Sezz who wanted to go slumming.

The footage of the kids with their eyeballs bleeding did not get much airtime domestically at first. But everyone else in the world was watching. It got out there on the alternet, and then it broke into the back channels of the Feed.

Then Nassra got an interview with Maxine Price, as she was dying from the aftereffects. She told them what really happened in November, and why.

There were a few people who actually cared.

And a whole lot of people ready to tear shit up.

115

TANIA LIKED TO CALL IT THE MARCH ON WASHINGTON.

It broke out two weeks after they fled New Orleans.

She was in the group that got out in one of the boats. Walker was on there, and Andrei. They went to Matamoros, then overland to Juárez, where Walker had another border blaster that had a dual use as armory and barrack. The crew waiting for them called themselves the Chisos Mountain Boys, except for the ones who were girls. Walker called them saddle leather Valkyries.

They took in footage of the riots breaking out in the big cities, and shaky clips from the fighting in rural areas, and put it back out over the air, through the border blaster and the foreign press.

They watched through binoculars across the valley that afternoon when three battalions of the First Armored Division and a full brigade of infantry deserted. The deserters took over Fort Bliss. Then they occupied El Paso long enough for the company waiting on the other side to come over.

Tania's crew went east through the empty expanse of the Transpecos, then north, up the I-35 corridor. She rode with Walker, in the Rover at first, until it broke down. Their convoy was more swarm than column, coordinated by distributed network connections rather than a centralized command. It made for more surprises, on both sides. Not to suggest there were only two sides. There were twenty, two hundred, or none, depending on how you counted.

She thought it would be scary. War. And it was. But it was also exhilarating, and less scary than when she first crossed over and betrayed the government. Now, like then, she convinced herself it was the only way she could truly fulfill her oath.

She helped Andrei with politics. She spin doctored for the network, missives from Max, inspirational aphorisms about the imminent rebirth of American democracy on a more authentically participatory model.

They followed an imaginary line through American mapspace they appropriated from the old fictions of Maxine Price. The original Tropic of Kansas. Walker said it was the line in our heads "where ingenuity runs into loco." To Tania, it was about riding on the cresting wave of the revolutionary impetus—the same energy that fuels a rock band, or a start-up, or a new religion, or a new American idea—before it gets co-opted by peddlers and power trippers.

Maxine's death was what the movement really needed, Tania realized. Maxine was right when she said the movements of the future only work without leaders, organized by their own network logic. And the Maxine they had found in the tower was no longer really capable of leading—even her messages from exile were barely coherent. Maybe that's why they worked so well—as oracular koans to be situationally interpreted, like horoscopes for an ailing nation-state. In her death she became something more like an authentic prophet, and the spread of the news worked like religious revelation, the call to a new communitarian congregation.

Law and order broke down quickly. The population was ripe. It didn't take much to light the fire in people weaned on myths of revolution and pent up with a century of media-induced numb.

It didn't take much to light the fire in people covered in petrochemicals by the kleptocracy and told it was actually freedom.

Walker's alternet was the sparkplug. Cells activated by test patterns, intelligence, and tactical plans shared through encoded spurts in the blanking interval. Until the feds took out the main relays and broke the network's spine.

Then young rebels hacked the Citizen Emergency Alert network and filled it up with disinformation and misdirection until *it* broke.

Tania's crew found sanctuary in Austin, which was already experimenting with distributed democracy. They set up camp and used it as a base of media operations for the movement. People from New Orleans and other cells were already there, and more came in their wake. That's where they picked Sig's trace back up.

Sig had stayed behind, occupying the occupiers while the others fled. With him were forty-seven bandits, his new buddy Newton Towns, and Nassra with her camera and uplink kit. When New Orleans was lost, they moved east into the ruins of Biloxi, then disappeared into the woods.

Sig, it turned out, was just the exemplar people needed to fill the vacancy left by Maxine. The replacement of talk by action.

They hijacked a C-130 in Mobile. They flew it to Wichita, loaded with explosives that took out the main build hangar of the Boeing drone factory. They gathered new forces by liberating Leavenworth—first the five hundred military convicts at the Armed Forces Disciplinary Barracks, then the two thousand political inmates at the federal penitentiary down the road. In Kansas City they broke open the vaults of the Federal Reserve and distributed the contents on the streets.

They moved fast through territory depopulated by drought, depression, and robotized agribusiness. Lands that thought they were protected by their importance to Mack's regime and their relative obscurity.

Sig's band killed the robots when they saw them along the way, and rogue makers followed in their path, harvesting the remains to be repurposed as counterdrones.

Government missiles took out the bridges across the Mississippi, so they forded it in big, slow barges that made easy targets. They lost half their people that day but found new cells self-activated and autonomously engaged on the other side, all up and down the economically decimated swath of the Ohio River Valley. The bands from Chicago were even more lethal, when they came down out of the high-rise projects ready to retake their own streets and then move east.

Appalachia was the real bulwark of federal power. The rebel armor got bogged down there, and the loyal divisions and agency forces radiated out from D.C. implementing defense plans developed and refined over 250 years of official paranoia. The autobots owned the roads, the skyways, the streets, and the networks, maintaining order along the eastern seaboard with inhuman mechanized tactics—deploying derivatives of algorithmic machine processes developed to manage massive livestock operations, remixed with surveillance and interception operations brewed in far-flung theaters of asymmetrical warfare.

When the robots started developing their own new models, it got weird fast.

Tania saw the footage when Tracer's cell was fighting for a BellNet network node in suburban Atlanta, and the thing came up out of the ground, like a giant octopus made out of chain saws. She turned her head the first time, but they made her watch it again to confirm ID. Tracer's head rolling onto the green office park turf, some life still visible in his eyes before the footage cut.

Tracer was an early indicator of how things would go that penultimate week of the push.

116

THEY CAPTURED SIG WHEN THEY BURNED THE REBELS OUT OF THE woods around the Occoquan Reservoir, east of Manassas and the battlefields of another civil war, where the waters of the blue hills found their way into the Potomac and on to the ocean. It was the first time a private country club with adjacent gated communities had been napalmed. The ground troops moved in from all directions behind the fires, accompanied by combat bulldozers and little motion-seeking drones that saw every stray dog, deer, or naked ape moving through the scraped battlescape.

Tania saw it live from their bunker. Andrei was there, and Walker, and even the Colonel, who had mostly recovered from her injuries. Fritz was there, too, and he kept them online as best he could. They were losing, and you could see it in the long faces hollowed by the yellow lights of the concrete cave.

They locked Sig and the other survivors in the brig at Quantico. There weren't that many survivors. They had resisted too hard, and too long, for that.

Newton Towns was one of the survivors, but they kept him hidden.

The brig at Quantico was famous as the place where the Reagan assassin had died under mysterious circumstances, way back in 1981. Since the attacks it had grown into a little gulag where temporary detention of dissidents for questioning turned into interminable extraconstitutional imprisonment. Most of the detainees were political types singled out in the Executive's periodic Beltway purges. Sometimes pictures of the brig 2.0, a windowless metal building behind a thirty-foot-high sharpened fence, showed up on the network. Tania had been there once for training, back in the day that seemed so long ago now, even though it wasn't. It was the place where they refined the particular type of enhanced interrogation techniques best suited to making journalists reveal their sources, and dissidents to name their fellow travelers. The guys in charge called it the Hotel. The D.C. streets called it the building where no one can hear you scream.

Sig was not a screamer.

So they trotted him out for public humiliation. General deterrence. Right out there on the runway where they bring in the planes with high-value detainees from other parts of the country. They invited cameras. Loyal network cameras. They even invited a few popular bloggers and commenters known for unwittingly relaying the State's unofficial fear meme with tabloid enthusiasm.

The counterrevolution would be televised.

The official narrative was this:

The man the streets knew mainly as "the Minnesotan" was an enemy combatant of unknown citizenship. They did not know his true name. In military and intelligence operations, Tania knew, representatives of the State frequently referred to him by the code name "Nomad." But for the public they called him Enemy Fighter N174. The Feed Nets went along, mostly, their producers well trained in the things you have to do to keep your access to the information that keeps eyeballs on and advertisers up. They talked about the different theories of Sig's background—that he was incubated in some foreign training camp, raised as a kind of superterrorist, or that he was a sleeper agent raised in America by alien spies who trained him from birth in service of his mission of destroying America. They explained how the entire rebellion by the "anticonstitutionalists" was in fact a campaign sponsored by foreign powers to destroy our way of life.

"So he's apparently almost like some kind of ninja, Charlie," said Kendra Clark, one of the evening news anchors on *American Sunset*. "Jungle warfare—in the suburbs."

The signal was rough, fracturing into broken pixels every few seconds, but Fritz was able to hold the feed.

"Yeah, every time he strikes, he disappears back into the woods," said the co-anchor, Charlie Owen. "But let's see if he can hide from this beast—the new hunter-killer from General Robotics."

"Whoa!" said Clark. "It's a walker!"

"That's just the beginning," said Owen.

Even then, in their bunker at what seemed like the end of the world—or at least the end of hope—as they watched the public execution of the figure who best embodied popular aspirations and effective tactics to achieve them, they managed to laugh. Because of course, in America, the end of the world had to be accompanied by banal color commentary, and used to sell ads.

They could laugh in part because they knew the movement still had a few tricks left to deploy, things they were cautiously confident would remain surprises to the regime.

However, they stopped laughing when the hunter-killer stepped tentatively but menacingly from the gangway of the self-piloted cargo prop on awkward hydraulic legs. Or at least they appeared awkward to Tania. Unnatural—a primitive robotic simulation of the musculoskeletal locomotion of a four-legged mammal. Its head came up on a strange coiled stalk, electronic eyes wrapped in a lidless white helm of bulletproof metal. It looked blind by the standards of nature, but you could see it was watching everything, assembling a complex model of the immediate tactical situation in the silicon brain that rode on top of its atomic heart. The beast had a patchwork exoskeleton of polished metal plate, mostly white but with a few off-color panels of red and black. Its call sign was a machine code laser-etched on its left rear haunch. It had a black box where the flag should have been.

"Is it armed?" asked Clark.

"I'm sure," said Owen. "It's a beta model battlefield interceptor straight from DADA, the Defense Autonomous Development Area in Nevada. So it's definitely meant to be combat-capable. Official moniker looks like one of those network-generated secure passwords, but apparently its human minders have given it a nickname: 'Argie.'"

"That thing doesn't have 'minders,'" said Walker. "It has servants. The robots are fully in charge, at the pleasure of the Prez."

"I think the President gave up control when he released the autonomous code clearance," said Tania. "And I don't even know why you take it for granted that the President is still even around."

"He's on TV every night, delivering his weird-ass curfew messages," said Walker. "*Good night, America.*"

"How do you know he's not a robot, too?" said Andrei.

Walker shrugged.

Argie had the lines of a warhorse, but as it walked past one of its human helpers, a guy in a yellow jumpsuit with black plastic sunglasses, you could see it was too tall for any man to mount. The hunter-killer stopped for the human, connected through some mode of communication you couldn't see. The man stepped underneath Argie and made some adjustments through a panel inside of one of the rear legs.

Argie seemed to focus in on the figure of Sig, who was being held by three guards and one smaller robot amid the crowd of soldiers and hoverbots a hundred yards down the runway. The head stalk whined, spun, pointed—and froze. And then, from deep inside its mechanical body, Argie emitted a sharp tone that ascended in volume until the people around were covering their ears—a robot howl pitched to destabilize human equilibrium. Bad enough to make Tania mute the volume, and cause Walker to start gagging.

And as she saw the intense pain on Sig's face, Tania remembered all her broken promises to keep him safe, and had the sudden feeling that everything that was about to happen was all her fault.

But she couldn't look away.

117

SIG FELT THE SONIC BLAST RATTLE HIS CELLS AND SLUMPED down in the arms of his captors. They did what the voice of the hoverbot instructed and let him slide to the ground, like a toy they were leaving for the giant dog.

The guards walked off as Sig tried to shake the jams. He got up on one arm. He was alone in the middle of a military runway, right on top of one of the center stripes.

Sig watched the four-legged robot as it watched him. It moved a lot like a moose, he thought, but without the natural grace, and definitely more predatory. It seemed ever on the verge of collapsing, as if each part of the body were run by a separate computer that barely managed to stay in contact and coordination with the other parts. The robot had no smell other than a faint whiff of electrical burn. It stepped toward Sig.

Sig stood up, just as the robot went into a crouch, each leg bending to bring its metal body down into contact with the tarmac.

And then it leapt, higher than anything that heavy should be able to jump.

Sig reeled, moved backward and sideways as the robot fell toward him from its zenith. The robot adjusted, but still missed Sig, landing with a spring just off the centerline, its ball-pointed feet indenting the asphalt.

Sig looked for weaknesses. He heard machines inside the beast whirring and clicking. He looked at the gaps between the armor plates. He saw colored wire nerves, metal tendons, and ballistic membranes. He saw the robot twitch, contract, and bound.

Sig was down before he could move, knocked back by the one-two flicks of well-targeted forefeet. It was playing with him. He tried to crawl backward and up onto his feet. The robot followed him, watched him, then swung back one long leg and hit him with real force.

The hydraulic kick of the atomic robot flung Sig into the air, high and far. He landed hard. He did not move for a long minute.

Eventually Sig sat up, slowly, winded and battered. Color bleached from the air around him, then bled back in. He could see the tear in his left arm and feel another one inside his shoulder.

His ankle hurt, too, the right. It was twisted, the foot bare. He saw the lost sneaker ten feet away, so he pulled off the other one.

As he recovered, Sig saw the handler in the background, watching his pet do the job he couldn't, making sure the thing paused for televisual drama rather than finishing Sig off too fast. Sig imagined that if he'd encountered this robot in the "wild," he would already be dead. Or maybe his friends were right, and the robots were the real masters now, smart enough to play for the camera.

Sig saw the brig where his comrades were locked up.

Sig saw the hangars where they kept the robot's avian kin. He saw some of the airbots overhead, flying low, providing patrol and live feed.

He saw the cameras.

He saw the crowd of people behind the cameras—reporters, soldiers, government officials, prisoners brought out to watch the execution and tell the demoralizing story to their cellmates.

Sig stood, slowly, at the edge of the tarmac. He watched the robot assess his movements. He studied its hydraulic twitches, trying to intuit its machine-code instincts. He wondered how much of its brain was written by man, and how much by new machine intelligence.

Sig tried to imagine what this robot's descendants would look like, three or four generations down the chain, and wondered if they would have their own human servants.

He wondered what autonomous robots made by humans would do to the woods, and the waters.

Sig stepped back off the tarmac, onto the patch of turf next to the runway. The earth squished between his toes as he stepped farther back, the soil still engorged from two days of heavy rain.

He turned and ran, zigzagging across the soggy ground.

He heard the sound of the robot leaping again. He turned to face it, staggering sidesteps. The robot tried to splay midair, too late. It planted like a giant cleat, hard metal slurp into mud as all four limbs penetrated the ground and immobilized the mechanical beast.

Sig mounted the robot, clambering up onto its back. The armored panels were easy to rip off. The head flailed as he tore wiring and cables from along the back—it was trying to knock Sig loose but coming up short. He used one of the shoulder plates as a primitive axe, hacking and prying at electromotor assemblies and then the sectioned metal spine until it cut clean with a liquid pop, adrenaline flooding out his broken pain. He stood, tossed the plate, reached down, grabbed the coil, and yanked with all the force of his body. He fell back, and the head fell back with him, clanging off his own body, the white helm bouncing off to reveal a thousand glass lenses and fiber optic points, all bleeding photons into the static of the air.

Sig stood back up, with the metal coil pulled over his shoulder, and dragged the robot back toward the cameras as the soldiers rushed to intervene.

THAT WAS ABOUT WHEN CLINT AND XELINA AND A CONTIN-gent of the hundred Texans had gotten to a high point across the river from the base. They had the thing it had taken them months to build on a big flatbed semitrailer. The team that put it together were Xelina's welder brother Luis, his tinkerer buddy Jerry, who used to work at NASA, and a real smart electrician named Connor. It was a mess of metal boxes, batteries, solar panels, and wires at the back of a big tube with a lens at the end. They called it the camping flashlight of the gods.

When they flipped the switch, it popped a flash against the back of everyone's eyeballs. All the lights went out from Fort Meade halfway to Richmond, and drones fell from the sky like big metal doves.

118

THE WHITE HOUSE WAS NOT BURNING ANYMORE, BUT THE LAWN was. A hulking armored personnel carrier smoldered on the edge of the ceremonial driveway. The giant double doors of the mansion were wide open now, breached by the people in the battles of the long night before. The grounds breathed wisps of black smoke from the flaming spilled fuel, shadow dancing with the scorch marks and hurried tags marring the building's exterior walls. From a block away, Tania could see rebel soldiers in the man-made haze. At first she thought they were trying to squelch the flames, until the gunfire and laughing made her realize they were trying to make them worse, taking turns seeing who could ignite the gas tank.

Tania remembered the last time she had been here. That seemed like a long time ago. A lifetime ago. Another person's lifetime.

It felt like some kind of spell had been broken. The haze over everyone's heads cleared out, the way it does after a big storm or a blackout or some other event that suspends normal operations of daily life. Too bad it took so much blood, though not as much as she would have imagined. Once people woke up, all the big institutions collapsed crazy fast. And when the machines of the State were grounded, the streets filled with people who were no longer afraid of the skies.

The President had tried to escape in the night as the rebels approached the federal city. He didn't get far. They got him in Anacostia, as he tried to reach one of the ships in the naval yard. A group of hoodlum kids saw him first, and pretty soon it was a mob. Everyday people came out of their houses and swarmed him and his detail. Tania heard they were holding him in the cell of a police precinct they had taken over in the chaos, neighborhood watch as self-directed rebellion, now negotiating its own terms with the UN representatives coming in to try to help restore order.

Tania navigated around the craters of Lafayette Square, past the altered statues of the German and French aristocrats who helped win the first American Revolution. Andrew Jackson was gone, dismounted for good, but his spirit lingered in the multitude converging on the open house to retake it as theirs. Tania saw them as she walked from the command camp they had set up on the high point of Dupont Circle. They were already starting to pour into the square from every corner. Tania passed a shirtless old man with a long white beard and dreads, dancing with a staff made of found materials, pointing it at the sky, reading the contrails and telling the people the news.

"The capital is liberated territory," said the message they sent out at midnight. The news traveled fast, even with broken communications networks.

Tania was coming from Georgetown, where she had gone looking for Odile. She found a neighbor, who told her Odile had been arrested, something about procuring false identities.

Odile's mother had left the country, as soon as New Orleans fell. She was in London, and had written her daughter off.

Tania wondered how she could find where they were keeping Odile. Some of the prisons were already being opened up, which was wonderful and scary at the same time.

Odile was one of the lucky ones. Mike was dead, killed by his own employer, and Bert had not resurfaced.

The wide lanes of Pennsylvania Avenue between the park and the White House were crammed with vehicles and the irregular soldiers who had used them to breach the barricades. Remodded civilian pickups were the most popular, but there was no shortage of others—stripped-down sports cars, meterless taxicabs welded over with Frankenstein armor, doorless minivans with off-road suspensions, plenty of motorcycles, and a handful of loaded-up luxury cars that had been appropriated by the network. Tania saw one soldier she recognized working his way through a six-pack with his buddies while they polished the chrome on a vintage yellow Mercedes. A celebratory hum ran through the crowd, making a cacophonous polyphony with the revving engines and cranked-up stereos playing the mash-up anthem of unexpected victory.

On the front lawn, as the fires dwindled and the smoke dissipated, Tania saw the bodies of the dead being collected. Uniformed Secret Service in their black and chrome, plainclothes agents piled up in their dark suits like infinite copies of the same prototype, a few federal police, and one mangled German shepherd, all mixed in with an even larger number of rebels, mostly in their own improvised gear, some in the uniforms of the official services from which they had defected. They would all be buried together.

A stencil of Maxine Price was tagged on the guard tower. And a new flag fluttered from the roof, the one that was made of a million stars to represent the idea of the Crowdrule.

A trio of well-armed drunks stumbled out of the front door of the White House bearing gunmetal, battle scars, and predatory smiles, breaking the funereal haze with a sports bar hip-hop variation on the theme to *Bravo Five Zero*. One of them, it appeared, was wearing several strands of the First Girlfriend's jewelry around her neck, the perfect scalp to garnish the full metal bandolier draped across her torso.

Tania dodged their stumbles and stepped into the mansion.

The formal red carpet of the State ran the length of the long entrance hall, now stained with blackening splatters of spilled blood, rips from stray bullets and vandalizing machetes, and mud tracked in from the battlefield outside. A gangly white kid with a sniper rifle and a burly Chicana with two pistols and a double-action shotgun guarded the hall, watching the mob of coup d'état tourists as they tried to find their way up to the President's bedroom before every last souvenir of this ephemeral moment was gone. A fat man enlisted his wife to help him pull the painting of Lewis and Clark off the wall, stopping when he felt the girl's shotgun in his gut. The rules were improvised, but one of them was that the old heroes were off-limits.

The porcelain was another matter. In the State Dining Room, they were throwing the last block party of Ragnarök. There must have been close to a thousand people crammed in there, shoulder to shoulder, cleaning out the pantries with daisy chains that ran down into every one of the undisclosed secure subbasements. The doorway exhaled an overload of spilled beer, indoor barbecue, and the body odor of an army on the move and the residents of a city that had gone five days without running water. You couldn't hear the music over the noise. Onstage, a group of rebel soldiers invented drinking games with the official china, tossing plates toward the ceiling for target practice.

One of the soldiers pointed Tania to a small hallway that led to the West Wing, which had been rebuilt from steel and concrete in the time since she had yelled at the President. Access to the working offices was still being controlled. The windows of the colonnade looked onto the long expanse of the South Lawn, where an even bigger party was getting going as thousands gathered under the fractured shadow of George Washington's broken monument. Soon the Mall would be packed, from the Capitol to the Lincoln Memorial, with the chaotic crowd that now needed to figure out how to govern itself.

The reporters were still there in the press room, joined by new colleagues without official credentials, all competing for access to the network connections enabled by the White House's underground generator. A bank of monitors screened live coverage of the events outside.

In the tiny offices of the West Wing, a nerdier class of soldiers was quietly collecting information from the mother lode—breaching networks, scanning files, and filling banker's boxes with paper.

A huge portrait of President Haig in his six-star General of the Armies uniform stared over the scene, unmarred, still scary in his paternal severity.

A camouflaged giant guarded the Oval Office, a big soldier with a massive red beard and a black baseball cap adorned with the silhouette of a combat sheepdog. Blue eyes sized up Tania from a long world away, and waved her in.

Tania noticed Xelina first, even though she was the farthest from the door, seated at the window behind the desk with a very long rifle.

Moco was there, inside the door, standing next to Clint.

Walker leaned back in one of the armchairs on the right, smoking a cigarette and helping himself to the presidential liquor.

Newton Towns was standing behind Walker with a hand-held vidcam, filming Sig as he sat at the President's desk, drinking a can of beer and carving something into the desktop with his knife.

"Decorating your new office?" said Tania.

Sig looked up. "No," he said. "Taking it back. This office is going to stay empty. The time for chiefs is over."

"Well, hurry up," said Tania. "We tried to reach you guys but couldn't get through. We need to leave. The British are coming."

119

IT WASN'T A JOKE.

The blue helmets came in after the Brits. French, Dutch, and Polish. The fighting was already over by the time the hovercrafts floated up the Potomac and the relief pods started dropping from the sky on big white parachutes.

It took a week for the different bands of rebels to sort out who had authority to speak for all of them. They settled on a triumvirate. A Texan from the St. Louis cell, the guy who led the Cabrini Commando from Chicago, and the Colonel for New Orleans. She took Sig with her as her bodyguard.

Nobody fucked with her.

The deposed regime was represented by the defense secretary. The Vice President had been killed, supposedly by friendly fire, more likely fragged.

A pair of senior senators and a congresswoman helped mediate the discussions.

The rebels agreed to go home. So long as they got autonomy when they returned. They won a sort of sovereignty, subject to free trade and open travel agreements, for an archipelago of territories, an idea that Sig suggested to the Colonel in a breakout, an idea he had gotten from Betty. The territories were mainly on the Mississippi—New Orleans from Bywater to the eastern edge of Echo Sector, most of East St. Louis, and some big swaths of the Tropic of Kansas—repatriated federal biofuel estates in Iowa, Missouri, and Minnesota. They threw in a couple thousand acres Walker owned in far west Texas, on a section of the Rio Grande that had gone dry. In those zones, seed-funded with what reparations they could extract, they could make their own rules. Beta-test experiments in political form that incorporated the capabilities of the network they had built, and were rebuilding, and making better.

They would need the beta tests, because the other major outcome was the calling of a constitutional convention. They would try to come up with a new national operating system, one native to the world that was emerging.

Figuring out how to let everyone in on the renegotiation of the social contract had sounded a lot more feasible when it was impossible.

One year later

ON HER WAY WEST TO PITCH THE CALIFORNIANS FOR FUNDING, Tania went to visit Sig. That involved a stopover in Las Vegas and a long drive out into the desert where the map went blank in the spot where they hid the Supermax.

It didn't look like much from the outside. A cluster of shimmering buildings behind four perimeters of tidily combed DMZ. Like the White House, the real deal was underground.

It took more than two hours to negotiate her way to the visiting area, not counting the long elevator down into the earth.

They gave her twenty minutes.

They talked through three layers of bulletproof glass, over a mic.

He was keeping his hair short now. It probably was not voluntary.

"We're working on a new deal," she said.

He nodded.

"Don brought in some better people in Washington. Been around. Says they are really confident about it."

"It's okay," said Sig.

"It's totally not okay," said Tania. "It's not what we fought for."

Sig shrugged. "It kind of is. At least you're out there. How's that going, anyway?"

"Okay."

"Not good."

"They're carving up the country."

"We started it."

"I know," said Tania. "But they're like . . . selling it."

"What did you expect? Bills to pay. Or didn't you see the mess we left."

"I just wish it would kind of hold together better. More balanced. Instead it's like half the places are giant co-ops and the other half are going to be company towns. Hard to confederate that."

"Walker straddles it pretty good," said Sig.

"Utopia as real estate speculation," said Tania.

"Better than what was."

"It's chaos."

"Creative destruction," said Sig. "It's the future. The short-term future. The long-term future is green. No matter what we do. Nature will be better off without us, whenever that finally happens."

"When did you get so glib?"

"Not a lot of visitors. They won't let press talk to me."

"I know. Don's working on that, too. And look, I know this is fucked up to say, but four years isn't that much longer."

Sig gave her the finger. He looked tired.

"They treat you okay?"

"They leave me alone."

He looked down at his hand.

"It would be good if they would let me go outside once in a while."

Tania looked at him as he looked away, and tried to contain the pain.

"Can I get you anything?"

He shook his head. "They wouldn't let you."

"It's not gonna be four years."

"Worry about making it worth it. Your job is the hard one. This one is easy."

Tania tried to see if she could tell if he was lying. But she knew he was right.

She wanted to talk about his mom, and how proud she would be, but it seemed corny now and anyway she had brought up enough stuff. She put her hand on the window, and tried to let him know that way.

THE SKY WAS SO CLEAR THAT NIGHT, YOU COULD ALMOST see the flares coming off the shooting stars. You could actually imagine a world you would really want to live in, even as you knew you were still in America.

Acknowledgments

I was greatly aided in writing this book by the critical insights of friends and colleagues who read early drafts and excerpts, especially Allen Varney, Richard Butner, Paul Miles, William Gibson, Pepe Rojo, Anil Menon, Jessica Reisman, Nisi Shawl, Nicky Drayden, Gavin Grant, Henry Wessells, and the participants in one hot summer's Sycamore Hill and Turkey City Writers Workshops—including Meghan McCarron, Jenn Volant, Catherynne Valente, Alice Sola Kim, Dale Bailey, Christopher Rowe, Don Webb, Derek Johnson, Dave Hardy, and Lawrence Person. I also owe thanks to Eileen Gunn, L. Timmel Duchamp, Bruce Sterling, Joe Lansdale, Christopher Priest, M. John Harrison, Kelly Link, Nathan Ballingrud, and Rick Klaw for invaluable provocation and encouragement along the way.

Thanks to the many folks who provided inspiration and information that informed the book, especially Eric Paulus, who told me what it feels like to be shot with a rubber bullet; Bill O'Rourke, who gave me a glimpse into life off of capital's registry; and my Mexican colleagues who showed me the view from the other side of the border wall we already have, especially Pepe Rojo, Bernardo Fernández, Deyanira Torres, Mauricio Montiel Figueiras, Miguel Ángel Fernández Delgado, and Gerardo Sifuentes.

Thanks to my agent, Mark Gottlieb of Trident Media Group, whose energy and enthusiasm made it happen; to my amazing editor David Pomerico, who had the courage to take it on and the editorial gifts to help make it the book it wanted to be; and to the rest of the team at Harper Voyager/William Morrow, especially cover designer Owen Corrigan, who translated the book's aesthetic into living color.

Family plays a big role in this book, and it did in the writing of it as well. Thanks to Bill and Sibyl for the belief. Thanks to Alex for the example, and to Billy for the feeling. Thanks to Katiti and Tristan for the love and strength. Thanks to my aunts and uncles, living and dead, for the views down other paths. Thanks to Virginia and Eliseo for sharing stories of how it can be. And most important, thanks to Agi and Hugo, whose love and support made it possible, as it does every day.

About the Author

Christopher Brown was nominated for a World Fantasy Award for the anthology *Three Messages and a Warning: Contemporary Mexican Short Stories of the Fantastic*. His short fiction has appeared in a variety of magazines and anthologies, including recent pieces in *MIT Technology Review*'s "Twelve Tomorrows," *The Baffler,* and *Stories for Chip*. He lives in Austin, Texas.